Prais

The Rom Con

"A rip-roaringly fun and sexy novel that calls into question our beliefs about vulnerability and connection. I felt every heartbeat in this one."

—Annabel Monaghan, national bestselling author of *Same Time Next Summer*

"Refreshingly smart, heartfelt, and laugh-out-loud funny. Daniels once again delivers an absolutely flawless rom-com."

—Lauren Layne, *New York Times* bestselling author of *Made in Manhattan*

"Perfectly encapsulates the whip-sharp hilarity and nostalgia of *How to Lose a Guy in 10 Days*, but for a modern audience. Masterfully paced, *The Rom Con*'s scorching slow burn will have readers giddily kicking their feet in anticipation. Consider me dazzled!"

—Amy Lea, international bestselling author of *Exes and O's*

"Sharp, witty, and fun. . . . The perfect reminder that you're at your best when you're being yourself."

—Lacie Waldon, bestselling author of *The Layover*

"If the Doris Day / Rock Hudson battle-of-the-sexes rom-com classics had a baby with *How to Lose a Guy in 10 Days*, the result would be *The Rom Con*. Devon Daniels has written a surprising, sexy slow-burn romance that's packed full of enough pop culture references to keep any romantic comedy fan happy."

—Kerry Winfrey, author of *Faking Christmas*

FEB

"With winks to *How to Lose a Guy in 10 Days*, *The Rom Con* strikes the perfect balance between feminine and feminist with its clever premise. . . . Readers will delight in the pop culture references from both the past and present, the delicious tension, and the witty dialogue. This hilarious and heartwarming love letter to classic romance movies and spunky grandmothers everywhere is going on my favorites list!"

—Meredith Schorr, author of *As Seen on TV* and *Someone Just Like You*

Praise for

Meet You in the Middle

"Sharp, clever repartee propels this irresistible, very modern, wonderfully warm and optimistic romance that asks the eternal question, Do opposites really attract?"

—*New York Times* bestselling author Jayne Ann Krentz

"More timely than ever. . . . It's the kind of book that will leave you feeling gleeful."
—*USA Today*

"Smart, sexy, and satisfying! Daniels has penned an engaging enemies-to-lovers contemporary romance set against a Beltway backdrop that gives an insider's look at the people and politics of Washington, DC, while maintaining the heart and humor of two people falling in love against all odds. I loved it!"

—*New York Times* bestselling author Jenn McKinlay

The ROM CON

Devon Daniels

Berkley Romance
New York

BERKLEY ROMANCE
Published by Berkley
An imprint of Penguin Random House LLC
penguinrandomhouse.com

Copyright © 2023 by Devon Daniels, LLC
Readers Guide copyright © 2023 by Devon Daniels, LLC
Penguin Random House supports copyright. Copyright fuels creativity,
encourages diverse voices, promotes free speech, and creates a vibrant culture.
Thank you for buying an authorized edition of this book and for complying
with copyright laws by not reproducing, scanning, or distributing any part
of it in any form without permission. You are supporting writers and allowing
Penguin Random House to continue to publish books for every reader.

BERKLEY and the BERKLEY and B colophon are
registered trademarks of Penguin Random House LLC.

Library of Congress Cataloging-in-Publication Data

Names: Daniels, Devon, author.
Title: The rom con / Devon Daniels.
Description: First edition. | New York: Berkley Romance, 2023.
Identifiers: LCCN 2023019631 | ISBN 9780593199237 (trade paperback) |
ISBN 9780593199244 (ebook)
Subjects: LCGFT: Romance fiction. | Novels.
Classification: LCC PS3604.A5327 R66 2023 |
DDC 813/.6—dc23/eng/20230501
LC record available at https://lccn.loc.gov/2023019631

First Edition: November 2023

Printed in the United States of America
1st Printing

Book design by Ashley Tucker

For two extraordinary women and exceptional matriarchs,
my grandmothers, Cassie and Lucy

The
ROM
CON

So, LET ME JUST MAKE SURE I'VE GOT THIS. You're telling me you can't come with me to my grandmother's party this weekend because Saturdays are *'for the bros'*?"

I stop short on the sidewalk, my voice—and spine—stiff with indignation. Brett and I have just arrived back at my apartment building after grabbing a late dinner, one of a handful of dates we've been on since meeting a couple of months ago at Skye Verde, a rooftop bar my coworker and roommate Natalia had insisted we try out for her twenty-ninth birthday. He'd impressed me that night, as much due to his easygoing personality and wry sense of humor as to the fact that I never once caught him checking out other women over my shoulder (a transgression that should be the exception but, as all women know, is far more often the rule). I peer at his face now under the glare of the streetlamp to confirm this isn't some misguided attempt at humor, but all signs point to him being serious. *Just great.*

Things had been going deceptively well until now, too. Brett's gainfully employed as a lawyer (who doesn't need

free legal advice?), more than holds his own conversation-
ally, texts back quickly, and hasn't sent me any unsolicited
dick pics. Perhaps not the highest bar, but he's definitely the
most impressive guy I've dated in months. I'd even been
hopeful enough about his potential longevity to extend an
invite to a family function—not a step I take lightly.

Brett massages the back of his neck, clearly annoyed. "I
warned you that Saturdays are off-limits. I haven't missed a
Hokies game in six years, and I'm not about to start now. I
was very up-front with you about this."

I blink and step back. *And to think I'd planned on inviting
him up.*

"Yes, I recall your dramatic monologue about 'Sacred
Saturdays.' I assumed it was satire."

"I don't joke about football."

"Evidently."

He raises his hands defensively. "Look, you wouldn't
want me there anyway. I'd be distracted the whole time."

I'm tempted to laugh. *So gaslighting is his weapon of choice.*
"Actually, I *did* want you there. Hence the reason I invited you."

There's a beat of silence as we face each other in a stubborn standoff.

"Sorry, Cassidy, but I refuse to feel guilty about this."
He crosses his arms over his chest, his body language anything but apologetic. *Strike two.* "Saturday's the one day per
week that's off-limits for me. Pick any other day."

I stare at him. "I didn't pick the day. It's her *ninetieth*
birthday."

"Just as easy to have a party on a Sunday as a Saturday."
Aaand strike three.

"Mm-kay." I rummage in my bag for my keys. "You know what? Forget it. You're off the hook."

He drops his arms and his face relaxes, relief replacing irritation. Easygoing Brett has returned. "Thanks for understanding. You wouldn't believe how many women won't cut me any slack on this. I'm always the bad guy."

This time, I do laugh. "I meant you're off the hook *permanently*. Consider your Saturdays wide open from now on. And your Sundays, and your Mondays, and every other day that ends in -*y*. We're done."

Now he's the one blinking at me. "Seriously?"

"Seriously. You made that decision very easy." I reach past him to grab the door handle. "But I hope you enjoy your game," I say, syrupy-sweet, and pat his arm before letting the door swing shut in his face.

And another one bites the dust.

I block and delete his number from my phone before I can second-guess myself, then shake my head in disgust as the elevator lurches upward to my floor. Despite my righteous indignation back there, I'm disappointed. Brett was the rarest of breeds: good-looking, smart, successful—and what's more, he actually seemed to *want* a relationship (practically an endangered species in the urban jungle that is New York). But if he doesn't know how important my grandmother is to me, then he hasn't been listening . . . and the last thing I need is to sign up for a lifetime as a weekend sports widow. *No thank you.*

I sigh as I key into my apartment, setting my purse down on the console table in our entry and calling out for Nat. There's no answer; not a surprise since she spends most nights at her boyfriend's in Williamsburg. I usually don't mind being home alone, though I wouldn't mind having someone to commiserate with right about now.

As I brush my teeth in our shared bathroom, I peer into Natalia's dark, empty bedroom, the pit in my stomach growing larger when I think about how close she is to getting engaged—and how I'll be forced to find yet *another* new roommate, my fourth in five years. It's become a running joke in our friend group: *"Want your boyfriend to pop the question? Just move in with Cassidy! You'll be engaged in no time."* I laugh right along with them, even if I'm crying inside. Don't get me wrong, most of the time I'm happily single and embrace my independence, but even the most confident among us would be unnerved by pulling bridesmaid duty six times in three years. It's not a great feeling to watch everyone around you stairstep into the next phase of life while you seem to be running in place.

Though my bed and Instagram feed are calling my name, I plop into my desk chair and open my laptop instead, forcing myself to tap out some thoughts before the memory of that Brett confrontation fades. While I don't much feel like wallowing in my disappointment, it's true what they say: Everything is copy (and by "they," I mean the queen herself, Nora Ephron). Emotional turmoil fuels creativity, and when the Muse knocks, one must answer. I close my eyes and channel my inner Carrie Bradshaw: *I thought I'd picked a winner, but when a man values football over family, I can't help but wonder—in the game of love, will I always come out the loser?*

Something Brett said niggles at my brain, so I open a new tab and google "Sacred Saturdays"—then groan out loud.

Of course.

"BOY, I'D GIVE my eyeteeth to have seen the look on your face."

"Right? I don't see how I could have reacted any differently."

"I might've added a smack for good measure. You'd be surprised how quickly a well-timed slap can knock some sense into a man." There's a mischievous glint in Gran's eye as she slices a hand through the air to demonstrate. "Besides, who would pass up the chance to meet *me*? I'm delightful."

I snort. "Obviously."

It's early Saturday evening and my grandmother's party's just ended, the last of my extended family members trickling out in a flurry of Tupperware, overstimulated toddlers, and goodbye hugs. I stayed late to chat and catch up—and rehash all the fresh family gossip, of course.

My grandmother and I have had a unique bond from the time I was young, perhaps because like recognizes like and she sees herself in my quiet bookishness. Growing up I often felt out of place among my extroverted sister Christine and my natural athlete brother Colin, but Gran always paid me special attention, never letting me fade into the background or feel like the introverted nerd I surely was.

While my dad loved to regale us with childhood tales of her exacting nature and authoritarian brand of discipline, we rarely saw that side of her. With us, she was gregarious and fun-loving and lenient, perpetually spoiling us and slyly encouraging our mischief (as all the best grandparents do). To me she always seemed glamorous and impossibly chic, from the collection of Chanel scarves she'd style a thousand different ways to the extravagant doll clothes she'd sew for our Barbies: faux fur coats with pearl buttons and evening gowns made of gold chain mail or luxe velvet. She was a stickler for things like manners and etiquette, but also cool, like when she'd teach us how to origami-fold our cloth napkins into bikinis or pour us glasses of wine when we turned eighteen and practically dare our parents to chide her for it.

I lean my hip against the countertop as she putters around the kitchen making tea. I'd offer to help, but I know better—she'd accuse me of treating her like an invalid, maybe even mock me by calling me *Thomas* (the name of her worrywart second-born son, otherwise known as my dad). She spent the entire day today assuring anyone who would listen that she's a "young ninety."

"Where are you even finding these boys, anyway?" she asks, then stops bustling long enough to hold up a finger. "Wait, let me guess. An *app*." She makes a face like she's just licked a lemon. "Why your generation entrusts their romantic futures to a machine is beyond me. If you think a computer can accurately predict chemistry, I've got some oceanfront property in Kansas to sell you." The kettle starts whistling and she moves to take it off the burner.

"It's how things are done now, Gran. I don't exactly have men lining up to fill my dance card at the sock hop."

She swats me with a tea towel. "Some might consider your ageist jokes elder abuse, you know."

"*Now* you're elderly," I tease as I squat down to pet her Himalayan cat, Pyewacket, so named after the feline sidekick in one of her favorite old movies, *Bell, Book and Candle.*

"Well, I'm sorry he didn't work out, honey. Did you like him a whole lot?" She pours the steaming water into a teacup, the lines around her eyes crinkled in concern.

I think about that as I wander out of the kitchen and over to my favorite spot in the house, the vintage tufted couch in her sitting room that she had re-covered in a sunny yellow velvet after my grandfather passed away twelve years ago. She said the color cheered her.

I sink deep into the cushions, feeling myself instantly relax. "Honestly? I'm not sure. I think I liked the idea of him more than I actually liked *him*, if that makes any sense. It was nice to have someone to think about and go out to dinner with, but he didn't exactly give me butterflies." Pye-wacket jumps up onto the couch and I scratch behind her ears as she curls herself into a fluffy ball on my lap.

"Never underestimate the importance of butterflies," Gran warns as she follows me out of the kitchen. "It'll eventually wear off, of course, but when the going gets tough, sometimes just the memories of the butterflies are enough to pull you through."

"Tell me a good Pop-Pop story," I beg, reaching out to take her teacup so she can get settled next to me on the couch.

"Oh, you've already heard all my stories," she says, waving me off, but I catch the tiny smile she's hiding. She loves any excuse to talk about my grandpa—which is why I asked her, of course.

"Come on, just one that'll restore my faith in men and prove that true love still exists."

"*Just* one of those, huh?" she says with a laugh, then hums as she thinks for a minute. "Let's see. There was this one time when we were newlyweds, and we'd just been transferred to a base in Texas. So we were in this brand-new place, didn't know a soul, and I caught some bug. Maybe it was food poisoning, I can't remember. Anyway, I got sick, and I mean *really* sick. You know, vomiting and . . . the other thing," she says, raising her eyebrows and giving me a wide-eyed look, and I have to stifle a laugh. She's so proper, she can't even bring herself to say the word *diarrhea*. "And in those days, we were very private about such things. None of this 'open door' stuff you kids are into. I'm not even sure he'd seen me without my face on before we got married!

"So I was really in a state, just terribly embarrassed," she continues. "I locked the door and tried to keep him from seeing me like that, but he wouldn't have it. He demanded I open the door, and then he sat with me, and rubbed my back, and brought me ginger ale. He doted on me," she says simply, the faraway look in her eyes tinged with sadness. "And I remember thinking, *Boy, did I choose the right one.*"

"Pop-Pop was a gem."

"True enough." She smiles at the memory. "So there's my advice for the day: Pick a man who'll hold your hair back."

"Duly noted."

She picks up her teacup again. "Now, enough of my blathering. What else is new with you? How's work?"

"It's good," I tell her, the question earning a genuine smile. "Busy as always."

For the last four years, I've worked as an editor at Siren, a female-run, female-focused news and entertainment website that covers everything from current events to fashion to relationship trends to pop culture. My boss, Cynthia Barnes-Cooke, founded the site out of her apartment nearly ten years ago, though today Siren employs more than twenty full-time editors and two hundred contract writers. We produce at a punishing pace, publishing more than two hundred pieces of content a day, and I love everything about it: the responsibility of managing a team of writers, the diversity of content I get to work on, helping shape the growth strategy. In our last funding round, the site was valued at more than $200 million.

"Any update on the book? How's it coming?" Gran asks casually, focusing studiously on dipping her tea bag instead of on me. Even so, I feel myself deflate.

Gran is one of the few people to whom I've confessed my ultimate career ambition: to write the next great American novel—or at least, something buzzy enough to get picked for Reese's Book Club or *O* magazine's list of "Summer's Hottest Beach Reads." Natalia thinks I'm psyching myself out by starting with such lofty expectations, but I hardly think I'm setting the bar too high (and as Gran's so impartially pointed out, Reese or Jenna or Oprah would be *lucky* to have me). The only problem? I have no clue what to write about. I know what it takes to stand out in the publishing world, and none of my ideas feels fresh or high-concept enough. What's the point of writing a book if it's just going to fade into the background like some sort of literary wallflower?

I'm a wannabe author with writer's block. I hate myself for the cliché.

"No update. Still searching for a topic that'll set the publishing world on fire."

Gran hums noncommittally, sipping her tea.

"I'm going to be in another wedding," I blurt before she can work her way up to a follow-up question I won't have an answer for.

"What number is this one?"

I wince. "Lucky number seven."

"Pretty soon you'll be the girl in that movie, with all the bridesmaid dresses." She looks tickled.

"I will *not* be that girl, because I sell all the dresses before the couple even gets back from their honeymoon." Thanks to a bridesmaid's best friends, eBay and Poshmark. "But you're gonna love this next part."

Her eyes light up. "Is it a destination wedding?"

"The Caribbean."

She claps her hands in delight. "Can I be your plus-one?"

"You know what, maybe. I'd certainly have more fun with you than as the perpetual third wheel with all my couple friends."

"I wouldn't want to steal the spotlight from the bride," she says, deadpan.

"With great power comes great responsibility," I respond, just as seriously.

"Or maybe you'll meet someone by then!" *Ever the optimist.*

"Maybe I'll win the lottery, too," I say dryly. And frankly, I'm gonna need to if I have a prayer of continuing to afford the never-ending merry-go-round of bachelorette parties, bridal showers, and tropical nuptials I'm forced to attend. I have half a mind to start a GoFundMe to finance my lifestyle as a serial bridesmaid. No one would be able to resist my tear-jerking backstory: destitution via wedding gift.

I heave a sigh. I hate that I'm starting to hate weddings. "Let's face it, weddings just aren't any fun without a significant other. It's like they're designed to make single people feel pathetic and inadequate. And you know I hate saying that out loud, because it goes against *everything* I stand for."

It's the truth. I've never bought into the narrative that life doesn't start until you meet "The One" or that I won't be

whole until I've found my "other half." In fact, I'm that annoying friend you can count on to trot out trite platitudes
like "A man can't love you until you love yourself" or "A
fulfilling life starts by being full."

But I can't deny that when I arrive back to my empty
apartment each night, I wish there was someone waiting inside for me. Sometimes I even imagine I'll see him when I
swing open the door, this phantasm who looks a little like
Henry Cavill or Scott Eastwood or maybe a *Magnum, P.I.*–era
Tom Selleck (there's just something about that mustache–
chest hair combo that gets my motor running). Someone
who'd be interested in the tiny, insignificant details of my
day, who'd take my side on every petty grievance, then
mount his steed and ride into battle, vowing vengeance on
those who dared to wrong me. Someone who'd ruin my
perfectly curated Netflix queue of time-traveler romance
and angsty teen dramas with sweaty man shows like *Reacher*
or *Yellowstone*. I ache for someone to curl my body against
on the couch, to fall asleep in the embrace of a man who'd
spoon me so tight I'd overheat.

"Wanting a partner isn't a weakness," Gran reminds
me, as if she can read my thoughts.

"I know that. I just feel like all these weddings have
turned me into this Bitter Betty, and that's not who I am.
Most of the time I *like* being independent."

"Maybe you're *too* independent," she muses thoughtfully. "Men like to feel needed, you know. Sometimes I
would pretend I couldn't open the pickle jar just so your
grandfather could feel useful."

I wave a hand dismissively. "Women in your generation
were different than mine. We don't have to make ourselves
small for men to feel big."

She freezes with the teacup halfway to her lips. "I'm sorry?"

Crap. I'm so comfortable with my grandma that I somehow forgot the first rule of journalism: *Know your audience.* "That came out wrong. What I meant was—"

"Oh, I know exactly what you meant." She bangs her cup down on the saucer so roughly, tea splashes over the side. "You think you've got it all figured out, Miss Modern Gal-About-Town? You think you have nothing to learn from the women who came before you? Never mind the hard-earned lessons learned from a nearly fifty-year marriage. What could this old fuddy-duddy *possibly* have to teach you?"

I hold up my hands in surrender. "Point taken. That was very judgmental. I didn't mean it the way it came out, and I'm sorry."

She pins me under her gaze, her expression shrewdly assessing. "You know, the world you're living in might look different than mine did, but the rules haven't changed. Men still want the same things."

I can't help myself. "Like what, to be waited on hand and foot? To have their laundry folded and dinner on the table when they walk through the door?"

Her eyes narrow. Pretty sure if I wasn't twenty-eight, she'd paddle me. "They want to feel like *men.* They want to pursue, provide, and protect. That's biological, no matter what you want to tell yourself."

"Maybe that's my problem, then," I muse. "I don't need a man to provide for me. And I can kill my own spiders. Heck, I can even have a baby on my own! Honestly, sometimes I think women have evolved past men entirely."

"Well, keep telling men you don't need them, and don't be surprised when you find yourself all alone."

Ouch. "That was harsh, Gran."

"The truth hurts, doesn't it? I swear, your generation needs a reprogramming. You're all too liberated for your own good. I should sign you up for *The Bachelor*," she mutters, then suddenly straightens and snaps her fingers. "Wait."

"You are *not* signing me up for *The Bachelor*."

She ignores me, squinting into the air as if racking her brain. "Yes, I'm sure I still have it. It's got to be in the study . . ." she murmurs, then gets to her feet, padding down the hallway that leads to the back of the house.

I resign myself to going along on this tangent and follow dutifully behind her, and eventually she veers off into her home office, heading straight for the floor-to-ceiling bookshelves spanning the back wall. She slips on the glasses hanging from a chain around her neck and starts grazing the spines with her fingertips, brushing past my grandpa's old engineering texts and Ludlum thrillers, and her own cozy mysteries and romance novels.

While she hunts for whatever it is she's looking for, I peruse the framed photos lining the shelves, which is akin to taking a trip through time via fashion. My favorite is the one of my grandparents all dressed up—he in his Navy dress whites and she in an off-the-shoulder red dress and fur stole that would fetch a mint in one of the city's upscale vintage shops. In a posed family portrait, she's every bit the stately matriarch in a boxy Jackie O suit and white gloves. There's one of my grandpa with his arms around their boys, the Jersey shoreline in the background, the sea air wreaking havoc on their windblown hair. And then I spot a picture of them with my siblings and me from a family trip we took to the Grand Canyon, my awkward stage on full display in braces and curly bangs. "Ugh, why is *this* the picture you chose to frame?"

She pauses her search to glance over, then clucks her tongue. "Oh stop it, you look adorable. A little gawky, maybe. But look at the swan you grew into."

"You used to tell me I looked 'gamine' instead of 'gawky.'" I remember this detail so vividly because it's one of the many reasons I fell in love with the written word, that just a slight variation in letters had the power to improve the mindset of an awkward, gangly teenage girl. "Anyway, it's a real mystery why I never heard back from those model searches I was constantly entering at the back of *Teen* magazine." I place the frame back on the shelf, stealthily nudging it behind a couple of others.

"Aha! I knew I still had it." She pulls a dark hardback from one of the lower shelves and hands it to me triumphantly—and when I see the title, I nearly choke on my tongue: *I Do: Rules & Etiquette for the Military Wife.*

"Oh my . . ."

I drift toward an overstuffed floral love seat set up in the corner of the room and switch on the reading lamp. Inside the front cover is a faded inscription on the flyleaf: *Welcome to the club, Joanie!* Everything about the book—from its worn linen cover to the thick card stock and its musty smell—appears ancient. I check the copyright: originally published in 1952. "Where did you get this?"

"Every woman who married a Navy man was given this book."

"You're telling me this was *government-sanctioned*? As in, required reading?"

"Oh, I don't know about that. It was a bit of a joke among the ladies, though I can't say we ignored the suggestions."

I start thumbing through the pages, noting the chapter headings with wry amusement—*Indoctrination of Wives; An*

Efficient Kitchen; Matri-Money—when a loose sheaf of papers falls from the back cover onto the floor. I bend to pick them up and unfold them gingerly, noting the signs of age in the creased and yellowed pages. They seem to be ripped from a magazine.

I read the headline on the top sheet and gasp. "Gran, you have *got* to be kidding me."

"What?"

I hold it aloft like a prosecutor presenting damning evidence. "'125 Tips to Hook a Husband'?!"

She squints at the page for a moment before breaking into a grin. "I'd forgotten I'd saved this." She plucks it out of my hand, skimming it and occasionally chuckling to herself.

"Okay, you need to explain yourself."

She waves a hand, as though such reading material is as normal and mundane as the Sunday paper. "It's just an article I ripped out of an old *McCall's* or *Ladies' Home Journal* a long time ago. Back when I was single."

I do some fast math. "You've saved this since the *fifties*?" I say, incredulous. "Did you use this to trick Grandpa?"

She recoils, affronted. "Excuse me? Of course I did not *trick* your grandfather! My goodness, you're really on a roll today," she huffs.

"Well then, why do you have it?" I ask, suitably chastened.

"What do you mean, *why*? I didn't meet your grandfather 'til I was nearly thirty! I was considered a spinster in most circles. I needed all the help I could get!"

I narrow my eyes, not missing her subtle dig—*I'm* nearly thirty. No one's better at camouflaging an insult than my grandmother. "Thanks for that."

She smiles innocently, passing the pages back to me. "You should take this advice. There are a lot of great tips in here."

I scan the list, then snort. "Like '*Read the obituaries to find eligible widowers*'?"

She shrugs. "It's not the *worst* idea."

"'*Learn to sew and wear something you've made yourself.*'"

"It shows him you're thrifty!"

"'*Ask his mother for recipes.*' I hate cooking."

She looks scandalized. "Whatever you do, don't tell a man that. *Or* his mother."

"'*Find out about the girls he hasn't married and don't repeat their mistakes.*'"

"That one's just a no-brainer."

"'*Point out to him that the death rate of single men is twice that of married men*'?!" I throw the pages down. "Gran, be serious."

"What? Statistics don't lie! No harm in instilling a little fear," she says defensively.

"I am not using these '*tips,*'" I say, my fingers locked in tight air quotes, "to trap a husband. They're ridiculous and antiquated and you know it." I scan the list again anyway, shaking my head. "Funny, though. I can't believe women actually used to do this stuff."

"Oh, I think you will use them."

I glance up. "Excuse me? How's that?"

A slow, devious smile blooms on her face, melting the years and lines of age away. It takes me a second to place the familiar glint of mischief in her eyes until I realize: It's the same teasing gleam I see when I look in the mirror.

"Because it's my birthday, and this is what I want as my gift."

I cross my arms and tilt my head, my body language

communicating: *You can't be serious.* She meets my gaze steadily, her smug expression confirming: *As a heart attack.*

"What, the *Hamilton* tickets weren't enough?"

She throws up her hands. "Cass, just read the book and give some of the tips a shot. What do you have to lose?"

"Uh, my dignity?"

"*Pfft.*" She waves a hand. "Overrated."

"You're actually suggesting I behave like a submissive 1950s trophy wife?!"

"I'm *suggesting* you consider that some of those tips might actually have merit. They say the definition of insanity is doing the same thing over and over again but expecting a different result, right? You're sitting here telling me you wish things were different, but you're not willing to change your behavior or consider another way." She raps the book cover with a knuckle. "Here's another way."

"I hardly think you blackmailing me into highly problematic, subservient behavior is a proportional response for my lack of a wedding date."

"Oh, 'blackmail' is such a strong word," she says airily. "Think of this as . . . an *experiment.*"

I open my mouth to argue further, but the word triggers something in my brain and I pause.

This article—one my grandmother's saved for *seventy* years—is exactly the kind of story we salivate over at Siren. Just reprinting these half-baked dating tips in all their ridiculous retro glory would generate a million clicks and even more shares, but what if we actually tested them on some unsuspecting suitors? I can see the headline now: *I tried these old-fashioned dating tips so you don't have to!* Subhead: *June Cleaver meets the modern Manhattanite.* We could even turn it into a recurring series. It's a content gold mine.

Gran's voice snaps me out of my reverie. "I know you wouldn't deny an old woman one of her last requests."

I laugh in spite of myself. "Please, you're going to out-live us all."

She wags a finger at me. "I won't be around forever! My clock is ticking. And I want to see you happy."

"I *am* happy."

"But you could be happier."

I groan and drop my head into my hands. "I can't win."

She shrugs, unrepentant. "I just call it like I see it."

"You should consider a filter."

"Nah. One of the few benefits of being ninety is that I'm allowed to say whatever I want, whenever I want. And pressure my grandchildren into doing my bidding, of course," she adds with a wink.

"I see. And how exactly do you think"—I consult the list—"'*Asking him to carry my hatbox*' or '*Dropping my handkerchief*' is going to secure me a significant other?"

She pats my hand. "You're smart and creative, I'm sure you'll figure it out."

"That's it, huh?"

"What, you need me to lend you a handkerchief?" I sigh in defeat as she starts for the door. "Now that we're agreed, I want some more of that cake," she tosses over her shoulder.

"I did *not* agree to this," I call after her—but I know I've lost before the words have even left my mouth.

Chapter 2

*S*O WHAT DO YOU THINK?"

I scan the faces of the women lining either side of the conference room table and stop on Cynthia, trying to gauge whether her expression indicates amusement or horror. Maybe a little bit of both.

I'm at our Monday morning editorial meeting at Siren's offices in Gramercy, where department heads give status updates on both the short- and long-lead pieces we're working on, as well as pitch and assign new story ideas. I've just explained my concept for the vintage-inspired dating feature I've cheekily coined "Operation Betty Draper." I spent my Sunday doing a deep dive into the *Military Wife* etiquette book Gran gave me (verdict: every bit as antiquated as I expected), fell down a rabbit hole of additional internet research into courtship customs of the 1950s, then somehow wound up inhaling an entire pint of birthday cake Halo Top while streaming YouTube clips from classic films of the era like *Pillow Talk* and *Sex and the Single Girl.* Between all that and the 125 tips to snag a spouse, I have more than enough material to work with (and a newfound appreciation for Doris Day, the "girl next door" rom-com queen of the golden age).

"I love it," Cynthia says immediately, and I beam. It's one of my favorite things about her leadership style, how direct and decisive she is. It's either "I love it, get to work," or "What else you got?"—nothing in between. And she has a pitch-perfect radar for which stories will hit, a skill honed over the course of her twenty-plus years in the always evolving, cutthroat world of modern journalism. She also has a built-in bullshit detector, which is why I come overprepared to every meeting.

She holds up the "125 Tips" magazine pages I've since encased in plastic sheet protectors. "These are gold." She slides them down the table for others to peruse before turning back to her laptop, fingers flying over the keyboard. "So you're thinking a long-form piece?"

"Yep, maybe a couple thousand words? I thought I could assign the actual testing of the tips to Hannah, since she did such a good job with—"

"Wait, wait, wait. *You're* not going to be the one testing them?"

Every head swivels toward me in unison like a pack of meerkats. "I—well no, that wasn't my plan. You know I don't typically do—"

"I really think it needs to be you," Cynthia cuts me off. "The heart of the story is your relationship with your grandmother and the generational divide, if you will," she says, peering at me over the rim of her cat-eye glasses. "As the reader, I want to see how you balance your commitment to your grandma with your more modern sensibilities. I want to *feel* your discomfort at this retrogression of gender roles. That's what makes this so relatable."

I nod slowly like I'm considering it even as my brain races to construct a convincing counterargument. This is *not* what I had in mind. "I understand what you're saying, but I really think it would be better to assign it to someone like Hannah. This type of undercover piece is her wheelhouse. Remember when she re-created Sarah Jessica Parker's strangest looks from *Sex and the City*? She wore overalls with a bra and a bird on her head for a week and no one even batted an eyelash." I grimace regretfully, like it's out of my hands. "I'm not an actress."

"But that's just the point, you don't need to be." She steeples her fingers under her chin, regarding me seriously. "This story is *you*. You can delve into the psyche of a late-twenty-something single woman because you *are* one. You can explore what her needs are now versus then, how societal expectations for dating and marriage have evolved across generations. What's obsolete, and what remains? The silly dating tips and how they play out is the setup, but I don't see this as just some throwaway farce piece. I think that's selling your concept short."

Did I say I loved her direct leadership style? I meant I hate it.

"Um . . . okay," I say slowly, beginning to panic now at the thought of putting myself out there so publicly. I write stories about other people; I don't want to *be* the story. "It's just a little more personal than I prefer to get." Not to mention that Gran will hobble me if she finds out I'm making fun of her advice.

"We can run it under a pseudonym?" she says expectantly, and I know I've lost this battle. Natalia kicks me under the table, and I plaster on a smile with clenched teeth.

"Sure. I guess I'm up for the challenge."

"I'll make sure she pulls it off," Nat offers unhelpfully, and I kick her back even harder. "She can practice on me. It'll be fun." She grins at Cynthia, ignoring the death ray I'm beaming into the side of her head. *Note to self: Kill roommate.*

"Perfect. You think you'll be ready to run it in a couple weeks?" She looks at me and I nod in affirmation. She glances back at her screen. "I also have you down as covering the Jessup cologne launch tonight, yes?"

"Yes, and I'll have a recap ready to run by ten a.m. tomorrow," I reply, switching mental gears. "My goal is to get a quote from Olivia the mystery fiancée. *If* she's in attendance."

While it may sound strange for a women's site to cover the launch of a men's fragrance, events in the personal life of Eric Jessup, recently retired star pitcher for the Yankees and New York's golden boy, have made him a trending topic among Siren readers. Known for the carousel of models and actresses he's paraded down red carpets for the last decade, he shocked the world last month by announcing his engagement to Olivia Sherwood, a pretty but decidedly non-famous schoolteacher and high school ex-girlfriend from his hometown in Louisiana. Speculation is rampant that it's a publicity stunt to rehab his reputation as a hard-partying womanizer.

While I'm curious about Olivia, I'm not exactly amped to spend my evening at yet another press event, which sounds exciting to outsiders but gets old fast: the bland, canned sound bites from the celebrity of the hour; the protective barrier of publicists preventing you from asking any *real* questions; the gifted but ultimately useless bottle of cologne I'll pass on to one of my coworkers with a boyfriend or husband at home. Still, the potential to see and maybe even speak with the elusive Olivia—a woman who hasn't granted a single interview or even been seen in public—is too compelling to ignore.

"I'm going too," Nat pipes up. "But my goal is for Eric to take one look at me and realize he proposed to the wrong woman." The group titters. "What? If Eric Jessup can fall in love with a commoner, then there's hope for all of us."

"You're practically engaged," I remind her.

She raises her left hand. "Do you see a ring on my finger? I'm keeping my options open," she says breezily.

I shake my head, turning back to Cynthia. "Anyway, tonight's covered."

"Great." She taps a few more keys, then turns to our relationships editor. "Jordan, *'Across the aisle to down the aisle: How I found love with my political polar opposite.'* How's that going?"

"Great. I'm interviewing this adorable couple, they work as rival Senate staffers in DC and their story is so entertaining, I swear it deserves its own book . . ."

I tune out as the meeting spools on, taking the opportunity to respond to some emails and approve a product roundup from one of our contract writers. A text pops up from Natalia: Legit starving. Placing a Serafina's order now. You want in? I text back in the affirmative as Cynthia starts recapping our stats from last week, a signal the meeting's wrapping up.

"Last week's biggest hit and the winner of this week's bonus is Daniela, with her piece about influencers inflating their numbers. Excellent work, Daniela," Cynthia says to the spunky brunette lifestyle editor, who preens and waves the crisp hundred-dollar bill in the air. "Shares were way up, it saw huge numbers on social and got a lot of pickups. If anyone has any follow-on story ideas there, don't be shy. Influencers behaving badly always performs." She mouse-clicks a few times and squints at her screen. "The equal pay for equal work story got a big traffic spike on Wednesday. Unfortunately, we have our friends at Brawler to thank for the assist with their classy rebuttal: *'But do women work equally as hard between the sheets? From the boardroom to the bedroom, by the numbers.'*" Jordan snickers under her breath and Cynthia gives her the hairy eyeball.

Ugh, Brawler—Siren's nemesis and the thorn in our collective side. Just hearing the word spikes my blood with adrenaline, bringing with it the memory of Brett's rejection like a fresh, still-stinging wound.

Originally founded a decade ago by a pair of college roommates as a site focused mainly on sports betting, Brawler unwittingly stumbled upon a substantial—and lucrative—untapped market: emotionally stunted manchildren hungry for validation of their sports- and sex-obsessed lifestyles. Once the site's scope was broadened to a more comprehensive "by men for men" format, they quickly amassed an army of rabid fans and never looked back. The content they churn out is about what you'd expect: sports scandals, toilet humor, click-through galleries of scantily clad coeds. With its provocative, clickbait-y headlines and misogynistic editorials designed to drum up as much controversy as possible, Brawler lives up to its name—and then some.

Siren's long-running feud with Brawler dates back years

before I worked here, and legend has it it's all because of George Clooney.

Here's the backstory: Not too long after Cynthia founded Siren, George proposed to Amal, and they married later that year in a splashy, star-studded Italian wedding. Their nuptials dominated entertainment news, with every outlet running near-identical versions of the headline A-LIST ACTOR AND NOTORIOUS BACHELOR GEORGE CLOONEY MARRIES LAWYER. Despite an accomplished life and impressive résumé, Amal was relegated to a nameless footnote, her identity immaterial, her only noteworthy accomplishment apparently taming an untamable man. Galled by the slight, Cynthia penned a wedding announcement of her own: TRILINGUAL, INTERNATIONALLY RENOWNED HUMAN RIGHTS LAWYER AND FORMER ADVISER TO UN SECRETARY GENERAL AMAL ALAMUDDIN MARRIES SOME ACTOR.

Overnight, Cynthia was crowned journalism's latest "It" girl, the feminist voice of the digital media generation, putting her and Siren squarely on the map. But just as her fledgling website was enjoying the warm glow of the spotlight, Brawler wrenched it back by publishing their own snarky hot take: bachelor George Clooney's *obituary*. And since the media loves nothing more than a feud, the headline tug-of-war and resulting press frenzy catapulted both sites into a battle of the sexes so intense, we've been locked in a death match ever since.

Cynthia slams her laptop shut with more force than necessary. "I hate them, but traffic is traffic. So let's all thank Brawler for spreading our message," she says, raising her hand to the window in a one-finger salute.

"Speaking of Brawler, have any of you heard of 'Sacred Saturdays'?" I ask as everyone starts gathering their things.

"Ugh, yes," Kara, a petite, freckled blonde and one of our beauty editors, groans from across the table. "My boyfriend thinks it's hilarious. News flash: You sound like an asshole."

"I made the mistake of dating a 'Brawler Bro' once," Jordan says as she twists her hair into a bun. "Worst few weeks of my life. He forced me to tag along with him one weekend when he went back to hang at his frat house. He was twenty-seven." She grabs her laptop and stands. "Never again."

"Thank you for validating me." I briefly summarize my run-in with Brett the buffoon and am gratified by their appropriately outraged reactions. "I guess I didn't realize Sacred Saturdays was a Brawler thing, but I googled around, and get this: They've *trademarked* it."

"Doesn't surprise me," Cynthia tosses over her shoulder, scrolling through her phone as she heads out the door. "If there's one thing those lowlifes at Brawler have figured out, it's how to monetize being a Neanderthal." She waves as she exits, her harried assistant rushing to keep up with her.

"They're like a cult," I muse to Natalia as the rest of the women file out. "With an army of brainwashed followers. Why does everyone pretend they're a legitimate news organization?"

"Because if you go after them, their fans go after *you*," she points out, looping an arm through mine and tugging me toward the door. "It's not worth the hassle."

"They're basically encouraging an entire generation of men to be the worst versions of themselves, and no one's going to call them out on it?"

"That's about the long and short of it," she says blithely.

"Listen, I'm seriously about to gnaw off my own arm. Can we go?"

"DO YOU THINK this dress sends the right message?" Nat asks later that afternoon, pirouetting on the pavement as we wait to get checked in. "I'm going for *I'm bold and beguiling, but won't upstage you in the press.*"

I fan myself, trying not to melt in the city's muggy late-August heat. "I think it says *I'm single and ready to mingle*, which you most certainly are *not*," I respond dryly, thanking the publicist as she waves us inside. "Does Gabriel know you talk this way?"

"Are you kidding? I sent him a selfie before we left and reminded him that Eric Jessup is number one on my hall pass list. A little jealousy goes a long way." She checks out her reflection in the mirrored glass walls as we walk past. "Can't have him getting complacent."

I chuckle, knowing her outrageousness is (mostly) for show and she'd never cheat on Gabriel, her devoted boyfriend of more than a year. They're so into each other, it's actually kind of disgusting. In fact, I've often wondered if she wishes she'd moved in with him instead of me, though at the time her rent was hiked and I found myself searching for yet another new roommate, it was too early in their relationship for cohabitation. Natalia Kimura was my best work friend prior to becoming roommates, and while I initially worried we might get sick of each other, her frequent sleepovers at Gabriel's quickly negated that concern—and despite our differing personality types, our living situation has proven surprisingly harmonious.

She's bold and brash to my measured and thoughtful; uninhibited to my introverted. I talk her down from flights of fancy, while she's the devil on my shoulder. We're opposite but complementary, like flip sides of the same coin. Even our appearances are a study in contrasts. Nat paints herself in loud colors and samples every trend; I stick to neutral palettes and pride myself on the capsule closet of sophisticated basics I've built over time. Her olive skin and dark features are the perfect canvas for every shade of lipstick; my fair skin burns even on cloudy days.

If her half-Japanese features are distinctive, I think of my own as distinctly in-between. My wavy hair falls somewhere between curly and straight, in a shade of burnished copper that's neither brown nor red. In some lighting my eyes trend toward green; in others, hazel. I'm neither short nor tall at five foot six, and I'm trim and toned but just shy of curvy (or at least lacking the generous bust my sister inherited). My most striking attributes are my wide smile and hearty laugh, which have been called Julia Roberts–esque—a comparison I pretend to be embarrassed by but secretly love.

While Natalia's fire-engine red dress is meant to draw attention, tonight I'm wearing my version of a work uniform: fitted black cigarette pants, my favorite trusty nude pumps, and a white blazer with the sleeves scrunched to the elbows. It's my own personal brand of New York chic, my sartorial suit of armor, appropriate for any and every industry event I'm called to cover.

I survey the restaurant, getting the lay of the land while the chill of the air-conditioning cools my skin. We're early, so the vibe is still relatively relaxed, with most attendees standing around awkwardly sipping the Jessup Julep, tonight's signature cocktail. Moody blue spotlights project the words FORCE BY ERIC JESSUP onto every available surface. Centerpieces featuring cologne bottles perched atop tiered glass pillars anchor each table, alongside spherical glass bowls crammed full of baseballs (for ambience or autograph signing, I'm not sure which). The room positively *reeks* of cologne. While the scent might be fine in moderation, the olfactory-straining superdose saturating the enclosed space is more potent than a sixth-grade stink bomb.

It's the calm before the storm, though I know that'll change the second Eric shows up and everyone's forced to jockey for exclusive sound bites. I tend to see the same group of familiar faces at these events—entertainment reporters, lifestyle bloggers, colleagues from our competitors Refinery29 and Bustle—but this crowd's different, skewing heavily male. Likely a bunch of sports writers coerced into covering the athletic-adjacent event—and not thrilled about it, judging by the restless looks on their faces.

"*Hellooo*, sausage fest," Nat says, nodding at a guy who very obviously checks us out as he walks past. "I'm a-likin' these odds."

"This is a *work* event," I remind her as I fish my phone out of my purse so I can test the voice recorder, which takes me a hot minute because my overstuffed tote rivals Michelle Pfeiffer's magic bottomless bag in *One Fine Day*. My sister Christine calls it my "diaper bag" despite me not having any kids.

"Not for me, it isn't. And as the resident singleton here, you should be paying closer attention. It's not every day you find yourself in a room chock-full of men."

"That reminds me—one of the 125 man-trapping tips is

to check census reports and move to a state with a higher male-to-female ratio. In case you were wondering, Nevada has 138 males to every 100 females. In 1958, at least."

She grabs my arm with a gasp. "OMG! We're totally going to try out some of those tips tonight!"

I fake-gasp back. "No, we're not."

"This is literally the perfect place to practice."

"How is a room full of our *colleagues* the perfect place to practice?"

I spot a couple of publicist types huddled near the kitchen and make a mental note to keep an eye on the back entrance. If Olivia is planning to attend, it would make sense that she'd try to sneak in to avoid the crush of photographers out front.

"Oh please, you don't know any of these men. A lot of them don't even look like writers. They're probably sports agents or batboys or something. Like . . ." She scans over my shoulder until her eyes brighten. "That guy over there. In the purple tie."

I roll my eyes but indulge her, subtly spinning in a slow circle until I spot our mark: a man in a suit standing by the bar, chatting with a couple of other corporate-looking types. Brown hair, average height, nothing too intimidating about him. A nice, approachable regular Joe.

I turn back to her. "He looks like a generic finance bro."

"Or he could be a wealthy cologne executive just *dying* to meet his soul mate. Maybe he even manages the entire Coty portfolio of fragrances."

"Or maybe he's Eric Jessup's even wealthier best friend," I say with phony enthusiasm.

"That's the spirit!"

I scoff. "Please."

"Do I need to remind you that this story was *your* idea? You have no one to blame for this but yourself."

As if I could forget. "Actually, I'm quite content to blame my grandmother."

"Come on, this is going to be fun! For me to watch, at least." She rubs her hands together like a cartoon villain. "Now, which one of the tips should we start with?"

I sigh in resignation and surrender to my fate, digging around in my bag until I come up with the plastic pages and hand them over.

She immediately starts snickering. "*'Cry softly in the corner and wait for him to ask you what's wrong.'*"

I raise a finger. "Not happening. I have my limits."

"Probably a bit over the top," she concedes. "How about this: *'Walk up to him and tell him you need some advice.'* That's perfect! Appeal to every male's overinflated ego. And then just play dumb about whatever it is he says so he can do some mansplaining."

I glance toward the front door, like if I just stare hard enough, Eric Jessup will magically appear and save me from this nightmare of my own making. "I'm not sure *my* ego can handle that."

She hums. "Alright, how about this one: *'Stumble into him, "accidentally" spilling the contents of your purse all over the floor.'* It doesn't get easier than that." She stares at me expectantly when I don't move. "Chop-chop."

"I can't believe I'm doing this," I grumble, reaching into my bag and unzipping my makeup pouch so as to achieve maximum spillage. *In for a penny, in for a pound.* "Our mothers burned their bras so I could set us back a generation."

Natalia inhales sharply. "Our target just left his group!

He's walking toward the bathroom. Hurry up, you can cut him off at the pass."

"Hang on, I don't want to drop my phone," I tell her, tucking it into my back pocket.

"Quit stalling, he's right behind you. *Go!*"

She gives me a shove, and she must not know her own strength because I go careening backward like a drunken sailor, my arms windmilling comically as I try to stay upright, but I'm no match for gravity (and neither are these heels). The ensuing chain of events registers in a slow-motion sequence: I watch Natalia's eyes pop wide as I collide with my unsuspecting victim. I hear his surprised *"Whoa"* and low grunt as my body collides with his. His arms lock around me instinctively as I topple him, and I feel the blunt impact of the floor even as his body breaks my fall. And I smell . . . well, I only smell Force by Eric Jessup, because it's overpowered every other scent within a five-mile radius.

As the hot flush of embarrassment sets in that *Yes, I just took out a random stranger accidentally-on-purpose,* I remember my original mission and mentally throw up my hands, deciding I may as well go all in—then upend my purse, sending stray pens, napkins, makeup, and assorted debris raining down upon us. From my prone position, I watch one of my lipsticks disappear underneath a nearby table and want to die. *The things I do for a story.*

"I am so sorry," I say, rolling off the poor guy, noting that—thankfully—he appears more amused than angry. "Are you okay? You're not hurt? I'm so embarrassed," I babble, quickly swiping a tampon that's wedged underneath his shoe and stuffing it back in my purse.

He chuckles good-naturedly. "I'm just fine. Are *you* okay? That was quite a spill," he says, passing me the travel-sized deodorant I carry in case of sweat-mergency. From the corner of my eye I spot Natalia watching from the bar, her entire body shaking with laughter. *She is dead to me.*

"I'm okay. And I really am sorry." I frantically collect the stray hair ties, hand sanitizer, dental floss, Imodium tablets, Tic Tacs, and egg-shaped lip balms littering the floor while pretending not to notice the gaping stares of onlookers. "I swear I'm not usually this clumsy."

"Must be my lucky day, then."

I snap my head up to find him grinning at me. *Flirtatiously.*

Oh, you have *got* to be kidding me. *There is no way this asinine stunt actually worked.*

"I'm Chase." He holds a hand out to help me up.

"Cassidy," I reply, standing and brushing off my pants. It's a damn miracle I didn't break an ankle in these heels.

He points to the keys I'm clutching in my hand, a bright yellow banana charm dangling from the key ring. "Interesting key chain."

I wave a hand. "Long story. An inside joke, really."

"How about I get you a drink and you can tell me all about it?" He flashes me another grin, eyes twinkling.

Unbelievable. Gran will be peacocking all over the place when I tell her.

"I don't usually drink at work events," I start to demur, then change my mind. "Actually, I think I've earned it, right?" Honestly, I probably should've downed a couple shots before committing to this harebrained scheme.

"You've more than earned it," he assures me. "Pick your poison."

"Anything—whatever they're serving. Beer, wine . . ." *100-proof moonshine.*

He tells me he'll be right back, and once he's out of eye-shot I glare at Natalia, who gives me a shit-eating grin and a thumbs-up. I roll my eyes and busy myself reorganizing my purse, doing my best to tamp down the lingering feelings of humiliation . . . that is, until I get the distinct feeling I'm being watched.

I scan the room casually, surveying the crowd, which has grown thicker now. Several men in my immediate vicinity send me pitying looks, and I wince theatrically so they know I'm in on the joke. It's not until my eyes sweep past a shadowy corner that I spot him: a tall, dark-haired man watching me with interest, head cocked to one side, a bemused expression on his face.

When we lock eyes I expect him to look away, but he surprises me again by meeting my gaze head-on. *A brazen challenge.* My heartbeat ticks up as I take him in, registering several things at once: his barely concealed smirk as he swirls a glass of amber liquid in his hand; the air of brash confidence he's wearing as comfortably as his midnight-blue suit; his brutal good looks, the kind that feel dangerous.

I fold first, breaking eye contact and feigning preoccupation with my bag, hoping that by the time I look up again he'll have trained that unnerving stare elsewhere. But I must have a sixth sense, because when I furtively flick my eyes back up to check, the mystery man has cut the distance between us in half and is headed straight for me with the cool, unhurried stride of a stalking predator. It's the kind of stride that says *I own the place,* or maybe *No one tells me no.* He's *sauntering,* really.

The second surge of adrenaline in as many minutes courses through my veins as he stops before me and pins me under his gaze. "What the hell was *that*?"

Chapter 3

I'M SORRY?"

"What. The hell. Was that?" He enunciates each word slowly, accusation thick in every syllable.

I feel my face heat, like a light bulb burning brighter and brighter until it shatters. "What was *what*?"

"That Three Stooges pratfall I just witnessed. If I didn't know any better, I'd think you were trying to pick his pocket."

"Excuse me? I *fell*," I say with as much dignity as I can muster—which, at the moment, isn't much.

"You fell, or"—he leans in and drops his voice—"you were trying to pick him up?" He arches an eyebrow knowingly.

I cross my arms and take a moment to study this cocky stranger (who's a little too observant for his own good). His dark hair is slightly mussed, like he attempted to style it but gave up when it refused to behave. His strong jaw is clean-shaven and jutted out slightly in practiced defiance. He's what the Regency romances I sometimes read would describe as "broad of shoulder," leanly muscled and tanned in a way that tells me he spends more time running outdoors than on a treadmill. He's standing close enough that I have to look up at him, and I get the distinct feeling he enjoys that power dynamic.

He has an honest face, but under the surface there's an unpredictability to him that has me on edge. He's like Jamie Dornan in every frame of those *Fifty Shades* movies—he prowls around with calculated restraint, but you just know at any moment he's going to snap and bend Anastasia over a table.

I match his conspiratorial tone, deciding my best course of action is to play along. "You got me. Throwing myself at him was the easiest way to get his attention."

I smirk at my own cleverness. They say the key to pulling off a convincing lie is to keep it simple. What's more believable than the truth?

He catches my eye and holds it. "Trust me, you don't need to try so hard."

I blink in surprise—and Chase chooses precisely that moment to reappear, a wineglass cradled in each hand. But before he can hand me one, my new companion intercepts it and passes it to me himself.

"Thanks for grabbing that for her," he says smoothly, reaching a hand out to a clearly confused Chase. "I'm Jack."

"Chase," he answers slowly, casting me a quizzical look as he accepts Jack's proffered handshake. I'm no help—I'm a deer in the headlights. "Are you two—"

"So what is it you do, Chase?" Jack cuts him off and takes a small step closer to me, wordlessly establishing dominance and staking his claim so shamelessly that I'm left speechless. *Who* is *this guy?*

Chase slides his eyes from Jack to me and back again.

"Uh . . . I'm in investment banking. The retail and consumer side." I would laugh at how accurately I pegged Chase but for the fact that I'm still openly gawking at Jack.

"No kidding?" Jack jabs a thumb over his shoulder. "I was just chatting with a friend of mine, you might know him. Neil Waltham?"

Chase goes bug-eyed. "Neil Waltham, as in CFO of Cohen Property Group? The largest owner of outlet malls in the country? He's here?"

When Jack nods in the affirmative, Chase looks a bit sheepish. "Could you . . . point him out?"

"I'll do you one better. Want an introduction? Neil and I go way back."

I watch the exchange in mounting disbelief, simultaneously appalled and impressed by how effortlessly this guy's managed to turn Chase into a pawn on his chessboard.

"Uh, *yeah*, if you're offering," Chase says eagerly, barely glancing at me, the now-forgotten footnote in their conversation. *Really, Chase? I nearly ruptured my spleen for you!*

Jack lightly cups my elbow and I startle.

"I'll be right back." He says it in the casual, *just checking in* tone of a significant other, and when I gape back at him, he shoots me a nearly imperceptible wink.

I take a generous gulp of wine as I watch their retreating backs and attempt to unscramble my conflicting feelings about this guy. His arrogance is completely obnoxious, that much is for sure. And yet, the ease with which he dispatched Chase was . . . pretty hot, if I'm being honest. I don't know whether I'm offended or turned on. Before I can decide, Jack's back at my side, his smirk somehow even cockier than before.

"Well, that was . . . something."

"Thank you," he replies seriously, like it was a compliment.

I eye him over the rim of my glass. "So what's your game?"

"Funny, I was going to ask you the same thing."

"You make a habit of running off perfectly nice guys?"

He considers the question. "How many's a habit?"

I let out a puff of air. "What if I liked him?"

"Come on, that guy? Really?"

We both swivel to look across the room at Chase, who's now talking the ear off a bored-looking older man. I think of a puppy wagging its tail.

"I am a little insulted by how quickly he gave up on me," I admit.

"And after that stage dive you took, too. So much wasted effort." He *tsks*.

"I *fell*," I groan in exasperation, then move to leave. "You know what, forget it."

He grabs my elbow to stop me, laughing as he holds his hands up in surrender. "I was just messing with you. Anyway, I did you a favor. You don't want a guy who's that easily manipulated."

I wonder how many times this guy's been slapped. "And I suppose *you* know what I want? You don't even know my name."

"Ah, now we're getting somewhere." He clinks his glass against mine in cheers. "I'm Jack."

I eye him suspiciously, and he grins in a way that tells me unequivocally: *I'm used to charming my way out of every sticky situation.* The question is, will I let him off the hook?

My internal battle seems to amuse him. "This is the part where you tell me your name. Or you don't, in which case I'll *definitely* think you were trying to pick his pocket."

I roll my eyes, but his challenge has the intended effect. "Cassidy."

"Cassidy." His eyes dance and I see they're a deep blue, sharp and intense and sparked with intelligence. "Nice to meet you."

"I'd say 'likewise,' but the jury's out on you."

He throws his head back and laughs, the rich sound washing over me, fermenting in my bloodstream. There's something intoxicating about this guy that I can't quite put my finger on. I *want* to like him, despite my gut sending up warning flares.

"Guess I'll have to work on changing your mind," he says, smiling like he's harboring a secret. "So what brings you here tonight, Cassidy?" He takes a swig of his drink, though his eyes don't stray from my face.

"Isn't it obvious? The free men's cologne."

He laughs again and I award myself another flirt-point.

"I'm covering this event for work. Though our readers are a little more interested in Eric's love life than how he smells," I confess.

"Ah, of course."

"So what do you think, is their relationship real or for the cameras?"

He raises a skeptical eyebrow. "Why would Eric Jessup need to fake a relationship for the cameras?"

"Oh, I don't know, because he could use an image overhaul? Maybe he's not getting the family-friendly endorsement deals he was hoping for."

He snorts. "He made twenty million a year for more than a decade. Pretty sure his bank account is just fine."

"Then why's he shilling cologne?" I counter.

He shrugs. "They're paying him millions to slap his

name on something and make a couple of appearances. I'd take the money and run, too."

"So you believe he's been carrying a torch for his high school girlfriend for the last fifteen years? Sorry, I'm just not buying it."

"What's so hard to believe about that? Maybe he never got over her. Maybe she's the one that got away." His eyes glimmer in the dim light and I know he's enjoying our sparring.

"Oh yeah, I'm sure he was crying himself to sleep every night while his supermodel of the week slept beside him."

He shakes his head sadly. "So cynical. And here I thought women were the ones who wanted to believe in the fairy tale."

"Remind me again, which fairy tale was it where the hero went off to sow his wild oats while his jilted ex-girlfriend pined away for him at home?"

"You know, we should ask Eric. And I think we're about to get our chance." He nods toward the door.

A current of energy ripples across the restaurant as the previously low din of voices builds to a fever pitch, and before I can blink, the crowd surges toward the front door like a tidal wave, nearly flattening Jack and me in the process. Eric Jessup has arrived, and I'm not ready.

I curse under my breath and try to join the throng, but before I can, a heavyset guy in a backpack elbows past me, clipping me on the shoulder and sending me hurtling to the side. Before I've even registered what's happened, Jack's grabbed a fistful of his backpack and shoved him away.

"Excuse you," he barks in a menacing Clint Eastwood–esque growl. I half-expect to hear him snarl, *Get off my lawn.*

Backpack guy mumbles an apology, avoiding my eyes as he skitters away.

"Damn," I mutter once I've regained my balance for the second time tonight. I abandon my wine on a nearby table and attempt to muscle my way into the mob, but I'm hopelessly boxed out, the wall of men now blocking my view even more intimidating than the one standing next to me.

"Can you see if he's arrived with anyone?" I ask Jack, hopping up on my tiptoes and craning my neck, but it's futile; I can't see a thing. I pray that Nat—wherever she is—has a better view.

"Nope," Jack says, looking amused.

"You didn't even look!"

He chuckles as he sets his empty glass on the tray of a passing waiter and thanks him.

"Come on, you said you wanted me to change my mind about you? Here's your big chance. Just throw a couple 'bows and get us to the front of that pack."

His grin grows wider. He's enjoying this. "How about we raise the stakes a little?"

I arch a brow while simultaneously keeping my other eye trained on the crowd. One of the guys in the back is manspreading; I might be able to army-crawl through his legs.

"I help you secure an exclusive quote from Eric Jessup, and you . . ."

He pauses for dramatic effect and I brace myself for some crude sexual favor he'd like me to perform. *Wouldn't be the first time.*

". . . let me take you to dinner," he finishes.

I slow-blink at him. "You want to take *me* out? The woman you suspect of being a con artist?"

He waves a hand. "That was so ten minutes ago."

I laugh out loud. "Gotta say, I didn't see 'blackmailing me into a date' coming."

"Not my usual approach, I'll give you that, but life is all about opportunity and timing. You gotta shoot your shot when you see an opening."

"My professional pain is your gain, huh?" Which brings me to my next question. "How do you even plan to get his attention? Are you going to create a diversion or something?"

"Maybe I'll take a dive," he says, wagging his brows. "Now come on, clock's ticking. Who knows how long Jessup's contractually obligated to stay?" He sticks his hand out, letting it hang in the air. "Do we have a deal?"

I eye him warily, sizing him up. I don't know how he's doing it, but it feels like this guy's been one step ahead of me since the second I spotted him in that shadowy corner. It's disconcerting that I can't get a good read on him. In fact, I'm nearly certain he's still messing with me, but what else can I do? It's not like I have a better option.

"Fine." I clasp his outstretched hand and his eyes flame like I've struck a match. "We have a deal."

"We have a *date*."

"Easy, tiger. I don't have my quote yet."

He grins rakishly and releases my hand. "I'll be right back."

I expect to see him shoulder his way into the fray, so I'm surprised when he heads in the opposite direction, toward the back of the restaurant where I saw the PR folks huddled earlier. I watch him exchange a few words with a woman dressed all in black, and when he points at me, I lift my hand in an awkward wave. She nods once, then starts speaking into an earpiece.

Jack strolls back looking so smug, he's practically spitting canary feathers.

"Who was that? And what'd you tell her?"

He shrugs innocently, but before I can follow up, the crowd parts and a different woman in all black emerges—this time, with Eric Jessup in tow.

How the hell did he pull that off? I start fumbling for my phone, but Jack brushes my elbow to stop me.

"He'll be chattier if you're not recording him," he murmurs in my ear, then puts his hand up to wave. "Rick!"

"You *know* him?" I hiss. Great, and I sat here going on about what a womanizing sleazeball he is. *Smooth move, Ace.*

"We share a publicist."

"You could've told me you know him!"

"Now where's the fun in that?"

Eric's upon us before I can answer. "Jackie boy!"

I watch them perform an intense bro-greeting ritual: hand-gripping pulled into a tight hug with a dash of aggressive backslapping. My shoulder spasms just watching them.

"Thanks for coming, man," Eric says.

"Wouldn't miss it. You know I've always dreamed of smelling like a jockstrap."

"Just for that, you're not going home with a gift bag." He turns to me and flashes his signature megawatt smile. "Hi, I'm Eric," he says, holding out his hand.

"Cassidy," I say, smothering a laugh. *Like I don't know who you are.* "Would you mind if I asked you a couple of questions?"

"That's what I'm here for, so shoot."

"Fantastic. First of all, congratulations on the cologne launch," I tell him, getting that out of the way. "It smells"—*awful*—"great. Very . . . potent."

"Some might even call it . . . *forceful*," he says, straight-faced.

"Right." I huff a laugh and make a mental note: *Eric Jessup makes puns!* "I was actually hoping to learn a little more about your recent engagement."

He grimaces. "Ah, sorry, we're not—"

"I know you're keeping things private, and I totally respect that," I barrel ahead, talking faster before one of the publicists circling us like sharks catches wind of my line of questioning and whisks him away. "It's just that our readers are dying to know more about Olivia and how you two reconnected."

I watch his face go carefully neutral. "Sure. Well, I'm very happy and looking forward to settling down."

I nod like he's said something groundbreaking while suppressing an eye roll. That kind of rehearsed, generic quote isn't exactly the headline catnip I'm after—and it won't win me any bonus cash, either. I rack my brain for another way to draw him out.

Jack breaks in before I can. "Oh come on, you can give her more than that."

I lock eyes with Jack and beam him a silent message: *Alright, you've earned that date.* He shoots me another wink.

Eric groans. "Look, I'd love to help you out, but Liv's really adamant about privacy." I file that little detail away, the casually intimate way he uses her nickname.

"How about this—if I give you my card, would you pass it along to her? I'm sure you've experienced this yourself,

but sometimes saying nothing just encourages more speculation. It can be better to just tell your own story rather than
let others tell it for you."

"I have tried explaining that to her," Eric admits. "I
don't see her changing her mind, but I'll take your card."

"I appreciate it. In the meantime," I press, pushing my
luck, "is there *anything* you feel comfortable sharing? Like
what are you most looking forward to about married life?
Will you stay in New York or move back to Louisiana? Is there
anything you wish the public could know about Olivia?"

When he eyes me warily, I add, "Trust me, no woman
would be upset to hear her fiancé publicly gushing about her."

Eric looks at Jack. "She's good."

Jack splays his hands like, *What can you do?*

He sighs. "Alright, here's what I'll say: I've been in love
with Olivia basically my whole life. She's the most beautiful
woman you'll ever meet, inside and out. I would've married
her a long time ago, but life got in the way a bit. I feel very
fortunate that we were able to find our way back to each
other."

*You mean you decided you were ready for kids and needed a
broodmare,* I think to myself, but I'm not about to quibble. It's
a quote I can use, and Siren readers will eat it up.

"Would you say she was the one that got away?" Jack
says seriously, and I nearly snort.

"Well, she didn't get away, now did she?" Eric replies
with a smug *If you know what I mean* expression, and I watch
them laugh and swap those cocky guy head-nods. *Ugh.* Another minute and I'll be witnessing a dick-measuring contest.

"Thanks, man. I know you're busy here, we appreciate
it," Jack says and claps him on the shoulder.

"Sure thing. Though if Liv gets pissed at me, I'm blaming you," he says with a laugh, then turns to me, jerking a thumb in Jack's direction. "How long you been working for this guy?"

"Oh, we don't work together," I quickly correct him.

He looks surprised. "No? Sorry, I just assumed."

"I'm with Siren," I tell him, handing over my card, and Jack goes very still beside me.

"Ah, now things are making more sense. Couldn't figure out why Brawler would care about my wedding. Thought you were goin' soft on me!" He punches Jack in the arm.

My jaw drops just as one of the hovering publi-sharks gets tired of treading water and appears at Eric's elbow, apologizing to us before murmuring in his ear.

"Duty calls," he tells us regretfully. "It was great to see you, man. And say hi to Tom for me. We should all go out for a drink, it's been too long."

"Absolutely. Name the time and we're there."

"Nice to meet you, Cassidy," he calls over his shoulder as he's led away, and he's swallowed up by the crowd before I can answer—which is probably a good thing, since I'm currently stunned silent.

As soon as he's out of sight, I spin around to face Jack accusingly, my face a flaming ball of fire. In fact, my entire body blazes with indignation.

"You're with Brawler?" I spit out the words like they've scalded my tongue.

He takes his time answering. "Well, actually . . ." he says slowly, "I own Brawler."

My temperature spikes; mercury showers everywhere. "You *what*?" I cry, barely recognizing the shrill sound of my own voice. "You're telling me you're Jack *Bradford*? Founder of Brawler?"

"Cofounder, but yes." He looks annoyed. "Is there a problem?"

My mouth opens but no sound comes out; my brain still hasn't quite caught up to the fact that the human embodiment of that god-awful hellsite is standing before me with a name and a face (a nauseatingly attractive one, at that). I'm simultaneously speechless and shaking with the need to hurl an insult at him that's both cutting and clever. I'm Meg Ryan in *You've Got Mail*, holding Tom Hanks at knifepoint after he's just compared books to vats of olive oil.

Before I can formulate a response, Nat pops up at my side, cheeks flushed and gripping a blue-tinted cocktail. "I cannot believe you just got a private audience with Eric Jessup! I tried to get over here but security kept holding us back." She sticks her free hand out to Jack. "Hi, I'm Natalia."

"Ja—" he starts to respond before I cut him off.

"This is Jack Bradford, founder of Brawler."

Her eyes go silver dollar–wide. "Whaaat? Seriously?"

"Wish I was kidding."

Jack's starting to look pissed now. *Good.* We'll match. "I'll repeat—is there a problem?"

"Yeah, Brawler's my problem. And by extension, *you* are now my problem." Natalia hoots and takes a noisy slurp of her cocktail.

I am righteously indignant. I'm standing up for wronged women everywhere. He has no idea what's about to hit him. I might even break out my Z-snap.

He stares at me impassively, a parent humoring a tantruming child. "So this is about the history between us and Siren? How is my friend Cynthia, anyway?"

I bristle. "She is *not* your friend."

He grins, clearly enjoying ruffling my feathers. He juts

out his chin, and I have to talk myself out of socking his perfectly chiseled jaw. "Oh come on, we all benefit from this little feud. What's good for the goose is good for the gander.
Cynthia knows that better than anyone." His eyes light in
recognition. "Wait, I know who you are now. Cassidy Sutton.
I've read your work." He nods approvingly, like I've passed
some sort of test I didn't know I was taking. "It's good."

"Thanks, I've been awaiting your validation," I say sar-
castically.

"You know, you should run a photo with your byline,"
he says, bypassing my hostility completely, and I narrow
my eyes. "You'd get a lot more clicks."

Oh, gross. "Maybe I don't want those kinds of clicks."

He raises a finger. "Now, that statement would be a fire-
able offense at Brawler. Clicks are king. I would think you'd
know that."

"I'll take my dignity over clicks, thank you."

He shrugs. "Suit yourself. Of course, that kind of emotional decision-making is probably why Siren's traffic has
stagnated."

"Hey!" Natalia is affronted.

I raise a hand to her as if to say, *I've got this.* "You know,
you're every bit as obnoxious as I imagined you'd be."

The insult seems to amuse him. "Funny, my partner's
usually called the obnoxious one. And I'm pretty sure you
didn't think I was so bad a minute ago." There's a lascivious
edge to his smirk, like he's seen me naked. I huff and tug
my blazer closed.

"Wait, what happened a minute ago?" Nat asks, trying
to keep up.

"He attempted to blackmail me into a date. I almost fell
for it, too."

"So this is the thanks I get for helping you out, huh?" He shakes his head, but he's still wearing that stupid smirk, like my ire entertains him. And it probably does, since life's all a big game to men like him. They can behave however they please and never face any real consequences. They can act like a cocky asshole at a bar and still walk away with a girl's phone number. They can get away with murder and the world will say, *May I offer you another victim?* "I hand-delivered you Eric Jessup's first on-the-record comments about his engagement, but somehow *I'm* the villain here? Please tell me, how exactly have I wronged you?"

"Oh, I wouldn't go there, buddy," Nat warns.

My blistering laugh could strip paint from the walls. "How have you wronged me? Oh, I don't know, maybe it's the constant stream of misogynistic articles you publish, many of which come at Siren's expense? Or perhaps it's that your site brands all women as either nagging harpies or sex objects? Or maybe"—I snap my fingers—"it's that you've inspired an entire generation of men to shout their chauvinism from the rooftops."

"I warned you," Nat singsongs.

Jack regards me calmly, his expression unfazed, almost bored. I'm having the exact inverse reaction—the more un-ruffled he appears, the more agitated I'm getting. "Brawler is a site where men can be men. You know, almost exactly like the website *you* work for?"

"The site we work for doesn't encourage its readers to troll and harass anyone who disagrees with them."

"We don't *encourage* harassment."

"You don't condemn it, either."

"I'm not responsible for the behavior of our readers any more than you're responsible for yours."

Our gazes collide in a fiery clash. I'm so frustrated, I could flay the skin off his bones.

I flog him with my words instead. "I can't believe you're actually defending what you do. You're shameless."

He's quiet for a beat, eyes narrowed, considering me. "You seem to be harboring some sort of personal grudge against me, but as a reminder, I haven't done anything to you."

"Oh no? Then I guess I must have just imagined the guy who told me last week that he couldn't attend my grand-mother's ninetieth birthday party because 'Saturdays are for the bros,'" I spit with derisive air quotes. "But I suppose that's not your fault, either, right? You're not responsible for any of the harmful ideas you put out on the internet to your little band of brainwashed sycophants."

My insult doesn't hit its target like I thought it would. In fact, Jack's eyes soften—and when I realize why, I immedi-ately regret revealing that detail of my personal life. I don't want his pity.

"For the record, that guy sounds like a dick." He pauses, as if to gauge whether his comment will thaw my iciness any, but I throw my shoulders back and raise my chin in a clear message: *I don't need your sympathy.* He sighs. "But you're blaming me for something that has nothing to do with me."

"Is that what you tell yourself so you can sleep at night?"

A muscle flexes in his jaw; his control's starting to slip. *Not used to women talking back, are you, Jack?* I inject that sat-isfaction directly into my veins; it fuels my outrage better than gasoline and a match.

"You know, the whole idea behind Sacred Saturdays was to give men a day to just be men, to recharge with their friends. I can't help it if some guy weaponized it as a way to dodge his obligations." His voice is razor-sharp.

I scoff, wishing I hadn't ditched my glass of wine. I could throw it in his face and it would be *so* satisfying.

"Wanting to drink a beer and watch the game isn't a crime, you know. In fact, I fail to see how it's any different than women having a 'girls' night out,' but somehow it's only wrong when guys do it." He's gaining steam now, clearly riding his own wave of self-righteousness. "Maybe if you weren't so busy vilifying us for it, you'd see that a little downtime actually makes men better partners."

Does anyone actually buy this BS? "So you're doing it all for us, then? I suppose we should thank you for your service? Wait, let me guess—your publicist fed you that line for situations just like this. When someone calls you out, just spew some crap about how you're actually *helping* women. Spot-on delivery, too. But hey, it's not a lie if you believe it, right?"

Nat drains the dregs of her cocktail in one long, judgmental slurp.

He cocks his head. "Have you ever actually been to our site, or are you just parroting back what you've heard about it?"

"You ran an editorial titled *'Why women should be seen and not heard.'*"

"It's called satire." His words are clipped. "As a writer, I'd think you'd be familiar with it."

"Your logo is a set of *boobs.*"

His eyes go a hard, wintry gray, like brushed steel, cold to the touch. A frisson of pride shivers down my spine that I've managed to get under his skin after all. Perhaps I should take his shift in demeanor as a warning to reel it in some, but I can't retreat now. I've got him on the ropes.

"Our logo is a *B*. For 'Brawler.'" His voice is arctic.

"Turned on its side."

We glare at each other, our gazes warring for victory as we wait to see who will back down first (or, more likely, just end this by leaving). The flinty resolve in his eyes tells me Jack isn't used to losing, though.

Well, news flash, Jack: *Neither am I.*

Nat breaks in. "Okay, you two. I'm not gonna lie, this has been really entertaining, but I think it's no longer constructive." She tugs on my arm, shooting me a pointed look.

I'm grasping for the perfect witty-yet-biting parting shot when one of the article's tips pops into my mind uninvited: *Never ridicule his masculine achievements or show contempt for his ideas. Building him up should be your highest priority.*

I cringe as I realize that Gran's meddling advice and those stupid tips seem to have infiltrated my brain against my will—but almost as quickly as the thought dissolves, a new one materializes in its place:

Use him.

The idea breaks through the clouds like a wartime airdrop; a sudden, providential gift delivered into my outstretched hands on a clear, sunny day. It's a brilliant beyond brilliant idea. Maybe the best one I've ever had.

But one thing's for sure: To pull it off, I'll need to perform the about-face of a lifetime.

"You know what?" I say, making my tone appropriately sheepish. "You're right. I'm sorry."

"What?" Jack and Nat say in unison.

I lock eyes with Jack and pray my face conveys regret rather than duplicity. "I don't know what I was thinking, blaming you for what happened with Brett. You're absolutely right, it has nothing to do with you. It's obviously still pretty raw—I must be looking for a scapegoat." I drop my head and look away, feigning embarrassment, and hear Gran's voice echoing in my head: *Men want to pursue, provide, and protect. They want to feel needed.*

I peek up at him from beneath my lashes, doe-eyed and repentant. He looks stupefied and more than a little suspicious. *Take pity on me, you big, strong man. I'm a delicate flower.*

"I took my frustration out on you, and that was wrong of me. It was probably that fall—I must've hit my head." I chirp a laugh like a potential concussion is hilarious. "I've been out of sorts. Nat will tell you."

I turn to Nat and she's gaping at me like I've just morphed into a werewolf. I send her a pleading message with my eyes: *Just go with it.*

She blinks and turns to Jack. "It's true," she continues seamlessly. "Brett was a total shit to her and she's been on the warpath ever since. Wild mood swings, snapping at people. It's like twenty-four-seven PMS. Don't take it personally."

I shoot her a look: *Really, was that necessary?* She splays her palms like, *What?*

I grind my teeth and turn back to a still-shell-shocked Jack. "Anyway, I apologize. I let a silly work feud get the best of me, but that's really between you and Cynthia. And also"—I lean into him like I'm confessing a grave sin—"I probably shouldn't admit this, but that recent piece you guys posted on equal work in the bedroom? It was actually really funny."

Just saying that last part burns my throat like bile. Frankly, I'm amazed I could even vomit the words up. *Please God, do not smite me for speaking with such a forked tongue.*

I pause to gauge my progress, assessing his body language to see how I'm faring. He's studying me carefully, his expression inscrutable. He hasn't spoken a word since I flipped the script on him, so I have no idea if he's buying this in the slightest. He probably thinks I have multiple personality disorder.

I don a coquettish smile. "I hope I haven't scared you off." I bite my lip and *Look at me, I'm pleasing and submissive and exactly the type of woman you want.* I lightly brush my fingertips along his forearm, and his eyes flare. "I'm still game for that date—that is, if you're still offering." I stop, my case rested, on tenterhooks now as I wait for his final verdict.

He wants to agree, I can tell he does, but still he waffles. Behind those navy eyes I can see his mind working, the gears spinning as he tries to make sense of my one-eighty. He's at war with his own intuition.

A lightning bolt of inspiration strikes me. Men like him—masters of the universe, kings of all they see—love a challenge. *Appeal to his manhood.*

"Of course, that's if you think you can handle me," I say suggestively, throwing him a sly grin and a wink for good measure. I'm *daring* him to claim me.

It does the trick. "Consider yourself handled." His eyes gleam and I know I've got him. "It's a date."

$\mathcal{S}$O THEN IT DAWNED ON ME—JACK IS MY story. These tips are just begging to be tested on *him*."

It's the next morning and I'm in Cynthia's office, relaying every sordid detail of my run-in with Jack while Nat provides pithy commentary from Cynthia's blush-colored love seat. Behind her, a wall of glass provides an unobstructed view of the newsroom floor, a hive of worker bees orbiting their queen, their low buzz of activity throwing off a lulling ambient noise. If I were the boss I'd want a little more privacy—good luck picking so much as a wedgie without someone seeing—but I think she gets off on surveying her kingdom like Mufasa.

"You should've seen how she had him eating out of her hand by the end of it," Nat reports gleefully, swilling her coffee. "Not an actress, eh? Could've fooled me."

I flush with equal amounts of pride and embarrassment. "Honestly, I don't even know where it came from. I felt possessed."

After I somehow managed to convince Jack to hop aboard

the crazy train, I practically threw my number at him while Natalia made some excuse and we hightailed it out of there as fast as our heels could carry us. Back at the apartment (and after I explained myself), Nat and I spent the rest of the night workshopping my new-and-improved plan for the vintage dating story. When we finally called it a night, I spent hours blinking at the ceiling, my brain racing with ideas, too keyed up to sleep. I woke up blurry with fatigue, yet somehow so jittery I was forced to eschew my morning coffee. An EKG machine would have a field day.

"I'll tell you where it came from," Cynthia says, matter-of-fact. "Your reporter's instinct. You recognized a once-in-a-lifetime story and went for it."

"What can you tell me about Jack?" I ask her, leaning forward in my chair. "We weren't able to find all that much by googling."

It's an understatement; "virtually nothing" would be more accurate. In an attempt to *know thine enemy*, my first order of business was to comb the internet for background information—past interviews, photos, anything I could use to paint a clearer picture of Jack Bradford—but for someone in such a prominent role at a highly publicized company, Jack's basically an internet ghost. He doesn't actually write for Brawler, so no past bylines to dissect. I couldn't find any public social media profiles (or private ones, for that matter). He's rarely quoted on Brawler's scandals du jour, instead leaving that dirty work to his cofounder and college BFF Tom "the Tomcat" Bartlett (who, to be fair, seems responsible for most of the dustups). From what I can gather, Jack seems to maintain a shadowy existence behind the scenes, pulling strings and operating beyond the glare of the media spotlight. How very *Wizard of Oz* of him.

The only in-depth profile I was able to find mainly re-counted Brawler's inception and meteoric rise. It's an origin story we've all heard a million times before—two guys in a dorm room, *blah blah blah*—but it also included some rare personal details about the founders and friends. I learn that Jack, along with an older brother, was born and raised here in the city and earned his degree from Penn's Wharton School of business, where he met Tom his freshman year after they were randomly paired up as roommates. It's heavily implied that the Brawler seed money came from Jack's father, a wealthy hedge fund manager, corroborating something I already suspected: Jack is used to getting what he wants.

"We cross paths every so often," Cynthia says, leaning back in her chair and raking her fingers through her chic black bob. "I'd say our relationship has been fairly cordial, all things considered. It's his horrible partner I avoid like the plague." Her face pinches in distaste. "Jack's always seemed pretty reserved to me, though I suppose it's easy to maintain a low profile when your Tweedledum cofounder is sucking all the air out of the room."

"Well, he definitely wasn't reserved last night," I tell her, remembering how smugly he called me out on my faux fall. "In fact, he was the cockiest guy I've ever met, and that's saying something. It's like he thinks he's the king of New York or something. I kept waiting for him to say, 'I'm Chuck Bass.'"

Nat snorts.

"So tell me what you're thinking here," Cynthia says, tapping the end of her pen on the desk. "How exactly would this work?"

I stand and begin to circuit the room, a prosecutor delivering her opening statement. "According to Brawler, the perfect woman is beautiful but compliant. She challenges a man just enough to keep him interested, but not so much that he has to try very hard. She's spirited and playful, but always defers to his judgment. She can be smart, but only in a nonthreatening way. They want the 'cool girl' who can hang with the guys but would never dream of talking back to her man."

I pause to survey my audience. Both Nat and Cynthia are leaned forward in rapt attention, on the literal edge of their seats. *Perfect.*

"For Brawler bros, women fall into one of two categories," I continue, drawing out the suspense. "Hysterical, uptight feminazis like yours truly"—I vogue with my hands framing my face—"or vapid, brainless arm candy who'll shut up and look pretty. Coincidentally, the 1950s housewife portrayed in that column matches up almost seamlessly with Brawler's ideal female archetype: polite, devoted, and submissive, leaving the male to assume the traditional dominant, decision-maker role. Really, these tips couldn't have fallen into my lap at a better time."

I stop at the glass window and peer out at the newsroom, observing my Siren coworkers: Some are on the phone or hammering away at keyboards, while others weave through the maze of cubicles or collaborate in small groups. These are my colleagues, my friends. They're clever and driven and impressive, the most inspiring group of women I know. No matter what Jack says about their site being "satire," Brawler has done real damage to these women in both obvious and insidious ways. I can't let him get away with it.

I spin around and lock eyes with Cynthia. "Jack thinks women should be seen and not heard? Well, he is in for a real treat, because I'm about to give him exactly what he wants: the perfect trophy girlfriend. And once he's fallen for it hook, line, and sinker?" I pause for dramatic effect. "I'm going to expose him for the misogynist he is."

Natalia holds out her arm. "I just got chills."

I see the exact moment it all slots into place on Cynthia's face. "A takedown of the founder of the most sexist site in journalism."

"You can see it, right? The story was already funny when I was going to test these tips on unsuspecting men, but testing them on an unsuspecting *villain*? It's chef's-kiss perfect."

Cynthia's got a taste for Brawler blood now, her eyes glowing Cullen-red. "And he'll fall for it, because what guy wouldn't? He'll think he's died and gone to heaven! He'll think he's found that elusive unicorn: a smart but subservient woman, sexy and flirtatious but pure as the driven snow."

"A lady in the streets and a freak in the sheets!" Nat crows.

"Exactly!" I realize it a second too late. "Wait, no—I'm not pimping myself out. Just the street lady part." I hear how that sounds. "I mean, he won't be seeing *my* lady parts." Not better. *Argh.* "Never mind. The point is, not only will Jack be embarrassed that he's fallen for such an obvious trap, but the fact that he's been duped by the *enemy*, the precise type of woman they claim to hate? The headlines write themselves. And if I get to torture him in the process, well." I grin wickedly. "That's just an added bonus."

"You're gonna give him exactly what he wants," Cynthia says. "Or at least what he *thinks* he wants—then expose them for the backward-thinking chauvinists they are. And the beauty of it is, this doesn't just embarrass Jack. It's a forced reckoning for the entire Brawler fan base." She looks at me approvingly. "Cassidy, it's brilliant. Well done."

Nat widens her eyes at me, neither of us accustomed to that degree of praise from our notoriously hard-assed boss. It's the Cynthia equivalent of throwing a parade in my honor.

"Thank you. I just hope I can pull it off." A giant *if*. "And on that note, let's talk about some of my concerns."

Nat groans and sags back against the couch. "Here we go."

I start pacing the length of Cynthia's office. "So okay, I was able to fool him for a few minutes while under the influence of adrenaline and proximity to celebrity. But could I really pull off a long con like this? Regardless of how Nat thinks I performed last night, I wasn't kidding when I said I wasn't an actress."

Cynthia considers me thoughtfully. "Or maybe you've just never had the right role."

I'm pretty sure she'd say whatever I need to hear right now; visions of page views dance in her head.

"The point is, this could all blow up in our faces. And I'd never want to do anything to hurt Siren." *Or my own career*, I add silently.

She hears what I'm not saying. "There's an element of risk in all undercover work. You'd have to be comfortable . . . *misrepresenting* certain facts."

I flop onto the couch next to Nat. "Misrepresenting is one thing; lying and publicly shaming someone is another. I was prepared to do some ridiculous things for this piece, but that was when they'd only embarrass me. I've never taken a story this far." Guilt churns in my gut; I'm not used to trafficking in deception. "Do we think this is crossing an ethical line?"

"Did Brawler have an ethical line when they ranked *'Sports' hottest side pieces'*?" Nat sputters, indignant. "Or how about when they body-shamed that cute sideline reporter who ended up being *pregnant*? Or when they congratulated that prick golfer who jilted his fiancé at the altar? Or what about that Locker Room Report where they described which Packers were packing the most heat?"

I cock my head at her.

"Fine, so I was a *little* interested in that one, but the others were highly offensive!" She waves a hand. "The point is, they're certainly not operating under any sort of journalistic honor code. You need to start thinking like *them*."

"She has a point," Cynthia says. "Maybe it's time we started fighting fire with fire. 'When they go low, we go high' is a nice idea in theory, but it sure hasn't stopped them from coming after us. I think they've earned a little duplicity on our part."

"They've *more* than earned it," Nat confirms.

"Besides, it's not like you're trying to hack into his bank account. A little fake dating?" Cynthia waves a perfectly manicured hand. "It's harmless."

"Totally harmless," Nat parrots. "Plus, Jack already knows you work at Siren. He's entered Taylor Swift territory now."

I look to Cynthia for help decoding that reference, but she seems just as mystified. "I'm sorry, in layman's terms?"

Nat sighs in impatience. "Any guy who dates Taylor Swift knows she'll eventually write a brutally vindictive yet insanely catchy pop hit that drags his name through the mud and trashes his reputation. Jack pursued you even *after* he knew you worked for the competition. You may as well have *Date at your own risk* tattooed on your forehead!"

"Gee, thanks."

She smacks my arm. "You know what I mean. The point is, Jack knows what he's getting into, and if he falls for it, he deserves whatever he gets."

"She's not wrong." Cynthia pushes out her chair and stands, navigating around the desk to perch on the edge. "And before you start feeling guilty, remember that Jack's in control of this whole thing. No one's forcing him to react a certain way. If he behaves like a Neanderthal," she says with a sniff, "he'll only have himself to blame."

I expected this, both of them egging me on; frankly, it's why I came to them. As I lay in bed last night second-guessing myself, wondering if I was crazy to think I could pull this off, I knew dangling the opportunity in front of Cynthia would make it impossible to back out. Still, this is way outside my comfort zone, and no matter how noble the cause or how much Jack and Brawler deserve their comeuppance, I know this whole scheme is morally murky at best.

Cynthia's watching me closely. "Listen, I would never pressure you to do this. It has to be your decision. But if it were me? I absolutely would do it. This could be a career-making opportunity for you, and you know as well as I do those don't come around very often."

In my periphery I see Nat suddenly straighten, like a ventriloquist dummy that's been jerked upright. I shoot her a look: *What?* Her widened eyes bore into mine, but she just shakes her head slightly.

Cynthia's waiting for an answer. She's right, of course—by a stroke of luck and good timing, this once-in-a-lifetime story has basically been handed to me on a silver platter.

Like her George and Amal piece, it could put me on the map. Is there even a choice here?

"Alright, I'm all in. Operation Rom Con is officially a go."

"*Yee-es!*" Nat jumps up, pumping a fist in the air. "This is giving me life already. I'll coach you up! I'll be in the ring with you every step of the way. We'll get in his head. We'll go ten rounds if we have to!"

I can't help laughing. "I don't actually think a coach is allowed to be in the ring with a fighter. And isn't it twelve rounds?"

"Okay, so I don't know anything about boxing. But good news, you're now dating someone who does!" She snaps her fingers at me. "Make a mental note: something to ask Jack about."

Cynthia's chuckling as she winds her way back around the desk. "We'll keep this one off the books. You can update me directly, and we won't mention it at the weekly meeting. We can't risk any leaks on this."

"I was going to suggest the same thing."

"Great." Her phone buzzes and she frowns down at it, then turns her attention back to me. "Dare I ask what you have planned first?"

"I've got a few tricks up my sleeve," I hint, dangling the carrot. "I plan to let the 125 tips be my guide."

"Make sure you agree with everything he says," she advises. "Laugh at all his jokes, even the unfunny ones."

"*Especially* the unfunny ones," Natalia pipes up.

"Flatter him constantly. Never complain."

"Offer to cook for him! And make sure to wear an apron."

"Act helpless. Always defer to him. Oh, and no cursing," Cynthia orders. *Shit, that'll be a hard one.*

"Should I buy him Knicks tickets and a love fern, too?" I joke.

Nat sucks in a breath. "I just thought of the perfect headline: '*How to Dupe a Guy in 10 Days*'!" She throws her head back and cackles, slapping the arm of the couch. Even Cynthia cracks a smile.

"Alright, laugh it up, you two, but I'm the one who actually has to pull off this little charade, okay? This is real life, not some cheesy rom-com."

Nat lets out a gasp. "You did not just call Kate Hudson's tour-de-force performance *cheesy*."

I laugh in spite of myself. "Well, honestly, I'll need to be Andie Anderson–level adorable if I even have a prayer of keeping Jack wriggling on the end of my hook. Don't forget, this whole thing hinges on him finding me irresistible, and I wouldn't be a bit surprised if I never heard from the guy again. I mean, you were there—I was *aggressively* hostile to him. Frankly, I'm shocked he even stuck around long enough to get my number."

It's a head-scratcher that prolonged my insomnia last night, as a matter of fact. Why *did* Jack hang around to be berated by a random stranger? I can't say I would have done the same in his position. In fact, the more I think about it, the more impressed I am that he stood there and took my verbal beatdown. Actually, scratch that, he didn't take it. He fought back, proving he must be just as headstrong as I am.

"*Pfft*, I'm not surprised," Nat says. "You're the ultimate challenge. You basically spit in his face. You treated him like crap and now he wants—no, he *needs*—to conquer you to set the universe at rights. It's how men like him work. He won't rest until he's won you over. Besides, he was clearly into you. I nearly choked from that fog of sexual tension when I walked up."

I cringe internally as Cynthia's eyes sharpen like a hawk's. "So you liked him, then?"

Thanks a lot, Nat.

"No!" I think of how I admired his bone structure and feel a stab of shame. "I mean, I didn't *like* him, like him." Now I sound like I'm in junior high. "I thought he was, you know, fine. Nothing special, really." I'm definitely making it worse. It's like a spray of word vomit I can't suppress. The two of them exchange a look and I fight the urge to fan my armpits. "I was just grateful that he made the introduction to Eric Jessup," I say desperately.

Cynthia holds up her hands. "Relax, I'm not judging you. He's a good-looking guy. But he's also a smooth talker and didn't get where he is by being dumb, so don't underestimate him. And *don't* let him derail you."

"I won't," I assure her firmly. "He's a story to me, nothing more." *See? I'm absolutely not attracted to him. I haven't thought at all about whether I'd classify his eye color as sapphire or indigo.*

She holds eye contact for a long beat. "You know, if he's as into you as Nat says, he'll be trying to impress you. He'll share things he otherwise wouldn't, so listen carefully. You may uncover things about Brawler. Damaging things we can use to twist the knife even deeper."

A cold fear arrows through me at her villainous tone, and I have to wonder if I'm in over my head with this. She's like a bloodhound that's caught the scent of a fugitive. I half expect her to cage her fingertips and cackle like Dr. Evil.

She dismisses us, but the second we're out of her office

Natalia grabs me by the elbow and hauls me into an empty conference room.

"Ow, what's your deal?" I ask once she shuts the door behind us.

"Didn't you hear what she said in there?" Nat hisses. "About how this could make your career?"

"Uh, yeah. No pressure, right?"

She flicks me on the forehead. "*Gah*, you are asleep at the wheel. Cass, this is your book idea!"

I blink at her, trying to catch up . . . and a little pissed at the flicking. "How is *this* my book idea?"

"Don't you see it? People love this shit! 'I'm tired of my life, so I did this wacky thing to shake it up.' I made every recipe in Julia Child's cookbook. I went backpacking in ill-fitting boots. I meditated in India, ate pasta in Rome, and fell in love in Bali. I got tired of modern dating and decided to live like a 1950s housewife." She squeezes my arm excitedly. "This is your Pacific Crest Trail!"

"In all those books they learn something deep and meaningful about themselves," I protest, massaging my arm pointedly. "I'm just trying to take down some sexist jerk. Hardly the warm and fuzzy aha moment people are looking for."

"You're underestimating this idea," she insists. "Think of how many women are completely disillusioned with modern dating. You should know; you're one of them! Men put in no effort because they know another woman's just a swipe away. I'm telling you, there are plenty of women out there who wonder if life would've been easier if they'd just been born in a different era. Who wonder if women had it better back then. Speak to *those* women."

I squint at her as I consider it. As crazy as it sounded at

first, she does have a point. For all the ease and convenience modern technology's offered my generation, online dating seems to have brought out the worst in men—or the ones I've matched with, at least. Like my Hinge date who showed up smelling like mothballs, admitted he'd lied and hadn't actually earned an architectural degree, then relayed his aspirations of becoming a "shoe-preneur." My expectations of men are so low that even a mediocre, ho-hum date counts as a smashing success. And while we may not need them to protect us or pay our bills, aren't we all looking for a man who dresses well, opens doors and pulls out chairs, and reaches for the check as a matter of habit? Who's actually interested in *us*, and not just a casual hookup? Don't we all wish chivalry would make a comeback? I'm not asking for a Disney prince or a carriage ride through Central Park, but would it kill a guy to give up his seat for me on the subway?

"I see the potential," I acknowledge, and she grins smugly. "I'll start thinking on it, but right now I need to focus on this story. And on that note . . ."

I motion for her to follow me, then push open the door and make my way down the hallway, the heels of our shoes clacking on the polished concrete floor.

"I decided I need an alter ego," I explain in a low voice as we walk, "so I started putting together a character profile." At my workstation, I start searching through the piles of printouts littering my desktop.

"What is all this?" Nat asks, lifting the top sheet off the nearest stack.

"Research."

She starts reading aloud. "'*Things to do with your hands that men like.*' Written in 1962. Huh. Maybe I should try these out on Gabriel." She skims for a moment. "'*Feel his muscles.*

Write him a love letter. Toy with his belt.'" She wags her eyebrows, then snorts. "'*Do needlepoint while he watches.*' Yeah, that'll turn him on."

She twists to lean on the edge of the desk. "'*Massage him with baby oil. Tie him up and tickle him.*' Getting a little kinky here in the swingin' sixties." She falls silent for a minute as she keeps reading, then straightens. "Wait, hold up. '*Pumice his calluses*'? '*Powder between his toes*'? '*Frolic in his chest hairs*'? What the hell am I reading?" She drops the page like it's blistered her fingertips. "Seriously, where are you finding this stuff?"

"I swear, these lists are finding *me* at this point. And you'd be surprised how much bizarre dating advice you can find on the internet. Apparently 'be yourself' is too logical," I mutter as I riffle through the papers. "Aha! Found it." I whip the page out of the stack and present it to her with a flourish. "Meet Betty."

"Betty?"

"Betty was a very popular name for women of courtship age in the fifties. What, you don't think I'm a Betty?" I strike my best model pose.

"I think you're a *total* betty, obviously." She winks at me, then starts reading aloud. "Let's see here, Betty do's and don'ts: '*Betty always dresses to the nines and would never be caught dead without her face on. She's a domestic goddess; presentation is very important to her. She eats like a bird, but always has dinner ready and waiting for her man when he walks in the door. Betty would never make the first move—only floozies ask men out.*'" She groans. "Seriously?"

"It's a direct quote from one of the articles!"

She shakes her head and continues reading. "'*Betty would never split the check and always ends phone calls first to keep him*" *wanting more. She's demure and pleasing and never makes demands. Betty lets her man take the lead and always puts his needs before hers. Her career comes second to landing a man.'"* She fake-gags.

I smirk. "What do you think? Good, right?"

"I think it's a good thing I'm here, because it's going to be near-impossible for you to say or do any of these things with a straight face. In fact, I'm not sure I could think of someone *less* suited to behave submissively. You're no June Cleaver. You're no Ana Steele! However." She holds up a finger. "I believe in you, and I'm here to help. I will put you through Betty boot camp. Like . . ." She scrunches up her face and thinks for a second. "When Jack texts you about your date, how does Betty respond?"

I'm ready for this one. "She doesn't."

"And why not?"

"Because cell phones didn't exist in the fifties."

She swats me with the printout. "*No.*"

I grin. "I was just kidding. Obviously, any self-respecting maiden of the fifties would expect more effort from her beau than some measly little text. A phone call, at the very least."

"Perhaps a meeting in the parlor between the gentleman caller and her father to secure his permission."

I crack up. "Wrong century, Scarlett O'Hara. This is the *nineteen*-fifties, not the antebellum South."

She waves a hand. "S'all the same. Anyway, this is going to be a ton of fun."

"Or a total disaster. Who can say, really?"

She slings an arm around my shoulder. "Either way, I come out a winner because I have a front-row seat for this shit show." She hip-checks me and grins. "Pass the popcorn."

Chapter 5

RUTH BE TOLD, I THOUGHT I'D HEAR FROM
Jack quickly. Based on the way we left things, I assumed I'd
get a text or a call within a day, two at most. But when a
couple of days pass without hearing from him, a seed of
doubt starts to take root and sprout.

You got way too far ahead of yourself, my brain admonishes
as I putter around the apartment Tuesday night making
dinner. *He saw through your whole charade and is probably writing his own exposé on you right now,* I fret as I sweat through a
spin class the next morning. *You should never have pitched
this to Cynthia before he actually made contact,* I berate myself
as I grab a midafternoon latte at Starbucks on Thursday. I
can't even reach out to him myself (not that I would; are
you kidding? Betty would *never*) because I didn't stay long
enough at that bar to get his number in return. I'm a pitiful
double agent.

To talk myself off the ledge, I run through all the reasons why he might be taking his time to call: he's a busy
guy at the helm of a major media corporation; he wants to

establish himself as the alpha by making me wait; he mis-typed my number; I have BO.

At least no one knows about this, I reassure myself. *If he ghosts me, I'll just go back to writing the original story. No harm, no foul.*

But I can't lie—I'm disappointed. I definitely got caught up in the idea of writing a big splashy takedown (and okay, perhaps even parlaying it into a buzzy bestseller). And fine, maybe I've got a bit of a bruised ego as well. Nat seemed so sure he was interested . . . heck, *I* thought he was interested. I like to think I'm decent at reading people; I guess I just pegged him wrong.

Or more likely, you scared him off by acting like a total psychopath.

By Thursday night I've just about decided he's a lost cause (and stopped checking my phone eighty-three times a day—*a watched phone never buzzes* and all that). I'm two glasses of wine in and halfway through a rewatch of an old *Outlander* episode (a super-porny one, too; the best kind) when my phone rings next to me and I glance down at it. An unknown 212 number flashes across the screen and I bolt upright.

Settle down. It's probably just a political robocall.

But if it *is* Jack, I need to stay in control. Act aloof, like I expected him to call.

I take a moment to slip into my Betty skin, pausing a shirtless Sam Heughan (my timing is impeccable), and let it ring once—twice—before answering on the third ring. "Hello?"

"Cassidy." A statement, not a question.

It's him, I know it immediately. I hadn't realized I'd committed his voice to memory, but the deep baritone and silver-tongued confidence, smoother than any salesman's, are instantly familiar.

"Yes?" I ask, infusing the word with a questioning lilt. Like I haven't been anxiously awaiting his call like a parent on prom night. Like there are so many unidentified men of marriageable age calling me, I can't possibly keep track of them all.

"Jack Bradford." There's a pause, and I don't rush to fill it. "From the event on Monday?" A tinge of uncertainty's crept into his voice and I have to squelch the urge to draw it out, see just how uncomfortable I can make him.

"Jack! Of course," I say instead, pouring diabetic levels of sugar into my response. "I'd almost given up on hearing from you," I scold in a playful singsong. Betty is an incorrigible flirt.

"Sorry about that," he says, and he actually does sound remorseful. "I've been out of town. Still am, actually."

See? I tell myself. *He's on a work trip. You don't smell.*

"Where to?" I ask, settling back on the couch and swirling the wine in my glass.

"Vegas. I head back tomorrow morning."

"Wow, Vegas. Tough job you've got there."

He laughs. "Right? Though I can assure you that Vegas for work isn't quite the same as Vegas for fun."

"I bet. I'll confess, though, I've been to Vegas for a couple of bachelorette parties, and that was enough for me."

"I can relate. After a trip, it always seems to take a couple of days for my ears to stop ringing."

I strain to hear some identifying background noise, like slot machines or the buzz of the casino floor, but it's as silent as a library at midnight. "Seems pretty quiet to me."

He lets out a low chuckle. "I'm in my hotel room."

It's an oddly intimate mental image—Jack, alone in a Vegas hotel room. I picture his tall frame sprawled across a hotel bed, the comforter thrown back and sheets mussed, his socked feet hanging over the edge. I wonder if he's the type to wear noisy patterns in hidden rebellion or if he sticks to muted solids.

"I read your Jessup story," he says suddenly, amid the quiet.

"Oh yeah? What'd you think?" I ask reflexively, then immediately hate myself for fishing for compliments.

"It was surprisingly sweet. Romantic, even. To read it, you wouldn't even know what a jaded fairy-tale hater you truly are."

I laugh, gratified by his praise in spite of the teasing. *Damn that universally disarming trap, flattery.* "Yeah, well, I know my audience. Gotta give the people what they want, right?"

"Not gonna lie, I was a little disappointed not to get a mention, but . . ."

I nearly snort. *Be careful what you wish for, buddy.* "Noted for next time. And contrary to popular belief, I'm not *actually* a romance hater," I say, dropping the world's most obvious hint.

He catches it seamlessly. "Oh no? Let's see you prove it."

"What'd you have in mind?" I volley back playfully, then clap a hand over my mouth to smother my laughter. This is almost *too* easy. And the best part is, he thinks he's the one in control while I'm busy pulling his strings like Geppetto.

"So I know I mentioned taking you out to dinner, but I thought I'd throw you a curveball and see if you like tennis."

Wait, what? My silent laughter cuts off like a record scratch. "Tennis, as in . . . a racket and a net?"

He chuckles, and the sound is deep and rich, like a smooth whiskey. "I was thinking more like tennis, as in the US Open."

I blink a few times. That's more than a curveball; it's an overhead smash. "You want to take me to a professional tennis match?" Of all the potential date scenarios I mentally prepared for, I did *not* see this one coming.

"Full disclosure: Brawler partners with the U.S. Tennis Association every year to promote the tournament, and one of the perks is a box at Arthur Ashe. On Sunday I've got to entertain some investors during the morning session, but it would really help me get through it if I had something to look forward to." He pauses, then clears his throat. "So if you're free in the afternoon, I'd love for you to join me."

There's a hint of vulnerability in his tone and for a moment I forget all about Betty and my subterfuge as my heart beats a little faster, those familiar first-date butterflies fluttering to life in my belly.

And then I catch myself. *This is* not *a first date. Jack is a mark, nothing more.* I clench my abs, and butterflies: exterminated.

Betty slides back into the driver's seat as I consider my response. *He's trying to impress you by throwing his money and connections around. He's fanning his peacock feathers. Act appropriately impressed.*

"Wow. Of course, I'd love to go," I gush—and to my surprise, I actually mean it. "I've never been to the US Open before." *Flattery, flattery.* I'm just a naive, blushing virgin, grateful to this big, strapping man for showing me the great wide world.

"Fair warning, there will be some other Brawler folks and their guests there," he continues, and I nearly choke on the mouthful of wine I've just swallowed. Five minutes in and he's already inviting me behind enemy lines to mingle among the Brawler inner circle? He may as well hand me the keys to his torture chamber right now. It's almost too good to be true. Cynthia will shit a brick. "So you may cross paths with a few members of the executive team, if that's, ah . . . I mean, if you're—"

"You mean, can you count on me to keep any hostile work-related outbursts to myself?" I rattle off a laugh, like the very idea is preposterous and didn't actually transpire a mere three days ago. "I promise, that was a one-off. I was just, um . . . hangry."

"It's more that I don't want to put you in an uncomfortable situation," he sidesteps neatly, neutral as a politician.

I decide to throw him a curveball of my own. "Actually, having other people around would be a relief for me. I typically prefer first dates to be with a group, rather than one-on-one."

The pause is long. "I'm sorry?"

"You know, like built-in chaperones? I know it sounds a little old-fashioned, but it was something my dad insisted on back when I first started dating, and I guess it sort of stuck."

There's an even longer pause and I have to hold the phone away from my face because my silent laughter's becoming not-so-silent. I'm practically wheezing.

"So . . . *huh*. Group dating. And that's not, like . . . weird at all?" He's incredulous, and at this point I'm seriously struggling not to lose control of my bladder.

"No, not really," I respond airily. This whole acting thing

might be fun after all. "Plus, having friends around helps with that first-date awkwardness, don't you think?" I pinch the bridge of my nose and try to think of sad things: Military homecomings. Olympics montages. That song "The Christmas Shoes." *Marley & Me.*

"Uh, sure," he says haltingly. "I mean, yeah, I guess I see what you're saying." He clears his throat and I can practically hear him questioning my sanity. If this phone call had a soundtrack, the lyrics would be *Oh, she's sweet but a psycho.* "Well, I'm glad I could deliver with the group date, however unintentionally."

I've got to hand it to him, he's making a valiant effort to act like this is a normal request and not some bizarre courtship monitoring ritual a la the Duggar family. Honestly, I'm impressed.

"Thank you for inviting me," I say, getting us back on track and remembering one of the tips: *Always end a phone call first.* I soften my voice a little, making it appropriately shy. "I'm looking forward to it." Betty's laying it on real thick. Is there such a thing as too much fawning? I feel like a fluffer.

"Me too," Jack says, and I imagine his ego expanding to fill the hotel room, escaping out the window and floating down the brightly lit Strip like a runaway parade float. "Looking forward to seeing you, that is."

I giggle bashfully. "Well, aren't you sweet." *Gag me.* "Have a safe trip back tomorrow."

"I'll do that. And I'll see you on Sunday."

"You sure will."

To your date with doom, I toast him silently and raise my glass.

Chapter 6

*Y*OU CANNOT BE SERIOUS."

Natalia's face lights up like a jack-o'-lantern. "It's perfect! I am *so* good."

I turn back to face the mirror. I wish I had a racket so I could smash it into a million spiderwebby cracks. "I cannot wear this."

"You can, and you will. I had to hit three vintage stores to score this stuff. You're welcome, by the way."

"I look like a Stepford wife!"

To fully commit to my role as a trad-wife-in-training, I somehow let Nat talk me into dressing "in character," which I'm learning means like some sort of retro pinup girl. The dress she's chosen for my tennis tryst is a sleeveless cotton fit-and-flare in a flashy banana leaf print, with a square neckline and fabric-covered buttons running down the bodice. It's garish and girly and not at all my style. I look like Blanche Devereaux's bedspread.

"Okay, first of all, that's the idea. And second of all, you look adorable! Like Audrey Hepburn or Natalie Wood." Natalia cinches the matching belt around my middle one notch tighter, nearly displacing a rib. "Look how tiny your waist looks."

"It better look tiny—you have me in a corset! I can't even breathe!"

She rolls her eyes. "It's a *girdle*, not a corset. If you're gonna pull this off, you need to at least learn the era-appropriate undergarment lingo." She cocks her head, eyeing me critically. "Something's missing."

"It's my pride. I left it on the floor of that bar."

She ignores my sass in favor of rummaging through her shopping bag, which looks ominously full. "It's going to be like ninety-some degrees. How about a parasol?" She extracts something lacy and cream-colored and holds it out.

"Nat, are you on drugs? I already look ridiculous enough without carrying a *sun umbrella*."

She blinks at me, unmoved. I change tack and appeal to her logical side. "We're sitting in a box, remember? I'll be in the shade."

She purses her lips, considering. "Fine, no parasol. But you need to use a small handbag, not your giant tote. And I found these cute raffia espadrilles to go with the dress . . ." She trails off, burying her head in the bottomless bag.

"You're enjoying this way too much," I grouse, loosening the belt a couple of notches while her back is turned.

"You should be glad I'm not making you wear pantyhose and gloves. Aha! Here they are." She brandishes the espadrilles with a flourish, and admittedly they are pretty fabulous. I silently thank Cynthia for agreeing to expense an entire vintage wardrobe. *I will gladly take custody of these shoes, thankyouverymuch.*

Nat eyes me approvingly. "It is an absolute travesty that

you don't wear more color. And that neckline does great things for your cleavage."

"The girls do look perky," I admit grudgingly. "But how am I going to explain this getup? People wear shorts and flip-flops to tennis matches. I'm going to stick out like a sore thumb."

"Girl, you're not part of the unwashed masses! You're rolling with the moneyed set. Haven't you seen what Kate Middleton wears to Wimbledon? You're not overdressed, you're *aristocratic*."

She stands behind me so we're both looking into the mirror, then squeezes the tops of my arms. "Look, I know you're nervous about pulling this off. You're not an actress, yada yada, I get it. But this whole thing"—she waves her hands down my body—"is going to help you stay in character."

I try to take a deep breath but only make it about halfway. "Does part of my method acting include passing out from reduced lung capacity?"

She smirks. "Think about it this way: with each shortened, shallow breath, you'll be reminded of the sacrifice you're making for women everywhere." She slaps me on the ass. "Now go get 'em, Betty Crocker."

Jack texted yesterday afternoon, offering to send a car for me. Though I felt rather bougie accepting, I wasn't about to turn down an air-conditioned ride in favor of a packed, sweaty subway car all the way to Queens. *No me gusta.*

I spend the first half of the drive giving myself a silent pep talk, and the second half gripping my own fingers so I can't tap the driver on the shoulder and beg him to turn around. As requested, I text Jack once we're five minutes out, and by the time we pull up I spot him right where he said he'd be: waiting outside the front entrance, looking tanned and Kennedy-esque in classic Ray-Bans and ever-so-slightly windblown hair. He's dressed in a pale blue oxford button-down and a sport coat, and I'm suddenly brimming with gratitude that I didn't wear my sensible shorts after all. I beam Natalia a telepathic thank-you for nailing the role of fashion fairy godmother.

When I step out of the car and give him a wave, he does a visible double take; I'm sure he wasn't expecting my costume. As I head toward him, I scramble for a plausible excuse as to why I'm dressed like a Golden Girl.

But he beats me to the punch. "You look gorgeous. For me?" he asks with a sly grin.

I can taste the flippant retort on the tip of my tongue. If it was Cassidy responding, I'd come back with something like *Nah, you never know who I might meet later*, or maybe *Some of these tennis studs might be single*. But since I'm firmly in the WWBD—What Would Betty Do?—camp, I flip through my mental Rolodex of tips and land on *Greet him with a warm smile. Be happy to see him!*

I flash him my biggest, fakest grin. "Of course! Who else would it be for?" I chirp in a syrupy singsong, then bat my eyelashes for good measure (because eyelash-batting *definitely* seems like something Betty would do). I immediately worry I've overdone it.

Incredibly, he seems to buy it. "I'll be the envy of every man."

He leans down to drop a kiss to my cheek and I stiffen, then attempt to mask it by smiling up at him. I'm straddling the finest of lines here—I need to pique his interest long enough to get my story while somehow keeping things as physically platonic as possible. A chaste peck on the cheek or some innocent hand-holding is fine, but anything beyond that is an ethical line I'm unwilling to cross. Threading this needle will be a challenge, but fortunately, I have a plan.

He offers me his arm with exaggerated gallantry, and I accept as he leads us into the stadium. I can't help but steal furtive peeks at him as he navigates us through the crowd, my eyes cataloguing details my memory must have missed: his profile, with high cheekbones and a strong, regal brow; the imposing set of his shoulders; the gold signet ring on his right hand that catches the sunlight; the way the hair at his nape curls around his collar. He moves with an ease and confidence no doubt established through years of pack leadership and good fortune. I don't miss the attention he attracts from other women, either—their gazes linger on him as we walk past, then skate over me, judging my worthiness, tight smiles masking thinly veiled jealousy. He really is *that* good-looking, proof that life truly isn't fair and God bestows certain gifts on the wrong people.

When we arrive at the suite, he opens the door and guides me inside with a hand to the small of my back. I take a deep breath, my inner monologue repeating *It's harmless* on an endless loop.

The interior layout is pretty standard for a stadium suite: a couple of high-top tables, a flat screen broadcasting a live feed of the match, a bar set up in one corner, a row of silver chafing dishes lining a buffet along the far wall. A handful of people mill about the room, a couple of small groups clustered in chitchat. Several people glance at us as we walk in, offering polite smiles before returning to their conversations.

"What do you think, enough chaperones?" Jack murmurs in my ear, his breath grazing my neck.

I shoot him a look of mock disapproval. "Are you going to make fun of me now?"

"I would never." He smiles innocently, and it's that get-away-with-murder look he's so good at. "Can I get you something to drink?"

I've already decided that Betty's signature drink is an old-fashioned (of course) served in a highball glass (obviously), but for the sake of making a low-maintenance first impression *(Don't be too fussy!)*, I tell him wine's fine.

I let my eyes roam over the buffet while the bar attendant is pouring. *Lasagna and sliders and éclairs, oh my!* I was too nervous to eat much of anything this morning and I'm paying the piper for that poor decision now. Saliva pools in my mouth.

Jack catches me ogling the food. "You hungry?"

Now there's a loaded question. *Obviously I'm hungry, Jack, but even if Betty were allowed to have an appetite, I couldn't possibly force a single calorie past this ridiculous corset. I'm sorry—girdle.*

"Oh, I'm fine," I say blithely, as though I couldn't possibly be bothered by such a basic human necessity as hunger. *I'll just have a few heaping mouthfuls of air, thanks.*

"Let me know if you change your mind."

I CHANGED MY MIND, my Cassidy-brain screams, but I mute her and paste on a demure smile as he hands me a plastic cup of wine, then accepts a bottle of water for himself.

"Hey, wait," I protest. "I can't drink if you're having water." A lush, Betty is *not*.

"I've actually been drinking since ten a.m., so you need to catch up." He winks, and I send him a petulant look, but ultimately decide it's not worth pushing back. *Above all, be agreeable!*

He motions toward the open-air seating and I let him lead me outside, where three descending rows of seats provide the suite's guests with an enviable view of the court. I pause for a moment at the top of the stairs, taking in the eye-popping grandeur that is Arthur Ashe Stadium, the most storied court at New York's premier tennis venue. The arena rises four tiers high, but it feels like forty, with stands climbing into the sky as far as the eye can see. Our suite is down low and center court, and I have to admit: as far as "first dates" go, this one is pretty impressive.

Jack's watching me with a crooked smile. "Pretty great, huh? This job does have its perks."

The Brawler reminder is a bit of a buzzkill, but I brush it aside and smile up at him—and this time, it's not even fake. While I may be here as a guest of the enemy, nobody said I couldn't enjoy myself. In fact, I get an evil thrill knowing that I'm profiting at their expense, not unlike the righteous satisfaction I feel when I shop local instead of on Amazon. If I'm going to debase myself for the cause, courtside seats are a great sweetener.

"No kidding. So what exactly did you do for the USTA? Hide a body?"

He laughs. "Well, it's not exactly charity. They're an advertising partner, and during the tournament we work with them to produce some additional content. Native ads and viral videos, things like that. Since tennis viewership tends to skew older, they're trying to tap into a younger fan base."

I nod; I'm intimately familiar with #sponcon. "What sort of viral videos?"

"This year, we filmed a spot where Tom tried out to be a ball boy."

I snicker. "Seriously?"

"I kicked those kids' asses, too," a voice booms from behind us, and I instantly recognize the thick Boston accent I've heard in so many interviews: Jack's cofounder, asshole extraordinaire and the man who puts the "brawl" in Brawler, Tom "the Tomcat" Bartlett. I turn, plastering on a smile to disguise the sneer lurking just beneath the surface.

"Cassidy, right? Tom," he says, holding out a hand. He's even more dressed up than Jack, in a dark suit and tie with a matching pocket square in a shade of lavender.

"No need for an introduction," I tell him as I accept his handshake. "Your reputation precedes you."

If he catches my veiled insult, he doesn't let on. "It often does, for better or worse," he says without a hint of apology. "As does yours, by the way. I've been anxious to meet the Siren spitfire."

Guess that answers my question of whether Jack relayed the details of my outburst. Tom's tone is casual enough, but I don't miss the unspoken challenge in it, or the sharp assessment in his gaze. *He's testing you, trying to determine if you're friend or foe. Prove you're not a threat.*

I look him dead in the eye, instinctively knowing the only way to deal with a guy like Tom is head-on. "I've earned myself a nickname already, huh? Let's see if I can live up to it."

There's a brief pause—before Tom barks a loud laugh. I exhale, relaxing a little. *Advantage: me.*

"I think you and I are going to get along just fine, Cassidy." He raises the beer bottle he's dangling by the neck and clinks it against the side of my cup. "And to think I was warned you might rip me a new asshole."

"I *never* said that." Jack turns to me, his expression pained. "I never said that."

I pat his arm reassuringly. "I wouldn't blame you if you had. Besides, I think we established that the Siren-Brawler feud is all in good fun, right?" My voice is spun sugar, double-dipped in honey. I'm the amiable arm candy of their dreams.

"We've had a lot of fun with Siren over the years," Tom admits, rocking back on his heels. "Your boss is a good sport."

"Well, she's certainly had plenty to be a good sport about."

It slips out before I can censor myself, and when Tom's eyes narrow, I curse silently. *No sassing the menfolk! You have got to learn how to hold your tongue. More Betty, less Cassidy.*

I'm preparing to backtrack when Jack steps in to save me. "Alright, no work talk. We're off the clock." I feel his hand flex against my back.

"I promised him I'd be on my best behavior," Tom confides conspiratorially.

"And you're failing miserably," Jack snaps back, annoyed.

I laugh in spite of myself, instantly diagnosing the *Odd Couple* dynamic between the two of them: Jack is the straight man, and Tom his outlandish foil. Jack's the Felix to Tom's Oscar; the Spade to his Farley.

"Oh, he's fine," I reassure Jack. "If you dish it out, you've got to be able to take it, right, Tom?" I toss him a wink.

"A girl after my own heart." He nods at Jack. "Think you might be punching above your weight with this one, bud."

I'm feeling pretty smug about how quickly I've won

Tom over. Didn't even break a sweat. He also just handed Betty a prime opening: *Compliment your man in front of his friends.*

"I think it might be the other way around," I coo sweetly, placing a possessive hand on Jack's arm and giving it a squeeze. When I glance up at him adoringly, I'm rewarded by his look of surprised pleasure, twin spots of color blooming on his cheekbones. Honestly, the aw-shucks routine from a guy this attractive is both absurd and adorable. *Is it possible that this cheesy, blatant flattery actually works?*

"Well, he's . . ." I trail off as Jack guides us to our seats, trying to come up with an appropriate adjective to describe that encounter.

"Insane?"

"I was going to say *a lot,* but your way works too."

"Tom is . . . an acquired taste." *Yeah, acquired like a bad rash.* "Trust me, there's nothing you could say about him that I haven't heard before."

He seems eager to change the subject, so I go with it, peppering him with questions about the match currently underway, the players' records, what the morning session was like. I play dumb about the rules of the game whenever possible (*Why do they call zero "love"? Is "deuce" a tie?*), which actually stings quite a bit, considering the couple of years I spent on my high school tennis team. *Allow him to shine and feel smart!* Le sigh.

I'm also melting. September heat in New York is oppressive, and within a few minutes I'm seriously regretting thumbing my nose at that parasol. I can't even imagine how Jack is surviving in his blazer. I go to dig my sunglasses out of my purse and catch a glimpse of my phone, noticing I've gotten a few texts from my sister. I scroll through them quickly, laughing at a couple of pictures she's sent of my nieces at some kid's birthday party, cake smashed all over their faces. *Ugh, I'd kill for some of that cake.* I wish I could teleport it through the phone, Wonka-style.

Jack leans over to peek at my screen, the fabric of his blazer brushing my bare shoulder. "Friends of yours?"

"My nieces," I tell him, angling the phone toward him so he can see better. "My sister's kids, Ella and Adeline."

He smiles at the screen. "Well, they're adorable."

"An adorable handful," I say wryly. "Honestly, they're a couple of holy terrors. But I love 'em to pieces." I give the pics a couple of heart tapbacks and slide the phone back into my purse.

"So you're the cool aunt, then?"

"Oh, absolutely. And I take my role *very* seriously. Not to brag, but I'm their favorite babysitter," I boast with exaggerated importance. "And just to annoy my sister, I buy them the most obnoxious toys I can find, like a microphone that only plays songs from *Frozen* and dolls that won't stop crying."

"So you have an evil streak."

"I think of it more as payback for a lifetime of big-sister torture."

He grins and cracks open his water bottle, draining half of it in a single impressive gulp. How do guys *do* that? "So you two are close?"

"We are. She lives in Connecticut, so I'm able to see her regularly. On the flip side, it's nearly impossible to have a phone conversation without being interrupted by the girls forty-seven times, so ninety percent of our interactions these days are via text." I shrug, accepting the stage of life we're in. "What about you, do you have any siblings?" I feel a pang of guilt asking him a question I already know the answer to, but I suppose that minor fib is the least of my transgressions right now.

"Just one. My older brother John."

"Two boys," I observe, sipping my wine.

"Yep. We even get along sometimes, too."

"Ouch." I grimace good-naturedly. "That doesn't sound too good."

He shrugs, though there's a resigned air to it. "It's mostly competitive brother stuff, but I think some people are just destined to butt heads. We worked together for a time, too, and that didn't help." He squeezes the water bottle, the plastic protesting his grip with a loud *cracking* noise. "There's just a lot of water under that bridge."

"Well, high tide eventually becomes low tide," I say reflexively.

He tilts his head, brow furrowed in question.

"Sorry, it's just something my grandma always says about the ebb and flow of relationships. Basically, all relationships have seasons, and sometimes people just need a little time and space. If you're patient, they usually come back around."

"Your grandma, huh?" he teases, not unkindly.

"I know, right? I'm really a ninety-year-old stuck in a twenty-eight-year-old's body." *If he only knew.* I let out a high-pitched giggle that resembles a horse's whinny. *Nope, I don't sound suspicious at all.*

He doesn't seem to notice. "Well, your grandmother sounds smart. What advice do you think she'd have if the rough patch had lasted, say, thirty-two years?"

"Hmm." I pretend to think about it. "She'd probably say . . . you need a therapist."

He coughs a laugh. "Touché."

He stands and shrugs off his blazer, draping it over the back of his chair before setting to work unbuttoning his cuffs and rolling the sleeves to his elbows. I keep my eyes trained forward, as though thoroughly engrossed by the rousing display of athletic prowess before me, but I hardly think I can be expected to ignore the forearm foreplay unfolding mere inches from me. Show me a woman who isn't turned on by that bare expanse of skin and I'll show you a liar.

"So are you happy at Siren?" Jack asks, interrupting my forearm fantasy.

"I am," I tell him, sitting up a little straighter. "I get to write what I want for the most part, and my pieces typically get a strong response. Each day and story are different, so I don't get bored. I've moved up to the point where I'm managing quite a few contract writers, and Cynthia's really great about seeking our input on the growth and direction of the site."

He nods, listening intently—and then I realize what I'm doing and give myself a mental kick to the shin. *This isn't a real date. Stop giving him real answers.*

I need to quit fixating on his foxy forearms and JFK Jr.–like charisma and remember why I'm here. What would Betty do? *Never let him believe your career is more important to you than marriage.*

I lean in and drop my voice. "But actually, my real dream is to be a stay-at-home mom."

His eyebrows shoot up. "Really?"

"I mean, not *tomorrow*, of course, but eventually. Once I meet the right person." I cast my eyes briefly away, faux coy, before sliding them back, doe-eyed once again. "Don't get me wrong, I like working. But don't you think raising a family is the most important work a woman can do?"

I've teed it up perfectly; all he has to do is agree. I'm giving him permission to say aloud what a man like him surely believes: that a woman's place is in the kitchen, barefoot and pregnant. *Let's hear those misogynistic thoughts in all their unvarnished glory.*

"You don't think you'd get bored?" he says instead, tilting his head. "You're so talented, and your career is just taking off. You'd really be okay giving all that up?"

I'm totally thrown by his response; I have to scramble to regain my footing.

"It's just that I've had a front-row seat to how difficult it is for my sister and her husband to juggle everything as a two-working-parent household," I explain, thinking fast. "She feels like she doesn't see the girls enough, she's only working to pay the nanny, she struggles with mom-guilt. I always thought if I had the financial means, it'd make more sense to commit myself fully to wife- and motherhood, keep things running smoothly on the home front. You know, have dinner on the table when my husband gets home, help the kids with their homework, make sure everyone's needs are met, that sort of thing."

I can't believe how easily this crap is falling out of my mouth. Honestly, I'm surprised the big man upstairs hasn't struck me down for such blasphemy. But Jack's not reacting how I expected. In fact, he's gone silent. *Did I take it too far?* It's hard to read him with his eyes hidden behind sunglasses—but judging by the crease in his brow, he's not buying it.

"What about your needs, though?"

I blink. *Okay, this is officially not going how I thought it would.*

"Don't get me wrong, I'm not judging your decision," he adds hastily, holding up his hands. "Staying home is certainly a selfless choice. I guess I'm just surprised. Can't you do both? From what I know about you, you seem really passionate about your work."

"I am, that's true," I say slowly, my mind grappling for ways to salvage this. "I guess I just see it as a different kind of work. You know, like the CEO of the household. And is there really anything you could be *more* passionate about than your children?"

I hear the words like they're coming out of someone else's mouth. I'm used to advocating for women balancing career *and* family, not choosing one over the other. And now he's forcing me to *defend* this drivel? He's got me twisted up like a pretzel.

"I hear what you're saying, and I respect that." He *respects* that? If I had a desk handy, I'd thunk my head against it. "I suppose my opinion on this is colored by personal experience. My mom stayed at home, but she was never very happy." He clears his throat, shifting his gaze back toward the court. "Though I suppose there were a variety of reasons for that," he mutters.

I eye him from behind my sunglasses and stay quiet, unsure how to react to that unexpected swerve toward the personal.

He seems to catch himself, casting me a wry grin. "Hoo, boy. That got a little heavy, huh? Guess my first-date etiquette's a little rusty." He lets out a stilted laugh.

I could let him flail, but I can't resist the urge to throw

him a life raft. "I could tell you some more about chaperones?"

He laughs again, though I can tell by the tense set of his shoulders that he's still embarrassed. *Diversion needed.*

I reach out and brush an imaginary hair from his sunglasses. "Oops, I smudged the lens. Here, let me fix it."

I hold my hand out expectantly and he passes them over, a faint smile curving his lips—and I pluck out the cleaning cloth I tucked into my bag for just this purpose.

Yes, I planned this. *Do little things to show him how you'll make his life easier,* the list instructed. *Catering to his comfort will provide you with immense personal satisfaction.*

"Good as new," I announce once I've finished buffing— but instead of handing them back, I slide them onto his face myself, then squint at him while pretending to check the lenses for dust. "Perfect."

It's a shamelessly flirtatious move, one that brings our faces within millimeters of each other, our mouths just a hair's breadth apart. I feel ridiculously obvious, brazen to the core, but he either doesn't notice or doesn't care because he holds my gaze, completely ignoring the scattered applause marking the end of a particularly spirited point. The corner of his mouth hooks up in a half smile and I mirror his expression, half smiling back at him.

He tilts his head. "You're different."

No shit, Sherlock! I want to scream. *I've practically given myself a lobotomy!*

"Oh yeah?" I say instead, feeling my stomach muscles constrict. *Is the jig up? Has he seen through my facade?* "Is that a good thing or a bad thing?"

I wish I could see his eyes. "Neither, really. Just an observation."

I wait, but nothing else is forthcoming. "Well, you can't just leave me hanging like that!"

He chuckles and shifts in his seat, angling his body toward me. "I think I just expected more . . ." He stops, searching.

"Ball-busting?" I supply after a beat.

He barks a laugh. "Kind of, yeah."

"I told you, you just caught me on a bad day."

He hums. "Wasn't all bad."

I stare at him. "Wait a minute. Did you *like* it when I was mean to you?"

He purses his lips, considering.

"You did!" I smack my forehead.

"Well, not exactly *mean*, per se," he says, still chuckling. "Though I suppose there was a novelty to it. I'm used to taking hits at my job, of course, but it's not often a woman calls me out to my face." He shrugs, a bit sheepish. "I guess I found your candor . . . refreshing."

Translation: He loves a challenge. Boy, am I tired of being *right* all the time. *Ugh, men. So transparent. So pathetically easy to manipulate.*

I toy with the string of pearls Nat insisted I wear, running my fingers over the smooth beads. "You like to be treated poorly," I say with a *tsk* and a mournful shake of my head. "I'm sorry, but that's a red flag."

He plays along. "Uh-oh. Any others you've noticed?"

Another golden opportunity for Betty: *Tell him he's handsome.*

"Too good-looking. Sorry, but I have a rule about dating men who are prettier than me."

"Ha! That's a funny one." He slaps his leg like I'm a real hoot.

I side-eye him to see if he's serious. "Um. Do you own a mirror?"

"Do *you* own a mirror?" he parries back.

"Uh, yes I do. And it's not the fun-house kind that distorts your body or plays tricks on the eye, either. Just a regular old mirror that shows my actual reflection."

He slides his sunglasses down his nose and peers at me over the rims. "Do you have Ugly Duckling Syndrome or something?"

"I'm *sorry*?"

"You know, like were you a late bloomer? Go through a prolonged awkward stage? Buck teeth? Ears that stuck out?"

I regard him suspiciously. "How'd you get ahold of my teenage photo albums?"

"Fascinating," he murmurs. "I've finally spotted one in the wild."

I smack his arm—then have to smother my reaction to the unexpectedly firm bicep hidden beneath his shirt sleeve. Is he *flexing*? "How dare you."

"The point is," he says, laughing, "I get the sense you don't know how other people see you. Remember the bar, when I came up?" I shrug in assent. "How do you think I knew you purposely took that guy out?"

I groan and let my head fall back, shaking a fist at the sky. "I *fell!*"

"Oh-kay." He folds his arms across his chest—*quit noticing his arms!*—and trains his vision back on the match, his voice aloof. "Let me know when you're ready to come clean."

I huff in disapproval, but I know when I've been bested. He's clearly not going to let this go, so I'm prepared to make a concession.

I sigh dramatically, as though chagrined to be giving in. "Fine, it was on purpose. Happy now?"

"Tell me something I don't know," he notes dryly, his gaze lazily wandering back to my face. "Like, for example, *why* did you take him out?"

"It was for a story," I admit, offering up the alibi Nat and I concocted for just this scenario. *Why lie when you can tell the truth?* "We were testing out some extreme pickup lines." *The partial truth, anyway.*

He raises a dubious eyebrow.

"You know, like *'Worst Ways to Meet a Guy'*? Crash into him and drop your purse. Get lost on a golf course or a military base. 'Accidentally' take a shower in a men's locker room. Play dumb at a shooting range. Pretend to be drowning at the beach."

He looks alarmed. "Pretend to *drown*? What kind of pickup lines are these?"

"The ridiculous kind, obviously."

He snorts. "No kidding."

"So ridiculous, in fact, they worked on *two* men." I smile with all my teeth.

He opens his mouth like he's going to dispute my version of events, then seems to accept he has no leg to stand on. "Not sure I can argue with that. Which brings me back to my original point, which is that the reason I knew you intentionally knocked that poor sap on his ass was because I noticed you well before I came over." He clears his throat. "From the second you walked in, in fact."

"You mean you noticed Nat in her fire-engine red dress," I joke. I'm used to her antics drawing attention wherever we go; frankly, she's hard *not* to notice.

He pulls his glasses off again, fully this time, revealing

his deep blue eyes—*indigo, they're definitely indigo*—and pins me with his gaze. I couldn't look away if I tried.

"No, I noticed *you*." The intensity in his voice makes something roll over in my stomach. "Some try hard to stand out, while others stand out without trying."

Chapter 7

*M*Y HEART STALLS IN MY CHEST, HEAT STEAL-
ing over my skin like the creeping glow from a fire. I blink
at him from behind my sunglasses, at a loss for words, all
my typical snappy comebacks completely deserting me.

It could be a line. In fact, it sounds exactly like a line some
slick Don Juan wannabe would use to try to pick me up at
one of those overpriced and overly trendy rooftop bars
Nat's always dragging me to.

And yet . . .

It didn't sound like a line coming out of his mouth. It
sounded honest and sincere and . . . earnest, even. It sounded
like he meant it. I mull it over as an unsettling swirl of emotions begins to gather in my gut.

You're supposed to hate this guy.

He's supposed to be awful. He's supposed to offend me
with his bad takes and worse behavior, not give me warm
fuzzies with his thoughtful, genuine compliments. I expected crass and shameless, not attentive and sensitive. I

can hear Cynthia's voice ringing in my ears: *Don't underestimate him. Don't let him derail you.*

Is acknowledging that I'm flattered the same as being derailed? Seems like a gray area.

Before I can untangle my tongue, Jack gets a tap on the shoulder—*saved!*—and I train my gaze on the court, letting out a slow, unsteady breath.

Thankfully, the rest of the afternoon passes uneventfully. I've never been on a date to a sporting event before—like Rose DeWitt Bukater, something about me must scream "indoor girl"—though it occurs to me that it's actually an ideal setting for a first date. Having the match as a distraction takes the conversational pressure off while also providing me with a convenient escape hatch: If there's ever an awkward silence, I can just pretend to be enthralled by the on-court action. *Easy-peasy.*

Though I find I never need to pull that rip cord. Jack's exceedingly easy to talk to, our conversation effortlessly skipping from one topic to the next like a smooth stone across a lake. Sharing the same industry means we speak a common language, and even I'm surprised by how quickly we fall into a natural shorthand. Frankly, if this was a real first date, it's the kind I could imagine spawning sappy, gag-inducing wedding toasts like *It was meant to be!* or *We kept finishing each other's sentences!*

If we're not chatting or watching the match, Jack's introducing me to other Brawler guests, which includes a seemingly endless array of investors, colleagues, and friends who stream in and out of the suite throughout the afternoon. While in any other context I might find the experience draining (the plight of the true introvert), I'm surprised at how *easy* it all feels.

We get along so well, in fact, that I'm surprised when I check my watch and see I've been here more than four hours. Knowing that a damsel of the fifties would *Leave him wanting more*—and let's face it, because another second in this girdle and I might pass out—I decide it's time to make my exit.

When I tell him, Jack immediately reaches for his jacket. "I'll call us a car."

Trapped in a car with him, alone, for a forty-five-minute ride into the city? *Abort!*

"Oh no, you stay," I insist, praying he won't push the issue, because on this, the tips are clear: *Let your man take the lead!* "I heard some of them talking about going on to get drinks, and I'm sure they want their fearless leader there. I'd feel terrible making you leave early."

He looks like he wants to argue, but whatever he must see on my face makes him reconsider.

"I probably should stay," he pivots seamlessly, granting me that gift, and I let out an internal sigh of relief. "But you can't stop me from walking you out."

I rearrange my features into a winsome smile. "I wouldn't dream of it."

I say my farewells to the group, and a few minutes later we're outside the stadium, a black SUV idling beside us on the curb as he tells the driver we'll be just a minute. I face him and swallow, my nerves a riotous mess at what I'm deathly afraid is coming.

He steps back onto the sidewalk and raises his eyebrows at me, a playful smile on his mouth. He's got to be the most confident man I've ever met, relaxed and unruffled even in the face of the dreaded end-of-date awkwardness. "Did you have a good time? I know it was a lot, meeting everyone."

"I had a lot of fun," I respond honestly—and I'm shocked to realize that I mean it. "Everyone was . . . really great, actually."

His eyes crinkle at the corners. "You sound surprised."

That's because I am.

"No, I'm . . ." I shake my head, then groan-laugh in embarrassment. "That came out wrong. Rewind."

"No offense taken." He winks, lifting his chin. "I'd like to see you again."

Whoa. Startled by his directness, I rock back a step, nearly tripping over my own espadrilles. "Oh! Wow, okay. Sure." Betty frowns at me in my mind's eye. "I mean, I'd like that too," I stammer, attempting to course-correct. *Better.*

He looks amused. "Were you . . . not expecting that?"

A middle-aged couple in matching fanny packs passes by, and I watch the woman glance back over her shoulder and give Jack a once-over, then raise her eyebrows at me and nod approvingly like, *Get it, girl!* I have to swallow the knot of hysteria bubbling up in my throat.

"Honestly? I'm just a bit more used to *I'll call you*," I intone in a man's low register. "And historically, I'd say there's only about a fifty-fifty chance of actually receiving said call."

"Ah." He nods, looking thoughtful. "So, something you should know about me: I'm past the game-playing stage of my life. I'm also not a beat-around-the-bush kind of guy. So if I say I'm going to call, you can trust I'm going to call. And if I say I want to see you again, then that's exactly what I mean." His eyes are steady on mine, clear as sea glass, determined as a gathering storm. "I won't make you guess."

My brain short-circuits as I gape at him, struck dumb for the second time today. *Is this guy for real? And how is he still single?* (Misogynistic job notwithstanding.)

My muteness seems to entertain him. "Have I scared you off? Didn't mean to put you on the spot there. You want to think about it and get back to me?"

"No!" It comes out more forcefully than I intended, and now he's the one who looks startled. "I mean, I don't need to think about it." I beam up at him adoringly. *Nice save.* Betty is pleased.

He's returning my smile when I watch his eyes flick to my lips and linger there for one second. *Two.* And it's that pause—a pause with *intent*—that makes me spring back just as he starts to lean forward.

"I don't kiss on the first date," I blurt, exhaling in a heavy gust. *Why am I winded?*

He blinks. "Really." *Blink blink blink.* "Well, that's a throwback."

You don't know the half of it.

"I know it's a little unorthodox," I babble, wondering if this will be the straw that breaks the camel's back, if said camel will finally spook and bolt down the Long Island Expressway. "And it has nothing to do with you, it's just one of—"

"Your rules," he finishes. "Like the chaperones."

"Exactly," I confirm, slowly dying inside. Saying these ridiculous things to his face is *so* much more awkward than over the phone.

"So." His mouth tugs up at the corner. Is he actually amused by this? "Any other rules I should be aware of?"

"Uh . . ." My mind's gone hideously blank. My heart's galloping like Seabiscuit. "Give me a minute and I'll come up with some."

"Is a hug too forward?" he says seriously, then snaps his fingers. "What about hand-holding? Or is that considered, like, third base?"

I refuse to laugh, instead donning a look of prim disapproval. I am an untouched vestal virgin, pure as the driven snow. This corset may as well be a chastity belt.

My reaction only makes his grin grow wider. He's having fun with this now. "So let's just say—and this is purely a hypothetical, of course—that I *was* interested in kissing you. Exactly how many dates would I be looking at?"

"Infinity, if you're going to make fun of me."

"So, three then?" His smile is irrepressible.

I'll be long gone by the time you make it to that kiss, buddy.

I peer up at him from beneath my lashes, simultaneously coy and seductive. Betty is a saucy little minx. "Stick around and maybe you'll find out."

It's the perfect response, really—ambiguous, yet just tempting enough to keep him in the hunt. I'm walking quite the tightrope here; my balancing act could rival Zendaya's in *The Greatest Showman*.

His grin lights up his whole face. He's a shimmering, flapping fish, hopelessly caught in my net. "You're definitely different than I expected."

"Gotta keep you guessing, right?" I throw him a wink, and something unidentifiable sparks in his eyes—surprise, perhaps, or maybe more like curiosity.

We stand there for a beat, quiet, until I raise my hand in an awkward wave and move to leave—but before I can, he catches my fingers and brings them to his lips, lightly brushing them against my knuckles in a featherlight kiss. I'm paralyzed in place.

His eyes meet mine over the curve of my hand. "Not *technically* against the rules," he murmurs, his voice a low, teasing rumble. "A gray area, I think."

I'm frozen in shock. An elaborately carved ice sculpture. I'm Princess Anna of Arendelle, forged in frost.

He takes a step closer to me and the space between us narrows to a sliver. "But it's probably best for you to learn now: I don't always play by the rules."

He gives my hand a gentle squeeze before reaching around my fossilized form to open the car door. "I'll call you."

I mumble something unintelligible and practically fall into the car, flattening myself against the backseat as the door snicks shut. My pulse hammers in my throat as the driver pulls away from the curb, and if I listen closely, I think I can make out its bleating warning, shrill as a Ross Geller primal scream: *DANGER!*

What is wrong with me?

Why am I so affected by this guy? It's like all he has to do is drop some not-even-terribly-original line or pin me with his bedroom eyes and I go comatose. It's mortifying, really; I'm not usually such a soft touch. It's like he's hypnotized me and I've forgotten the wake-up word to snap myself out of it. I can't remember the last time I've felt this off my game, this jittery around a man—and I know it's not just the stress of the story and this scam I'm running.

No, in the worst development imaginable: I am genuinely attracted to Jack Bradford.

I groan and grope for the door controls, suddenly desperate for oxygen. I consider sticking my head out the window like a dog, but this humid, muggy air would totally ruin my pricey blowout. I draw the line at self-immolation.

So he's good-looking, I acknowledge, attempting to rationalize away this epiphany. Like an addict, the first step is admitting the problem. *Big deal. Plenty of men are attractive.* It changes nothing about my plan . . . or my intended outcome.

I need to get my act together—literally. I can't be going starry-eyed and weak-kneed every time he says something remotely flirtatious or this whole thing will be over before it even began. I need to deflect his flattery and compartmentalize his compliments and resist his (admittedly strong) gravitational pull.

I definitely need to stop thinking about the naked interest in his eyes.

One thing's for sure: I need to regroup—but first things first.

I lean forward and tap the driver on the shoulder. "Excuse me, sir? Could you pull over at the nearest McDonald's?"

Goodbye girdle, and hello Big Mac.

Chapter 8

"SO YOU GOT NOTHING."

Cynthia peers at me from across her desk with one eyebrow raised, her piercing laser-stare practically burning a hole through the chic acrylic and gold office chair I'm currently occupying. She's intimidating on a normal day, but right now? Her midnight-black bob and blood-red lipstick are giving off serious Angelina Jolie in *Maleficent* vibes.

"I mean, not *nothing*." I shift in my seat, the backs of my thighs sticking to the Pinterest-popular but decidedly uncomfortable plastic chair. "I made inroads with the Brawler team, for one thing. Granted, Jack didn't take the bait on some of the things I thought he would, but I'll just have to get more creative."

She leans back in her chair, nonplussed. Cynthia's used to instant gratification—understandable, considering Siren survives and thrives on tight timelines and quick turnarounds—but this story requires flexibility. *Finesse.* She needs to grant me some breathing room.

"Besides, he was on his best first-date behavior. Once he

lets his guard down, I know his true personality will come out. I just need a little more time." I think I'm trying to convince myself as much as her. "Plus, I was on his turf—his event, his scene, his people—and I have some ideas for the next date that'll help tip the scales my way."

She brightens. "So there is a next date, then?"

My gut pinches as I flash back to the cast-iron certainty in his voice: *I'm past the game-playing stage of my life. I won't make you guess.*

"It's not officially on the books yet, but he made it clear he was going to call." *Clearer than those sea-glass-blue eyes.* Still, I can't find it in me to disparage this particular personality trait of his—despite his unjustly pretty face, his directness might be the most attractive thing about him.

As if on cue, there's a knock on the door and Talia, one of our receptionists, pokes her head in. "Cassidy, there's a delivery for you."

"For me?" I echo, accepting the large square box she hands me. Once I thank her and the door's shut, I shoot Cynthia a tight-lipped smile as I open it up—then inhale a breath.

It's one of those jumbo-sized souvenir tennis balls, emblazoned with the US Open logo and scribbled with an autograph, and it takes me a moment to realize: It's signed by the winner of our match. *Holy cow.* I spot a note in the box and grab it to read, knowing Cynthia's eyes are tracking my every move.

Cassidy,
This is my subtle way of letting you know I had a great time yesterday. Looking forward to more ball-busting

on a second date (bad pun, sorry). I'll call you tonight,
but if you want to beat me to it, the ball's in your court
(worse pun, sorry again, can't help myself).
Jack

I laugh out loud before remembering where I am and
who I'm with, then wipe the smile off my face in a hurry.

Cynthia's watching me closely. "Looks like whatever
you're doing is working."

"It's just how he is," I stammer, stuffing the ball and the
note back into the box. "You know, showy. Go big or go
home." *You are a terrible liar.*

She must hear something in my voice because she tilts
her head, studying me appraisingly. "You still okay with
this?"

"I am," I respond firmly. I don't need to give her any
reason to doubt I can pull this off.

She eyes me for an extra beat before nodding. "Okay.
Well, keep at it and let me know how it goes."

I assure her I will, then escape her office, grateful to be
out from under the glare of her spotlight and even luckier I
was able to avoid admitting the truth:

She's right, I got nothing.

I confessed as much to Natalia last night, who pounced
on me the second I walked in the door.

"How'd it go?" she screeched before I could even kick
off my espadrilles. I slingshotted the girdle at her in response.

She gasped. "Oh no. Don't tell me he *literally* charmed
the pants off you?"

"Don't be ridiculous. But I'd rather be drawn and quartered than wear that thing again," I called over my shoulder as I swept past her into my bedroom to change.

"So what'd you think of him?" she asked a few minutes later, once I'd exchanged Betty's ~~straitjacket~~ dress for my own buttery-soft sweats. I'd felt like a lizard shedding its skin.

"He's different than I expected," I admitted as I lounged on the couch, relishing the feel of my full, unrestricted stomach. I'd never take breathing for granted again. "Honestly, he's hard not to like. Easygoing and funny; flirty without crossing the line into creepy. He clearly knows how to play the 'charming' card, but I saw glimpses of a more serious side." I thought about the bits he let slip about his mom and his relationship with his brother, though I stopped short of sharing them with Nat. Something about dissecting the details of his family history felt off-limits to me. *Well, would you look at that? I still have a conscience.*

I yawned and stretched and started massaging the balls of my feet. The shoe designers of yesteryear had a lot to learn about arch support. "Now Tom, he's *definitely* what I expected. Loud and obnoxious. Pompous and arrogant. There's sort of a 'good cop, bad cop' dynamic going on between the two of them."

"You think it's an act?"

I considered that. "It could be. Who knows? Anyway, what does it matter? If Jack can be friends with someone like that—*best* friends, no less—how good of a guy could he be, really? You are who you surround yourself with."

She grinned wickedly. "Did he smell good?"

"Did he—*what*? I don't know! I was too busy trying to avoid getting close to him."

Nat side-eyed me knowingly. "I bet he smelled like money. Rich guys always smell good."

"Stop it."

I intentionally left out the details of my car-ride epiphany, which I'd already begun recasting in my memory as a momentary lapse in judgment. Whatever fleeting attraction I may have felt toward Jack was likely just a result of proximity and pheromones, or chemistry, or whatever you want to call the inability of attractive, unattached adults to maintain a platonic relationship in the face of potential future nudity. I can hardly be held responsible for the thousands of years of natural human instincts baked into my DNA. Meg Ryan and Billy Crystal settled this debate thirty years ago.

"You want to know something that surprised me?" I offered instead. "How nice it felt to be out of the driver's seat for once. Letting him make all the decisions and just following his lead was . . . pretty freeing, if I'm being honest."

She stuffed a pillow under her arm, getting comfortable. "Explain."

"I haven't fully processed it yet, but I guess it just made me realize how often I'm the one doing all the work. Like with Brett, I made all the plans, I coordinated our schedules, it was always my job to pick a dinner place. And maybe that's my fault or it was a red flag I missed, but . . . it's like, you know that feeling when you're talking to a guy and you're stressing out trying to keep the conversation going? And you're already queuing up your next question so there are no awkward silences?"

Nat groaned. "Ugh, the worst."

"Right? So today was like the *exact* opposite of that. Instead of being forced into planning mode or having to lead him by the nose, I just sat back and let him do all the heavy lifting. And I'm not saying I never want to make another decision again or anything, but honestly, I could get used to not carrying that load."

"You need to put this in your piece," she said thoughtfully. "Something our grandmothers got right."

"Maybe," I allowed, picking at a loose thread on the couch cushion. "I need to think on it some more. But right now I have a more pressing issue to deal with."

"Like?"

"Like the fact that he didn't fall for my shtick at all! And I thought I did a pretty good job setting him up, too." I was indignant at the injustice of it. How dare Jack turn out to be decent?

She waved a hand. "Maybe he's just saying what he thinks you want to hear. Gabriel does that all the time."

"If that were the case, he would have *agreed* with the nonsense I was spewing, not pushed back on it." I shook my head. "I don't think this is going to be as easy as we thought. He's just not as . . . manipulatable as I expected. Is 'manipulatable' a word?"

"Think it might be 'manipulable'?" she guessed. "Let's check. Hey, Alexa," she called out, and I smirked—as writers, this was the type of thing neither of us could let go. "Is 'manipulatable' a word?" We both listened intently as Alexa confirmed that it was, in fact, a word. "Thanks, Alexa, you're a sweetheart," Nat said graciously.

"Anyway, I think I'm gonna have to come at this from another angle, though I do have an idea on that front."

"Oh yeah? What's that?"

I flashed her a grin. "Call for reinforcements."

Double date with a happily married couple—let him see what it's like!

"Hi, give me a second to find my earpiece," my sister's voice rings out amidst a din of chattering background noise.

"No problem," I reply, sidestepping a mountain of trash bags piled high on the sidewalk as I make my way home from work later that afternoon.

"Alright girls, I'm talking to Aunt Cassidy now. That means I don't want anyone to interrupt me for the next few minutes. Okay?" It comes out as more of a threat than a question, and I stifle a laugh.

"Okay, I'm here," she says, sounding harried. "Warning, this is the witching hour, so I'm not sure how long they'll give me." I hear a loud banging noise in the background.

"How are my sweet little nieces doing?"

She snorts. "Sweet, right. Do 'sweet' children cut a chunk out of their sister's bangs when their mom is in the shower, then tell you it's fine because Rapunzel did it in *Tangled*?"

"Oh no," I say, trying—and failing—to contain my laughter. "How bad does it look?"

"Pretty darn bad. I'll send you a pic."

"It almost sounds like something you would have done to me," I say pointedly. "She's her mother's daughter."

"I wish I could deny that. *Hey, I'm watching you,*" she says loudly, and I know I've lost her again. *"Yeah, you, girlfriend with the Scotch tape. If you keep pulling that much out, you're gonna run out.* Sorry," she says, returning to our conversation. "I had the bright idea for the girls to help me wrap Greg's anniversary gift. Already regretting it." She exhales a loud breath. "I'll tell you what, I am so looking forward to our night away on Friday. The countdown is on. You're still meeting us, right?"

To celebrate their anniversary, my sister and her husband are coming into the city for dinner and a show, then staying overnight at a hotel while my parents watch the girls. Christine invited me to meet them for dinner, though I'd planned to stay only for a drink, not wanting to party-crash their rare night out.

"That's why I was calling, actually. I have kind of a weird favor to ask." I've reached the subway but the call will drop if I go underground, so I detour over to a nearby park bench and plop myself down. "How would you feel if I stayed for dinner after all, and brought someone with me?"

There's a brief pause. "Shut the front door! You're seeing someone new? Well, this is *exciting*! Who is he?"

I hold a hand up in a "settle down" gesture despite knowing she can't see me. "Okay, so this is where the weird part comes in. I'm not exactly *seeing* him, per se." I take the next few minutes to fill her in on everything: my deal with Gran, the story, Betty, and finally, on Jack.

She whistles when I'm finished. "So you're telling me you want to go out on a double date with me and Greg where you'll attempt to trick this guy into saying or doing something incriminating?"

"It sounds bad when you say it like *that*." I belatedly look around to see if anyone can overhear me. "But that's the gist of it, yeah. And before you say it, yes, I know how ridiculous this sounds, and of course, you're allowed to say no—"

"Say *no*?" she interrupts, then lets out a crazed hyena-cackle. "You must be joking. Cass, do you know how boring my life is? Last night I took the girls out for ice cream on a school night and it was the most excitement I've had in weeks! You're offering me the chance to go undercover for a story and participate in a sting operation. It's like something out of a movie!"

A loud laugh bursts out of me and an old man shuffling past on the sidewalk jolts in fright. I mouth *"Sorry"* at him. "But do you think Greg will be up for it? I hate to turn him into an accomplice . . ."

"Pshh, we're not telling Greg! That guy can't keep a secret to save his life. Trust me, it'll be much easier if we leave him in the dark."

"Are you sure?" I ask doubtfully. "Because I'm going to be saying some wacky stuff that's very out of character. Pretty sure he'll know something's up."

"Nah, he won't even notice," she says dismissively. "Now, I think I need an alter ego, too. Who's my character going to be?"

I groan-laugh. "Stop it, no! I need you to be the normal one here. I need you to back me up whenever I say something outlandish, help refocus the conversation if it goes off the rails, that kind of thing." *Provide a human buffer so I don't have to be alone with Jack,* I add silently.

"So you get to have all the fun, then?" she pouts. "Doesn't seem very fair to me."

"Can't you ever let me be in charge of *anything*?" The perpetual lament of a younger sibling.

"I can't help it. Your life is so much more exciting than mine and I'm jealous."

I'm about to correct her when I hear a crashing noise in the background, followed by a wail so loud I have to jerk the phone away from my ear.

Christine swears under her breath. *"Ella, what are you*

doing? *You can't swing the wrapping paper roll around like that! You just hurt your sister!"*

"She should've got out of the way, then!" Ella's little voice hollers back, and I snort.

"Cass, I gotta call you back," Christine says, sounding stressed. "But I'm totally on board and can't wait for Friday." *Click.*

I chuckle and shake my head, grateful that she didn't feel the need to chastise me for what's clearly an ethical breach—though I suppose her unwavering loyalty is one of the reasons I called her. Christine's always had my back, from the cradle to the . . . hoodwinking of unsuspecting suitors, I guess. She's who I'd want by my side in a knife fight. She'd be my first call if I needed to hide a body.

One down, one to go.

Since it's nice out and I'm not in a hurry, I decide to call Gran right there from the park bench.

She answers on the fourth ring, sounding out of breath. "Is this my favorite granddaughter?"

I'm already laughing. "I'd be flattered if I didn't know for a fact that you call *all* of us your favorite."

"You can have more than one favorite," she says defensively.

"By definition, I don't think you can. But what do I know, I'm only a writer," I tease. "Am I interrupting something?"

"Oh no, I was just finishing up my tai chi. And I did it for about five minutes, so I think that's about enough working out for the day."

I smile to myself. "Well, I'm calling for a couple of reasons. I wanted to give you an update on your birthday assignment-slash-blackmail, and also, I need your help."

"I'm listening," she says, and I hear her sliding glass patio door open and close.

"So I really hate to admit it," I tell her, "but you were right. I tested out a few of those tips, and they actually worked. This is my mea culpa."

"I knew it!" she crows. "Let this be your lesson that your grandmother is never wrong."

I fill her in on Jack, our mishap-turned-meet-cute at the bar, and our subsequent tennis date, though I leave out the details of my con job. I know she'd never approve, and I'd rather ask forgiveness than permission.

"So here's the thing: We're going out on a second date, and I need more ideas. Teach me your ways," I plead humbly, knowing that flattery will get me everywhere.

"Like intentionally forgetting your sweater at home so you can ask for his jacket?" she offers, a smile in her voice. "Or asking him if he likes your perfume so he'll lean in close?"

Jackpot. "Yes, exactly like that," I tell her, pulling up my Notes app. "What else have you got for me?"

Chapter 9

RUE TO HIS WORD, JACK CALLS ME ON MON-
day night and, after a bit of back-and-forth, asks when I'm
free this week—giving me the opportunity to turn the tables and invite *him* on the double date. In the brief pause
that follows, it occurs to me that a) I have no fallback plan in
place in the likely case he already has plans for Friday, and
b) asking him to meet my family on the second date is liable
to scare him off.

But he only chuckles. "More chaperones, huh?"

Cringe. "If it's weird to meet my family so fast, I totally
get it," I backpedal, hoping I haven't completely botched
this. "I just thought, since I was already going—"

"No, no, I'd love to meet them," he interrupts, amusement in his voice. "I appreciate the invitation."

"Okay. Great," I say, relaxing a touch. "It should be fun.
My sister's a real trip. So's her husband, actually. They're . . .
entertaining."

"Oh yeah? Anything I should know about them ahead
of time?"

"Not really. They're college sweethearts, so they've been together forever. Greg's like a brother to me. My two little nieces I showed you the pictures of? Those are their daughters. Oh!" I snap my fingers. "Whatever you do, do *not* ask my sister if they're going to try for a boy. She will cut you."

He laughs. "Noted."

Since we'll both be coming from work, we agree to meet at the restaurant. Jack even offers to call in a favor and book us a reservation at Constitution, a restaurant so exclusive and hard to get into, I'm pretty sure you have to sacrifice a limb or your firstborn to get on the list. Possibly both.

The rest of the week both speeds and crawls by, each minute ticking closer to our date like a doomsday clock. Before I know it, it's Friday night and I'm standing outside the Midtown hot spot, simultaneously excited to see my sister and anxious about the plethora of ways this night could go comically, disastrously wrong. I take a deep breath and gird my loins before pushing through the heavily lacquered wooden doors, immediately spotting Christine and Greg at the bar, a few minutes early as per our plan to rendezvous ahead of Jack's arrival.

I weave my way through the sea of bodies until I reach them. "Happy anniversary to my favorite sister and brother-in-law," I trill, greeting my sister first with a hug.

Before I can pull away, she holds me there, her expression grave. "I'm afraid I have to apologize in advance."

Uh-oh. "For what?" I ask, hanging my purse on the back of her barstool.

She jabs a thumb toward her husband. "For Greg. I made the mistake of mentioning your date's name to him and—"

"I can't believe you're dating the founder of Brawler!"

Greg bursts out as he crushes me in a bear hug. "How dare you keep life-changing news like that from me?!"

"Well, hello to you too, Greg," I say wryly, then catch my sister's eye over his shoulder and raise an eyebrow in question: *How much did you tell him?* She shakes her head slightly. *Our secret is safe.*

"I'd love to know how this is life-changing for *you*," I tease once he releases me, then swipe my sister's martini to steal a sip.

Greg looks incredulous. "Jack Bradford could end up as my brother-in-law, and you didn't think that was an important detail to share with me?"

I laugh and hold up a hand. "Whoa there. This is only our second date, so you may want to hold off on that wedding gift."

"Cass, I don't think you understand—the perks of being directly related to Jack Bradford would *drastically* improve my quality of life. I mean, the guy has access to every sporting event in the world. He's best friends with Tom Brady!" I make a face and he groans, exasperated. "I need you to tell me something."

"What's that?" I ask warily as I pass my sister's drink back.

He clasps my shoulder, regarding me seriously. "What can I do, personally, to help make this happen?"

Oh, for the love. "Are you going to be able to be cool tonight?"

"Not a chance," Christine answers for him. "He's been running his mouth about this for twenty minutes now. He has absolutely no chill."

"Hey, I can be cool," Greg says defensively. "In fact, I'll be so cool, Jack Bradford will want to be *my* friend."

"That would be more convincing if you didn't keep using both of his names."

He shoots me a wounded look while Christine nudges him toward the bar. "Hey, cool guy, why don't you cool *off* and go order Cass a drink?"

Greg sighs dramatically. "Fine. You want your usual pinot grigio?"

"Actually, how about an old-fashioned?"

"An old-*fashioned*? Like, with bourbon?" He looks dubious, and I can't blame him—I've been drinking the same thing since he's known me.

"Yeah." I school my expression, not wanting to raise his antennae. "Just feel like changing it up tonight."

He casts me a funny look, but dutifully raises a hand for the bartender. "If you say so."

As soon as his back is turned, Christine pulls me away a few paces. "Okay. Any last-minute directions? Changes? Warnings?"

"Nope. Just be normal, and back me up any time I say something bizarre."

"I have plenty of experience with that." I roll my eyes, and she finally seems to register my outfit, giving me a once-over. "What are you *wearing*?"

"You don't like it?" I ask, striking a pose.

Despite feeling as out of place as Elle Woods in a Playboy bunny costume, I actually don't mind tonight's getup: a blue tweed pencil skirt paired with a sleeveless white silk blouse that ties at the neck. And pumps, of course, because: *Wear high heels as often as possible—they're sexier!* Armed with my Brigitte Bardot–inspired hair (per Gran's latest advice: *"Tease it to Jesus!"*), I'm ready. Nat deemed the look "very Grace Kelly in *Rear Window*." I called it "secretarial chic."

"You look like a librarian." She slurps her martini.

"Thanks a lot." I smooth the bow at my throat, fingering the antique gold-and-rhinestone brooch I dug out of my jewelry box. It's a piece I admired as a teenager on Gran, who unpinned it from her sweater and gifted it to me on the spot.

I stroke it now like a talisman. "Anyway, that's fine, because I don't want to give him any ideas."

"Well, you've succeeded. A handmaid shows more skin."

I'm swatting her when I see Jack duck through the door. "Crap, there he is." I throw my shoulders back, slide on a smile, and begin my mental metamorphosis into Betty.

"*That's* Jack? Whoa, he's *way* better-looking than you let on."

Gah. "Not you too! Look, just remember that he's built his entire professional career on demeaning and degrading women." I catch his eye and wave him over.

"I think I might let him degrade me."

"Please act normal," I hiss through clenched teeth as he cuts his way through the crowd.

"I hardly think *I'm* the one who needs to be reminded to act normal," she mutters under her breath just as he reaches us.

"Ladies," Jack says in greeting, before turning the full force of his smile on me. "Cassidy. It's great to see you." I find myself drawn into a hug, and before I can pull away, he presses a kiss to my cheek.

"Watch out, I just blew past first base," he murmurs in my ear, and I barely have a chance to react before he's reaching a hand out to my sister. "You must be Christine?"

"That's me," she says, accepting his handshake. "And my husband Greg is—"

"Right here!" Greg pops up from behind us and hands off my drink. "Great to meet you. I'm a big fan," he says, vigorously pumping Jack's hand. I shoot him a warning look, which he expressly ignores. "I can't believe you're not at Yankees-Mets tonight."

I blink at them both for a moment, confused, before connecting the dots. "Oh, shoot—I didn't realize there was a game tonight. Is it a problem that you're missing it?" *Betty is nothing if not supportive of her man's job. Remember: His career comes first!*

"Nah, I got a better offer." He throws me a wink.

I squirm inside my skin, flustered by his overt flirting... or maybe it's that I can feel Christine's eyes on me, studying my body language like a forensic psychologist. To distract myself, I take a deep swallow of my drink—then immediately start coughing, nearly spitting it all back out. *Good lord, this is strong.* It tastes like battery acid. With a hint of orange.

Jack looks concerned. "Are you okay?"

My eyes are stinging. "Oh, fine," I manage to splutter, before lightning strikes. "Actually, you know what? I got this for you." *Two birds, one stone.*

His eyebrows lift. "For me?"

Always have a drink waiting when he walks in. After a hard day's work, he'll appreciate you anticipating his needs.

"Yeah, you know—you've had a long day, I'm sure you could use a drink. You like bourbon, right?" I present it to him as earnestly as an engagement ring.

He blinks at me, a twelve-point buck frozen in headlights. "I don't want to take your drink," he protests, casting Greg an uneasy glance. "I'll just order something once we sit down."

"No no, I insist. Really." I hold it out until he's reluctantly forced to take it.

I watch the internal battle play out on his face before etiquette wins out. "Alright. Well, thank you very much," he says, raising the glass in cheers and taking a hearty swig. *Better him than me.*

"Would you look at that? How come you never have a drink waiting for me?" Greg ribs Christine.

She folds her arms across her chest. "Um, maybe because you get home from work before I do? Why don't you ever have a drink waiting for *me*?"

There's an awkward pause. "Uh . . . now that we're all here, why don't we go see if our table is ready?" Greg suggests brightly. "Can I carry your purse for you, honey?"

He throws a pained *Help!* look over his shoulder as he steers Christine toward the host's stand, and Jack laughs quietly as we follow a few paces behind them.

"Told you they're entertaining."

"You did. They seem great, though." He leads me forward with a hand to my back, then dips his head toward mine. "You look very nice tonight."

Maybe he has a naughty librarian fetish. "Thanks. You don't look so bad yourself."

It's an understatement. He's dressed similarly to how he was at the bar that first night, in full business attire: white button-down, perfectly coordinated striped tie, and a steel-gray suit that's cut as impeccably as his hair. With his high-voltage smile and godlike bone structure, he's easily the best-looking guy in this restaurant. Maybe for miles.

He has an ugly soul, I remind myself.

"I didn't picture Brawler as the type of office where people dress up for work," I confess as we navigate our way

The Rom Con * 123

through the restaurant's main dining room. In my mind, Brawler's headquarters are akin to a grimy frat house, full of degenerate men in shapeless hoodies and sporting a sticky, beer-stained floor.

"It isn't, but these days I'm constantly in meetings with investors and finance people," he says as we arrive at our table. "Not exactly a jeans crowd." I thank him as he pulls out my chair, ending up with him on my left and Christine to my right.

As everyone gets seated and settled I take a look around the restaurant, appreciating the vibe of the place, the decor a blend of modern industrial and traditional steakhouse. There's exposed brick and funky oversized chandeliers made of metal and glass, but the comfy leather chairs and moody lighting ensure the overall feel is cozy, not cold.

"Jack, thanks so much for getting us the reservation here," Christine says, accepting a menu from the hostess. "I feel very VIP."

"It's no big deal," Jack says, brushing off the praise. "A friend of a friend runs the parent restaurant group. All I did was make a phone call."

This time I'm the one studiously ignoring the pointed looks Greg's beaming across the table. *Alright, I get it. The man has access to perks.*

"Well, it's a big deal for us," Christine continues. "We don't get out much."

"It's your anniversary, you deserve to celebrate in style," Jack says graciously, tapping his knife on his water glass in jest. "How many years?"

"Eight, but we've been together for twelve." They moon at each other like horny honeymooners and I can't help feeling a pang of envy.

I can barely remember a time when Christine and Greg weren't together, which basically means I've idolized their relationship for a decade. They're truly best friends—the embodiment of #couplegoals—as well-matched and secure in their relationship as Cory and Topanga. In fact, I blame them for giving me unrealistic expectations. Because of them, I always assumed I'd meet my soul mate in college and live happily ever after, too. Talk about a letdown.

"Your daughters are adorable," Jack says as he unfurls his napkin. "Cassidy showed me some photos."

"Meh, they're alright," Christine jokes. "They're also—"

"Not here!" Greg finishes, and they high-five each other. At Jack's confused expression, she clarifies. "We have a policy of not talking about our kids on date nights."

Jack laughs at that. "Fair enough."

Our server interrupts to take my drink order, and this time I wise up and request my usual pinot. *Betty can bite me.*

"Do you have any nieces or nephews, Jack?" Christine asks, sipping her martini.

He shakes his head. "No. It's just my older brother and me, and he and his wife divorced before they had any kids."

"Ah. Well, if you're bored or hate sleeping, we have a couple we're willing to lend you."

Jack chuckles. "Sign me up."

"So, how'd you two meet?" Greg asks.

Jack's face lights up and he turns toward me. "Well, it's a funny story, actually—"

"That we don't need to get into right now," I cut him off instantly.

"Oh come on, there's nothing to be embarrassed about. It's a great story." When I make no move to share it, he turns back to Christine and Greg, his now-captive audience of two. "You could say she fell into my path."

I slant him a look. "You could also say he blackmailed me into a date."

"She was blowing a little hot and cold," he tells them conspiratorially.

"The details aren't important," I say hastily, desperate to wrest back control of this conversation. "Long story short, we crossed paths at a cologne launch party for Eric Jessup a couple of weeks ago that I was covering for Siren. Jack happens to be friends with Eric, and he was kind enough to help me get a quote." *Downplay your professional competence so he doesn't feel threatened*: check!

Greg coughs. "Friends with Eric Jessup? Huh. That's cool." He eyes me over the rim of his glass as he takes a long swig of his drink. Pretty sure the poor guy's head is about to explode.

"I apologize for my husband," Christine tells Jack, patting Greg's hand consolingly. "I didn't give him enough notice about your identity, and he's very starstruck. He's trying so hard to be cool and just failing miserably."

Jack chuckles. "I promise, most of the Brawler stuff is not nearly as exciting as it looks from the outside. Most days it's just a job like any other."

Greg considers that for about half a second. "I don't believe you."

Christine smacks his arm but Jack only laughs, clearly used to having this conversation. "Fine, the connections part is useful, I'll give you that."

"And the access to every major sporting event," Greg points out.

"And that."

"And the personal friendships with the greatest athletes in the world."

"Fine, those too," he concedes with a grin. "But there's also unflattering media attention, constant lawsuits, employee headaches, a perpetually dissatisfied board of directors that complicates every decision we try to make . . . trust me, it's not all Super Bowls and Stanley Cups."

I can't help myself. "Come on, you don't get to complain about negative media attention when *you're* the ones courting controversy."

"Ah, there she is! That fiery, slightly unhinged woman who told me off at a bar." Jack's eyes spark as they fix on me. "I wondered where she's been hiding."

Crap. I realize my mistake the second my brain catches up with my mouth: I've broken character again. *Betty would never talk back to her man.* But hot damn, staying silent and submissive is *so* much harder than it looks.

"She's been here the whole time," I say eventually, meeting his gaze head-on.

"Has she, though?" His dark eyes are lit in challenge and I'm reminded that he *likes* this push-pull dynamic between us; he enjoys being provoked. The site is called *Brawler*, after all.

So I give him what he wants: a heaping dose of Cassidy. "She has. Guess I just didn't expect you to play the 'poor little rich boy' card. Not sure it suits you."

I keep my tone playful, careful to ensure I can pass off the dig as flirty banter. He doesn't flinch—not visibly, anyway—but when I look closer, I see a shadow reflected in his eyes, and for one blink-and-you'll-miss-it moment, I think I've scored a direct hit. Strangely, the knowledge doesn't give me the satisfaction I thought it would.

Before he can respond, our server, a young guy with a man bun, returns with my wine and sets it down in front of me. "Are you all ready to order, or would you like more time?" When Greg answers in the affirmative, my stomach tightens at what I know I have to do next.

I reach over and rest my hand lightly on Jack's forearm. "Would you mind ordering for me?"

He blinks at me once. Twice. "Order *for* you?"

"You've been here before, right? I'm sure you know what's best." I smile guilelessly.

His eyes flick to our waiter, currently busy with Christine and Greg, then back to me. "Are you . . . sure?"

"I'm sure I'll like whatever you like." I sound like the queen-to-be in *Coming to America*.

"Uh . . . okay," he stammers after a beat, then reaches for his discarded menu, knocking over a saltshaker in the process. He's delightfully rattled. "How hungry are you?"

I shrug airily, helping him exactly zero percent. "So-so."

When it comes to the 125 tips, the rules for dining are actually wildly inconsistent. One says to *Order a steak rare*, while another espouses the "cabbage soup diet" as the secret to a trim waistline. *Choose the most expensive thing on the menu*, but *Show him you can have fun on a cheap date! Experiment with meals that have the spirit of adventure*, but also *Cook him foods that are basic and familiar, like his mother made*. (I'm deliberately ignoring the tips that veer into fat-shaming: *Go on a diet if you need to*, or *If your mother is plump, tell him you take after your father. If he's fat too, tell him you're adopted!*)

Rather than try to parse through that contradictory advice, I made a pregame decision to place the ball squarely in Jack's court, giving him a golden opportunity to mansplain the menu while assuming the presumptuous, male-dominant role he was born to occupy. It's a twofer.

But Jack bypassing my carefully laid bait seems to be becoming a theme. "Do you eat meat? Or are you more of a salad person?" He's trying valiantly to pass this ridiculous retro test, but he's definitely sweating.

"Surprise me. I trust your judgment," I reply magnanimously, giving him absolutely no guidance whatsoever. It's a challenge to keep a straight face, but I'm nothing if not committed.

Our waiter clears his throat expectantly, pen poised over his notepad. A faint pink hue's started to bloom up the back of Jack's neck, broadcasting his discomfort. It's such a treat to see him squirm.

"She eats meat," Greg offers helpfully, and I howl internally. "And you can't go wrong with the crab cakes, she loves those."

Damnit, Greg! I can't decide whether to strangle him or thank him (since I did, in fact, want the crab cakes), but seriously—can't *anything* go the way I need it to? I want to stomp my feet under the table like a tantruming toddler.

As soon as the server leaves, Jack makes quick work of shucking his jacket (I was right; totally sweating), then takes a long pull from the old-fashioned. "You caught me off guard there," he admits in a low voice, setting his drink back down.

"What do you mean?" I am all puppy-eyed innocence.

"You don't seem like the type of woman who'd want a man ordering for her."

"That's because she's not," Greg says flatly. He jerks

abruptly and I'd bet money Christine just kicked him under the table.

"I am sometimes," I counter.

"She is sometimes," Christine echoes, shooting her husband a stern look. Greg makes a face at her in answer.

Jack's unconvinced. "You just seem more, I don't know . . . independent."

I nod like this is a novel observation I'm considering for the first time. "Sometimes it's just nice to not have to think for yourself, you know?"

I deliver the line flawlessly, but this one truly hurts coming out, like I'm regurgitating a cactus. *This isn't me!* I want to shout to the restaurant at large. *If you're overhearing any of this drivel, please disregard!*

Jack considers me thoughtfully. "Actually, I do know. Decision fatigue is very real when you run a business. I have to make a thousand different decisions every day, and by Friday? Forget it, I can barely remember my own name." He leans back in his seat and flashes me a grin. "How about next time we switch and you can order for me? It'll be like menu roulette."

ARE YOU KIDDING ME? Why can't Jack just react how I need him to even *once*?

I somehow manage to gin up a smile, but behind my polite veneer, I'm seething. Also, suspicious. No man could successfully dodge *every single* trap I've laid for him, could he? Has he somehow discovered what I'm up to? That's how it works in *How to Lose a Guy in 10 Days*, right? Both Matthew McConaughey and Kate Hudson falsely assume they're the only ones doing the double-crossing. Maybe someone's tipped him off and he's trolling me with these letter-perfect responses. Maybe Nat's a double agent!

It's about here I realize I'm losing my marbles.

"Ooh, Cass—awkward couple at four o'clock."

"Hmm?" I'm so lost in my paranoid delusions that I completely missed what Christine was saying.

"That couple over there," she says impatiently. "What's their story?"

Ah. Jack tilts his head at me quizzically.

"It's sort of a party trick of mine," I explain to him. "I can tell you the backstory of every couple in here—who's on an awkward blind date, their professions, et cetera."

"It's her superpower," Christine boasts.

"It's just something silly I do for fun," I clarify, feeling a little self-conscious now. "It's more of a writing exercise than anything else, just to get the creative juices flowing."

He looks intrigued. "Alright, let's hear it. What's the story with those two?"

I purse my lips, observing them for a moment. "First of all, definitely a first date."

"How can you tell?"

"Stiff body language, for one. And she's got her interview face on. You know, bright-eyed, fake perma-grin. She seems more into him than he is to her, so I'd bet they matched on Bumble." Jack looks lost. "You know, because that's the one where the girl makes the first move?"

He shakes his head. "I've never done any dating apps."

"*Never?*" That shocks me. "How can that possibly be? Are we part of the same generation?"

Greg snorts. "Duh, because he's Jack Bradford. He doesn't *need* dating apps."

Christine makes a gagging noise. "Should Cass and I leave you two alone? I swear, you're more excited about him than you are about having hotel sex later."

He thinks that over. "It's a tie."

Poor Jack is going red. "It's not like that. I'm just weird about my privacy. I have a hard time trusting people. It's much easier for me to spot someone with ulterior motives when we're face-to-face."

My pulse starts to speed, fast and furious.

"How can you be sure Cassidy doesn't have ulterior motives?" Greg jokes, and a bead of sweat breaks loose from my hairline.

Jack laughs. "She made it very clear that my being the Brawler guy was definitely *not* a point in my favor."

Greg gasps theatrically in my direction. "How dare you."

We all laugh this time and my anxiety drops a notch.

"Anyway, I know my strengths," Jack continues. "I'm much better in person than via text. Plus, it gives me a chance to deploy my own superpower."

"And what might that be?" *So sue me, I'm interested.*

He wags his brows. "Cheesy pickup lines."

"Oh, geez." I ball up my napkin and throw it at him.

He catches it seamlessly, his grin only growing wider. "There's a real art to it. You've got to pick a detail—her appearance, her job, something you know she cares about—and tailor it to her just so."

"Did you fall for this?" Christine asks me, incredulous.

"No!"

"She would've, if I'd gotten the chance to lay one on her." There's a candlelight gleam in his eye as he looks at me, and I know he meant for me to catch his double entendre.

"You know, there's such a thing as *too* cocky," I tell him, and he shrugs like, *Sorry not sorry.*

"Let's hear one now," Greg eggs him on. "What would have been Cassidy's pickup line?"

I can't help myself. "Let me guess. *'Are you a pickpocket?'*" Jack rolls his eyes and I flash him my widest smile.

"I don't get it," Greg says.

"Never mind," Jack continues smoothly. "Knowing that Cassidy's a writer, I might try . . ." He squints at me for a moment before taking my hand and staring deeply into my eyes. "Your eyes are like an open book, and I can't wait to dive into this page-turner."

Greg hoots.

"You got the cheesy part right," I tell him as our appetizers arrive.

"It's a gift," he says simply, releasing my hand so Man Bun can set down my salad.

"Speaking of, how's the book progress?" Greg asks, grabbing a roll from the breadbasket and tearing off a hunk with his teeth. "When are you gonna let us read some?"

"You're writing a book?" Jack says in surprise, and my stomach plummets like one of those rides that drops you twenty stories. This is dipping dangerously close to him learning actual, personal details about my life. *Knowing the real me.*

"Um," I hedge, trying to figure out how to respond without offering more information than necessary. Christine grimaces and mouths "*Sorry*" at me. "Sorta? I'm not really ready to talk about it yet," I say vaguely, scanning the dining room for a diversion. *Aha!* Man Bun is retreating. I grab him by the elbow before he can. "Sorry, could I get another glass of wine?"

His eyes flick to the nearly full glass in front of me, so I grab it and knock back half its contents in one aggressive swallow.

He eyes me and I eye him right back, daring him to say

something. He gets the message. "Sure thing." *You just earned yourself a hefty tip, pal.* "Can I freshen any other drinks while I'm at it?"

"Sure, I'll have another . . . what was this?" Jack asks me, pointing to his nearly empty tumbler.

"An old-fashioned."

"Ah. How fitting." He smirks and turns to Greg. "Did Christine put you through the ringer too? How many of your dates did dear old dad have to chaperone?"

I lock eyes with Christine in a panic as Greg echoes, "Chaperone?"

"Oh, he wouldn't remember," Christine intervenes, leaping to my rescue. "Anyway, that's really more of a Cass thing. She's pretty traditional."

Greg looks bewildered. "Since *when*?"

She shushes him. "Eat your salad."

"She just means I prefer to date men who open doors and pull out chairs," I clarify, and on this, I realize Betty and Cassidy are in agreement. "Respectful, old-fashioned courtship. Is it so wrong to want that?"

"I've always treated you respectfully, haven't I, honey?" Greg says, squeezing Christine's thigh playfully.

She snorts. "Sure, yeah. When we're in bed and you have to fart, you face your butt the other way."

Greg looks to Jack for backup. "I think that's pretty considerate."

Maybe double-dating with these two wasn't the best idea.

"Well, I find your principles refreshing," Jack says to me, suppressing a smile. "I like a woman who knows what she wants."

Of course he does. I close my eyes and count to ten. When that doesn't do the trick, I repeat it in Spanish.

"As fun as it is fun to watch Cass squirm, I'd rather put you on the hot seat, Jack," Christine redirects quickly, sensing my impending meltdown. "We already know all of her secrets."

Jack straightens, lacing his fingers and turning them inside out in a fake stretch. "Is this where the sibling interrogation comes in? I came prepared to be grilled."

"Excellent, so the arm-twisting I'd planned on won't be necessary." She grins and shushes me with a hand, ignoring my protestations. "So Jack, in the event Greg and I both die, Cassidy will gain custody of our kids. Therefore, it's important for us to know what kind of father figure you'll be."

Omigod. I drop my head into my hands and wish for a swift death.

"I completely understand," Jack says, nodding solemnly. I can't believe he's playing along with her shenanigans. "I take that responsibility seriously, so ask away."

"Do you smoke or do any kind of recreational drugs?"

"No."

She side-eyes him. "Not even cigars?"

He hesitates. "If they're disqualifying, consider them gone."

"Have you ever been convicted of a crime?" She's ticking things off an invisible checklist.

"No. Though I have been accused of thoughtcrime."

Greg bellows a laugh and smacks the table.

Christine regards them both wearily. "Have you ever ghosted a woman?" *Ooh, that's a good one.*

Jack casts a guilty look Greg's way. "We all do dumb things in college."

Christine shakes her head sadly. "That's disappointing to hear, Jack. I expected better from you."

I snicker as he hangs his head. It's one of the things I love most about my sister—she's totally fearless, intimidated by no one. Not even Jack's charm can faze her.

"Have you ever changed a diaper?"

He thinks for a minute, then grimaces. "Shit, no. Is that a deal-breaker?"

"We'll see." Greg mouths *"No"* over her shoulder, then pretends to be studying the ceiling when she whips her head around to give him a warning look. "How long does it take you to return your mom's phone call?" *Another good one.* She's on a roll.

I smirk and look to Jack for his response, but there it is again—that shadow. A pinch between his brows that promptly vanishes when he notices me studying him. It's there and gone, faster than a flash of lightning, so fleeting you wonder if you even saw it to begin with.

"Same day is the only acceptable answer to that, of course," he answers smoothly. *A little too smoothly, if you ask me.*

Christine considers him for an extra beat, which tells me she's picking up on the same less-than-truthful vibes I am. I make a mental note to revisit this later. "How long was your last serious relationship?"

Okay, this has gone far enough. "Christine, stop. Over the line."

"Over the line? I haven't even requested his credit score, W-2, and medical records yet." She leans toward Jack conspiratorially. "I'm also going need to see your browser history and the past three years' worth of your Amazon purchases, but you can get me all that later."

"It's fine," Jack says, brushing his hand over mine in reassurance, and my knuckles tingle like he's sprinkled them with fairy dust. "It lasted about a year and a half. And it ended a little over a year ago," he adds preemptively.

I sit up a little straighter. *Now that is new and interesting information.* Christine smiles smugly like, *You're welcome.*

Her eyes take on a diabolical glint. She's a dog with a bone now. "Who ended it?"

"*Christine.* That's enough." I murder her with my eyeballs. "Greg, control your wife."

He barks a skeptical laugh. "You of all people know how futile that request is."

Jack holds up a hand. "I ended it. And before you ask why, I'm fine to tell you." He refolds the napkin on his lap before leaning forward and resting his forearms on the table. "When we first started dating, I was looking for someone who understood how demanding my job was and wouldn't require too much of me. And she didn't." He laughs ruefully. "She gave me the space I asked for. Sometimes we wouldn't see or speak to each other for days. And that was fine for a while, until I realized that I *wanted* someone to require more of me."

He turns to lock eyes with me, the warmth in his gaze whispering across my skin like a tropical breeze. "I realized I could live without her. And I want someone I can't live without."

The din of the restaurant fades to the edges as he holds eye contact, the tension between us fogging thicker than vapor in a steam room. In fact, I may as well be in a sauna, the way I'm cooking under the heat of his gaze, the effort it's taking to drag in a full breath. The look he's giving me is charged and private and loaded with hidden meaning. This look needs to get a room.

"Now *that's* a pickup line," Greg declares, and the moment is broken by our laughter.

I finally tear my gaze away from Jack and reach for my water, needing to cool myself down (or plunge myself into an ice bath, one of the two), when I catch sight of Christine and I'm jogged out of my Jack-trance right quick. Her eyes are sharp on mine, narrowed, her penetrating expression the same one she used to reserve for interrogations about whether I'd borrowed her clothes without asking. I'm under the sister spotlight now, and she's got twenty-eight years of experience in seeing right through me.

When she tilts her head and smiles meaningfully at Jack, I can pinpoint the exact moment I've lost her as my partner in this particular crime. "I've got just one more question for you, Jack."

Dread trickles through me. *What is she up to?* "Christine, come on. Enough."

"This is my last one, I promise." She won't look at me, instead keeping her eyes trained on Jack, and I'm seized with panic. *Is she about to blow my cover?* "Why are you interested in my sister?"

I let out my breath. *That's not so bad.* Guess I misread her.

"Besides the obvious?" Jack says brazenly, and my cheeks flush red as a ripe tomato.

"Of course," she says immediately, and I want to crawl under the table and expire. *This must be what a show pony feels like.*

Jack's grinning. "The truth is, your sister captivated me." He shifts his gaze and now he's speaking directly to me, as though Christine and Greg aren't sitting mere inches away, hungrily hanging on to his every word. "And the more I learn about her, the more I like. She's smart and bold and intriguing, and as it turns out I seem to have a weakness for that *exact* combination. I knew about thirty seconds after meeting her that I needed to find a way to see her again." His dark gaze drags slowly over mine and my stomach does a backflip. "And so I did."

My throat is scorched dry. Christine and Greg are practically drooling.

"So did I pass your test?" Jack picks up his old-fashioned and nonchalantly brings it to his lips, and I have to admire this man's swagger. He's got them eating out of the palm of his hand.

"Uh, *yeah*," Greg answers. "If Cassidy won't marry you after a speech like that, I will."

Chapter 10

*A*N HOUR LATER WE'RE OUTSIDE ON THE sidewalk, saying our goodbyes so Christine and Greg can make it to their show in time for curtain. The rest of the meal went fine—which is to say, the three of them got on like a house on fire while I silently smoldered over my total failure to get anything remotely damaging on Jack *again*.

"You're a sweetheart, Jack," Christine is saying, ignoring my icy glare. "I know I speak for Greg when I say we hope this works out." She goes up on her tiptoes to give him a hug while I mentally draw a chalk outline around her body. "Take care of my sister, okay?"

She releases him to Greg, and while the guys do some macho backslapping routine, I squeeze her extra tight, not at all trying to cut off her air supply.

"What do you think you're doing?" I hiss in her ear. "'*I hope this works out*'?"

"Hush, I did you a favor," she says, speaking into my hair. "This guy really likes you, and I think you like him. If you go through with this story, I know you'll regret it." She pulls back and squeezes my hand. "Think about it, okay?"

Before I can formulate a response, she links her arm through Greg's. "Let's go, babe, I don't want to be late. Love you, Cass. Be good, you two!" She winks at us, and with a final wave from Greg, they head off arm in arm and we're left alone on the sidewalk.

I turn to face Jack, feeling a fresh wave of nerves now that my human shields are gone. Christine's words ring in my ears like a skipping record: *I think you like him. I think you like him.*

"So have they permanently scared you off?" I joke as we start ambling down the sidewalk side by side. Part of me hopes they have; it would certainly make my life easier.

He laughs. "They're a trip, you were right about that. But in a good way. Honestly, it's refreshing to be around a family that genuinely *likes* one another."

It's the second time he's referenced a less-than-ideal upbringing, so I put on my camo bucket hat and go on a little fishing expedition. "Oh yeah? What's it like in your family?"

He makes a low humming noise in his throat. "More like . . . a lot of tense silences. Or shouting. Not much in between." He attempts a smile that doesn't reach his eyes. "We don't really get together unless we're forced."

Yikes. "I'm sorry to hear that."

He shrugs like it doesn't bother him, but his body language tells a different story. He may be a worse actor than I am. "I'm used to it, for the most part. But you're very lucky. Not everyone has a family like yours."

"But surely your parents must be proud of your success?" *However ill-gotten it might be.* "How often do you see them?"

"You could never be successful enough for my dad. Anyway, I'd rather hear more about your book," he says, expertly dodging my line of questioning. It's one of the things I've noticed about him, how adept he is at pivoting the conversation away from himself. *And here I thought these hotshot types loved talking about themselves?*

"I wish there was more to share," I admit, deciding that if I want him to open up, I'll need to take the first step. "My dream is to be a novelist, but I've started and stopped so many times, I've lost count. I can't ever seem to get past the first few chapters. I can't even decide on a genre. Should I write a thriller with a shocking twist? A sweeping family saga? An epic love story where the sexual tension is just steaming off the page?"

"I'd read it." He guides me around a subway grate, correctly guessing it would be a problem for my stilettos.

"You read a lot of romance novels, then?" I tease, calling his bluff.

"Fine, you caught me. I tend to stick to nonfiction and business books. I'm sure you find that pretty boring, though, huh?"

"Nah, I would never judge what someone else reads. But hey, you know who else likes nonfiction? My dad."

He groans. "Thank you for that. Real nice."

I can't help laughing; he's fun to mess with. "I'm just kidding. I think everyone should read what they want to read."

"Well, I'd read *your* romance novel." The corner of his mouth curls up. "I could probably learn a few things."

"*Every* man could learn a few things from romance novels," I say firmly. "Why more men don't take advantage of what are essentially instruction manuals for women is beyond me, though I suppose that's a conversation for another day."

He cants his head as if to say *Touché*. "So what do you think is holding you back? From writing, I mean."

Now I'm the one who wants to change the subject. "Oh, you know, the usual suspects: Fear of failure. Unrealistic expectations. Perfectionism. Inadequacy. Self-doubt."

"Just those, huh?" he teases.

I think of how to explain it. "Writing a two-hundred-word article is simple for me. I do it every day—multiple times a day, actually. Easy-peasy. But writing an entire book? Coming up with a plot that'll hold someone's attention for a hundred thousand words? Creating a story that's memorable, that will resonate, that someone will love so much it'll become their favorite book? It's incredibly daunting. It's such a high bar to clear."

"And if you don't try, then you can't fail," he says pragmatically.

"Exactly." It takes me a second to hear what he actually said. "Wait, no."

He chuckles, his eyes twinkling like he's pulled the sparkle straight from the stars overhead.

"You think I'm too scared to do it," I say accusingly. How dare he . . . peg me so accurately? *Damnit.*

He throws me a sideways grin. "Are you?"

"Of course I'm not scared!" How insulting. I huff like a marathoner on their last mile. "I'm just . . . taking my time figuring things out."

He presses his lips together and nods seriously.

"You know what, I'm not falling for whatever this reverse psychology is you're using on me, Mr. Smooth Talker. You can just forget I ever said anything." Greg and Christine are dead to me for bringing this up to begin with. "And how did this even get turned around on me, anyway? I was the one asking *you* uncomfortable questions."

The surge of righteous adrenaline puts some extra spring in my step, and I end up striding ahead of him—only for him to grab me by the crook of the elbow, haul me away from the curb, and shift me to his other side, depositing me on the inside of the sidewalk.

I gape at him, but he keeps right on walking as if nothing at all just happened. "Ahem? What was that?"

"What was what?" He's the picture of innocence.

"You just moved me to the other side of the sidewalk."

"Did I? Hmm. S'pose I did."

I wait, but he doesn't elaborate. "And *why* did you do that?"

His shrug is blasé. "Just in case."

"In case of *what*?" I make a show of looking around the quiet, mostly empty street. "Is Pennywise going to climb out of the drain and drag me into the sewer?"

He clamps down on his smile like he *really* doesn't want to admit he's amused by me. "Women aren't supposed to walk next to the street."

Now that perks my ears right up. "And why's that?"

He opens his mouth, then hesitates, tilting his head. "You know what? I'm not actually sure. It's just one of those things I've been raised to know, like how to throw a spiral or drive a stick. A man should never let a woman walk next to the street." He shrugs like, *Sorry, I don't make the rules.*

"You know that if a car hopped the curb, it'd be just as likely to take me out if I'm only three inches to your right."

He considers that. "But if it was raining and a car drove through a puddle, I'd be the one to get splashed, not you." He looks quite pleased with his loophole.

"Maybe I like to walk on the wild side."

"Sorry, not on my watch." He splays his palms as if to say, *It's out of my hands.*

"So what would you do if I, say . . . entered a crosswalk before the light's changed?"

"Pull you back by the scruff of your neck," he replies without missing a beat, and I crack up.

I haven't been paying attention to where we've been walking, but all that changes when the quiet street we've been meandering down spits us out into the belly of the beast: the blinking neon screens and blinding strobe lights of Times Square.

I immediately throw my forearm up to shield my eyes and search for an escape. "Get thee to a subway."

He stops me before I can flee, catching me by the hip. Heat spreads through me, his hand like a brand.

"Let's keep walking," he says casually, and my blood pressure spikes. "It'll be fun."

I peer at him like he's just suggested we stroll through a deserted cornfield in a slasher movie. "Are you serious? What self-respecting New Yorker actually chooses to hang out in Times Square?"

"Oh come on, it's not that bad."

"Not that *bad*? It's one giant epileptic trigger!"

He smirks like a mischievous teenager out past curfew. "You have to admit, the people-watching can't be beat. Who needs Broadway when Times Square is *right* there? I'm telling you, this is the real show."

Somewhere, a piece of Lin-Manuel Miranda's soul dies. "I know you did not just compare Times Square to Broadway. That is beyond sacrilege."

He chuckles, the low, velvety sound dancing across my skin.

"You seem to be experiencing some confusion. You must've had too many drinks at dinner. Are you unwell?" I reach up to feel his forehead with the back of my hand. "I think we may need to get you home." *And I can regroup and figure out where to go from here.*

He snags my wrist. "Or maybe," he says, his voice distinctly rougher, "I'm just not ready for the night to be over."

I flush, a mixture of fear and flattery spiking my blood. It's a confusing combination. "Oh."

"Unless you're trying to get rid of me." His eyes search mine with interest.

What I'm trying to do is pretend not to notice how your hand feels pressed against my skin.

"No!" *Yes.* "Not at all." *Gah.* How am I going to tap-dance my way out of this one?

You're not, Betty pipes up. *Accept every invitation with gratitude. Let him be the decision-maker!*

So I paste on my own second-date perma-grin, link my arm through his, and let him lead me out into the intersection of Bright & Brighter, accepting my soon-to-be-damaged retinas as the price I pay for a story.

To prove I'm a good sport, I start playing tour guide. "You were so right about the unique charm and distinctiveness of Times Square. To our right, you'll see such esteemed

New York landmarks as the Hard Rock Cafe and M&M's World." I motion toward the creepily costumed characters milling about aimlessly. "If you want, we could get your picture taken with a few off-brand superheroes or beloved characters like 'Winnie the Pooch' or 'Mikey Mouse.' They may look a little shifty, but I'm pretty sure they've never killed anyone." I gesture to the restaurant on the opposite side of the street. "Oh! And if you're still hungry, nothing says 'only in New York' like the Olive Garden."

Before I can react, his arm's shot out and grabbed me by the waist, and he's tickling me within an inch of my life. I shriek and writhe as I try to escape, but it's a long, torturous few seconds before I'm able to twist out of his grasp.

I point at him with my arm extended, like I'm holding him at sword's length. "Don't even *think* about doing that again," I wheeze, still catching my breath.

His eyes are alight with humor. "I don't think I'm the only one who had too many drinks at dinner."

He's not wrong; I am feeling a little fuzzy at the edges. Against my better judgment—and spurred on by the giddy adolescent energy that always seems to accompany a night out with my sister—I indulged in more wine than was probably wise given the circumstances. The easy, natural camaraderie of our foursome only served to blur the line even further. There were times tonight when I nearly forgot that Jack is my sworn enemy. *Forgot this isn't a real date.*

I think I'll also blame the booze for the fact that when he grabs my hand and starts swinging it between us as we walk, I don't let go.

There's loud music blaring up ahead, a group of people gathered around observing something, and when we make it to the edge of the crowd I spot the main attraction: an elderly couple is dancing in the center of the circle, and it's the most wholesome spectacle I've ever seen in Times Square. We stand and watch as the thin, slightly stooped man twirls his gray-haired partner in a spin, and the smile she aims back at him is so adoring, my heart melts like soft serve in humidity. "Wow. How cute are they?"

He nudges my shoulder. "And to think, you would've missed this."

I pull a face, but I can't even pretend to be mad. "I love this song," I tell him, humming a few bars of "Cry to Me."

"Solomon Burke is one of the best."

I blink at him, surprised. "You know your golden oldies," I say approvingly.

"Motown's my mom's favorite. It's all we listened to growing up."

"Your mom has good taste." I can't help swaying back and forth. "This song will always remind me of *Dirty Dancing*. Gosh, it's such a great scene." It's also one of the steamiest scenes in the movie, but I leave that part out. I can hear Jennifer Grey's heartfelt confession now: *"Most of all I'm scared of walking out of this room and never feeling the rest of my whole life the way I feel when I'm with you!"* Pretty sure the rest of us felt the same way about Swayze and his bare chest. *Hungry eyes, indeed.*

"Don't you feel like that era of music is so much better than ours?" I muse aloud, snapping my fingers to the beat. On this, Gran's generation wins hands down.

He doesn't answer, and when I glance over at him I see he's watching me with amusement.

"What?" I ask, immediately self-conscious. I've been told I dance like Phoebe Buffay runs, and I do not need to be showing Jack that side of me.

He nods his head toward the silver surfers. "Should we give them a run for their money?"

"You're joking."

He arches a brow.

"You're *not* joking." He grins wickedly. "Jack, we can't do that!" I hiss.

"Pretty sure there's no law saying you have to be over eighty to dance in Times Square. Unless, of course, you don't dirty dance?" His eyes flicker with mischief.

Very funny. "Don't you think we should watch respectfully, then clap politely at the end?"

He purses his lips like he's considering it. "Nah, I think we should take 'em."

I meet his eyes, which somehow look both heated and dark. "You're trouble."

"I've *definitely* thought the same about you." He holds out a hand. "Come on. Let's be the embarrassing tourists now."

As his invitation—and hand—hang in the air, out of nowhere my mind flashes to a long-forgotten childhood memory.

As kids, my sister and I were obsessed with *The Sound of Music* (to the point where our brother would beg us to watch something—*anything*—else). But we could never get enough of the singing and dancing, the yodeling marionettes, the playclothes stitched from curtains. We were hopelessly devoted to Julie Andrews and just as hopelessly in love with Christopher Plummer's Captain von Trapp, and utterly enthralled by his transformation from stern authoritarian to besotted paramour.

But our most favorite part—the scene we watched again and again until we had every step memorized—was when the captain exited the ballroom to discover Maria teaching Kurt the Laendler, the Austrian folk dance. We'd swoon over the way he adjusted his gloves as he prepared to cut in, certain there was nothing more romantic than the way his eyes tracked Maria's every move, his smug grin when she took his hand, the restrained passion with which he twirled her around the marbled patio. I used to dream of the day when a man would look at me with such intention, such raw desire in his eyes. *The way Jack's looking at me right now.*

As the memory shimmers and fades around me, I find myself taking his hand and letting him tug me out into the center of the circle, and then I'm in his arms and we're doing an improvised foxtrot in the middle of Times Square.

I don't even have to heed Betty's nagging reminders to *Let him lead!* because Jack's doing that all on his own, pressing me against him with one hand low on my back and the other clasping my palm to his chest. When he spins me out unexpectedly I let out a squeal of surprised delight, and it's just the thing to help me shed any lingering self-consciousness and surrender to the moment. Honestly, I'm not sure it gets more "only in New York" than this; I feel like I'm in a movie montage. I half expect a flash mob to break out.

You said you wanted chivalry, Betty singsongs, and I suppose she's got me there.

He must sense the change in me, because when he reels me back in his hold on me is stronger, more assured; his gaze more intense; his hands, well . . . *handsier.* He moves with such an easy grace and innate rhythm that I can't help but wonder how his skill would translate to the bedroom.

I immediately banish the thought.

"You're pretty good," I tell him, trying to distract myself from my illicit thoughts. It only half works. "Did your mom teach you how to dance, too?" *There you go, talk about moms.*

He does some complicated spin move that tangles our arms up like a pretzel. "Not quite, but she'd be pleased to know all those years of cotillion didn't go to waste."

I glance over at our competition, and if I've felt self-conscious about "showing them up," I shouldn't have—they're lost in their own world, with eyes only for each other. For a moment, my mind flashes to Gran and how tickled she'd be to see me doing something so spontaneous and carefree. She always says she sees herself in me, but the truth is, she's bolder and braver than I've ever been. I'm a rule follower, a type A stickler who rarely colors outside the lines, while she's always done whatever strikes her fancy—and she's never cared who's watching.

I have to pause that train of thought, though, to address a more pressing concern: this pencil skirt, which is so fitted that it's actually restricting my range of motion. Not a huge deal when I was sitting at a table, able to disguise the slight wiggle-walk it forced me to adopt; a much larger issue, however, while trying to be the Ginger Rogers to Jack's Fred Astaire. I'm forced to cling to him like a second skin or risk toppling like a tipsy penguin. For someone playing the purity card, it's a mixed message I do *not* want to be sending.

It's like he can read my mind. "This is sweet," he says, toying with the bow at my neck. "Like a present." He casts me a naughty look, then starts tugging on one of the ends.

I smack his hand away like a nun with a ruler. "Undressing me is *definitely* not second-date material," I scold in the primmest, churchlady-est tone I can muster, and he throws his head back and laughs at the sky.

I can't deny it: I'm enjoying myself. Everything about this "date"—this whole night, really—has been a pleasure. In a shocking twist I never saw coming, Jack is proving to be—*dare I say it?*—a gentleman. Sure, I may have started with rock-bottom expectations, but if I'd randomly matched with him on some dating app I'd be rating it five stars, writing a glowing review, and forcing all my friends to join.

Looking at him now with fresh eyes—his face crinkled in laughter, his mood contagious, the summer air causing his hair to curl up and wing out a bit at the ears—I can't help but wonder if my sister is right, if I like him more than I'm willing to admit to myself, if I'm missing what's right in front of me. *If I'm making a huge mistake.*

I can practically hear Gran's prodding voice in my ear: *Give him a chance. What do you have to lose?*

Everything, I lament silently. *My job. My credibility. My pride.* The idea that my judgment could be so off—that I could have gotten him *this* wrong—is terrifying, and my blood runs ice-cold despite the late-summer heat.

The song winds down, and as the crowd—some of whom have joined us in our spur-of-the-moment dance-off—begins to applaud, Jack bends me back in an exaggerated dip. I'm forced to tighten my grip on his biceps—*whoa, someone's been eating his Wheaties*—and when he pulls me back up, we're awash in a chorus of *Awww*'s. Everyone's a romantic.

As the spectators disperse, Jack holds me in his arms for an extra beat, and here it is, the picture-perfect fairy-tale movie moment: our first kiss, bodies silhouetted against the iconic backdrop of a glittering New York City skyline. It couldn't be more perfect if I'd scripted it myself.

Jack's watching me intently, eyes aflame, and when his

gaze drops to my mouth I know at just the slightest hint from me—if I leaned forward even a fraction of an inch—his lips would be on mine.

I absolutely cannot allow it to happen.

Panic sets in, and for once I'm sending out a Betty Bat-Signal, begging her to rear her retro head and offer me some of her heirloom pearls of wisdom—but of course, now that I actually need her, she's nowhere to be found.

~~Why buy the cow~~
~~Modest is hottest~~
~~Pet your dog, not your date~~
Learn where to draw the line, but do it gracefully. That'll have to work.

I move to step back, but his firm grasp—and this damn pencil skirt—won't allow it, so I raise my eyes to his and give my head the slightest hint of a shake. His hands flex on my hips as he exhales a ragged breath, his eyes briefly closing, and I have to wonder when he'll hit his breaking point, if there's a limit to this man's patience.

And if there's a limit to my resistance, as well.

"When can I see you again?" His voice is a husky scrape, like loose gravel on an unpaved road. "Alone?"

I have no idea how to respond. I'm so sick of lying, but I can't admit the truth: that I *want* to see him again.

"It'll be our third official date, you know," he adds before I can answer. There's an unmistakable gleam in his eye, and unfortunately, I know *exactly* what he's getting at.

"Not that you're counting," I quip, trying to sidestep that land mine.

"Oh, I'm counting."

My blood pressure ratchets up.

"But it's interesting," he says, catching my hand before I

can think to snatch it away, and I have no choice but to stare up into his eyes. They're dark as a roiling sea and just as deep. "I've realized there's something to be said for delayed gratification." He strokes his thumb across the back of my hand and I barely suppress a shiver. "I can't remember the last time I've anticipated anything quite this much."

He sounds as surprised as I feel—and just like that, this doesn't feel like a game anymore. This relationship no longer feels fake. The stakes are too high and I'm in *way* over my head.

And later, when I'm lying in bed without the bright lights of Times Square to distract me, I no longer know if I'm doing this for a story . . . or if I'm doing it for me.

Chapter 11

$\mathscr{T}$HWACK.

The magazine lands on top of my knuckles, forcing me to stop typing. When I glance up to see the source of the interruption, I find Nat, looking triumphant.

"What's this?" I slide off my noise-canceling headphones and pick up the magazine.

"Your next date idea," she announces. "You're going to make Jack 'Engagement Chicken.'"

"I'm going to do *what* now?"

She taps a perfectly polished coral fingernail on the page. "Engagement Chicken! According to this article, any woman who uses this recipe on her boyfriend can expect a proposal shortly thereafter. It has a proven track record of success and everything! Meghan Markle even used it to get a proposal out of Prince Harry. Allegedly." She raises a finger. "And it's *absolutely* something Betty would do."

I groan and spin around in my chair. "This is the *opposite* of what I need! I told you, all these tips are doing is backfiring on me! What am I supposed to do while the chicken is roasting—ask if he has any socks that need darning? Invite him to a Tupperware party? He'd probably accept and thank me for the invitation!" I blow out an exasperated breath. "If I had to turn in the story right now, he'd coming out smelling like a rose. My only hope at this point is that he lets something damaging slip about Brawler, but so far, I've got nothing."

Nat flashes some *settle down* hands. "You didn't let me finish. The Engagement Chicken is just your ticket in the door."

"In *what* door?"

Her grin is Elphaba-wicked. "His apartment."

Fear trickles through my veins like ice water. "I really don't want to be alone with Jack in his apartment." *Talk about a danger zone.*

She tilts her head. "Don't you, though? Think about it— what better way to discover his deepest, darkest secrets than by infiltrating his lair?"

I stall, unsure how to respond without showing my hand. So far I've been able to keep my muddled, not-exactly-platonic feelings for Jack under wraps, and I don't want to admit to Nat (or anyone else, for that matter) just how out of control this situation has begun to feel. Jack's made no secret of his intentions; an intimate night alone at his apartment would surely be asking for trouble.

On the other hand, her idea is a good one—and it's also the *only* idea on the table, since I've come up with precisely zilch in the week since our double date. I've spent the last few days taking rain checks on his date requests and dodging his calls like a total coward. (A true test of willpower when he's texting me adorable things like an article explaining the historical significance of men walking street-side. Turns out, it has something to do with runaway horse-drawn carriages back in the day. Who knew?)

I don't know what to do. I'm bewitched, bothered, and bewildered by him, and the laugh is definitely on me.

"Are we at all worried that this is taking things too far?" I ask in a low voice, mindful of our coworkers within earshot. "Invading his home sort of feels like crossing a line."

Without a word Nat reaches over my shoulder, tilts my monitor in her direction, and starts typing, her fingers flying over the keyboard. When she angles the screen back toward me, I see she's pulled up the Brawler home page.

She points at a headline midway down the page and starts reading aloud. "*'Rate my rack! Who'd you rather motorboat? Cast your vote!'* Shall we click through the gallery?"

I wince and cover my eyes.

"Or how about this lovely blog post: *'How to hook up with your friend's sister without losing a limb.'* And let's not forget the Meme of the Day: *'She's a 10 but she expects me to watch women's sports.'*"

I wave my hands in front of the screen as if to block it out.

Her smile is gloating. "Still feeling guilty?"

I sigh in resignation and pick up the magazine again. "Engagement Chicken, huh?" I rock back in my chair, scanning the article. "This is so ridiculous." *So ridiculous, in fact, it just might work.*

"Ridiculously genius, you mean. Emily Blunt even used this on John Krasinski! And we both know Emily Blunt can do no wrong."

Well, that much is certainly true.

Nat leans a hip against my desk. "Come on, what guy

doesn't love a home-cooked meal? Just ply Jack with some food and booze and he'll be singing like a canary."

I bite my lip. "You really think so?"

She nods definitively. "Be a good little Suzy Home-maker and roast your man a chicken."

I snort and toss the magazine back on the desk. "I think we're overlooking one minor detail here: I can't cook."

"What are you talking about? You make great break-and-bake cookies."

I narrow her a look.

"Fine, I actually had the same thought, but this recipe literally has five steps. It's so easy, not even you can screw it up."

"Gee, thanks." My calendar dings and a reminder pops up on my screen. "Oh my gosh, I forgot to tell you! I'm interviewing this woman from Nebraska I found on YouTube who—get this—lives her *entire* life like she's in the 1950s. We're talking everything from retro hair and makeup to a full vintage wardrobe. She only uses recipes from vintage cookbooks. Every bit of her home is authentic to the era, down to the appliances. Her husband even drives a classic muscle car."

Nat's eyebrows have shot up to her hairline. "This whole trad wife trend has gotten totally out of hand."

"She said she believes the fifties were an 'idyllic time in history,'" I explain as I pull up my interview questions. "And apparently, she's not the only one out there doing this. I found a whole bunch of TikTok accounts devoted to 'vin-tagecore.'" I don't mention that I lost several (very entertaining) hours of my life to #VintageTok under the guise of said research. The song "Mr. Sandman" has been stuck in my head all day as a result.

"They're so committed to authenticity that they're on social media, huh?" Nat says with an eye roll, and I shrug. "I suppose life might feel idyllic if the most stressful part of your day was choosing what to cook for dinner," she muses as she slides off my desk. "Never mind the fact that you couldn't open a bank account or get a credit card without your husband's permission."

"Or work outside the home as anything other than a secretary," I add.

"Maybe you two can exchange fashion tips," she ribs me.

"You know, that's not a bad idea. I'd love to know how she manages to walk in a pencil skirt," I mutter, making a mental note.

She gives me a dead-eyed stare. "I was joking."

I avoid eye contact as I unplug my laptop and set off for an empty conference room. "Uh, yeah. Me too."

AS PREDICTED, JACK immediately accepted my offer to cook him Engagement Chicken (which I innocuously framed as "dinner"), and if he thought this was a peculiar activity for a third date, he didn't let on. Honestly, he sounded so relieved that I finally called him back that he probably would've said yes to BASE jumping. He even had me send over the list of ingredients so his assistant could stock his kitchen in preparation. I wanted to ask if his assistant could recommend a dry cleaner that specializes in vintage clothing, but figured that might raise a red flag.

Jack lives in a brand-new, luxury high-rise condo building overlooking Central Park, which, I'll admit, is a wee bit intimidating. Most of my colleagues are like me: barely scraping by, living paycheck to paycheck while eking out a living doing the noble but financially unrewarding job of journalism. Although I've dated men with income levels all over the spectrum (and grew up comfortably middle-class myself), Jack's wealth is in a different echelon altogether. And I don't know, there's just something about the "old family money" crowd that's always made me uncomfortable, with their Nantucket summer homes and needlepoint belts and upper-crusty, seemingly impenetrable Ivy League caste system. It all seems designed to make you feel less than, like even if I became super-successful in my own right, I'd never *really* be accepted into their exclusive club.

But I force myself to set those feelings aside as I enter his building, politely greeting the uniformed doorman holding open the wide double doors. The lobby is just as grand as the posh exterior: soaring ceilings, a tastefully appointed sitting area with high-backed chairs and plushly upholstered couches flanking a sleek double-sided fireplace, an imposing gold-and-crystal chandelier that casts a perfectly flattering shade of light on the room. My heels click across the marble floors as I make my way toward the older gentleman manning the concierge desk. He's got thick eyebrows and hair that's more salt than pepper, and I watch his eyes brighten as I approach.

He smiles warmly at me, a gold nameplate reading CLIFF winking at me from his chest. "Miss Sutton?"

Now that's what I call service. "Now how could you possibly know my name, Cliff?"

He laughs at my dumb joke, and I fall in love with him instantly. "Mr. Bradford let me know a beautiful woman would be arriving, though I'm afraid he didn't do you justice." He comes out from behind the desk and offers me an arm. "Right this way."

He leads me to an elevator bank, and once he keys in a special code for Jack's apartment—he's got the entire floor, *gulp*—and I'm zooming upward, I attempt to shake off my nerves by recapping my goals for the night:

- *Get him talking and see what he'll let slip.*
- *Don't fall under his spell no matter how good he smells or how twinkly his eyes.*
- *Less Betty, more Cassidy.* He seems to open up more when I'm myself.

The pressure's on because this is it—my last-ditch attempt to find something incriminating. If I can't get anywhere tonight, I'm out of ideas and out of time. I need to pin him down and peel away his layers—and prevent him from Houdini-ing his way out of sharing anything personal.

I think of Gran's latest tips—and not the silly ones like *Kiss him even if he's sweaty* or *Offer to rub his shoulders*—but her real ones, the good-faith relationship advice she gave me that's worth its weight in gold: *Make him feel special. Be your best self for him. Support and encourage him. Dressing up for him isn't inauthentic or putting on airs; it's showing him he matters. Considering your partner before yourself isn't subservience, but an act of love.*

I take a deep breath and smooth my dress, fingering the frilly secret weapon that's tucked discreetly into my purse. I'm ready for a night of playing house.

Jack's waiting for me as soon as the elevator doors slide open, his face lit with the anticipation of a kid standing at the threshold of a candy store.

"Hey, you." He envelops me in a hug before I can even step out, and I get a lungful of his cologne, a clean, forest-fresh scent that makes me think of alpine lakes and sturdy redwoods, like he regularly bathes in naturally occurring springs or majestic waterfalls. I wish I could place it exactly, but the only scent I can reliably identify is Acqua di Gio (those high school memories run deep). One thing I can say for sure, though: It is definitely *not* Force by Eric Jessup.

"I'm happy to see you," he says when he pulls back, eyes shining with pleasure. He has serious golden retriever energy tonight. "And looking beautiful, as always."

While this evening's strategy may be more about letting the real Cassidy shine through, I'm still dressed like Betty, this time in a sleeveless pink linen shift with an embroidered neckline that Nat swears is an exact replica of one Jackie O once wore. And while there's plenty to complain about between the corsets and cone bras, I've come to appreciate just how chic and timeless that era of fashion actually was—so much so, in fact, that I've decided to embrace my mid-century makeover for the duration of this experiment. I refuse to admit it to Nat, but the infusion of color into my wardrobe has actually added some pep to my step. And no, I absolutely did not use some of the tips from those TikTok tutorials to give my auburn hair some soft Rita Hayworth–inspired pin curls. That would be taking things too far.

I know, I know, I have sartorial Stockholm syndrome. But as they say, "When in Rome"—or, er, *Roman Holiday*.

In a nod toward "more Cassidy, less Betty," I did, however, ditch the dainty handbags in favor of my trusty overstuffed mom tote. While I highly doubt Jack (or any guy) would notice such a subtle change, I worried it might cause whiplash if my character shift was too jarring, if I suddenly went from Elizabeth Taylor to Taylor Swift overnight.

Of course, Jack's experiencing no such style dysmorphia. Tonight, he's dressed casually in a pair of broken-in jeans and a charcoal gray T-shirt that's stretched tight around his biceps—so tight, in fact, that the seams appear to be clinging on for dear life. Either his muscles are larger than the average male's (I chance a glance at them—*yep*), or whoever designed this T-shirt did women everywhere a solid by botching the sleeve-to-torso fabric ratio. I silently salute said couturier for their service.

I suddenly realize this is the first time I've seen him out of a suit, and it should come as no surprise that he wears the laid-back look just as well. I take a moment to sight-see, admiring the ruggedly handsome view. He's still rocking some serious *Big Man on Campus on his home turf* energy, but there's a looseness to him tonight, a quieter, more relaxed confidence that's new—and frankly, refreshing. I immediately sense that this stripped-down model is the real Jack, that the besuited power broker I've grown accustomed to must be his own costume, a suit of armor disguising his true self from the world.

"So what do you think?"

"Hmm?" I tear my eyes from where they've settled on the smooth, corded muscle of his bicep. I think I've been wetting my lips without realizing it. "I'm sorry, what was that?"

If he noticed me drooling, he gives no sign. "Would you like a tour?"

"Oh. Yes, please." I smile up at him.

I follow him down a hallway, and it's like I've been photoshopped into one of those aspirational home decor accounts I follow on Instagram. There are creamy white walls and tall arched doorways; thick molding lining the ceilings and baseboards; wide-plank oak floors stained the perfect shade of chestnut; large-scale artwork that's the quintessential mix of modern and masculine. Every step screams *luxury*. It even smells expensive, like one of those overpriced home stores in Soho where I love to browse but can't afford to actually buy anything.

There are a couple of guest rooms in addition to the primary bedroom, a space I skitter past with only the briefest of peeks. It's like my brain instinctively knows that any more than a cursory glance might spark the fuse of my already oversexed imagination. From just one quick glimpse, I'm able to gather that Jack has a giant bed (for acrobatic, Cirque du Soleil–style sexual activity?), crisp white hotel linens (for comfortably sleeping in the nude?), and a classic mid-century modern chest of drawers (for housing boxers or briefs?). *Must. Redirect. Thoughts.*

His office is the only room that isn't immaculately styled. His desk is strewn with papers, crumpled receipts, and piles of mail; file folders lay askew in messy stacks. An old coffee mug sits forgotten alongside a large computer monitor, a dozen sticky notes stuck to its frame. *He must really only work and sleep.*

I start absently flipping through a leadership book that's out on his desk before noticing he's using our US Open ticket stub as a bookmark. When I hold it up with raised eyebrows, he just smiles, unembarrassed.

Like an alien called home to its mothership, I'm immediately drawn to the built-in bookshelves covering one wall that stretch all the way to the ceiling, spines stuffed into every nook and cranny. There's even a *Beauty and the Beast*–style rolling library ladder. I want to hang off it like Belle and belt, *"Bonjour!"*

We continue the tour, though I glance behind me long-ingly as he leads me back out to the hallway. I'd love to steal back in there and rummage through his files, but it's not like I can just slip away without him noticing. My mind shuffles through plausible cover stories: Pretend I need to make a phone call? Challenge him to a game of hide-and-seek? Feign diarrhea?

We end up in a high-ceilinged great room with floor-to-ceiling picture windows offering stunning panoramic views of the city. In the center of the room is a conversation area set up in an inviting vignette: a pair of club chairs upholstered in a subtle, soft plaid flanking a long butterscotch-leather couch I'd bet costs more than I make in a year. An interior designer has definitely been here, because I don't know any straight men who'd have coffee table books stacked on their sideboard with an organically shaped wooden bowl perched on top.

It's beautiful. Meticulously so, really, but the thought that comes to mind is *model home*—technically flawless, but devoid of any unique character or distinguishing details about its inhabitant. If I'd thought I was going to glean all these new insights into Jack's psyche by handling his knick-knacks or poring over his personal photos, I was sorely mistaken.

I swallow this setback as I step closer to the window to take in the incredible multimillion-dollar view of Central Park, which looks like a lush carpet of green treetops from this height. "Wow," I murmur. *So this is how the other half lives.*

I can feel him come up behind me, my skin prickling with awareness. "Right? It's the reason I chose the place. Hard to feel sorry for yourself with this view."

I swivel my head one hundred and eighty degrees just

so I can give him some side-eye. "And what possible reason might you have to feel sorry for yourself?"

He raises and lowers a shoulder. "You'd be surprised."

I tuck that vague answer into my back pocket for the time being, then continue to turn in a slow circle like I'm surveying the room . . . but what I'm actually doing is casing the joint, *mwa-ha-ha*. I have no idea what I'm expecting to find—a file folder left unattended on his coffee table conveniently labeled *Brawler Top-Secret Blackmail Material*?—but it's intimidatingly clean in here. Spotless, actually, like he's stashed a live-in housekeeper under that ginormous couch of his. Argh. *What's the point of infiltrating enemy territory if I'm forced to retreat empty-handed?*

My brain sparks with an idea, and I saunter over to the sideboard, skimming my fingertips over his coffee table books. "So are you always this neat? Or did you stuff all your skeletons in the closet before I came over?"

He gives me an *Aw, shucks* expression. "I'm afraid you've uncovered my dark secret: I'm actually quite boring. I don't have anything to hide." *Ha! I'll be the judge of that, mister.*

I cast him an impish look and reach for one of the cabinet knobs menacingly. "So if I opened up this cabinet right here, I wouldn't find anything incriminating? No Spice Girls or Barry Manilow CDs? No notebooks full of angsty teenage poetry? No collection of Beanie Babies or blow-up dolls? No creepy taxidermy?"

"Nah, I keep that stuff at the office."

I snort a laugh.

"But now I'm kinda wishing I had something in there that would shock you." His eyes dance with amusement as he nods his head. "But let's live dangerously—go ahead and see what's behind door number one."

I keep my eyes trained on him, slow-playing it for dramatic effect, before throwing the door open with a flourish. *"Board* games?" I clap a hand over my mouth to stifle my laughter.

It's a *lot* of board games, too. Neat stacks of everything from Sorry! to Scattergories to Boggle to Operation fill the cabinet to bursting. I feel like I've stepped back in time to the childhood playroom in my parents' house. I crouch down to get a closer look and laugh when I see there's even a Trivial Pursuit: *F·R·I·E·N·D·S* edition.

"Oh, my . . ." I pull out Rummikub as a steady stream of memories washes over me. "This one takes me back. We used to play this for hours at my grandparents' house when they'd babysit us." I replace it on the top of the stack and shudder at Perfection, a game that always terrified me. It's a panic attack in a box. "Why do you have all these? Do you host a lot of game nights?"

"Not exactly." He presses his lips together like he's trying to decide how much to divulge. "I'm a bit of a board game enthusiast." He says it seriously, like it's an academic pursuit akin to pursuing a PhD.

"A board game *enthusiast*? Oh, wow. Geez, okay. I only just realized."

"Realized what?"

"That you're a huge nerd."

He barks a laugh and palms the nape of his neck self-consciously, and I can't help but notice how the pose makes his bicep bulge. He's a male pinup poster come to life, like the kind my girlfriends and I would have clipped from the side of an Abercrombie shopping bag and tacked up in our dorm room. Silhouetted against the window with the city at his back, it's the second view I'm salivating over tonight.

"You are. You're a giant nerd and this whole 'big shot' persona of yours is just a cover for your *severe* nerdiness."

He's laughing. "Not doing so hot tonight, am I? So far we've established that I'm boring *and* a nerd. And to think, this whole thing"—he motions to his cabinet of wonders— "was supposed to impress you."

I mimic his serious nod. "I am impressed. By how you've managed to fool everyone into thinking you're cool."

His eyes narrow playfully. "Keep it up and I'll be forced to tickle you again."

"You wouldn't dare."

He raises his eyebrows in challenge as tension and anticipation and unspoken thoughts neither of us is willing to voice dance in the air between us.

Eventually, he clears his throat. "Shall I show you to your domain?"

"My domain?"

He quirks an eyebrow. "The kitchen?"

I'm instantly offended, steam shooting out of my ears cartoonishly before I remember—*Duh, Cass, you're supposed to be making him dinner.*

My swell of righteous indignation deflates like a leaky balloon. "Oh, right. Sure, of course."

I follow him back down the hallway, through a door— and into a kitchen that would make Nancy Meyers weep. When Jack flicks on the overhead recessed lights, bathing the room in a soft glow, I nearly swoon. Dark soapstone countertops extend along the room's perimeter and climb up the wall in a dramatic coordinating backsplash. A marble island stretches as long as a football field; I could turn cartwheels across it. The live-edge wooden barstools look like they were carved from a five-hundred-year-old tree trunk. Every appliance is stainless steel or shiny chrome and unnervingly high-tech. The overall effect is modern, striking, and sophisticated . . . and totally intimidating. Like a museum—and not the cool, hands-on kind my nieces are obsessed with. The *look but don't touch* kind.

You can cozy it up, Betty urges. *Make his house a home!* I banish her to a locked room in my brain. *You're not welcome here.*

"Wow, Jack," I say, running my palm along the cool soapstone. "This is . . . incredible."

Somehow, he hears what I'm not saying. "But?"

"But nothing!" I quickly chirp. *Don't insult him!* Betty squawks. "It makes my place look like a hovel. My entire apartment could fit in your kitchen. With room to spare." I fiddle with the handle of an expensive-looking brass pepper mill and think of my own tiny, cluttered apartment, with its hodgepodge of mismatched IKEA furniture cobbled together over the years courtesy of my revolving door of roommates. They move on up to deluxe, dual-income apartments with fresh-off-the-registry furnishings while I shelter in place, the "lucky" recipient of their unwanted castoffs. Jack can never see my apartment.

And he never will, because this is your final date, remember?

He leans back against the island, crossing his feet at the ankles. "But?" he prompts again, a half smile playing on his mouth.

I hesitate, debating. *Remember, more Cassidy.* "I guess it's just not what I expected? Not that I necessarily expected anything. It's just . . . I don't know. Fancy." I press a button on his *Jetsons*-esque coffeemaker, and when it makes a chorus of angry-sounding beeps, I shrink back. "You just seem like a simpler guy."

"Well, I am a poor little rich boy," he says pointedly, and I wince.

"I'm sorry about that. I shouldn't have—"

He waves me away, pushing off the island to navigate around me. "It's fine. It's not untrue; I did have a privileged upbringing."

I catch his arm to stop him, looking him straight in the eye. "No, it's not fine. It was unkind, and I shouldn't have said it."

He blinks at me, something passing between us wordlessly before he drops his gaze to where my hand grips his forearm. When his eyes rise to meet mine again, he nods once. *I'm forgiven.*

"I've been called worse," he admits. "Today, even." He wags his eyebrows good-naturedly. "Anyway, you're not wrong that this place is a bit 'fancy,' as you put it, though it's not really my doing. I hired a design firm that handled everything."

"I sort of figured."

He shrugs, unbothered. "I only have so much bandwidth for nonwork stuff, and home decor is definitely not one of those things, so I was happy to outsource it. I think they just decorated it how they imagined a single bachelor would want it? So I'm not offended if you hate it."

"I don't hate it!" I insist, and he chuckles. "It's just a little intimidating compared to the shoebox I live in. But I can work with it." I mime pushing up my sleeves.

He leans in conspiratorially. "Can I tell you a secret? I'm intimidated by it too."

"Oh stop it, you are *not*," I say with a laugh, then start unloading the sack of groceries that's set out on the island: a bag of lemons, onions, red potatoes, carrots, olive oil, salt and pepper, plus bunches of fresh rosemary, sage, thyme, and parsley. *Gang's all here!*

"I'm serious! It's not like I'm some Michelin-starred chef. I think the most I've done in here is reheat takeout? In fact, I'm pretty sure this is the inaugural run for this oven, which is why I'm so excited to see you do your thing." He grins, and I feel his pleasure like sunlight, warming my skin.

I think we're all excited to see what magic's about to happen here, Jack. "Right. Well, let's dive in, shall we?" I say brightly, doing my best to project a confidence I don't feel.

I remember my surprise, the good-luck charm I'm hoping will carry me through tonight's gambit: a ruffled, cherry-print hostess apron with a sweetheart neckline and edged in red rickrack that I scored at Hamlet's Vintage, where Nat and I stopped in last night after work. When we spotted it mixed in with a bin of scarves, we both agreed it was an essential ingredient on tonight's menu. My favorite part: the monogram embroidered on one of the slanted side pockets, *LSH*, a detail I find utterly endearing. As I loop it over my head, I channel *L*'s (Lucille, Lettie, Loretta's?) spirit—and, hopefully, her culinary skills.

I glance over at Jack as I start tying the back straps and his face is *priceless*—so priceless, in fact, I nearly break right then and there. To hide it, I quickly spin around so I can mask my expression, but he takes the gesture to mean I need his help managing the backward tie.

"Here, let me."

He comes up behind me and I surrender the waist straps, our hands brushing in the process, and my pulse starts to speed, the temperature in the kitchen rising by a few degrees. He takes his time with it, his fingers grazing my lower back, and when his knuckles sweep higher, skimming my spine, I suck in a breath—a physical reaction that's impossible to conceal with him standing barely an inch away in this silent kitchen.

His hands stall for the briefest of moments—a short eternity—before resuming and tightening the bow in one final tug, then traveling upward to free my hair from the loop around my neck, his fingers repeatedly stroking my bare skin. When I realize I'm surreptitiously breathing him in, reveling in his intoxicating scent, I quickly spin back around—only to find I'm now *facing* him from barely an inch away.

His eyes are smoldering blue embers as he stares down at me. "Perfect."

"Thanks." It comes out breathy, barely above a whisper. I quickly clear my throat and rock back a step, knocking directly into his space-age refrigerator, and the touch screen on the front panel blinks to life. I half expect the display to read: *SHAME.*

Oo-kay, let's reset. I throw open the refrigerator doors and take a deep, cleansing breath, letting the cool air hit my face and chill my over-sensitized skin while I take a moment to reorient myself.

Settle down.

Don't get sidetracked.

Don't let him derail you.

I blink a few times, the shrink-wrapped bundle in front of me suddenly coming into focus. *Right, the bird. You're making Engagement Chicken, remember?* I wrestle it out of the fridge and over to a cutting board that's set out on his island, acutely aware of Jack's eyes on me.

"Let me help you with that," he says and starts toward me, but I wave him off.

"I've got it. You just relax on one of your lumberjack-chic barstools over there and leave it to me."

He laughs but makes no move to sit, instead standing there and watching me with a lopsided grin. His surveillance is making me nervous, so to busy myself I start inspecting the stainless-steel roasting pan that's set out on his range like I'm some sort of cookware connoisseur. *Mmm, Calphalon. Nice.* Of course, I take it a step too far by picking it up and shaking it, like I'm testing its weight.

I catch Jack's mouth twitching out of the corner of my eye. "Your staring is making me self-conscious," I warn.

He chuckles again and circles the island. "How about I get us something to drink?" he offers, already opening the door of what looks like a well-stocked wine fridge.

Wine! I could hug him. "Yes!" I practically yell. Anything to take the edge off my awkwardness.

"This okay?" he asks, holding up a bottle of pinot grigio, and when I see it's my favorite brand—the one I ordered on our double date with Christine and Greg—I blink in surprise.

"Wow, you have a good memory."

He doesn't respond, just grins smugly as he works to uncork the bottle, his biceps flexing with the effort.

"Or wait, this is all part of your pickup line thing, right? Paying attention to the details."

He grins wider as he pours. "Can't get anything past you."

"I see what you're up to."

He winks, sliding me a glass and holding up his own, and we clink them together. I take a sip, savoring the flavor, then sigh in contentment as it hits my bloodstream. "It's a nice move," I concede.

He laughs and sets his glass down. "If you think that one was good, you're gonna love this . . ."

He pulls his phone from his back pocket and starts tapping, and a few seconds later the opening strains of Sam Cooke's "You Send Me" fill the kitchen, the music wafting down from speakers embedded in the ceiling.

"Wow." I throw the back of my hand to my forehead, mock-faint. "That was very smooth, Mr. Bradford. I might swoon."

"I had a little help from Motown radio on Spotify," he says modestly.

"And speakers in the ceiling, huh? I totally have that at my apartment too." I mouth *"Fancy"* at him while he laughs. "Now stop distracting me or we're never gonna eat."

I locate the requisite cooking utensils with Jack's help, then lay the recipe printout on the island and survey the ingredients again, making sure everything's present and accounted for. Okay *fine*, I'm stalling. *Why couldn't this recipe have been for something simpler, like "Engagement Pasta" or something?*

It's like he can hear my thoughts. "Do you make this often?" he asks, leaning his forearms on the island.

"Oh sure, all the time. It's one of those recipes that seems difficult, but is actually really easy," I bluff, as if the single Ina Garten YouTube video I watched last night makes me some kind of expert. Even with her bound and gagged, I can feel Betty's silent judgment for this dereliction of my feminine duties.

Come on, you can do this. You've seen Julie & Julia *countless times. "If you can read, you can cook," right?*

If you say so, Julia.

I follow the recipe exactly. I start by preheating the oven, then wash the chicken in cold water, taking out the gizzards (gross) from its cavity (grosser), then stuffing it with lemons (grossest). I season the whole thing with salt and pepper, then baste it with more lemon juice. I even truss it, tying the legs up with string, before adding the sliced-up veggies to the roasting pan. By the time I'm done, I'm strutting around Jack's kitchen like a *MasterChef* contestant. Gordon Ramsay's got nothing on me.

While I'm meal-prepping, Jack's serving as my personal peanut gallery, providing running commentary and peppering me with questions about my childhood, college experience, and early years in the city. It doesn't escape my notice that yet again, he's learning more about me than I am about him, but this time I have a plan to turn the tables.

I pop the chicken in the oven and set an alarm on my phone (I'm not even going to try to locate the timer on this futuristic contraption), then say a prayer to the cooking gods that everything turns out okay. *Rachael, Giada, and Martha, don't fail me now.* I even throw one up to Snoop for good measure.

"It has to cook for ninety minutes," I inform him, untying the apron and setting it on the island. "So we have some time to kill."

Jack's face immediately turns mischievous. "Hmm. Whatever shall we do to pass the time?" He rises from his perch on the barstool and saunters over, leaning a hip against the marble countertop, his body angled toward mine meaningfully. He's invading my personal space now, and if he thinks that's going to unnerve me . . . then he is absolutely right. *Damnit.*

I place a hand on his chest. *Time to flip the script.* "Oh, I know *exactly* what I want to do."

Chapter 12

IS BROWS SHOOT UP AND HIS FACE GOES slack. I've surprised him.

"You do?" His gaze briefly flicks south, snagging on my mouth. "And what's that?"

I pause, drawing out the suspense. "I want to kill you at F•R•I•E•N•D•S Trivial Pursuit."

There's a beat of silence before a shocked laugh bursts from his chest. "Is that right? Well, I have to warn you—I'm not the type who'll let you win just because you're a girl."

Aww, his overconfidence is cute. Misguided, but cute. "And I'm not the type who'll let a guy win just to boost his ego."

His eyes glimmer with amusement. "The wager?"

I think for a minute before a light bulb blinks on. "If I win, Brawler has to print something complimentary about Siren."

He lets out a low whistle, nodding approvingly as if to say, *Well played.* "Ruthless. And if I win . . ."

"You won't."

The corner of his mouth hooks up. "*When* I win," he

amends, and when he reaches out to tuck a stray lock of hair behind my ear, it takes all my willpower not to shiver. "You let me kiss you."

This time I'm the one letting out a strangled laugh. "Jack, come on."

"What? That kiss is happening and you know it. Third date, remember?" he says and wags his brows, like I need to be reminded of this looming disaster.

I narrow my eyes. "Sounds like a waste of a wager, then."

"Call it insurance."

Our gazes lock and he lifts his chin, a determined glint in his eye. He's daring me to back down, even as his lips curve into the confident smirk of a man who knows he's irresistible. And I'm sure history's on his side, because what woman could ever resist those eyes, that face, these lips?

I break eye contact first, sighing dramatically. "Fine. This whole thing is moot anyway, because when it comes to *Friends* trivia, I can't be beat."

"And by that, I assume you mean it's a 'moo point.' Also known as a cow's opinion."

Shit, I may have underestimated him. "I see what you did there, but I'm still not afraid of you." I follow him back into the living room while he pulls the game box from the cabinet.

"*'There's such a thing as too cocky,'*" he tosses over his shoulder, using my own words against me.

"So you watched a lot of *Friends* growing up?" I ask him, kicking off my kitten heels and getting comfortable on his couch—and holy moly, is this thing comfortable. It's not cold or stiff like the leather couches I'm used to, but soft and supple and beautifully broken in. I sink into it like a cloud and suppress the urge to yawn. *Whoever said money can't buy happiness never met this couch.*

"Actually, no. I probably caught an episode or two growing up, but I really hadn't seen it much until college, when Tom got me into it. I guess his sisters were obsessed with it, so he always had it on, said it reminded him of home. Did you know he has three sisters?" He takes a seat next to me on the couch and starts pulling out the game pieces.

"He *does*?" I exclaim much too loudly, and Jack casts me a funny look. "I mean, no."

How can a guy with three sisters be so crude and sexist? Make it make sense!

"Huh," I comment blandly. I don't get it. When it comes to Tom, I have more questions than answers.

Once we've picked our game pieces (Chandler's vest for me, Monica's turkey head for him) and gotten our cheese wedges ready, Jack hands me the dice.

"Ladies first," he offers generously.

I roll the special dice and it lands on blue, which apparently corresponds to Seasons 7–8, and I shake out my neck. *I've got this.*

Jack draws a card. "In the episode where Rachel is pregnant and feeling 'erotically charged,' she goes to a doctor's appointment and flirts with her OB-GYN. What is the doctor's name?"

I blanch. "Are you serious? How is anyone supposed to know that? He was a minor side character! Does he even *have* a name?"

He smiles condescendingly. "Do you need to forfeit?"

Grr. "No. Um, let's see, he had brown hair. I can picture him, that cute guy. It's the Evander Holyfield episode." Jack pointedly checks his watch. "Uh, Dr. . . . ." I hem and haw, hoping for a lightning strike, but I'm coming up empty.

"Dr. Cute Guy?" he says seriously.

"Oh, shut up. I don't know, Dr. . . . Smith?" I toss out uselessly. *Pathetic.*

"Wrong, but you're actually not too far off. It's Dr. Schiff."

I throw up my hands, huffing in frustration. Jack smirks and takes his turn to roll while I grab a card.

"Okay, yellow. Your question is: Where did Chandler claim to be moving so he wouldn't have to get back together with Janice?" I slam the card down on the coffee table. "Are you *kidding* me with this? That's so easy! Did you rig these?"

"Yemen," Jack says immediately, grabbing a yellow wedge for his cheese wheel.

"These are stupid, unfair questions," I grumble as he goes to roll again.

"Hey, don't blame the questions," Jack mimics in a spot-on Ross impression, and I laugh in spite of myself.

Our back-and-forth continues in this vein, and I succeed in learning something new about Jack: He's a competitive trash talker. Not exactly useful for my article, but entertaining all the same. He also knows *way* more *Friends* trivia than I thought he would. I have the edge, but it ain't by much. Once it becomes clear that I'll be coming out the victor (to my relief and his chagrin), I prepare to make my move.

I select a card and pretend to read. "What is Jack Bradford's biggest regret?"

His brows draw together. "That can't possibly be what it says."

I exhale loudly and flick the card at him like a Frisbee. "I'm ready for some Jack trivia," I tell him, and he makes a face. "What? I feel like you know all this stuff about me—heck, you've already met my family—and I only know superficial things about you. I've learned more from Google than the horse's mouth."

He looks disturbed. "Please do *not* google me."

"Fine, I won't . . . again."

He groans and lets his head fall back against the couch.

"I don't know what you're so worried about, it's not like there's anything to find. Anything *real*, anyway."

He peeks one eye open, lolling his head toward me.

"Come on, spill it. Every time I ask you a personal question, you . . . well, you *pivot*." I smirk and lean over to grab my glass of wine from the coffee table.

"Do I? I don't mean to. I guess I've spent so long trying to protect my privacy and stay out of the news that I don't always realize when it's doing more harm than good." He sits up and rolls his shoulders, like a runner limbering up. "I'm an open book. For you, at least." He flashes me an easygoing grin and I feel that familiar pang again: *guilt*. "What do you want to know?"

Was that too easy? "Anything, really. Tell me something I don't know about you. Actually no, wait. You said you've never done a dating app before, right? Let's pretend we're setting up your profile. Give me the full rundown: likes and dislikes, favorite food, favorite place to travel, whatever. I want the 'Jack in a nutshell' executive summary."

His cheeks go a little pink, and it's then I realize just how unused to the spotlight he really is. "Jack in a nutshell, let's see. I was born and raised in New York, so clearly I'm a bit of a homebody. I have to stay on top of basically every sport for work, but I really only like playing golf and going for runs. I couldn't possibly pick a favorite song. My mom made us learn the piano as kids even though I would've rather played the drums, but she couldn't handle the noise. Oh, when I was in middle school I tried out frosted tips. It wasn't a good look for me."

"Or anyone," I quip.

He bobs his head in agreement. "My favorite subject was history, and I love doing nerdy stuff like touring historic sites or presidents' homes. I get excited about data and metrics. I get cranky if I don't get enough sleep. I have a temper, especially when people disappoint me. I have a red tie I wear when I want to feel intimidating. I love ketchup and spaghetti sauce but hate tomatoes. If I could eat anything it'd be Italian, specifically the chicken parm from this amazing hole-in-the-wall restaurant in Little Italy I stumbled across years ago. I'll have to take you." His eyes flick to mine, a little shyly, and he clears his throat. "I also love a good hotel continental breakfast. I don't really have a sweet tooth. If I could vacation anywhere, it would probably be Greece." He finally breaks for a breath. "How'd I do?"

"Not bad. I'd probably swipe right on you. Extra points for not mentioning hiking, CrossFit, or craft beer."

He laughs out loud, and we grin at each other while Doris Troy croons in the background about falling *so hard, hard, haaaard in love*, the music filtering through the room at just the right volume. A feng shui expert was paid thousands to determine this exact decibel level. It's romantic as hell.

I tuck a knee beneath me and watch his eyes slowly trail over the exposed skin of my thigh, and his expression is . . . well, I can only describe it as *longing*. I decide to do something quite cruel and shift slightly, making my hemline ride up even farther, and now *he's* the one shifting in his seat, leaning over to grab his wineglass and tossing back its contents in a single swift gulp.

I decide to take advantage of the mood and his candor and press my luck with the next question—though I admit, it has nothing to do with the story. *This one's all for me.* "Still an open book?"

Apprehension darts across his face. "Sure."

"I'd love to hear more about your family. You've made some comments about them that have me a bit curious."

"Ah." He blinks a couple of times before breaking my gaze, his eyes flicking back to the game board. "I think I'm going to need some more liquid courage before I answer that one."

He gets up to go to the kitchen, and when he comes back, he's got the wine bottle in one hand and a crystal tumbler half-full of amber liquor in the other, one large spherical ice cube floating in the glass. *He even has fancy ice.*

"Switched to the hard stuff, huh?"

"This story requires something stronger," he says as he refills my wineglass, and once he's resettled on the couch, he begins. "So, my family. Not necessarily my favorite topic, because honestly, they would scare off any sane woman." He eyeballs me, gauging my reaction, as though I might bolt off the couch and make a break for it right this very second.

"Is your dad actually Charles Manson?"

He smiles briefly. "No."

"Part of a notorious crime family?"

"Not that I'm aware of."

I wave a hand dismissively. "Eh, serial killers and mob bosses are my only real deal-breakers."

"A low bar, that's good." He clears his throat. "So, my

mom and dad were introduced by mutual friends after college and dated for a year or so before getting married. Their families both ran in the same social circles, so it was considered a good match. At that point my dad was working at an investment bank and my mom was in fashion, though she quit when my brother was born." He pauses. "They named him John Jr. and me Jack, if that gives you any indication of my father's ego."

"If it makes you feel any better, my parents named us Colin, Christine, and Cassidy. The triple C's are about as nineties as you can get."

He laughs wryly. "Since you've *googled* me," he says, making it sound like a dirty word, "then I'm sure you've read about my dad. He's obsessed with money: making it, spending it. He also uses it as a weapon by withholding it when he sees fit. He's ruthless and manipulative, and once I was old enough to figure that out, I did whatever I could to stay out of his way. He enjoys wielding his power and influence over everyone, including his family. *Especially* his family." He pauses. "He's also a serial philanderer, which you probably didn't read about."

My jaw drops. "Oh, geez. Jack, I'm sorry. You know what? Forget I asked about this. It's none of my business."

He waves away my objections. "No, you should know what you're getting yourself into. My family is . . . not the Cleavers. More like the Bluths. Only more dysfunctional."

"Is your mom—I mean, how does she . . ."

"How does she feel about being repeatedly cheated on?" He lets out a humorless laugh. "When we were young, they would get into these crazy fights. Screaming matches and blowups, and then she'd give him the silent treatment for a few days. Eventually things would go back to normal, and then the cycle would repeat itself. By the time I was a teen-ager, she was self-medicating as a way to deal with it." He looks pained. "I know she did the best she could for us under the circumstances, and she didn't deserve the way my dad treated her, but she also refused to leave him, which never made sense to me. It's like she made a decision that she was going to look the other way, that she'd rather live a lie than blow up her life, and it didn't matter if we were all miserable as a result." He blows out a breath. "It's taken me a long time to stop resenting her for it."

Whoa. He takes a heavy swallow of his drink and I see now why he wanted the extra fortification. "What about your brother?"

He makes a low noise in the back of his throat. "Our re-lationship is . . . complicated. My dad would pit us against each other, encourage us to be competitive. You don't al-ways understand that when you're young, and by the time we caught on to it, the die had been cast. And then when Brawler started taking off, I thought it would be a great idea to bring him into the fold. It seemed like a perfect solution—I could surround myself with people I trusted and fix our relationship. What could go wrong?"

This story is starting to make me sick to my stomach. "Oh no."

"Exactly. Here's a tip if you ever start your own busi-ness: Don't hire your friends and family. It will blow up in your face."

"Wow." I shake my head, at a loss for words. "Jack, that's a lot. That's really tough."

"It wasn't great." He exhales. "Years of therapy so I could learn to say 'It wasn't great.'"

I cough a laugh. "Well, I'll tell you what—despite all

that, you seem pretty darn put together. From where I'm sitting, at least."

"Thanks. I suppose we have the therapist to thank for that, too."

We both chuckle this time, and I'm quiet for a moment as I consider how best to approach this next part. *Time for the sixty-four-thousand-dollar question.*

Nothing left to do but rip off the Band-Aid. "Since you brought it up, how exactly does Brawler fit into all this?"

"Like the early years? How we started?"

"Sure, yeah."

He shifts on the couch, stretching his legs out in front of him. "Well, initially it was purely a sports betting operation. Tom and I both needed the cash, and the Penn dorms were the perfect place to find a bunch of guys with money burning a hole in their pockets."

"Wait, I don't understand. Why did you need money? I thought . . ."

He shakes his head. "When I left for college, I promised myself I'd never take another dime from my father. I told him so, too, so I'd be forced to stick to it. And that *really* pissed him off, since money was his only leverage over me at that point."

I'm still confused. "But I thought your dad provided the seed money for Brawler?"

His brows pull together and he frowns. "You read that stupid profile." He curses under his breath. "I swear, that thing will *never* stop following me."

"It's the only interview I could find," I admit.

"That's because I haven't done a single one since." He violently rakes a hand through his hair, clearly agitated.

"That asshole writer completely misrepresented everything about us. At the time, Tom and I thought a big, splashy profile would help legitimize the business, but they framed the whole thing like it was some pet project of my dad's. He never had a thing to do with Brawler. In fact, he's embarrassed by it. He thinks it's beneath me."

He's not the only one. I practically draw blood biting my tongue on that one. "So I'm going to guess that making it successful became even more attractive to you."

"Bingo. It was a giant *fuck you.*"

All the puzzle pieces are starting to fit together. "I think I'm starting to better understand your relationship with Tom. If you don't mind me saying so, I haven't really understood why . . ." . . . *you'd be friends with such a crass misogynist.* "I mean, he's so . . ." . . . *offensive in every way.* I collect my thoughts and try again. "You seem very respectful of women in general, and my boundaries specifically. Tom's whole persona is . . . basically the opposite of that." *There.* That's about as diplomatic as I can put it.

"Tom's not who people think he is."

I scoff. "Come on."

"Fine, he's not *only* who people think he is. He knows his role in the business is to be the outrageous one who says shocking things, and I can't exactly complain about that when it's allowed me to fly under the radar."

"And made you a lot of money," I add pointedly.

He slides me a sideways glance but lets that one go by. "We've been through a lot together. I'm closer to him than my own brother. He's taken a lot of bullets for me."

I make a face, still unconvinced.

"You know the Brawler fund, where we raise money for

veterans and first responders? And how we expanded it to help keep restaurants open during the pandemic?"

Of course I do; it's one of the few truly decent endeavors Brawler's spearheaded. They rallied their audience for donations and persuaded their network of professional athletes to match them, eventually raising more than forty million dollars and saving hundreds of restaurants from permanent closure. "Yeah?"

"I wish I could say that was my idea, but it was all Tom. He's got a big mouth, sure, but he's got an even bigger heart."

Hmph. "Guess I'll have to take your word for it." I'm not buying that Tom's some sort of misunderstood do-gooder no matter what Jack says, but there's no use debating the point with someone who's so obviously determined to view him through rose-colored glasses. "Anyway, I guess I thought you were this 'Mr. Popular, everyone's best friend' type, but I'm sensing that your life is . . . simpler than I thought." *Lonelier.*

"A lot of people *think* they're friends with me—and of course, socializing is a big part of my job—but I can count my actual friends on one hand. Which, honestly, is just fine with me. I'd rather have four quarters than a hundred pennies."

I smile to myself. *I like that.*

"What?" he asks, seeing my face.

"Just sounds like something my Gran would say."

He grows serious. "Just what every man wants to hear: that he reminds you of your grandmother."

I giggle, and his eyes gleam. I think he likes making me laugh. "So, now that I've shared my most damaging childhood memories, shall I show you to the door?" He's joking, but there's real vulnerability in his voice.

I reach out and give his arm a comforting squeeze—though let's face it, fondling his bicep is more of a treat for me. I want to pet him like one of those touch-and-feel board books I read to my nieces. "Nah. What's a little family drama? Anyway, this confession is nothing compared to the guy who told me he'd been collecting his toenail clippings since college."

He throws his head back and laughs. "No way. I refuse to believe it."

"Okay fine, it was part of a story I did about worst app dates, but it really did happen to a coworker of mine."

He's laughing harder now, his voice husky and deep, and something about the combination of the music, the wine, and this absurdly attractive man whose lap I'm practically sitting in—not to mention his unabashed, palpable interest in me—has me loosening up, dropping my guard, and relaxing into the rare, heady feeling of a date that's going well. *Really* well.

"Quick, tell me something awkwardly personal about you so I feel less pathetic." He stretches his arms over his head, and I find my eyes lingering over his midsection, hoping to catch a fleeting glimpse of his abs. I get another whiff of his man-scent and I have to fight the urge to inch closer to him, to press my nose to his neck and bask in his body wash. I can only hope the smell will permanently brand itself on my sense-memory to enjoy long after I leave tonight.

"Awkwardly personal, hmm." I rack my brain, trying to ignore the gnawing attraction building in my stomach. "I don't really have any deep, dark family secrets, though there is something . . . but I can't possibly tell you, because it would definitely scare off any sane man."

He perks up instantly. "Try me."

I'm absolutely going to regret this, but here goes. "So you've heard the saying, *Always a bridesmaid, never a bride*?" He nods, waiting for the punch line. "Well, pretty sure whoever coined that phrase had me in mind. Guess how many weddings I've been a part of in the last few years."

"Four?" he guesses.

"Try seven."

"*Seven?*" He winces. "Ouch."

I sock him in the shoulder. "You're not supposed to make me feel worse!"

He laughs, blocking my blows with a throw pillow. "I was just kidding. Anyway, who cares? It's not like *you've* been married seven times. You're not Ross."

I shoot him a look. "Come on. Seven weddings in the last few years, and I'm no closer to one myself. What does that say about me?"

He blinks. "That you have a lot of friends?"

I smile faintly. "Or that other women are marriage-worthy, and I'm not."

It's a shocking thing to say aloud—especially since it's one of those deep-seated fears I only allow myself to brood over when I'm several glasses of wine deep during that time of the month. *What's wrong with me? Will I be alone forever?* And the one that scares me the most: *Am I unlovable?*

I'm too proud to voice these feelings to my sister or all the other smug marrieds in my life, so to bare my soul like this to Jack of all people is humbling, to say the least. But I think a larger part of me wants to hear how Mr. Perfect, *I have an answer for everything* will respond to this confession—especially since he has unique insight into the collective male psyche most others don't.

"You don't actually believe that, do you?" He's incredulous.

"I don't know. I never used to, but when you hit your fifth wedding, you start to wonder."

He nods slowly, thinking that over. Strangely, I appreciate that he doesn't immediately try to placate me with some knee-jerk rebuttal or forced compliment. If there's one thing I'm tired of hearing, it's: *Your day will come!* (A close runner-up: *It'll happen when you least expect it!* I've been *not* expecting it for a decade now, thankyouverymuch Aunt Carol.)

"What about me?" he asks. "I'm not married, is there something wrong with me?"

"You're what, four years older than me? Thirty-two?" He nods. "Then probably, yeah."

He snorts.

"I'm kidding. Anyway, it's different for men. You not being married is a choice, and no one's going to give you a hard time about it. Women don't have that luxury. I have to hear, '*Why don't you have a boyfriend? Are you being too picky? You're not getting any younger! But what about kids?*' from every distant relative or random acquaintance of my parents' until my ears bleed. And you know what the worst part is? I ask myself those same questions."

He raises an eyebrow. "You think I've never been asked those questions?"

"Oh please, it's hardly the same. If a man isn't married, it's because he's 'focusing on his career,'" I say, fingers clenched in angry air quotes. "If a woman isn't married, it's because no one's picked her. And don't even get me started on how women are called 'spinsters' and 'old maids' while men get sexy nicknames like 'distinguished' and 'silver foxes.' I did a whole story on this."

"I know, I read it."

That pulls me up short. "You did?"

"Of course. I read everything of yours I could find." He starts reciting from memory. "'*When they graduate, men are told they have their whole lives ahead of them, while women are told their clock is ticking.*' That was a great line."

I stare at him, mouth agape. *Jack's read my work?* I suppose I shouldn't be that surprised; I certainly investigated him, so it stands to reason he'd do the same. Still, the idea of him scrolling through years of my writing (and apparently, committing some to memory?!) is both flattering and mortifying. My words are like a window into my soul; despite us never having kissed, he may as well have seen me naked.

"Wow. Uh, thank you," I stammer. I think of that line from *When Harry Met Sally*: '*Nobody has ever quoted me back to me before.*' I'm totally thrown. "Anyway, I got off track there. What was I . . . ?"

He looks amused. "Weddings, I think?" he offers innocently, swilling the tumbler so the ice clinks against the crystal. He's clearly enjoying that he's flustered me, the deep blue of his eyes awash with humor. They remind me of dark water; a pool at night. I want to dive into them and never come up for air.

"Weddings," I echo, trancelike, then shake myself. "I'm sorry, no, not weddings. I mean, it's not *just* about weddings." I tear my eyes away from his; it's like they're hypnotizing me. "I just feel like this stage of life isn't all it's cracked up to be. We're constantly being told that our twenties should be the best time of our lives, but if that's the case, then I'm *definitely* doing something wrong."

He sits back and drapes his arm across the back of the couch. "Explain."

"First of all, I'm constantly stressed about money. I work all the time, but I'm barely keeping my head above water financially. When you just got up to refill your drink, I had to stop myself from digging in your couch cushions for loose change."

He chuckles.

"And then there's the work. When I first started at Siren, it was exciting and everything felt important. And don't get me wrong, I'm proud of what I do. But does any of it *matter*? People read it, then click away and forget it. It's not changing anyone's life. Now, writing a book, that matters. That *lasts*. But I can't seem to actually start.

"And the weddings thing just adds insult to injury. All my single friends are dropping like flies, and once they are married, they fall off the face of the earth. They're either hanging out with other couples, or they get pregnant and only seem to have time for their mom friends."

To illustrate my point, I stand and head over to his credenza, where I've set my purse. While I rummage through it, I catch a glimpse of my reflection in the oversized round mirror: eyes alight and vibrant, skin flushed, cheeks tinted with the type of natural glow makeup brands would kill to replicate. I'm a vintage photograph come to life. I'm Reese Witherspoon in *Pleasantville*, slowly colorizing in a black-and-white world.

I finally find what I'm looking for—my keys—and hold them aloft. "You see this banana key chain?"

He nods, looking both amused and bemused about where this is all going.

"My friends got it for me at the end of a girls' trip we took to South Beach years ago. It was a gag gift, really—at some point during the trip, I claimed that piña coladas were made with frozen bananas, and they had a field day making fun of me for it. Anyway, they came across the banana key chain at some souvenir shop and couldn't resist."

I think back to that trip and how bright-eyed and optimistic we were, reunited for the first time since we graduated and moved into new apartments, new jobs, and new relationships. How we stayed up late swapping stories of horrible bosses and money stressors and dating woes. How it had felt like there weren't enough hours in each day to finish all the conversations we started. How we swore we'd make the trip an annual thing, committed to prioritizing our friendships no matter what.

"Anyway, that was the first and last girls' trip we took before weddings and babies took over. I've been carrying around this stupid banana for *six years* and I can't decide if it's more depressing at this point to leave it on or take it off." I toss the keys on the coffee table and sink back down into his luxurious couch cushions. "I really don't want to be someone who begrudges other people their happiness, but sometimes I just feel . . . I don't know, stuck in between. Or left behind. Do you ever feel that way?"

I finally pause for breath, and when I glance over at him, he's quiet, his face expressionless. I can't really read him. I'd like to think he's just being thoughtful, but he's probably trying to figure out how to politely remove me from his apartment. I seem to have careened right past "awkwardly personal" and straight into TMI territory.

I immediately regret my honesty. Why on earth am I telling him all this? I sound like some desperate husband hunter; a wannabe bridezilla on steroids. This is a rant best left to my single friends who can commiserate, or people who have no choice but to listen to me complain, like my mom.

It's Dating 101: Never whine about being single. Betty wags her finger in disapproval—*Girls who whine stay on the vine!*

I let out a self-conscious laugh and attempt to course-correct. "Sorry, got a little carried away there. Was that the kind of oversharing you were looking for? Rant over, I promise." I seize my glass and shotgun the rest of my wine.

He holds up a hand. "Don't apologize. Obviously, I can relate."

I almost laugh out loud. *I just bet Jack Bradford sits home alone, lamenting his singledom and crying into his beer.* "Somehow I doubt that."

He looks affronted. "Whose friends do you think all your friends are marrying?"

This time I do laugh, though my face still stings with embarrassment. I look around the room for a weapon I could use to put myself out of my misery. The aged-concrete lamp on the credenza looks heavy enough to do some damage.

There's a ghost of a smile on his lips. "But seriously, you think men never have these kinds of thoughts? The things we worry about might look a little different, but I can assure you, we have insecurities too."

"Oh yeah? Let's hear 'em."

He tilts his head, considering. "Just trying to figure out what women want is a huge source of stress. How do we show we're interested without coming on too strong? What if we say the wrong thing? What if we misinterpret intent? Does she want someone better-looking, more athletic, smarter, funnier? Can we afford the life she wants? What if you don't end up as successful as you'd hoped?"

"Well, *you* obviously don't have to worry about that."

"No, I get to worry about the opposite. Is she only interested in me for my money? Or because of this job and who I know?" He pauses. "Or in this case, will my job be a deal-breaker?"

Oh boy. He's giving voice to the question I've asked myself countless times since this whole charade began—and despite my soul-searching, I'm no closer to an answer. I decide to give that last part a football field–sized berth and focus on the first part of his statement (and mess with him while I'm at it).

"Hmm." I pretend to think about it. "For me it was mostly about your looks, but now that I know you know famous people, why don't you hit me with a list of names and I'll let you know how interested I am?"

He shakes his head sadly. "Terrible. You're terrible. Making fun of a guy who just admitted to being insecure."

"Oh please, you're the least insecure man I've ever met. You're about as insecure as the Dos Equis guy."

He casts me a sidelong glance. "You'd be surprised." It's the second time he's said that tonight.

"Prove it."

He eyes me for a minute, as if weighing the wisdom of whatever he's considering revealing, before nodding once. "Okay. Are you seeing someone else?"

It's a good thing I finished that wine, because if I'd had any in my mouth, it would now be soaking the front of his T-shirt (which, come to think of it, would be a highly appealing visual indeed). "I'm sorry, *what*?"

"And look, I realize you don't owe me an answer. You'd be well within your rights to tell me it's none of my business. But I'd just like to know what I'm up against."

Am I seeing someone else?! If he only knew how preposterous that idea is! I can barely keep my current multiple personalities straight without adding *another* human being to the mix. Honestly, I'd think he was kidding if he didn't look so serious. Jack Bradford—he of the model-perfect bone structure, certified alpha male, a literal leader among men—is insecure about *me*?

"What you're . . . Am I . . . Jack, you're . . ." I can't form sentences. I'm stuttering through the alphabet. I stop and start again. "May I ask where this is coming from?"

He exhales a breath. "You're very hard to read. You wait days to text me back. In fact, I'd just about decided you were ghosting me when you called and offered to cook me dinner. I couldn't figure out if I should be taking the hint or trying harder." He's ticking them off on his fingers. "I tried to pin you down all week but you said you needed a rain check, then very specifically *didn't* say what you were doing. Not that I'm entitled to an explanation of your whereabouts, but it makes a guy wonder. Wouldn't be the first time I assumed the wrong thing and paid for it later." Whatever he's referring to seems to disturb him, and he shakes his head. "I guess I thought we were on the same page after Times Square, but this past week I felt like I was back to chasing my tail. It's messing with my head." He swallows and I watch a muscle tic in his jaw, tight as a drum. I'm tempted to trace it with my index finger. "This is going to sound obnoxious and I don't mean it to be, but I'm not used to having to *guess* if a woman is into me."

Whoa. I blink a few times, caught off guard as much by his honesty as by my own tangle of emotions. My heart's doing something funny in my chest, leaping and fluttering against my ribs like a butterfly on a sugar high. *Jack is jealous! He doesn't want you seeing anyone else! He's a knight mounting his steed, ready to vanquish the enemy for your heart!*

Despite my vow to hold him at arm's length, I can't pretend I'm not flattered by his attention any more than I can pretend I'm not *wildly* attracted to him. Every cell in my body is begging to touch him, to taste his lips, to bury my face in his neck long enough to identify that scent once and for all. But almost as quickly as I acknowledge that startling truth, my giddiness is replaced by something else entirely: *guilt.*

I've been so desperate to paint Jack as the bad guy that I've managed to rationalize away all my lies and misbehavior, but that heartfelt speech just held up a mirror, and I do *not* like what I see. I've taken a man who's treated me with nothing but kindness and respect, who's opened up to me in good faith, and what have I done in return? Plotted against him, scoffed at his decency, toyed with his feelings, and abused his trust. Trust that clearly isn't freely given.

Gah! Could I have picked a worse time for an attack of conscience? I should feel triumphant. I should be *elated.* Jack just said it himself: I'm messing with his head. I'm driving *him* crazy. After all the times and ways Brawler has gotten under my skin, I've finally given him a taste of his own medicine. I've beaten him at his own game! I should be taking a victory lap around this cavernous living room.

But all I feel is shame.

No matter what I used to believe of Jack, I now know that he's more than his work, more than some petty website. He's a real person with bruises and battle scars and a beating heart—a heart I came dangerously close to exploiting for my own gain.

Who exactly is the bad guy here?

The realization is a kick-ball-change to the gut. I let my eyes roam over his face, registering the earnestness of his expression and the sincerity in his eyes, and I suddenly know with deep certainty: *I am not writing this story.* I think I've known it for a while. I may have known it all along.

I let out a shallow, shaking breath, desperate to stabilize my heart, which feels simultaneously like it's being squeezed and about to swell right out of my chest. At the same time, I feel instantly lighter, the weight of my deception melting away—and taking what's left of my resistance with it.

We're already sitting so close that our knees are touching, but that microscopic point of contact doesn't feel like nearly enough anymore. I reach over and rest my hand on his denim-clad thigh before drawing my gaze up and looking him dead in the eye. I don't want there to be a shred of doubt in his mind that I'm telling him the truth. "Jack, I'm not seeing anyone else."

Those few words are all it takes for his hand to land on mine, his fingers wrapping around my palm and squeezing with gentle pressure. It's as though I can feel his whole body relax through the flex of his hand.

"The night I needed a rain check was because I was going to a Celine Dion concert with some girlfriends. I didn't share it with you because it's the kind of thing that guys love making fun of us for, and I wasn't about to hand you live ammunition." His lips start to twitch and I raise a finger. "And before you open your mouth, do not speak a *word* against Queen Celine."

He clamps down on his smile. "I would never."

I side-eye him skeptically as I ponder how to address his other concerns—namely, my erratic behavior—without exposing my duplicity in the process. If I'm not going to write the story, there's really no reason to come clean, right? Frankly, there isn't even anything to come clean *about*. Sure,

I may be letting myself off on a technicality, but I think this lie falls under the "for his own good" category. And technically, it's not even a lie. It's more like . . . a sin of omission. A justifiable half-truth, if you will. A victimless crime!

Alright, *fine*, I'm chickening out. I'm being a gutless, yellow coward. Right on cue, "The Great Pretender" starts streaming in the background, and I could howl at the irony. *Even Spotify is calling me out.*

But I can't help it. *I can't let him hate me.*

I clear my throat. "As for the texting and my general . . . elusiveness, I'm sorry if my behavior's been confusing." He tries to break in but I won't let him. "No, you've been upfront about your intentions from the beginning, and you shouldn't have to wonder about mine. And I . . . I'm . . ."

I trail off, losing my nerve, but it's like I can hear Gran whispering in my ear, prodding me forward with her invisible hand: *Keep going, Cass. Say the scary part out loud.*

I take a deep breath. "I'm not sure how to explain myself except to say that you've caught me by surprise. I . . . well, I didn't expect to like you this much." It's the understatement of a lifetime, but it's also the naked truth—and it's such a relief to finally admit it. "The truth is, I've met plenty of men who seem great at first, but I always seem to wind up disappointed. So if I feel a little distant, it's because I know better than to get attached too quickly. Especially to a guy who appears a little too good to be true." I nudge him with my shoulder, feeling so exposed and vulnerable I could die. "A girl's got to guard her heart around a guy like you."

I don't think I realized the reality of it until this moment, that I've been holding myself back for reasons beyond Betty and this story—namely, that I'm scared shitless.

The thing is, men like Jack are dangerous. He's the

Prince Charming you dream about when you're little, the one you're sure doesn't actually exist, who's so full of appealing traits that you'd stack them together like a living, breathing paper doll if you could. He's literally tall, dark, and handsome; smart and successful; both interesting and interested. He's generous but modest, never flaunting his wealth or connections. He's been patient and gentlemanly, even with the near-Amish restrictions I've placed upon us. He's the type of man who acknowledges waitstaff by name, then looks them in the eye to thank them; who stocks your favorite wine even after you've blown him off for a week. He willingly met my family on our second date, for crying out loud. He's practically perfect in every way, as Mary Poppins would say. You could fall in love with a guy like Jack before you even know what's hit you.

He's the kind of man who'd hold your hair back when you're sick. Gran's words echo in my ears and my heart nearly stops, awareness knocking the wind out of me:

I have real feelings for Jack. I may even be *falling* for Jack.

I think I'm gonna be sick right now. My stomach is seizing and my palms are slick with sweat, which I belatedly realize he must know since he has yet to let go of my hand. Frankly, the way he's looking at me is enough to give me a hot flash.

He is lit from within. His smile is so dazzling that I briefly wonder if I've just confessed my feelings aloud before realizing that he must be able to see it in my eyes. He reaches up to cup the back of my neck, drawing me closer until we're breathing the same air. His thumb strokes a featherlight path along my jawline and my nerve endings detonate like a row of fireworks. We're a tinderbox ready to explode, and I'm holding a lit match.

And it's in that moment—our faces an inch apart, our breath gone shallow—that we both notice the same thing at the same time.

"Do you—" I start to say.

"—smell something burning?" he finishes, and before the words have even left his mouth, we've bolted off the couch and made a mad dash for the kitchen.

I manage to get there first, only to find smoke billowing out the sides of the oven. "Oh, fu—" I start to say, until Betty jabs me with a cattle prod. "—dge."

Jack goes to open a window while I throw on the oven mitts and pull out the now-charred bird, skin blackened and burnt to a crisp. To add insult to injury, the smoke detector starts blaring, and it's so loud that I start panicking about fire trucks showing up. I imagine being frog-marched out of the building in disgrace by Cliff the kindly doorman and have to talk myself out of crawling into the oven myself and ending it all. Somehow I don't think the FDNY—or Jack's richie-rich neighbors—will be amused by my tale of Engagement Chicken gone wrong.

The Joy of Cooking, my ass.

Jack fans a dish towel in the direction of the alarm, his forehead creased with concern. "I thought you said it needed to be in for ninety minutes? It hasn't even been an hour."

"That's what it said!" I say defensively. "I followed the recipe exactly."

He abandons the dish towel and bends over the oven display, squinting at the screen and frowning.

"I don't understand what could have gone wrong," I insist weakly, inspecting the outer layer of char. Maybe it only looks ruined. Maybe I can skim it off like a *Silence of the Lambs*–style skinsuit. "This has never happened before." It's

not technically a lie; the fact that I'm a poultry-roasting virgin is neither here nor there.

He makes a noise like *hmph.* "Well, I think I may have
diagnosed the problem—it was set to broil, not bake." He
presses a couple of buttons and the screen goes dark.

*Are you freaking kidding me? His stupid space-age oven con-
spired against me?!* I don an appropriately sheepish expression, but inside I'm unleashing a stream of profanity that
could rival a Scorsese movie. If karma is real, then this oven
better wind up stripped for parts and rusting at a junkyard.

But almost as quickly as the anger burns me up, humiliation takes its place. Tonight wasn't supposed to turn out
like this. This recipe was supposed to be foolproof—*so easy
a child could do it*—and like everything else pertaining to
Jack, I've screwed it up royally. Suddenly, this still-smoking
carcass symbolizes just how far this stupid scheme has gotten away from me, how out of control this situation has become. *How much trouble I'm in with him.*

What am I supposed to do now? What am I going to
tell Cynthia? Is there a way out of this without hurting anyone? *Can* I even walk away from Jack? I feel the hysteria
mounting—and to my utter dismay, my eyes start to smart.

Jack immediately senses the change in mood. "Hey, it's
alright. Really, this is no big deal."

I squeeze my eyes shut and shake my head, refusing to
look at him. I'm on an emotional tightrope and I'm hanging
on by my fingernails.

"Hey. C'mere." He tugs me over and gathers me into a
hug, fitting my head into the nook of his neck—and I surrender, wrapping my arms around his back, oven mitts and
all. "No sense crying over burned chicken."

I let out a laugh-sob, furiously blinking back the tears

pricking at my eyelids. I bury my face in his chest and breathe him in, letting his addictive, calming scent fill my lungs. "I'm overreacting, I know, it's just . . ." I heave a watery sigh. "I just wanted to do this one thing right, and I'm mad at myself for messing it up."

He's quiet for a minute as he strokes my hair, and I let myself enjoy how it feels: safe and taken care of and *right*. Like I could belong here. "Look, it's obviously my fault. This never would have happened if my kitchen weren't so damn fancy." I huff a laugh into his shirt. "Anyway, this is why we live in New York, right? We can get whatever we want delivered in ten minutes."

I brave a glance up at him. "That wasn't the point, though."

"No," he concedes, then leans back in, voice lowered. "But I'm gonna let you in on a little secret." His lips brush the shell of my ear and goosebumps bloom on my skin. "Your culinary skills are very low on the list of reasons I'm attracted to you."

The rough growl of his voice makes my toes curl. "That's probably a good thing," I manage—and right then, mercifully, the alarm stops bleating.

He grins down at me, and just as I'm registering that we're still hugging, our bodies locked together like magnets, the song changes and Otis Redding's bluesy baritone floats through the kitchen.

These arms of mine, they are lonely . . .

Jack raises an eyebrow at me, and without waiting for an answer, starts swaying in time with the music. I decide to go with it, replacing my head on his chest and melting into his embrace—but not before I slide off the oven mitts and toss them to the floor, which makes him laugh, the deep, rumbling sound vibrating against my cheek.

Time stands still as we slow-dance, the angst of the last few minutes fading away as I dissolve into his chest—though I suppose if we're splitting hairs, what we're actually doing is closer to cuddling than dancing. If this was a movie montage, it'd be the scene engineered to tug at viewers' heartstrings: just me and Jack, all our pretenses and posturing stripped away as we rock back and forth in charged silence, oblivious to everything but each other.

. . . They are burning from wanting you.

We sway that way for ten . . . twenty . . . thirty more seconds, before he slows and pulls away slightly, and I lift my head to look up at him.

His gaze is a scorching heat; a dark, raging fire that burns right through me. His eyes search my face, lingering on my mouth, and my throat goes bone-dry. He lifts his hands to cradle my face, tipping my chin up, and I nearly stop breathing. My pulse pounds a relentless drumbeat in my neck; he must be able to feel it.

I know what's about to happen and I'm powerless to stop it. He lowers his head slowly, deliberately, and it's as though he's saying: *Now's your last chance to pull away.*

Instead, I meet him halfway.

I push onto my toes and press my lips to his, and the world ignites in a shower of sparks. He makes a noise when our mouths finally connect, a low groan of satisfaction, and my entire body blazes to life. My hands scrabble at his back until I grab twin handfuls of his shirt, bunching the fabric in my fists and tethering him to me. His thumbs frame my cheekbones as he gently tilts my face and tastes me, his tongue meeting mine softly at first, then bolder, with more authority, more possession. He's branding me, making me his. He's going to make me forget any kiss that's come before.

I pull him closer, fusing our lower halves, while our mouths savor what we've both been craving. We're perfectly matched and equally consumed. He nibbles on my lower lip while I nip at the corner of his mouth. His hand cups the back of my neck, fingers threaded in my hair, while I run my palms over the bunching muscles of his back. He gives and takes, then gives some more, his lips spilling secrets his voice has yet to share. It's simultaneously chaste and indecent, his touch somehow both tender and insistent. In fact, he's kissing me with such intensity that neither of us notices I'm moving until my backside collides with the edge of the marble island, and we laugh softly into each other's mouths.

Frankly, I'm trying to keep from moaning. I knew Jack was in shape and I certainly fantasized about what his body might feel like, but imagining isn't the same as *knowing*. Everything about him is strong and solid and male, from his firm torso to his muscular biceps to his broad shoulders. I mold myself to his frame, my breasts pressed to his chest, every nerve ending alive and tingling with delicious friction. My arms find their way to his neck and I tangle my hands in the thick hair at his nape, and when I tug on it a little he lets out another grunt of pleasure. The guttural sound stirs something deep in my belly and I'm in danger of swooning.

I knew I was attracted to Jack (okay fine, more like super-horny and turned on at all times in his presence), but even I'm surprised by how powerfully my body responds to him, how desperate my hands are to know every inch of him. Prudish, well-bred Betty is a distant memory, replaced by a feral cavewoman driven by the most primal instinct there is: *lust*. I want to rip off this Jackie O dress and embrace my inner Marilyn. I want to serenade him with a slutty rendition of "Happy Birthday."

Between kisses he murmurs things like *"You're so . . . "* and *"Finally,"* and I flash back to what he said in Times Square—*"I've never anticipated anything quite this much"*—and I know he's right, that our delayed gratification has made this encounter infinitely more explosive, more passionate than I ever could have imagined. I made him wait, but he used his time wisely. He saw my hesitation and raised me some patience. He took my unusual demands in stride, charming and disarming me with some good old-fashioned romance. He burrowed under my skin and fought his way into my heart, shattering my defenses in the process.

He skims his knuckles down my side, his thumb just grazing my breast, and when I tremble in response I feel him hesitate. I can almost hear his thoughts: *How far is too far? Will I scare her off? Should I stop?* So I lean into his grip, his large hand fanned against my rib cage, and kiss him thoroughly in wordless answer. I find myself desperate to know if he has a dusting of chest hair underneath that perfectly fitted shirt, or if his torso is as smooth and velvety as glazed honey. My fingers itch to find out, and yet I somehow have the presence of mind to know that would be crossing a line, that I'd be starting something I'm unprepared to finish.

Or unable to stop.

It's too much. It's sensory overload. The heat of his skin, the weight of his arms caging me against the counter, the sandpaper scrape of his jaw, the rich flavor of malted whiskey on his breath, this sultry, soulful bump-and-grind playlist—it's all building toward something that will almost certainly lead to my destruction. I'm flying too close to the sun.

I should put a stop to this. I should pull away before it goes any further. And yet, in this moment I'd rather die than stop. I want to stay right here in his arms, treasuring his kisses and reveling in the feel of him and believing for just one night that this could be *right*. That Jack could be the man I've been searching for all this time.

Right now, he's the *only* thing I want.

So I close my eyes, press into him, and hurtle myself toward the sun.

Chapter 13

I CAN'T STOP THINKING ABOUT #98 ON THE "Tips to Hook a Husband" list: *Turn wolves into husband material by assuming they have honor.*

I thought about it as I left Jack's apartment last night, the promise of another date hanging in the air between us like a strand of twinkling Christmas lights. I thought about it as I tossed and turned in bed, giddy and restless and horny as hell. And I'm thinking about it now as I reluctantly head to Cynthia's office, feet heavy as cement blocks, a prisoner on her way to the guillotine.

I have no idea how she'll take the news that I'm dropping the story. She'd be well within her rights to fire me, and honestly, I'm not sure I could blame her. I've been working on this for weeks and not only do I have nothing to show for it, but now I've found myself in bed with the enemy (metaphorically, at least). I'm irrevocably compromised, both professionally and ethically. I'm sure I've exposed Siren to some sort of liability, too. I know lying itself isn't a crime, but should Jack find out about my ulterior motives he'd probably have grounds to sue Cynthia for invasion of privacy or emotional distress or defamation. (Or is it slander? I can never remember the difference. Cut me some slack, I'm not a lawyer.)

One thing I know for sure, though: My subterfuge ends today. If I'm going to move forward with Jack in good conscience, then this story needs to be a distant speck in my rearview mirror.

I knock once and enter when she invites me in, the chatter of the newsroom fading ominously as the door snicks shut behind me. In a blatant attempt at buying her mercy, I picked up a cup of her favorite overpriced coffee and a chocolate croissant from the fancy French bakery next door, though the bribery is about as transparent as these damn acrylic chairs. My thighs are already clammy at the sight of them.

"Hey there," Cynthia says, holding up a finger as she continues to type feverishly. I take a seat at her desk, and when she finally pushes her keyboard away, she makes a little chirp of appreciation at my sweet treats. *So far so good.*

"So a vague, last-minute meeting request," she says, pulling the croissant from the bag and tearing off a corner. "Do I take it there's been a break in the case?"

"Sort of." I rethink that. "Well, not exactly." I roll my lips together. "Actually, sort of the opposite?"

"What does that mean?" she asks around her mouthful. "Don't tell me he figured it out?"

"No, nothing like that." I gnaw on my lip, stalling.

Her brow furrows as she waits a beat. "Well? Spit it out. What's going on?"

I take a deep breath. "I need to call it off."

She leans back in her chair, index fingers tented, chewing

silently. This thousand-yard stare is one of her superpowers—I've watched her win countless face-offs just by staying quiet the longest. "Why?"

"First of all, he hasn't said or done anything offensive, so as of now it'd be a pretty boring story." It's a lame attempt at humor, and she rewards me with crickets. I forge ahead. "If I haven't found anything incriminating by now, I just don't think there's anything to find."

"Of course there's something to find. Everyone has skeletons in their closet, including me." She peers at me over the rim of her glasses. "What's really going on?" Great, I've tripped her bullshit detector.

I sigh. "I just don't feel comfortable with this anymore. I've gotten to know him, and he's not who I—who *we*—thought he was. Sure, maybe it was funny at first, but now it just feels wrong. And frankly, cruel. That's not who I am, and it's not the kind of journalist I want to be."

She continues to stare at me, her face unreadable. I don't even think she's blinked once. She's going to make me—and my sticky thighs—sweat this one out. "You let him get under your skin."

I know what she's really asking. I don't want to lie to her, but I'm also not ready to share the true nature of Jack's and my relationship—especially since *I'm* not even sure what that is yet.

So I sidestep. "He's a good guy, and he doesn't deserve to be ridiculed."

She tuts and shakes her head, her mouth in a thin line.

"I'll write the story the way I originally pitched it," I offer desperately, a sick feeling gripping my insides like a fist. I've never said no to Cynthia before; I've rarely even pushed back. I'm a team player, a model employee. I do what I'm tasked, no questions asked. "I'll test out the tips on unsuspecting men and it'll be hilarious, I promise. I'll do whatever it takes to make the story a success." I swallow past the knot in my stomach, hoping those words don't end up biting me in the ass. "I just need to leave Jack out of it."

"I see," she says after a long pause, pursing her lips. "Whatever it takes, hmm? In that case, I'd like you to do something for me."

I gulp. *The regret came faster than expected.* "Okay . . ."

"You can wipe that petrified look off your face. Who am I, Miranda Priestly? Some kind of tyrant? I'm offended, honestly."

I let out a stunned laugh and bury my face in my hands, relief spilling over me.

"This isn't a movie, okay? I can't make you write something you don't want to write."

"You could fire me, though," I point out.

"Fire one of my best writers? That would be a bad business decision, and I don't make those." She lifts the coffee to her lips and takes a slow, deliberate sip before setting it back down. "But I am going to be brutally honest with you about something, because I think you need to hear it: I expected this of you."

An entirely different type of anxiety washes over me. "What do you mean, you expected this?"

"It means you never take on risky, boundary-pushing stories. When you first pitched me this idea, I didn't believe you'd actually follow through with it. You seemed committed, though, so I hoped you'd prove me wrong this time."

Her words hit me like backhanded slap to the face. *She thinks I'm a coward? Some sort of gutless quitter?*

She sets her hand on mine, as if to soften the blow of her

insults, and I fight the urge to yank it back. "Cassidy, this is your MO. You come up with great ideas, really creative and unique ideas—and then you assign them to someone else. You have incredible instincts, but you're not willing to take any risks yourself. You can't play it safe in this business, not if you want to get noticed. Not if you want to make an *impact*. If I hadn't taken the risk to start Siren ten years ago, I'd probably still be wasting away at some dying newspaper, barely making enough to scrape by.

"Listen, you're smart and you're driven and you have amazing potential, maybe more potential than anyone else here. But your unwillingness to put yourself out there and really go for it is holding you back. Something is stopping you from stepping up and claiming your success."

"That's . . . that's not what this is," I mumble, so hurt and caught off guard I can barely speak. There's a freight train between my ears, a high-pitched ringing so loud it might split my skull. *I need to get out of here.*

"Of course this would have been a big story for Siren, but it would have been an even bigger break for *you*. You've gotten comfortable here, and as your boss, that's fine for me—I know what to expect from you. But I was really hoping you'd surprise me this time. I was hoping you'd surprise *yourself.*"

She pauses, as if to give me a chance to respond, but I'm stunned silent. I'm simultaneously tingling and numb with shock. I feel like one of those *Glee* kids after they've gotten a slushie to the face.

"Look, I don't need to know the details of your personal life. That's your business. But from what you've said, it sounds like you've gotten too close to your subject and you're letting some personal feelings cloud your professional judgment." I bring my head up and meet her eyes, refusing to confirm what she thinks she knows—that I'm giving up my chance at glory for a guy. I won't give her the satisfaction. "I think you need to ask yourself: If this same opportunity was in front of Jack, would he be sacrificing himself the same way you are?"

I want to say yes so badly. I think of how Jack's eyes tend to linger on my face a few seconds longer than necessary; the way he touches me, his hands both possessive and protective; the way he listens, *really* listens, when I talk; the genuine relief on his face when I told him I wasn't seeing anyone else. I desperately want to believe that if push came to shove Jack would choose me over his work, but the painful reality is, I can't say so for sure.

"Whether or not you write this story is your choice, Cassidy. It's always been your choice. But you don't get these opportunities back." She holds eye contact. "I'd hate for you to regret it."

"SHE BASICALLY CALLED me a coward. A spineless pushover. A weak-willed wimp! Do you think she's right?"

After I fled Cynthia's office, red-faced and humiliated, I sent Nat an SOS text to meet me around the corner at one of our favorite dive bars, known for its vibrant happy hour scene and reliably heavy pours. I've spent the last half hour railing against the injustice of it all, Cynthia's harsh feedback burning in my gut like a shot of cheap tequila. Like a true friend, Nat's been letting me rant without interruption or judgment while I drown my sorrows in this (very stiff) martini.

"I think she's trying to get in your head, and it's working." Nat motions over my head at our server, pointing to my empty glass. *A true friend, I tell you.*

"I don't know, I don't think of Cynthia as manipulative. She may be ruthless, but she doesn't lie." I wish I didn't respect her as much as I do; it would make her criticism so much easier to dismiss.

"If that's how you feel, then I guess the more important question is: Do *you* think she's right?"

I gulp. It's the million-dollar question, but putting my own behavior under the microscope like this is excruciating. "I do assign a lot of my best story ideas to other people."

Nat flicks a dismissive wrist. "You're an editor—it's your job to assign stories. You can't write every one yourself."

"What about the fact that I can't seem to get anywhere on my book? I've been talking about it for years now and have nothing to show for it."

"Well, maybe it's time to change that. Why don't you take this righteous anger you're feeling and use it as motivation? Channel it into your writing and prove her wrong."

I blow a raspberry. "Right now, I just feel like having a pity party."

She flashes a palm in solidarity. "Understood. I will stop offering productive solutions to your problems. Vent away."

"Thank you." Our waitress returns with the plate of fries Nat ordered and my refreshed drink, which I grab right out of her hand. "You know what I was doing before you got here? Scrolling through old articles to see if I could classify any of my work as 'risky.' Spoiler alert: nope."

"You know, looking at it another way, one could say that you're 'risking it all for love.'" She laces her fingers under her chin and bats her eyelashes theatrically.

"Oh please, we've only been on three dates. You can't be in love with someone you barely know."

"Speak for yourself! If Gabriel had asked me to marry him on our first date, I would've said yes."

I fake-gag, then throw her a smile to let her know I'm kidding. "But that's you."

"Exactly. That's *me*. I'm impulsive and reckless. And I have this idiotic butterfly tattoo on my ankle to prove it." She sticks her leg out in proof. "I go with my gut, and you think things through. Neither is wrong." She pauses. "Well, this tattoo was definitely wrong," she mutters.

I sigh and stare down at the table, ripping my soggy cocktail napkin into tiny pieces.

"Cass, tell me the truth about what's going on with Jack," she says gently. "You obviously have feelings for him. What really happened last night? No one here is going to judge you."

I exhale a breath. I purposely only shared vague details of my date-gone-wrong-then-right last night (torching the Engagement Chicken makes for an entertaining anecdote, after all), but if I'm planning to seriously pursue something with Jack, I'll need to bring Nat into the circle of trust sooner or later—and at this point, I desperately need someone to confide in.

So I confess it all: the attraction I've felt building since our first date at the US Open, how different he is than I expected, the crushing guilt of lying to him, and my epiphany about my feelings for him, all culminating in the steamy kitchen hookup I can't seem to stop replaying in my mind on an endless loop. Just recounting it fogs up the windows of this bar.

Nat's eyes are wide as cake plates as she leans back in

her chair and whistles. "*Wooow*. I had no idea things had gone this far. I just thought you had some sort of schoolgirl crush!"

It's such a relief to finally come clean; I didn't realize how badly I needed to unburden myself. "Last night, in his kitchen? I'm telling you Nat, it was the hottest moment of my entire life. And I don't mean 'since Brett,' or 'since my college boyfriend'—I mean *ever*. And all we were doing was kissing! Fully clothed kissing, at that. In fact, I think one of the reasons it *was* so hot was because—"

"You set his kitchen on fire?" She grins wickedly.

"*No*." I ball up what's left of my napkin and chuck it at her while she snickers. "It was because I knew he wasn't going to try to take things any further. Who knew delayed gratification was such a turn-on? It's like the more he respects my boundaries, the more I want to jump his bones. It's the strangest, most effective form of reverse psychology ever."

"You're living a real-life slow burn," she says cheekily, sipping her wine.

"I am! And the weird thing is, I feel like I know Jack better after three dates than after three *months* of dates with Brett. How is that even possible?"

"Anything's possible with the right guy," she singsongs, her dark eyes twinkling.

I level her with a stern look. "Let's be clear: Jack Bradford is not the 'right' guy. In fact, he's precisely the *wrong* man for me to be falling for. Cupid has a twisted sense of humor," I grumble as I slurp my drink. *Stupid Cupid*. "It's not fair."

"If life were fair, every dress would have pockets."

I snort, inhaling my drink in the process and setting off a prolonged coughing fit.

She slides me my water and leans forward. "Listen, you've been resisting this since the very beginning. I think you need to let go of all these guardrails you've put up and allow yourself to explore what an actual relationship with Jack would be like. You need to find out how you truly feel about him without it feeling 'forbidden' or off-limits. It's the only way you'll know for sure if there's something real there."

I consider her words thoughtfully. It's essentially the same conclusion I've already come to, though I don't think I realized how badly I needed to hear her vote of confidence. Or *any* vote of confidence, really. My judgment's been so out of whack lately that I don't even trust myself to see things clearly anymore.

She's studying me, the corner of her mouth curved up. "Did you know you smile when you say his name?"

My cheeks heat. "I do?"

"Totally. Your face gets all flushed and dreamy." I bury said face in my hands, embarrassed. "What? It's sweet! You like him, there's nothing to be ashamed of."

"Isn't there, though? Aren't I essentially choosing a guy over my career? I don't want to be known as 'the girl who didn't go to Paris.'"

We exchange matching grimaces, the pain of LC choosing Jason Wahler over a summer internship at French *Vogue* still fresh.

"And the thing is, Cynthia's not wrong; I am a little blinded by my attraction to him," I admit. "After all, he's still the guy who runs Brawler. That hasn't changed."

"But your opinion of him *has* changed. You said it yourself, he's nothing like the site, nothing like you thought he'd be. Evolving your position based on new information is a sign of strength, not weakness."

I huff a laugh. "You'd make an excellent politician."

"Are we really all that different, though? They're playing to their audience just like we are. Brawler gives Siren a hard time, and we give it right back. We're not exactly saints here." She pops another fry into her mouth. "Come to think of it, a little healthy competition makes for great foreplay." She waggles her eyebrows suggestively.

"Well, I hope foreplay's enough to satisfy him for a while, because . . ." I trail off, second-guessing that dash of honesty. Nat won't understand this.

"Because what?"

I drag a fry through the ketchup, stalling. I don't know why I'm embarrassed to admit this. "Because I actually like the pace we're moving at. It feels nice, you know? Getting to know him slowly, giving myself the chance to look forward to things. I haven't been pursued like this since . . . well, *ever*." I think of how to explain it. "Everything about the way I've handled this relationship has been different, and since it seems to be working out pretty well, I've decided to stay the course."

She sits back in her chair, giving me a *looong* look. "I don't believe it."

"What?"

She points her fry at me. "You're turning into Betty."

"What?" I attempt a laugh, but what comes out is a noise that's never occurred before in nature. "No, I'm not."

"You are." Her eyes are alight with the thrill of scientific discovery. She's Edison, and her prototype light bulb has just blinked to life. "She's gotten into your head. You think the tips are working, so you're turning into that crazy Nebraska lady!"

"Okay, first of all, Nebraska lady has a name, it's Tami. And she is *not* crazy, she's sweet as cherry pie and has been very helpful to me, so I will not abide any Tami slander." Nat rolls her eyes. "Second of all, you're being ridiculous."

"*I'm* being ridiculous? Let's consider the evidence, shall we?" She's gesticulating so wildly with her fry that a blob of ketchup plops onto the table. "You got a subscription to *Good Housekeeping*. You're watching black-and-white movies constantly. You pitched a story the other day about the comeback of pantyhose. *Pantyhose!*" she repeats, pounding the table for emphasis. She's a lawyer making her case; the fry is her laser pointer. "You followed a bunch of Rock Hudson fan pages on Instagram, and you're singing oldies in the shower. And now you're embracing *celibacy*?!"

I wave off her concerns. "All of that stuff is for research and you know it."

"Oh really? Have you even noticed what you're wearing today?"

I glance down—a gingham midi skirt, matching boatneck tee, and ballet flats. *An adorable ensemble, if I do say so myself.*

"I've never seen you wear that color before. I've never seen you wear a *pattern* before! You look like Doris Day's body double. And you wore this to work, so you can't blame it on a date with Jack."

Who is she, the fashion police?! "First of all, comparing me to Doris Day is not the insult you think it is." I want to clarify that this particular outfit was actually inspired by Brigitte Bardot in *Come Dance with Me*, but I refrain. *Not the time.* "And I don't know what you're getting at with this, but since you're clearly desperate for me to admit to something, then fine—I love my new wardrobe. There, I said it! These clothes are classy and feminine and wearing them is an instant mood booster. Happy now?" I grab my martini and start guzzling it like water.

She presses her lips together in amusement, covering my hand with hers. "I'm not giving you a hard time for the sake of giving you a hard time, okay? I'm just looking out for you. Are you doing this to fit some mold for him? Because you think that's what he likes? I just want to make sure Jack's getting to know the *real* you."

"Oh. Of course he is," I assure her, softening a touch at her concern. "Sure, I've said some silly things in service to this story, but I've been truthful about all the stuff that matters. My family, my job, my frustrations . . . I even unloaded on him about wanting to get *married*. I don't think it gets more brutally honest than that." A fresh wave of humiliation washes over me at the memory. I wouldn't mind getting that one back. "This?" I motion to my clothes. "Is just window dressing. I'm still me. If anything, I think I'm just finally starting to understand what my grandmother's been talking about all this time."

"And what's that?"

Before I can answer, my phone dings with a text and I glance at it.

Jack: Hey you. What are you up to?

"Is that him?" Nat asks, and I nod. "Know how I knew? You're already smiling."

I groan and cover my face with a hand.

"Well, what are you waiting for? Text him back!"

Me: Getting a drink with Nat. How was your day?

Jack: Confession: I can't stop thinking about you. It's extremely distracting, I can't get anything done.

Me: Wow, can't even play it cool for 5 minutes.

Jack: I thought we established that I'm a boring nerd? Playing it cool isn't really my thing.

Me: Lucky for me 😍 And confession: I missed you today too.

Jack: I know we made plans for this weekend, but it's too far off. How about tonight? I'll come pick you up and take you anywhere you want.

I refuse to acknowledge Nat, who's smirking at me over the rim of her wineglass—and I don't even bother trying to wipe the smile off my face.

Me: I thought you had a work thing tonight?

Jack: My Cassidy thing tonight is much more pressing.

Me: I can't be responsible for you bailing on your work obligations!

Jack: What's the point of being the boss if you can't bail on work? Anyway, Tom can handle it. It's one of the perks of having a partner.

Jack: Now, is that a yes?

Me: It's a yes, under one condition.

Jack: Name it

I bite my bottom lip, deliberating. I'm not usually so brazen, but today's events have lit a fire under me, driven me to take the bull by the horns and step outside my comfort zone in a way I never have before. *Cynthia thinks I'm a coward? I'll show her.*

Me: I want you to kiss me the second you see me.

The three typing bubbles appear for all of about one second before his reply comes across.

Jack: TEXT ME YOUR ADDRESS.

Chapter 14

*T*HE NEXT FEW WEEKS ARE A BLUR—A BLISS-ful, romantic blur. If I'm not at work or asleep, I'm with Jack. It's almost strange how quickly we become inseparable, how easily we fall into a shared routine, like we've been together years, not days. In the past I've resented when friends have gone radio silent the second they start seeing someone, but I find myself understanding them in a way I never have before. When you find someone who sets your world on fire, you want to be with them as much as possible. It's as simple as that.

Jack and I see each other almost every day, sometimes for a quick lunch, more often for a lingering dinner, and I look forward to each meal like a kid counts down to recess. Our weekends are spent doing a random hodgepodge of things—brunch in Hudson Yards, an outdoor concert in Central Park, taking in a Giants game—and despite the warnings about his demanding workload, he seems to have no problem making time for me.

While his relationship with his mom may be thorny, she

clearly did something right—there's an old-school, gallant quality to Jack's courtship style that could only be the result of a mother's touch. He leads me through doorways with a hand to my back; helps me into my coat; walks beside or behind me, never in front; shields me from rain; refuses to let me carry (or pay for) anything. He's affectionate and attentive, as generous with his time as he is with his money. While it's a bit of an adjustment dating someone with an income so disparate to mine—no restaurant is too nice and no tickets too expensive, which is about as far outside of my penny-pinching, budget-controlled lifestyle as it gets—Jack is so unassuming about it all that any self-consciousness I may have felt quickly melts away.

While I may not have his resources, I do my best to spoil him with the one thing I *can* give him in return: my attention. Eager to make up for my past hot-and-cold behavior, I create a revised romantic punch list and start checking things off one by one. I hide sweet (and sometimes spicy) notes around his apartment for him to find later. I snag him gifts from the steady stream of press samples that pour into the Siren offices, like an advance copy of a memoir written by an entrepreneur I know he admires. I compliment him openly and often, and ogle him shamelessly. I curate an oldies-themed Spotify playlist of our greatest hits and surprise him with it. I start monitoring sports headlines so I can converse with him semi-intelligently about his workday. I swallow my pride and give the Engagement Chicken another shot, and this time, I nail it. I even bake him a batch of my specialty break-and-bake cookies for dessert (what, you thought I'd make 'em from scratch? I haven't changed *that* much).

But watching his reaction to these small acts of kindness is my favorite part. An adorable carousel of emotions plays out on his face every time: surprise (widened eyes; raised eyebrows), pleasure (a boyish grin; flushed cheeks), followed by affection (his hands on my hips dragging me closer; lingering full-body hugs; leisurely, bone-melting kisses). He's clearly not used to people doing things for him, which could break my heart if I think about it too long. Even more surprising? How gratifying these acts of service are for *me*.

I'm the happiest I've ever been.

With every one of his playful texts and dimpled smiles and goodnight kisses, I feel the world shifting beneath my feet. It's not lost on me that the man I once dismissed as undateable is now responsible for the healthiest relationship I've ever been in. Gran's guidance is resonating more deeply than I ever could have imagined: *Let him know you're thinking of him. Make him feel cherished. Never stop trying to win his heart.*

It's a Sunday afternoon, and Jack and I have just finished hitting up a street fair, a fall-themed affair bursting with hay bales and spiked cider and wild children hopped up on kettle corn and face paint fumes. It's hard to believe it's already October, but the changing leaves and brisk air nipping at my forearms don't lie. Now would be the time to borrow Jack's coat, but like an idiot I actually had the foresight to bring my own. Somewhere, Gran is trolling me for the missed opportunity.

We're strolling through the Upper West Side now, and I'm introducing Jack to one of my favorite (free) activities: stoop-spotting (which is basically just an excuse for me to drool over the brownstones I love so much). I point to the one in front of us, its steps piled high with colorful pumpkins and squashes and funky-looking gourds of indeterminate origin. Matching cornstalks flank either side of the dramatic arched doorway while galvanized steel buckets brimming with mums crowd the threshold. It's a picturesque autumn vignette straight out of *Hocus Pocus*. "This one's definitely my favorite."

Jack snorts. "You said that about the last one."

"I really mean it this time, though."

"You said that too."

I blow out a puff of air, mock-wounded. "I think you're missing the point of the game, sir. They're *all* my favorite."

He hooks his index finger into my belt loop and tugs me back against his chest, wrapping his arms around me from behind and enveloping me in one of his signature full-body hugs. I flash to something Nat said a couple of days ago: *If you turn into one of those sickening couples who walk around with their hands in each other's back pockets, I'll have to kill you.*

I relax against him and grip his forearms, staring up at the house wistfully. "If I could live anywhere in the city, I'd pick one of these brownstones."

"Oh yeah? Why's that?" His breath is a curl of warm smoke against my ear. It's pumpkin spice and everything nice.

"Have you ever been inside one? They're so dreamy, so quintessentially New York. They have so much character—creaky floors, two-hundred-year-old millwork. The banisters alone! I just love everything about them."

"They're probably all haunted."

"Meh, living with ghosts is a small price to pay. My dream is to curl up in a window seat in comfy socks, reading or writing, listening to the rain pelt the window. Can't you just picture it in a winter storm? Like you're inside a snow globe." I sigh in contentment at the thought of it.

He hums and flexes his arms, squeezing me tighter. I'm steeped in his scent, cloaked in his embrace. Mummified in Jack. "Where am I in this fantasy?"

"You're making me dinner. Or rubbing my feet. Either is acceptable."

He laughs, and I nod decisively.

"That's it, we're definitely coming back to this house in December. You know they'll go all out for Christmas. Lights, wreaths, trees . . . I'm calling life-sized nutcrackers, too."

We resume our ambling, his arm curved around my lower back, my head nestled into his shoulder. Now that I'm thinking about it, it's very tempting to snake my chilly hand into his back pocket. I could even cop a feel while I'm at it. "What do you do for Christmas?"

"Me? I usually plan a trip. If I stay in town, I get guilted into a formal dinner at my parents' country club. My brother and I used to have a bet to see who could eat and escape the fastest." He grimaces and shakes his head, as if to rid himself of the memory. "How about you?"

"I go home to Connecticut. Stay with my parents, celebrate Christmas morning with Christine and Greg and the girls. Nothing like watching kids rip through gifts their parents stayed up half the night wrapping to make you feel better about being single and childless." I grin, thinking of how bleary-eyed and haggard Christine and Greg always look, their tight smiles when I gift the girls things like karaoke machines and slime. *Good times.* "My mom makes a huge breakfast: eggs, pancakes, waffles, Danish, sausage and bacon, mimosas. And everyone goes to Gran's on Christmas night, all my aunts and uncles and cousins. There's caroling if people get drunk enough. My Uncle Rich tripped once and ended up in the hospital with a broken ankle. Ahh, memories."

Now he looks wistful. "That sounds so normal. Maybe that's my fantasy. You think your parents would adopt me?"

I pretend to think about it. "They have been known to take in strays, but I think it's generally frowned upon to date someone you're related to."

We pause to appraise a stoop with thick cobwebs stretched across the railings and shrubbery. Two pirate skeletons in eye patches sit in chairs on the landing, goblets raised toward passersby in cheers. I give the tableau two very enthusiastic thumbs up.

"Tell me more about your parents," he says once we're walking again. I wave at a toddler being strollered past who's grinning up at us with a gummy smile.

"My parents? Let's see. First of all, it was a very cookie-cutter upbringing. You know, white picket fence on a dead-end cul-de-sac, the whole nine. In fact, I like to hassle them that my childhood was just too darn stable and happy for me to be able to do any gritty, serious literary writing. But then I remember that I hate stuffy literary writing, so it all works out."

He chuckles, shifting me over slightly as a delivery guy whizzes past on a bike.

"My mom loves nothing more than having all her kids and grandkids surrounding her. Like if there was a way she could force us all to relocate and live together on a compound, she would absolutely do it. She tries to bribe me to come home more by offering to do my laundry, even though she knows my apartment has a washing machine." He laughs again. "She hosts a family dinner every Sunday, a standing invitation for anyone who can come. I try to make it as often as I can, but *someone's* been monopolizing my time lately."

Jack gives me a *Who, me?* face. "And your dad?"

"Oh, he's fun. Always in a good mood, never has a bad day. He's constantly stuffing twenty-dollar bills into my purse when I'm not looking. Loves doing crosswords. He's also Siren's most dedicated reader. He reads every article I write, then sends me emails highlighting his favorite parts. And he's a big guy, so it's extra funny to think of him reading makeup tips. He was very intimidating for past boyfriends. But he loves sports, so you might be okay," I tease.

We reach the street corner and he pushes the button for the crosswalk, then flashes me his most dazzling smile, the one he knows I can't resist. "You should invite me home to meet them. I make a really good impression."

I should be thrilled by the offer—it's what I've wanted this whole time, isn't it?—but instead, his words trigger an unwelcome flashback and I stiffen.

His smile slips. "Is it something I said?"

I let out a caustic laugh. "In a word? Yes." His brows draw together. "The last time I invited someone home to meet my family, I was told '*Saturdays are for the bros.*' And now here I am, dating Mr. Saturday himself." There's no mistaking the bitterness in my voice. "So you'll have to forgive me for being a little gun-shy."

A look of resignation slots into place on his face. "Ah."

I cross my arms and look away, intently studying the street traffic over his shoulder. *Who needs the rugged landscape of his chiseled jawline when I can stare at some rusty old taxis?*

"Maybe we should clear this up, since it's obviously something that's still bothering you."

"It's not *bothering* me," I mutter, scuffing the toe of my bootie into the pavement.

He takes a step toward me, tilting my chin up with a finger, and I'm forced to meet his eyes, which are somehow both soft and imposing. "Cassie."

And that's another thing: He's started calling me Cassie. He's the only person who's ever shortened my name that way—I've always been called Cassidy or Cass, never *Cassie*. The first time he did it, my heart leapt in my chest; I worried I'd need a defibrillator to get it back in rhythm. It lit me up like the Griswold family Christmas tree. But right now, it grates. Like he's trying to butter me up.

The light changes and he clasps my hand firmly in his, leading me across the street and into a nearby park. All around us the world is exploding with color, the sky painted in oranges and golds; it's the romantic, stylized version of New York you see in the movies. I only wish I was in a better mood to appreciate it.

Jack plops me down on a bench before taking my hand again and twining our fingers together. "Now, why don't you tell me what you're thinking but not saying? I'd rather you just be honest with me." When I don't immediately speak, he nudges me. "I'm a big boy, you know. I can take it."

I blow out a breath. "Fine, it does bother me. I don't like the site. I don't like what you do."

There. My not-so-secret feelings are out. Betty may be fanning herself on a fainting couch, but damn, does it feel good to finally say that out loud.

His lip twitches. "You don't say."

"And I know how hard you work. You've built a successful business and you employ a ton of people, which is an incredible thing, Jack. And I just want to be supportive of you and proud of what you do, but you make that really difficult sometimes."

"You've been biting your tongue so hard I'm surprised it's still in your mouth." His expression takes on a lascivious edge. "Don't get me wrong, I'm glad it is . . ."

I groan. "Come on, I'm being serious. This is a legitimate ethical dilemma for me. I'm exhausted by the mental gymnastics I have to do to separate you from the sexist crap on your site." It's so incongruent, how someone as chivalrous and respectful as Jack could run a site that's so . . . well, *not*.

"You think I never have to do that for you? Why don't you take a look at Siren's home page and see how many times it refers to men as 'toxic'? I could be offended by that, but I choose not to be because I know those articles aren't for me."

"So that's how you justify it? It's not meant for me, so I should just close my eyes and pretend it doesn't exist?"

"I'm not justifying anything; I'm *explaining* it. You don't like the content on the site? Frankly, I'd be concerned if you did." He rakes a hand through his hair, clearly frustrated. "Let me put this in terms you'll understand. Brawler's largest audience is males between the ages of sixteen and twenty-four. College guys. We tailor the majority of our content to appeal to that age group. Is the humor crass and immature sometimes? Sure, because college guys are crass and immature. Am I thrilled about everything that's on the site? No, but I'm also not our target audience anymore, either."

He drags a hand through his hair again, mussing it adorably, pieces sticking up every which way. *How is it possible to want to both kiss and kill someone at the same time?*

"Look, it's been ten years. I'm not the same kid who started the site with his friend in a dorm room. I'm not even in charge anymore! We have a board of directors to answer to, investors to satisfy, revenue targets to hit. Brawler employs *hundreds* of people. The site stopped being about Tom and me a long time ago. And I won't be doing this forever." He seems to want to say something more here but stops short. "The point is: I am not the site, and the site is not me."

I desperately want to believe him. I want to pretend this elephant in the room doesn't exist, that his work isn't directly in conflict with mine, but how can I? I don't want to rationalize away his faults any more than I want to ignore my own principles. It's a dizzying paradox to navigate, like I'm tiptoeing around a house of cards, holding my breath for fear of sending it all crashing to the ground.

On the other hand, I know a job doesn't define someone; their character does. And Jack is a good man, full stop. Is he perfect? No, but he's also so many things I never expected him to be—gentlemanly and evolved, insightful and empathetic, unselfish in both word and deed. He's solid and rock steady in a way I didn't even know I was looking for but now can't imagine living without. It's painful to know that just a few weeks ago I would have written him off, as certain of his flawed character as I was that my grandmother and these old-fashioned tips had nothing to teach me.

Maybe life is thinking you have all the answers, then realizing you know nothing at all.

I stare at our entwined fingers and think about how many things had to fall into place exactly the right way at exactly the right moment for us to be sitting here together. Against all odds, this relationship is thriving. We're like two orphan puzzle pieces that somehow magically, inexplicably fit together.

"So in other words, I don't have to like the site. I just have to like *you*."

The corner of his mouth hitches up. "Tall order, I know."

"Indeed." I purse my lips like I'll have to think about it, then angle my face up to his.

The kiss starts slow, his mouth meeting mine, his lips chasing away my reservations like sunlight chases away fog. But what began as chaste and restrained quickly escalates into something more, something deeper; a needy, urgent intensity neither of us can seem to control. This is more than a kiss. It's a promise, an unspoken acknowledgment that this relationship is different from any others we've had. I can feel his commitment as strongly as I can feel my own. Our connection is a living thing, growing by the day, its roots twisting a winding path through me and wrapping around my heart.

When he finally pulls away there's a question in his eyes, and it's the same one I see every time we kiss. I can hear it on his lips; taste it on his tongue. He wants to know when I'll be ready for more, what's holding me back . . . but I also know he won't ask. The man seems to have a bottomless well of patience, matched only by his stubbornness. And as much as my body is screaming to take that next step, I find myself at a similar impasse, albeit for entirely different reasons. How could I possibly justify being intimate with him when there are so many lies still between us? My deception is a splinter that digs a little deeper into my psyche each day, perniciously infecting our relationship, and yet I know extracting it would cause even worse harm. Every time I consider confessing the truth, I picture

Jack's face, lit with joy at some silly, insignificant good deed I've done for him, and I can't go through with it. I can't be another person in his life who's let him down; who's betrayed him. It's a plot hole I can't seem to write my way out of.

But there is one thing I can do. "So I've been meaning to ask you something."

This is not precisely true; it was more that I couldn't decide whether to ask him at all, and it's not until this exact moment that my decision has become clear.

"There's an event next week. A work event, I mean. It's Siren's 'Women of the Year' dinner? That we host annually? Maybe you're familiar with it?" I need to stop speaking in question marks. Jack blinks at me and I shift gears, a torrent of words spilling out in one long, rambling gush. "Anyway, I'm allowed a plus-one. I've never actually invited anyone before, but Nat's bringing Gabriel and I thought maybe you'd want to go, but then I wasn't sure if it would be awkward for you or if—"

"Of course I'll go," he cuts me off, squeezing my hand.

Oh. "You will? Okay." A heavy breath gusts out of me. "Are you sure?"

"Are *you* sure?" He's gently amused.

"Yeah! I mean, yes. I just, you know, I wasn't sure if you would feel weird coming to a Siren event. Not that you *should* feel weird, I just . . . argh, you know what I mean."

Is it a bold choice to pick Siren's biggest event of the year as a coming-out party for me and Jack? Without a doubt, which is precisely why I've been obsessing over this decision for the past couple of weeks. Keeping our relationship under wraps made sense at first; I needed to find my footing, give myself the space and time to confirm this was real.

But the longer I've waited, the more wrong it's felt. Jack welcomed me into his life wholly and without reservations—heck, I met his friends and coworkers on our first date—and I haven't exactly responded in kind. It's time for me to step up to the plate. Besides, I'm finally dating someone I'm excited about, who makes me happy, and I'm tired of hiding it. I *want* to show him off. I want to prove to Cynthia and everyone else that Jack was worth the risk.

"Let me make this easy for you: I don't feel weird if you don't feel weird. I have a cordial relationship with Cynthia, and I promise to be on my best behavior." He is all wide-eyed innocence; a class clown trying to sweet-talk his way out of detention. "And I'd be honored to be your arm candy for the night."

There's pride in his voice, and it's hard to believe there was ever a time I thought he would say something demeaning or regressive; he's never been anything but my biggest cheerleader.

"Come on." He presses a kiss to my temple and stands, pulling me up. "And for the record, I know you hate the whole Saturdays thing, but how can I be sorry for it? If Tom and I hadn't come up with that nifty little catchphrase way back when, you'd probably still be wasting time with what's-his-face instead of here with me." He rubs my upper arms, eyes shining with mischief. "Remind me to thank that guy, actually. What was his name? Butt?"

I slant him a look, swatting his chest. "His name was *Brett*."

He waves a hand as if to say, *Same difference*. "Am I supposed to be sorry that Butt was an idiot? Butt's loss is my gain."

I refuse to laugh; it'll only encourage him. But speaking

of butts . . . *You know what? Screw it.* I slide my hands into his back pockets and squeeze. *Mmm.* He's got a highly squeezable heinie. "I'm so glad my pain and suffering is amusing for you. Maybe next time I can raise the stakes and be publicly humiliated."

"Next time, huh? Already planning to get rid of me?" He doesn't give me a chance to answer before lowering his mouth to mine, claiming it—claiming *me*—for his own.

Never, I think to myself as I wrap my arms around his neck and lose myself in him. *I'm never letting you go.*

There's something about kissing Jack that eclipses everything else. I lose time when it's happening; I dream about it when we're apart. He's passionate yet tender, hungry but still gentle, his touch somehow both inflammatory and healing. It's like I'm hypnotized, but I've also never been more awake. It's the most intoxicating dichotomy. I can't get enough of it. I can't get enough of *him*.

When we finally break apart I feel woozy, unsteady on my feet. I have to drag my eyes open and come back to myself, so thoroughly have I forgotten where I am (you know, in public, in broad daylight, with small children around). It's getting harder and harder to stave off this feeling, to satisfy this craving I have for him. Attraction is one thing, but this is like an addiction. I've never felt such a staggering *need*.

"Speaking of public humiliation," I mention casually once I'm able to stand upright without assistance and we've resumed walking, "your buddy Eric Jessup's been in the news this week."

Jack tips his head back and groans at the sky. "I knew the *I told you so* was coming on this."

"Why would I need to say that when *I'm always right* sounds so much better?" I taunt.

The story dominating the gossip headlines this week is the Eric Jessup–Olivia Sherwood engagement, which (if you believe the tabloids) has apparently imploded in spectacular fashion. The prevailing theory cited for the split is that Eric "wasn't ready to settle down," with sources describing Olivia as "devastated" by the breakup. I have to admit, I was disappointed to hear it. Maybe it's this blissful honeymoon stage I'm in, but I actually wanted to believe in their fairy tale.

"Look, am I happy that Eric Jessup has proven himself to be just another womanizing creep who screwed over his loyal, long-suffering hometown girlfriend? No. But I'm also not surprised."

"We don't actually know if it's true," Jack points out as we maneuver around a dog walker struggling with a giant tangle of leashes. "He hasn't confirmed it."

"He hasn't denied it, either, which may as well be a confirmation."

He shrugs in concession. "Well, if it is true, then I feel bad for the guy. It didn't seem like a fake relationship to me." He snaps his fingers. "That reminds me. There's a playoff game next week and I thought I'd see if Greg wanted to go, if you're cool with it?"

"Is that even a question? I'll be sister-in-law of the year. Are you sure, though? Don't get me wrong, it's really sweet of you, I just don't want you to feel obligated . . ."

He waves a hand. "I always have to see the same people at these things. Trust me, it'll be way more fun for me to hang with someone who actually *wants* to be there."

We've arrived back at his building now, and as soon as I see Cliff's on duty I tug on Jack's arm to wait, then start digging through my bag. "I found you a really good one," I tell him gleefully.

"You spoil me," Cliff says, rubbing his hands together as he comes out from behind the desk.

I've been at Jack's apartment so much lately that Cliff is basically my new best friend (and a major reason why *Make enough money to live in a building with a gently paternal, elderly doorman* has rocketed up my list of life goals). During one of our nightly exchanges I learned that he keeps an extensive matchbook collection, so now I do my best to nick one from every restaurant Jack and I visit.

"It's embossed," I tell him, presenting my spoils as reverently as a bronze star.

"Ooh, those are the big bucks," he says and holds it up to the light, scrutinizing it like a rare coin.

Jack's shaking his head at us. "Here I am thinking I'm dazzling her with my scintillating dinner conversation while she's plotting how to score you matchbooks."

"A woman after my own heart," Cliff says, shooting me a wink. "Don't let this one go, sir."

The elevator dings and I wave goodbye as Jack tugs me inside—then yelp as he hauls me against him.

"I don't intend to," he murmurs, lowering his face to mine as the doors slide shut behind us.

$\mathcal{I}$T'S ONE WEEK LATER AND I'M STARING INTO my bedroom mirror, dressed to the nines for the Siren event and feeling equal parts excited and sick to my stomach. Was this such a good idea? *Guess we're about to find out.*

This week's been ridiculously busy, with all Siren employees working around the clock to prep for the event, which seems to get a little bigger and more prestigious every year. When Cynthia first conceived of the idea, it was as much about building Siren's name recognition as it was as an excuse to get a bunch of influential women into one room. Now, years later, it's grown from honoring one woman annually to spotlighting a handful of trailblazers and tastemakers in the categories of technology, music, entertainment, entrepreneurship, and philanthropy. It's a thrill to have the opportunity to rub elbows with so many powerful and inspiring women, but it's also an insane amount of extra work on top of our regular responsibilities. I've stayed late every night this week, writing and editing the extended profiles on each honoree, weighing in on endless drafts of Cynthia's remarks, coordinating PR opportunities with our marketing team, and on and on it goes.

As a result, I've barely had a minute to spare for Jack, so I'm extra excited to see him tonight. I miss his face. (Not that I think he's suffering too much. Last night was the aforementioned baseball game with Greg, and I got a late-night text from Christine that read: I think my husband's gonna leave me for your boyfriend, so I'm guessing it went well.)

"We're pouring some champs out here!" Nat calls from our front room. "Quick toast to all our hard work before we go."

I stick one final bobby pin into the loose, wispy side bun I've fashioned at the nape of my neck, then grab my purse and head out to our main room, waving a greeting to Gabriel, who's in the kitchen popping the cork. Nat's pulling the champagne flutes from the cabinet, and when she sees me, she gasps. "Cass, that dress is *perfection.*"

For an event like this I'd typically rely on my trusty companion Rent the Runway (a godsend for the twenty-something serial wedding guest), but when Nat determined that she had to have a new dress and convinced me to run into a few stores with her, I ended up spotting this one on a mannequin and it was love at first sight.

If ever a dress was made for me, this would be it: a black halter neck with a low back, a gathered waist, and a pleated chiffon skirt that flutters around my knees in the softest, most feminine way. It's sophisticated yet understated and somehow both modern and timeless; the kind of dress that never goes out of style. If I've ever prided myself on my capsule wardrobe, then this is its capstone. Nat called it my "little black dress" moment a la *Breakfast at Tiffany's,* but the silhouette is actually much closer to Marilyn Monroe's iconic white subway grate dress in *The Seven Year Itch*, which is fitting, I suppose—the merging of Betty and Cassidy is now complete.

I accept the flute she hands me and clink it against hers. "It really is perfect. As always, I owe all my impeccable fashion moments to you," I acknowledge, giving her a little bow.

"Well, I'm no Edith Head, but I am damn good." When I tilt my head questioningly, Nat groans, exasperated. "Edith Head, only the most famous costume designer of all time? Responsible for just about every iconic look in all those Old Hollywood movies you've been watching nonstop?" She sighs when I shrug. "You disappoint me."

I chuckle and reach up to give Gabriel a hug. "Don't you look dapper," I tell him, and he does—he's model-handsome in his dark suit and tie, his longish, unruly hair slicked back into a slightly-more-ruly style. When he's paired with Nat in her off-the-shoulder emerald-green gown, they look like they've stepped out of the pages of a fashion magazine. "You guys are so attractive, it's ridiculous. I can't even imagine what your kids will look like."

"Hopefully just like her," Gabriel says, eyeing Nat appreciatively.

"You are *so* well-trained," Nat teases, slipping an arm around his waist.

"I'm looking forward to finally meeting Jack," Gabriel says, taking a swig of the champagne. "And selfishly, I'm glad I'll have someone to hang out with while you guys go off and do your thing."

"I'm looking forward to you meeting him too," I say pointedly, stealing a glance at our oven clock. Jack is now officially late. He was supposed to meet us here so we could all ride over to the hotel together, but we're cutting it close.

I decide to shoot him a text, but when I fish my phone out of my purse I see I've already gotten one from him.

Jack: Something came up at work. Need to meet you there

Huh. Well, that sucks. Maybe it's silly, but I was really looking forward to showing up with someone on my arm for once.

Nat reads my face. "What's up?"

"It sounds like Jack's going to have to meet us there." Disappointment sinks in my stomach like a stone. "Which is fine."

I pretend not to see Nat slide her eyes to Gabriel, silently communicating in couple code that all is decidedly *not* fine.

There's something else about Jack's text that's nagging at me. Maybe it's that he didn't share any details of what exactly came up. Or that he didn't offer an apology for his tardiness on what he knows is an important night for me—actually, for *us*. Or maybe it's the brusque tone of his text, so unlike his usual affectionate, flirtatious messaging demeanor. Something is off.

This is not what I need right now. This is not the night I want to start second-guessing Jack, picking apart his text messages and analyzing them for coded undertones and hidden meanings. It's the type of mind games I thought I'd left in my past, the kind that have been totally absent from my relationship with Jack. Until now, at least.

I decide I'm reading too much into it. *"No sense creating problems where there aren't any,"* as Gran likes to say. (Of course, my Pop-Pop always used to say, *"Early is on time, on time is late, and late doesn't happen,"* but somehow I don't think texting that to Jack would be helpful right now). I tap out a response (No problem, see you there), then throw my phone back into my purse.

"Okay if I tag along with you guys?" I ask lightly, hating how pathetic I feel in this moment. *And just when I thought I was done being a third wheel.*

"Of course!" Nat says quickly, tossing back the rest of her champagne. "You know you're always welcome with us."

"And I get two gorgeous dates instead of one," Gabe adds, gamely offering me his other arm, and my heart glows with gratitude for these two despite my disappointment.

It's stupid to care about something like this, right? Jack's a busy man with a lot of responsibilities and even more people depending on him. This surely won't be the last time an inconveniently timed work emergency crops up; I should probably get used to it now.

So I swallow my frustration, paste on a smile, and grab my handbag. "Ready?"

THE HOTEL BALLROOM looks stunning; I feel like I just stepped into the first-class dining room on the *Titanic*. Elaborate brass chandeliers dripping with crystals cast intricate light patterns on the walls, while extravagant floral arrangements explode across every surface. Each table is lavishly set with enough silverware to make Jack Dawson's head spin. Cynthia holds court near the entrance, greeting every VIP and guest who enters, while David, her longtime partner and the Stedman to her Oprah, stays glued to her side.

I end up chatting with a group of my friends from work—Nat and Gabriel, Jordan, Kara, and Daniela, along with their significant others—while we pretend not to rubberneck all the celebrities milling about the room. But despite all the famous eye candy, there's really only one person I care about seeing tonight, and his continued absence is the one glaring hiccup in an otherwise seamless evening. At this point I'm just hoping he shows up before the speeches start.

Nat catches me checking my phone for the umpteenth time. "He'll be here," she murmurs in my ear, and I squeeze her hand.

"I know."

We're well into the cocktail hour when I finally see him duck through the door, and for a moment I forget all about how irritated I am and just admire how striking he looks in his crisp black suit and tie, his hair flawlessly tousled, his lightly stubbled jaw locked tight as he pauses to search the crowd for me. His photo could be filed in the encyclopedia under *Man in His Prime*. I want to cast his cheekbones in bronze. He's like an NFT—I can't explain what it is, but I'd gladly overpay to own it exclusively.

He's still halfway across the room, but my body reacts reflexively: My pulse quickens and my breath shallows, my nose already tingling in anticipation of his cologne hitting my sinuses. There's a defiant, devil-may-care energy in his stride as he stalks toward me. He's a debonair man on a determined mission, and dangerously handsome, like a suave Cary Grant, a smoldering Gregory Peck, and a rebellious James Dean all rolled into one.

I've definitely been watching too many Turner Classic Movies.

"Hey, you made it," I greet him once he reaches our

group. "Thought I was gonna have to send out a search party." I reach up to give him a kiss, but at the last second he turns his head and I end up grazing his cheek.

I pull away slightly to look at him, and he gives me a tight smile in return. I smooth my hand down his lapel, wondering what the heck happened at work. I've grown adept at reading his moods, even learned how to laugh him out of a funk when he's stressed, but it's hard to get to the bottom of whatever's bothering him with an audience. *Right, our audience.*

I turn back to the group, taking a minute to introduce Jack to my friends. "Everyone, this is Jack Bradford, my"— *Should I call him my boyfriend? Is that too sixth grade?*—"uh, my date." He eyes me oddly and I wilt a little.

"Nice to finally meet you," Gabriel says, reaching out to grip Jack's hand. "Cass tells us great things."

"Get out of here. Brawler, right? Big fan, man," Kara's boyfriend Cody breaks in, and he and Jack exchange a fist bump.

"Did you say Brawler?" Kara says, looking from Cody to Jack to me in confusion.

"I'm sorry, are you two *together*?" Daniela blurts out with palpable shock, and I cringe internally. *Maybe I should've given people a heads-up.*

"Sure are," Jack replies without missing a beat, deliberately ignoring the shade in her tone. He throws an arm around my shoulders and squeezes, crushing me against him so hard my ribs crack. "The old ball and chain."

Now I'm the one giving him side-eye. *Ball and chain?!* Is this his way of poking me for my awkward introduction? I glance at Daniela; she looks like she's just swallowed a handful of rusty nails.

I decide to laugh it off, like I'm in on the joke. "It's pretty new," I say by way of explanation, patting Jack's chest mildly.

"Not *that* new," Jack counters. "Of course, Cassidy likes to take things slow, really *dig* into a person before she commits. Isn't that right, honeybuns?"

I freeze, slow-blinking at him in disbelief. *Is this his idea of making a good impression? Because he's failing miserably.* "Um . . . mm-hmm," I manage to croak, my cheeks flaming in embarrassment.

Registering my distress, Nat comes to the rescue. "Guys, I think Mindy Kaling just walked in!" she says, pointing, and every head whips toward the door. *Thank God for Nat.*

With them distracted, I tug Jack off to the side and lower my voice. "What is going *on* with you?"

He crosses his arms. "What do you mean?"

"I mean is everything okay?"

"Why wouldn't it be?" The belligerence in his tone makes me flinch.

"I meant at work." His response is a blank stare, so I clarify. "Whatever kept you late?"

He lets out a beleaguered groan. "Great, here we go. Are you going to nag me about being late now? I'm here, aren't I?"

Over Jack's shoulder, I lock eyes with Gabriel, who's monitoring our exchange with a frown. I shake my head slightly: *Stand down.*

"Have you been drinking?" I ask in a hushed voice. It's the only way I can explain his erratic behavior.

"No, though I see you've started without me," Jack responds at full volume, nodding at my wineglass. "Guess I need to catch up. But I'm sure you already have a drink waiting for me, right babe? Or is that one for me?"

Before I can react, Jack's grabbed the glass from my hand and drained its contents in one stiff swallow. The others have stopped talking and are openly gawking now, watching the scene unfold like the train wreck it is. Daniela's glaring at him like she'd like to massage him with some barbed wire.

He sees her face and laughs, holding up his hands defensively. "It's okay, this is just one of Cassidy's rules for dating. She likes to always have a drink ready and waiting for me at the end of the day. It's one of my favorite things about her, how devoted she is to taking care of her man." He grins down at me, his eyes cunning and sharp, and something pricks at my subconscious. "She even cooks for me! Talk about every man's dream, amirite guys?"

The men laugh nervously, shuffling their feet and casting uneasy glances at their significant others, most of whom have steel in their spines and daggers in their eyes. But I can't worry about their reactions for long because I'm too busy having an epiphany of my own:

He knows.

I'm as certain of it as I am that his eyes are blue—and it's those same eyes that ultimately give him away. The look he just cast me—the devious gleam and focused intensity, the antagonism and steely resolve—is the very same one he wore the night we met. We're back in that bar and at each other's throats in a ruthless battle of the sexes, only this time, one of us won't make it out alive. It's a fight to the death and Jack's just thrown down the gauntlet. Honestly, I'm surprised it took me this long to figure it out.

Sabotage. That's what tonight's been all about. I have no idea how he figured it out or how long he's known, but he's obviously been planning this—and it's not like he's trying to hide it. Indeed, as awareness dawns and the diabolical motives behind his antics sink in, Jack's villainous smile only burns brighter, as though pleased that I've finally caught up. He wants a willing and worthy adversary because where's the fun in besting someone who's oblivious to the fight? No, he intends to embarrass me, and he wants me to watch. He wants me to preside over my own defeat, thrashing and flailing on my way down. It's payback time, and if he has his way, I will pay dearly.

Welp, be careful what you wish for, Jack. If a fight is what he wants, then he's about to get one. Two can play at this game, and he's overlooking something crucial: I've had a weeks-long head start at acting like I'm a few fries short of a Happy Meal.

I tuck myself against his side and gaze up at him adoringly, splaying my palm on his chest possessively. "Oh no, sweetie—*you're* the one who's a dream." I tug lightly on his tie and imagine choking him with it. "I often think, how is it fair that one man can be so handsome and smart and funny, all while doing such important, admirable work—oh wait." I snap my fingers. "Scratch that last part. Oh well, can't have it all, can we, ladies?"

His smile tightens, jaw flexing, and I can practically hear the enamel grinding off his clenched teeth. We're nose to nose now, his narrowed eyes locked on mine and pinning me in place—twin blue flames that singe my skin.

Behind me, I hear Kara lean over to Jordan. "Is this some weird form of foreplay? Because I don't get it."

Cody clears his throat. "So did you two meet through work, then?" God bless this guy for trying to salvage this social interaction from the jaws of hell. We are *thisclose* to storming the stage and scream-singing "You're So Vain."

"We sure did," Jack says, brimming with phony pride, and I've got to hand it to him—his "devoted boyfriend" act is convincing. "And it's been such a blessing to be in a relationship where my partner understands the unique stressors of the industry. Working in media is crazy, as you can imagine, but Cassidy is *so* supportive," he says dotingly, and I brace myself for whatever grenade he's about to pull the pin on. "Our work even crosses over from time to time. Of course, Brawler isn't much for fashion and diet tips," he says with a condescending, good-ol'-boys chuckle, and my blood blasts from simmering to a full boil.

I bring the heel of my stiletto down very deliberately on his foot and am gratified by his wince. "But if you're looking for fratire or dick-lit, he's your man!" I boop him playfully on the nose.

His eyes are razors, slicing me to ribbons. "Speaking of fashion tips, that dress is a little revealing, don't you think?"

I rear back like I've been slapped. *How dare he insult the dress! Now he's gone too far.* I'm about to charge him like a bull when Nat cuts me off at the pass. "I'm sorry, *revealing*?"

He looks me up and down, making a show of his appraisal. "Just seems like she's advertising something that's not for sale."

Nat stares at him unblinkingly, and I genuinely fear for his life. With Nat, silence is impending violence. If looks could kill, Jack would be wearing a toe tag. "Her dress is gorgeous, just like her." Her voice is hypothermic.

"I agree," Gabriel says flatly, arms crossed. He's a bouncer ready to toss Jack out of here headfirst, *Fresh Prince of Bel-Air*–style. He may even throw in an Oscars-esque sucker punch for good measure.

A uniformed server passes by with a platter of hors

d'oeuvres and I snatch a few off the tray, barely identifying what they are before cramming them down my throat. Apparently, psychological warfare works up the appetite. Jack gives me a patronizing smirk and I can practically hear the next degrading insult trip off his tongue: *You sure you want to eat that? A moment on the lips, a lifetime on the hips!* To beat him to the punch, I take my next bite in slow motion, moaning in pleasure with some excessively suggestive *Mmm*'s. He has to cover his mouth with a hand, and I nearly had him there.

He clears his throat, attempting to recover. "Cassidy is beautiful, there's no doubt about that," he says with tenderness, his eyes briefly softening, and for a moment I wonder if he's going to call a cease-fire—but when they sharpen again, I know he's about to deliver the knockout blow. "Of course, if you think she looks good now, you should see her in an apron."

There's a chorus of muted gasps and I suck in a breath. Unfortunately, I completely forget that my mouth is full of appetizers and I inhale spinach spanakopita down the wrong pipe, sending me into a coughing fit—and because the universe hates me, Cynthia chooses that moment to materialize at our sides.

"Jack Bradford." The two of them size each other up like Olympic rivals while I choke on phyllo dough. "Can't say I ever expected to see you at a Siren event."

"I like surprising people," he says without a hint of irony. "Though I certainly appreciate the invitation."

"It's not me you should be thanking." She sends me a meaningful glance while Nat beats my back. "Cassidy speaks very highly of you."

"Does she now?" He swivels his head to catch my eye, a

sinister Joker grin climbing his face, and now I'm panicking. It's one thing to act out in front of my friends, but to do so in front of my boss is taking things too far. I defended him to Cynthia. I put my dignity, my credibility—heck, my entire *career* on the line for him. These histrionics might be fulfilling some petty need he has for revenge, but this is my real life we're talking about. It's all fun and games until someone gets fired—and since I'm the only one here who doesn't sign their own checks, I'm the one who will pay the price.

"I do." I take his hand and squeeze tightly, imploring him with my eyes: *You've made your point. Please don't do this.* He tilts his head at me, feigning ignorance.

"That's my girl. You've always got my back, haven't you, babe? And I've got yours." The vindictive gleam in his eyes belies his innocent words, and I know there'll be no white flag waving on his horizon.

Where is that waitress when I need her? I'd like to stab him in the thigh with a chicken skewer. "I need some air. Jack, would you mind joining me outside?" I ask tersely. *Translation: Join me outside or else.*

"In a minute, sweetie." He pats my hand dismissively and I indulge in some internal screaming. "So, Cynthia, things at Siren must be going pretty well these days." He makes a show of looking around the sprawling ballroom, whistling through his teeth. "This is quite an event."

"They are, thank you," she preens. "Cassidy here has certainly had a big hand in that. Though from what I hear through the grapevine, you've got some big things happening yourself." She raises an eyebrow and Jack stiffens slightly, something unspoken passing between them. *What is she talking about?* "I suppose congratulations are in order."

"For what?" I ask, genuinely confused.

Jack's jaw tics, and Cynthia holds eye contact with him for another beat before turning to me. "On this new relationship, of course! Jack, you seem to have somehow won over one of my star writers. Well done." Though her tone sounds more accusatory than congratulatory.

He dips his head in acknowledgment. "I'm a lucky man. Now if only I could figure out how to win her over professionally," he says in a flippant, half-teasing but not-really-teasing way. "Brawler could use more strong female voices, and I'm not above using all the tools at my disposal to poach her away."

I goggle at him like gargoyle horns have just sprouted from his forehead. Me, work at Brawler? Is he *high*?

Cynthia seems a little shell-shocked herself. She looks from him to me, her expression concerned. "Is this true? Are you considering leaving?"

"He's just kidding. I'm very happy at Siren," I assure her firmly, beaming him a death glare.

"Are you, though?" Jack drawls lazily. He's a serial killer about to strike; a cat batting around a mouse before devouring it whole. "Because I seem to remember you saying something about the work feeling unimportant. Or was it uninspired?" He snaps his fingers. "Wait, I remember now. You said it wasn't exactly changing anyone's life. That you were killing time until you could write something that matters. Yeah, that was definitely it."

This must be what it feels like just before you drop dead of a heart attack: dizzy and short of breath, limbs numb, blood pulsing in your ears while a dull, heavy ache slowly expands to fill every space from which you might draw air. I can't think or speak or even move. Anger and regret tangle around my heart, squeezing until I think it might rupture under the strain.

But I think what hurts the most is that he took something personal between us—something I trusted him with, something that was *ours*—and twisted it into something ugly. *Something meant to hurt me.* Despite what I've done to deserve his vitriol, I can't believe he would take things this far.

"How could you." It comes out in a hoarse whisper. I brush away a tear that's managed to break through, and I watch his face change, remorse finally making a long-overdue appearance.

I can feel everyone's eyes on me but I can't bear to look at them, to see their stunned expressions or the judgment in their eyes. I can't face Cynthia, or Nat and Gabriel, or anyone else here.

So I turn and rush out.

I hear his voice calling my name and telling me to wait but I don't stop, pushing through the crowd and tearing out of the ballroom like my feet are on fire. I've almost made it to the elevator when his hand grasps my elbow. "You don't get to run away from me," he says roughly, out of breath.

"Oh really, so I should stick around for some more abuse? Thanks but no thanks." I wrestle past him to the elevator and stab the DOWN button a couple of times, willing it to arrive and whisk me away from this nightmare I can't seem to wake up from.

"You know, I'm pretty sure that in this situation, *I'm* the one who gets to act betrayed, not you."

I whip around. "So you're the innocent victim and I'm the bad guy, do I have that right? Despite the fact that I'm not the one who just *humiliated* you in front of your boss, your coworkers, and your friends. In fact, I never did anything to you at all. But congratulations Jack, you got what you wanted. I likely won't have a job tomorrow, but you can rest easy knowing you got your revenge." I punch the button a few more times for good measure while hot tears blur my vision.

"*You* feel humiliated? Well, join the fucking club, Cassidy. All those people in there have been laughing at me behind my back for God knows how long, and you brought me here tonight so they could do it in person!" His anger is a visceral thing; it's rolling off him like radioactive waves.

"That is *not* why I brought you here." He snorts in derision. "Jack, I don't know what you think you know—"

"Here's what I know," he cuts me off. "You've been lying to me since the day we met. I have no idea who you are or if anything you've told me is true. I don't even know if this relationship was ever real."

"It was real," I insist, to myself as much as him. "It *is* real." *It's the most real relationship I've ever had.*

"You'll forgive me if your word doesn't mean much right now." He palms the back of his neck, twisting away from me to glance back at the ballroom. "I don't understand why you're even out here right now. I just gave you everything you needed for your story. That is what you were looking for, wasn't it? For me to act like some sort of ignorant asshole? Some chauvinistic caveman?"

I feel sick. "Who told you?" I whisper.

He looks incredulous. "That's it, that's what you have to say to me? Who *told* me?"

"No, I'm . . ." My head is spinning and I'm having trouble forming cohesive thoughts. I'm in the eye of the storm, an emotional tornado that's plucked me off the ground and spit me high into the air. "No, that's not all I have to say." My phone is going crazy in my purse, but I ignore it.

His eyes flash with temper. "So you're not going to bother denying it, then? No more lies?"

I take a deep breath. "No, I'm not going to deny it. You deserve the truth." Just saying the words out loud makes me want to weep with relief. Despite the intensity of the situation, to finally be honest with him feels like a two-thousand-pound weight's been lifted off my shoulders.

"*Now* I deserve the truth." He laughs bitterly, crossing his arms over his chest. "So tell me, Cassie, because I'm not exactly clear. What was your big plan here? To embarrass me? Ruin my business? Or just to rip my heart out?"

Tears well in my eyes as my own heart cracks right down the middle. I can't stand to see the hurt in his eyes, especially knowing I'm the one who put it there. It's the inevitable outcome I feared all along.

"Jack, no. *No*." He shakes his head in disgust and starts to walk away but I grab his arm before he can, dragging him into a nearby alcove and away from prying eyes. "You want the truth? Here it is, okay? I did go out with you intending to embarrass you. I thought if I acted a certain way, I could catch you . . . I don't know, being a jerk, or behaving badly, and then use it for a story. I gave myself three dates to come up with something incriminating I could use against you and Brawler."

He's still shaking his head, face turned away like he can't bear to look at me. Which is just as well, I suppose; it helps that I don't have to look him in the eye as I confess my sins.

"It's not an excuse, but I'd just been hurt and I thought you deserved it. It was stupid and ridiculous, I see that now, but I wanted to get back at you for all the times Brawler's gone after Siren, for all the obnoxious 'Sacred Saturdays' crap we're always dealing with. I even convinced myself it was *noble*, that by taking you down I'd be righting a wrong for women everywhere. I thought I'd write my story, shame Brawler and all the men who read it, then go on my merry way." I swipe at the tears that are gathering more quickly now. I shudder to think of what my face must look like, watery tracks running through my meticulously applied makeup. "But that was before I knew you. And somewhere along the way I—"

"Grew a conscience?" he sneers.

"No. I mean, yes, but . . ." I let out a ragged breath. "Jack, somewhere along the way I realized that my feelings for you weren't fake. I wanted to be with you as the *real* me, not the silly caricature I came up with. But I knew if I told you the truth, you'd never speak to me again. So I convinced myself that it didn't matter how we'd met, that I could just kill the story and pretend the whole thing never happened." I dash away another tear that's broken loose. I'll be able to raft down this river of tears soon. "I know it was wrong. I *know* that. I just . . . I didn't know what else to do." Despair is mounting in my chest. "I couldn't let you hate me."

He stays stoic, his expression giving nothing away. I want so badly to touch him, to grab the hand flexing at his side, but it feels selfish. I'd be doing it to comfort myself as much as him, and that's not fair to him.

He'll barely look at me. "I can't believe how stupid I've been. I told you things I never tell anyone, and you just lied to my face over and over again. You've lied about everything since the day we met!"

"That's not true. I lied about stupid things, like needing chaperones for our dates and knowing how to roast a

chicken. Not the things that matter." My phone starts ringing again and I curse, pulling it out and glancing at the
display—Nat, unsurprisingly—before shutting it off completely and tossing it back in my purse.

"Why should I believe a word you say?" There's pain in
his voice now, defeat, which somehow feels worse than his
anger. *Like I'm losing him.*

Desperation seizes me. "Because it's the truth! Jack, the
second I knew I had feelings for you, *real* feelings, I called
the whole thing off. I told Cynthia I refused to go through
with it. I told her she could fire me."

He continues to shake his head, saying nothing, and I
throw my arm toward the ballroom.

"You don't believe me? Go in there and ask her! Go find
Cynthia and ask her when I walked away from the story. It
was *weeks* ago, Jack. Doesn't that count for anything?"

"Is that supposed to make me feel better? That you only
lied *half* the time?" He drags a hand through his hair and
strides a few paces away before turning back again. "Jesus,
Cassie, were you *ever* going to tell me the truth?"

"I don't know," I say miserably, hating this. Hating *myself.* "Would you have forgiven me?"

He doesn't respond, but he doesn't have to. We both
know the answer.

"Jack, I'm sorry. I'm sorry for lying to you and betraying
your trust, and for giving you reason to doubt that what I'm
telling you now is anything but the truth. You have every
right to be angry with me. But don't you remember what
you said to me before, about Brett and the whole Saturdays
thing? You said, *'How can I be sorry for it when it brought us
together?'* Well, I feel the same way. I'm sorry but I'm also *not*
sorry, because without this stupid story I never would have

seen you again after the night we met in that bar. I would've cursed your name and walked out of there and never looked back. I would never have gotten to know you. I would never have learned what an amazing man you are. I would never . . ."

I hesitate, my voice faltering, and I nearly lose my nerve, but I'm determined to get this out. I owe him at least that much.

I swallow and meet his gaze, clear-eyed. "I would never have fallen in love with you."

Chapter 16

I WATCH HIM ABSORB MY DECLARATION, A medley of emotions reflected in his eyes: surprise, relief, wonder, then hesitation. Or maybe it's doubt. *Maybe he doesn't believe me.*

This time, I do reach out and touch him. I step forward and take his hand, lacing my fingers through his. I need to lay it all out there for him.

"I tried so hard not to love you, but you swept me off my feet anyway, with your silly board games and your cheesy pickup lines and your chivalry. With your patience and your generosity and your good heart." I smile at him, feeling my soul rattling around in my chest. It's both terrifying and exhilarating to make myself this vulnerable. "It's kind of funny when you think about it, isn't it? I gave myself three dates to bring you down, but I'm the one who fell." I laugh wryly. "Pretty damn inconvenient of you to be the man I've been searching for my whole life."

His eyes flare, and I raise our joined hands and place his palm on my chest, letting him feel my racing heartbeat.

"I've been just as scared of loving you as I've been of losing you, but I realize now that I've never been in control of either one. I can stand here and tell you I love you and you could still walk away, and I'd have to accept that." I curl my fingers around his and squeeze. "But I hope I won't have to."

His silence is excruciating. He's staring at me, his eyes full of emotion, but I'm not a mind reader. Is anything I'm saying affecting him? He can't possibly think I'd lie about this, can he?

"*Say* something," I implore him. "Please, I don't care what it is. Yell at me, curse at me, tell me you hate me, I'll sit here and take it if—"

My words cut off when he steps forward, taking my face in his hands and crashing his lips against mine. The force of it backs me up several steps, my spine hitting the wall behind me, but the discomfort barely registers because I'm so overwhelmed with emotion, so overcome with relief and hope and hunger for him. I cling to him, kissing him back passionately, thoroughly, roughly, desperate to show him how much I love him—but this time as *me*, with no secrecy or deceit standing in our way.

It's like all our restraint, all the lust we've kept banked is unleashed in a torrent, the dam broken, his mouth claiming mine as his hands slide possessively over my skin, moving anywhere and everywhere, like he doesn't know where to start. I fist my hands in his shirt, wishing I could get my paws on the bare skin of his torso, but he's so tightly bound up in his suit and tie that I can't defile him the way I want to. I want to rip his shirt open at the placket and send buttons flying. I want to savagely muss his hair until it looks like it's never seen a brush. I want to shuck off his pants and see if what's underneath is as impressive up close as it feels pressed against my stomach. I want to climb his body like it's my own personal jungle gym.

I whimper into his mouth. All of my long-suppressed sexual energy needs an outlet, and the clock has timed out on my patience. My body is locked between him and this wall and it is *not* working for me. I need to be let loose, wild and untethered, free to ravage him the way I've longed to for months.

I think he must crack my unspoken code because one minute I'm nibbling his neck and panting into his ear and the next we're in a hotel room, like it's *Bewitched* and all I have to do is wiggle my nose to magically teleport myself to another location. (Realistically, it likely had more to do with my impatient hands fumbling at his belt buckle and his desire to keep us from being arrested for lewd and lascivious conduct, but, you know, *details*.)

My arms are wrapped around his midsection from behind, my cheek pressed between his shoulder blades as he keys us into the room. I let go of him so he can shrug off his jacket, then head to the window, pushing aside the heavy drapes so I can take in the view. There's nothing quite like the city at night: bright and dazzling, with glittering lights as far as the eye can see. "Wow," I murmur.

"My thoughts exactly."

I turn and catch his eye, flushing slightly when I realize he's been watching me. I set my purse down on the desk in the corner and pat at my hair, my artfully undone updo now just undone, with pieces pulled loose from their bobby pins, a casualty of our frantic urgency and his greedy hands. I'm feeling shy all of a sudden, self-conscious . . . or perhaps it's more like unprepared. Normally I'd plan a night like this down to the tiniest detail, preselecting the perfect aphrodisiacal meal, sultry background music, and lacy lingerie set designed to make him forget his own name.

As usual with Jack, though, nothing goes the way I think it will.

He smiles and holds out a hand. "C'mere." He always seems to be able to read my mood.

When I take his hand he immediately pulls me into his arms, and I melt into him, resting my head against the shelf of his shoulder.

"Hi," he says softly, his nose nuzzling a path along my cheekbone, and I hum in response. "What are you thinking about?" His lips tickle my earlobe, sending goosebumps straight to my toes.

"That I wish I wasn't wearing chicken cutlets."

His mouth stills in its path. "I'm sorry?"

"You know, the kind of bra you have to wear with a low-back dress? Also known as sticky boobs?" He pulls away, looking perplexed. *If this freaks him out, it's a good thing I'm not wearing one of Betty's bullet bras.* "Never mind. I just meant I don't have lacy underthings ready to wow you."

He drops his forehead to my shoulder and laughs into my skin.

"What's so funny?"

"You are." He presses a soft kiss to my clavicle before straightening. "Cassie, this whole time I thought you were a virgin."

What?! I flush with embarrassment, feeling doubly self-conscious now—though I suppose I shouldn't be surprised. With how skittish I've been, why *wouldn't* he think that? "You did seem extraordinarily patient."

"I thought you were working up the nerve to tell me. I even practiced acting surprised."

I chuckle at the thought before a new concern takes its place. "Are you . . . disappointed that I'm not?" I ask hesitantly. It taps into my greatest fear, that he might actually prefer the pure and perfect Betty version of me to the real me.

His eyes search my face. "Are you kidding? Of course not."

"It's just that you haven't seemed to mind taking things slow, so I thought maybe . . . stop laughing!" I swat his chest as he laughs huskily. "Don't act like you don't know what I'm talking about, okay? There are plenty of men out there who go for the sweet and innocent type."

His eyes twinkle with humor. "Hi, were you there the night we met? I don't think anybody's mistaking you for *'sweet and innocent.'*"

I pinch his bicep through his sleeve. "Are you trying to run me out of here?"

He grabs my hand and clasps it to his chest before growing serious. "It was never about fast or slow. Cassie, my only goal was to keep you with me." He swallows, his other hand flexing on my hip. "From the very beginning I knew something was different about you. Or about *us*, I guess. I couldn't explain it. I still can't explain it, really. I just knew it felt right, to be with you. You felt it too, didn't you?"

I swallow past the lump in my throat, managing a nod.

"But I also knew that one wrong move on my part would scare you off, so I decided early on I was just going to follow your lead. I'd take whatever you were willing to give and wait as long as it took for you to feel comfortable with me." He squeezes my hand, his gaze charting a heated course all over my face. "And I think my plan worked out pretty well, don't you?"

His confession steals the breath from my lungs.

"Do you remember when we were in my kitchen, that first night you came over?" he continues, saving me from having to speak, which is a good thing because I have no idea what to say. Words, normally my currency of choice, have completely deserted me. "You were jumpy and hilarious and just . . . *so* damn beautiful. I couldn't stop staring at you. And I remember watching you across the kitchen and thinking, *What can I do to make sure she stays?* I'd give anything for her to just . . . *stay.*" He huffs a short breath. "I still think it every time I look at you. I'm in love with you too, you know. I've *been* in love with you."

My throat is raw with unshed tears as I stare up at him, so steadfast and ardent and handsome, more handsome than any man has the right to be. He's bathed in moonlight, the planes of his face cast in shadow, the pinprick reflections of the city lights sparkling in his blue-black eyes. It's unfathomable to me that there are people behind every one of those lit windows, living and breathing and going about their lives while my world is so seismically shifting on its foundations. I'm standing on a fault line, the magnitude of his revelations like an earthquake, upending everything I thought I knew.

It occurs to me that I asked him the wrong question before, about whether he was disappointed—or rather, that the person I should have been asking was *myself.* I've never regretted my past relationships, always believing they existed to help teach me something, but standing before him now as he reveals the depth of his commitment, the extent of his patience—proving his fidelity before I'd truly earned it—I wish I could wipe my slate clean. I wish I had waited for him, that I had seen him in my future, that I could have given him that gift. It's yet another epiphany for me in all this, and a testament to how profoundly I've changed: that once you find your last, you'll wish they were your only.

His expression turns mischievous, his mouth curving into a deviant smirk. "But if you really want to know the 'type' of girl I go for . . ." He tugs me to him by the hips, and I can feel his desire pressing strong and solid against my stomach. "She's about five foot six. Hazel eyes. The softest skin I've ever felt." His hands skim up my arms, feather-light, and I shiver. "Hair that leans brown or red depending on the time of day." He pulls one of my bobby pins loose and my hair starts to unravel from its messy knot. He makes a low grunt of approval and removes a few more, the rest of my hair cascading down and brushing my bare shoulders.

"She's crazy smart. Passionate." His fingers whisper across my collarbone, sensitizing my skin, and I try not to tremble. "Gorgeous." In a blink, his mouth replaces his fingers and he's pressing light, fluttering kisses along my décolletage, a slow and tortuous trail, and when his teeth nip at the hollow of my throat, a groan slips out. I let my head loll to the side to give him better access, and I can feel his smile against my skin as he winds a curving, leisurely path up my neck.

"Mouthy," he murmurs, then captures my lips, kissing me long and slow, our tongues tangling and hands grasping until we're nothing but heated skin and panting breaths and pounding hearts. Adrenaline courses through my veins; throbs at my pulse points. He slips a hand beneath the hem of my dress and starts teasing his way up my thigh, stroking and squeezing, torturing me with agonizing slowness. It feels like years pass before he reaches the thin silk at the apex of my thighs, and when he runs a finger along my wetness, I nearly disintegrate in his arms.

"Jack," I moan into his ear, and it's a plea; a warning. I'm swaying on my feet, clinging to him for dear life. *Aching* with want. Hearing his name must rob him of his restraint because he mutters an oath, roughly pushes my panties aside and sinks a finger in to the knuckle.

I groan his name again and arch my back, shuddering, surging, bucking as my hips seek further connection to his hand. I'm a bundle of raw nerves, every sense electrified, a frenzy of unfulfilled lust desperately seeking relief. My brain's emptied of all rational thought and there is only Jack's touch; Jack's heat. His finger swirls around, strong and unrelenting, and I dissolve into him, a writhing heap of nerve endings and sensations. It's so intense I have to choke back a sob. *Has it ever felt like this?* I may actually die from the pleasure.

He continues to obliterate me for an untold amount of time, his mouth swallowing down every one of my mewling cries until I'm near collapse, his strong arm wrapped around my back the only thing still keeping me upright. When he starts to withdraw slowly, devastatingly, I whimper at the loss of him, and he gives my backside a tender squeeze in consolation. He gradually slows our kiss but doesn't pull away, his lips resting just a hair's breadth away from mine.

I feel drugged. I'm in a Jack-trance and I never want to wake up. It takes superhuman effort to drag my eyes open, and when I do I know he's seeing directly into my soul. Every one of my thoughts is exposed, mined from the depths and drawn to the surface, his for the taking. I may still be fully dressed, but emotionally, I'm laid bare.

"Now what are you thinking?" His voice is husky and rough; a scrape of sandpaper against stone.

Is he actually expecting me to *speak* right now? I can barely form a coherent thought, let alone string words together. "I'm thinking . . . take me to bed or lose me forever."

He barks a laugh like I'm joking, but I've never been more serious. I want to kiss him until my lips are bruised. I want to imprint myself on his skin like invisible ink. I want to have marathon sex with him until we both need electrolytes and a Gatorade shower.

His tie is askew and his top couple of buttons undone, collateral damage from my haste to get my hands on him. He glows with health and virility, golden bronze skin peeking out from beneath his shirt, begging me to run my hands all over it. I want to ice him like a cake and lick him clean. I want to devour him whole.

I unbutton the rest of his shirt while he works to unknot his tie, the two of us grinning at each other like idiots in our race to disrobe. I'm a little giddy, but who could blame me? There's a profound relief in knowing Jack and I are finally on the same page, that there are no more secrets between us, no more emotional barriers—and soon, no physical barriers, either. This is the outcome I've dreamt about, one that seemed impossibly out of reach just a few short days ago. This is our long-awaited reward, and damnit, we've earned it.

He tosses his tie on the desk just as I unfasten the last button, and once I peel his shirt off, I press my palms to his bare chest and sigh. "Finally."

I've changed my mind; I'm no longer in a rush. The emotional roller coaster of the last hour's leveled off, our frenzied energy eased, and now I want to take my time, explore him in painstaking detail, prolong our pleasure until we're wrung out and shaking. I trail a finger from his shoulder down his biceps, taking a circuitous route around his tri-

ceps and deltoid. I trace a raised vein across muscular ter-
rain. I map his torso with my fingertips, marking every
freckle, every hair, every scar. I caress him with my hands,
learning every inch of him, committing each detail to
memory.

He starts to unbuckle his belt but I reach a hand out to
stop him. "Please let me."

My movements are not smooth or practiced. In fact,
they're clumsy and inelegant, but perhaps I'm doing it on
purpose, something inside me wanting to extend our agony,
drag out the suspense just a little longer. The jangling of his
belt buckle provokes a Pavlovian response—my mouth simultaneously waters and goes dry, my pulse breaks into a
sprint, my nipples pebble. The sound is music to my ears; it
makes my blood sing. I feel him growing even harder under
my fumbling hands and my stomach tightens in anticipation.

His suit pants have slipped low on his hips, and the
sight of his Adonis V disappearing into his waistband is so
tantalizing, I could scream. I make quick work of his zip-
per, yanking both his pants and briefs down in one fell
swoop, finally freeing him—then stare in admiration. *So
good looks aren't the only thing Jack's been blessed with.* The
man's won the genetic lottery.

I think my eyes must be big, because he chuckles. "Cat
got your tongue?"

I clamp my trap shut so drool won't spill out. "No, just
the opposite—I'm congratulating myself."

He chuckles again as he steps out of his pants and kicks
them out of the way.

"I'm trying to figure out how you've been walking around
single all this time." I let my eyes tiptoe down his body in a

shameless head-to-toe appraisal, stopping to linger on his very enthusiastic erection.

"And I'm trying to figure out how I'm naked right now and you're not," he says pointedly, reaching for me.

He won't get any argument from me—I'm desperate to feel him, skin on skin. This dress may be classy and proper, but some decidedly *im*proper things are about to go down in this hotel room, so it's got to go.

His eyes are smoldering blue fire. "Arms up."

I raise an eyebrow and then my arms, teasing and provocative, peering up at him seductively from beneath my lashes. His gaze stays locked on mine as he grabs the hem of my dress, lifting it up and over my head in one fluid movement. I'm nearly naked now . . . except for one thing.

"They really do look like chicken cutlets," he marvels as I rush to peel off the sticky boobs, giggling and batting his hands away as he tries to get a closer look. "Fascinating."

I fling them in the direction of the desk, then launch myself at him, throwing my arms around his neck and planting my lips on his—and there it is, skin-to-skin contact at long last. *Finally.* I'm enveloped in everything hard—his muscular arms flexing around me, his strong abs, his stiff arousal——and yet the way he holds me is gentle, tender, sweet. He has one hand cradling my face, fingers threaded into my hair, and the other braced against my rib cage, his large palm fanned over my breast, his thumb teasing my nipple and sending lightning bolts of desire straight to my core.

I let out a moan, and I think it triggers him to pick up the pace because his arms tighten around me and he walks us backward, guiding us toward the bed. His hand moves down to knead my ass, and now he's the one who's clumsy as he tries to tug my panties down my hips one-handed.

"These need to go," he growls against my lips, and as soon as I kick them off we tumble into the sheets, a cloud of soft linens puffing up around us, shielding us from the world.

Sensations swirl and collide in an erotic, all-consuming blur. Jack lavishes my body with attention, caressing my breasts and tracing my collarbone with his tongue, his stubble tickling my skin. I straddle his hips and nibble his ear, grinding against him while my breasts skim his chest. He kisses up my spine; noses across my navel; fists a hand in my hair. I nip and bite my way down his torso, savoring the salty-sweetness of his skin, stroking his shaft until he groans me for me to stop. He drops his head between my thighs and tastes me until my back arches off the mattress, fingers clenched and scrabbling at the sheets. His tongue is like fire licking up my skin; I'm surprised I haven't burst into flames.

Seeing him like this now, unconstrained and unleashed, I'm realizing just how much he's held himself back, how thoroughly he's subjugated his needs for mine all this time. He's insatiable and demanding, as dominant in bed as he is in life. He's indefatigable in foreplay in a way I can hardly withstand. He's taking his time, cherishing every inch of me, and it makes the rusty hinges on the door to my heart crack open that much wider. I feel *wanted*, body and soul. It's like he won't rest until he's unearthed every one of my hidden emotions, drawn out all of my deepest desires and claimed them for him and him alone.

"Please," I plead, and I'm not even sure what I'm begging for at this point—for him to end my torment, yes, but also to obliterate me, to fill this space in my soul that only he can fill, to take my heart, brand it with his initials, and never give it back.

He must hear the desperation in my voice because he settles me back against the pillows, blanketing my body with his and caging me in with the strength and sinew of his broad shoulders. Sweat's gathered at his temples, one unruly lock of hair fallen onto his forehead, and for some reason that little detail makes my heart squeeze in my chest.

He grabs my hand and pulls it above my head, lacing my fingers through his. "Don't close your eyes, okay? I want to see you."

I swallow thickly and nod, a powerful swell of emotion threatening to pull me under, and if possible, I fall deeper in love with him. *This is the most intimate moment of my entire life.*

I do as he says, staring into his eyes as he slowly guides himself inside me, inch by glorious inch—but it's when he breathes out a hoarse *I love you* that I lose all control, grabbing the back of his neck and slamming his lips down on mine. He jerks into me, burying himself to the hilt, and when I clench around him he groans into my mouth.

He starts to rock against me, his rhythm steady and deliberate, and I surrender to the pleasure, knowing he's got me, that I'm safe in his arms. Jack makes love like he does everything else—he's in control, confident and authoritative, yet still earnest and devoted in a way that makes me weak in the knees. I seem to have stumbled upon a unicorn of my own: a guy with serious alpha male energy but none of the ego that typically comes with it. He's my white whale. I've found the perfect man.

Everything I'm discovering about him sends me tumbling further down the love rabbit hole. He has a spray of freckles stippled across his shoulders that's like a hidden constellation for my eyes only, and I trace a path along them like it's my own private star chart. I'm addicted to the noises he makes—his panting breaths, broken grunts, the low groans that come from deep within his chest, as melodic and captivating as any musical notes. I press a fingertip into the dimple in his cheek, noting that I seem to have unlocked a new, boyish version of his smile. It's extraordinary to me that despite staring at his face for weeks, there are still things I'm seeing for the first time. I hope I never stop.

He moves over me, spoiling me, learning my body and minding my reactions, but it's torturous—he's setting a loose, languid pace when all I want him to do is annihilate me, press me into the mattress, suffocate me with his weight and his kisses. I writhe against him in an underhanded attempt to steal his control, but he doesn't give an inch; he won't be rushed. I think this must be part of his master plan—he wants me mindless and pliant, holding nothing back, so wild with lust that I'm twisting out of my skin, screaming his name, begging for mercy.

And maybe I'll give him what he wants. Our relationship has always thrived on competition, the push-pull dynamic between us as intoxicating as any drug, but maybe this is where I let him lead. Maybe this time, I'll let him take me where he wants to go while I relax and enjoy the ride. Going head-to-head and toe-to-toe with him has been fun, but I think I've finally found a kind of submission I can embrace. *Betty would be proud.*

Once I make that decision, it doesn't take me long to break.

Jack continues his carnal assault, his hands and tongue and body relentlessly pushing me to the limit, taking everything I have to give, and I surrender it all until I'm nothing but a quivering mass chasing release. This is the most intense sexual experience of my life, and I tell him so.

His mouth curls up. "For me too." And then: "Tell me what else you're thinking."

So I do. I tell him how sexy he is, that I've never been so attracted to someone. How I've ached for him since the night we met, and how difficult he's been to resist. I tell him what a good man I think he is, how strong and capable and admirable. I tell him how long I've fantasized about being right here, pinned beneath him and sheltered in his arms while he learns me inside and out. I tell him when he hits a spot that feels so good, so intense, I think it might split me in two.

He growls at that last one and thrusts harder, his speed picking up, hips grinding into mine until there's no more in and out, no separation between our bodies. There's only deep and deeper, our hips permanently fused, and I cry out, feeling my peak bearing down on me with each subsequent thrust—and then I'm yelling his name and gripping his biceps, body clenched and locked tight as I sail over the edge, breathless and euphoric as he joins me in finding his own release.

We lay there afterward, catching our breath and coming down from the high, and I'm almost comatose. The emotional whiplash of the day has finally caught up with me and I'm utterly spent. I'm breathless and boneless; a runner who's collapsed just past the finish line. I let out a sigh of contentment that morphs into a yawn, and Jack chuckles.

"You gonna make it?" He kisses me on the forehead and starts to withdraw, and I whine my disapproval.

"Unclear," I slur drowsily—though I manage to muster

up enough energy to roll over and ogle his naked backside as he pads over to the bathroom. "But I do know I want us to do that every day of the week and twice on Sunday."

He barks a laugh and I hear the sink turn on. "That can be arranged."

I roll onto my back again and stretch out, basking in the afterglow, luxuriating in these ridiculously soft sheets. I am never leaving this bed. We could move in here, stay forever. I wonder how long the contents of the minibar would last us.

The bathroom light flicks off a minute later and then he's walking toward me in the dim light, godlike and perfect. He's totally un-self-conscious even in nothing but his birthday suit, muscles and planes and, *ahem*, appendages all jockeying for my attention. He's the statue of David come to life, and I give myself a mental high five for landing this delicious piece of man candy. Vitality and testosterone radiate from his pores. I'd swear his skin is glittering like a fictional vampire, but I think that's just my love-goggles talking.

"That's quite a look on your face," he says.

"Shh, I'm mentally objectifying you."

He chuckles as he climbs back into bed, snuggling me against his chest and tucking the covers around us. I'm in a million-thread-count cocoon. "You know, you should be careful what you wish for. I've got months of pent-up sexual energy and you've barely scratched the surface. You won't be able to stand once I'm done with you."

"Don't threaten me with a good time." He laughs again, and the growly timbre of his voice liquefies my insides. "Actually, joke's on you, because my love language is 'acts of service.'"

He arcs an eyebrow as if to say, *And?*

"Which means I expect you to *service* me once a day, duh."

His lips twitch into a naughty smirk. "Only once a day?" His hand drifts south under the sheets, skimming over my derriere, and his lips find my neck. "That all you can handle?"

And it's funny—all of a sudden, I get a second wind.

Chapter 17

𝒲HEN I AWAKEN, I'M EXACTLY WHERE I was when I drifted off: in his arms, curled up against his side, absorbing his heat. My nose is smashed into his armpit, like even in sleep I'm desperate to soak up his pheromones. And you know what, I apologize for nothing. I'd hook myself up to a Jack IV drip if I could.

I have no idea what time it is, but I also don't really care; I'm in no hurry to leave this dreamy love-bubble we're in. I snuggle closer to him, warming all over when his arm tightens around me reflexively. I graze my fingernails through the smattering of dark chest hair dusting his torso, then have to stifle a laugh as I remember one of the weirder tips. *Frolicking in his chest hair, indeed.*

"Morning," I murmur.

"Mmm," he mumbles, and his gravelly, sleep-drenched voice instantly becomes my favorite sound in the world. He turns his head and kisses my hair without opening his eyes, and I bloom under his affection. I feel like we've been doing this for a hundred years.

I watch his chest rise and fall for a full minute, feeling deeply content. *Happy*. "How'd you sleep?" I ask, drawing lazy circles on his abdomen.

He peeks one eye open. "Is that a real question? Best night of sleep I've ever had. Totally uninterrupted. Nice long stretch."

I giggle as he brings my hand to his mouth for a kiss, and I know we're both replaying our late-night exertions, the ones that kept us up half the night until we finally collapsed in exhaustion, sweaty and sated. In fact, I'd be a total zombie right now if not for the potent post-sex adrenaline still humming through my veins. The whole night has taken on a surreal, dreamlike quality, with steamy flashbacks spooling through my mind like a silent movie.

I start grooming his mussed hair, finger-combing his bedhead. I can't stop touching him. "You have this rebellious little tuft in the front here that just doesn't want to behave." I make a few more attempts at taming said tuft before giving up.

He swipes at it with a coarse groan. "It's extremely annoying."

"No, I like it. It's a rule breaker. You're always so put together and on point, it's nice to see you this way." Unguarded and vulnerable—a side of him only I get to see.

It's something I've been thinking about a lot lately, that I want to lighten his load, give him permission to slack off, be a source of fun and play in his life. Barring last night's theatrics, he's always so buttoned-up and controlled, rarely stepping out of line, forever carrying the weight of the world on his shoulders. It must be exhausting to be the responsible one all the time.

He yawns and stretches, and I study the way his ab

muscles flex and bunch like I'll be tested on it later. "What do you want to do today?"

"This."

He laughs and rolls to face me, a smile in his eyes. "I feel like we'll eventually need to eat."

I pout at the idea of leaving this bed. So much for those change-of-address forms I've been mentally filling out. "How about room service?" I suggest hopefully. A bulletproof compromise if I've ever heard one.

"We could probably use some other clothes," he says pragmatically, and honestly, his logic is getting annoying.

"Ugh, fine." I'm tempted to sing that he's a party pooper on par with *Father of the Bride*'s George Banks, but because I am mature, I refrain.

I throw off the covers and roll out of bed, and when I stand and stretch his eyes track over my body in a look so heated, it singes my skin. "Could you do that again? Maybe just a little slower?"

"I'm sorry, but *someone* has to eat," I say with exaggerated emphasis as I cross the room. "Someone is *starving*." I retrieve my panties from the desk and bend over provocatively, sliding them on in super-slow-mo.

I'm gratified by the choking noise he makes behind me. "Now that's just cruel."

I toss a satisfied smirk over my shoulder and grab my purse from the desk before heading into the bathroom, helping myself to the plush white robe hanging on the back of the door. *Is this cashmere? My word.* I wonder how hard it would be to smuggle this thing out of here—though without a suitcase, I'm guessing pretty hard. Maybe I can throw it on over my dress and pass it off as a couture coat. *It's called fashion, people.* Honestly, it'd be worth the funny looks just to get an upgrade from the cheap waffle-weave number I've been rocking since college. *This is the kind of fanciness I can get behind, thankyouverymuch Jack.*

I do my business, then wash my face and attempt to tame my mane, which is an unmitigated disaster following last night's erotic escapades. Thank goodness for small favors because there's a complimentary toiletry kit set out on the sink that miraculously includes a toothbrush. *All hail swanky hotels.* I could get used to this.

I give up trying to make my hair look presentable and pull out my phone, wincing with guilt when I realize I never checked in with Nat after last night's spectacle. She probably thinks I've been out burying Jack's body—and knowing her, she's got several airtight alibis locked and loaded.

The phone starts vibrating and dinging with messages as soon as I boot it up, and *whoa*—sixty-three text messages, twenty-three voice mails. "What the . . ."

I scroll through my call log first—there are several voice mails from Nat, three from my sister, one from my parents, and a ton from unknown numbers. *Did Nat call everyone I know looking for me?* Great, now I'm queasy at the thought of having to explain my disappearing act. *Sorry everyone, I was too busy having multiple orgasms to answer your calls?* No.

I switch over to my text messages. As expected, a slew of them are from Nat: Where are you? Are you okay? and CALL ME and Seriously, call me right now, 911. But I zero in on one from a college friend I haven't heard from in months—since her wedding last year, in fact—and click on it.

Sarah: OMG Cass, is this true? I couldn't believe it when Doug showed it to me!

Beneath her text there's a link to an article from *Page Six*, and I click on it with a mounting sense of dread. I sink down onto the closed toilet lid while the page loads—then gasp when the headline pops up.

BRAWLER FOUNDER HAS MELTDOWN AT STAR-STUDDED SIREN PARTY

Top names in media were shocked Friday night when Brawler founder Jack Bradford got into a heated public argument with another guest during Siren's glittering annual Women of the Year gala.

The famously private cofounder of the controversial men's lifestyle website and digital media company stunned onlookers when he and his rumored girlfriend, identified as Siren writer Cassidy Sutton, got into a fiery spat right in the midst of the flashy festivities.

Sources at the party told Page Six that Bradford appeared belligerent and possibly intoxicated, loudly berating Sutton while her stunned coworkers, an assortment of celebrity honorees, and a who's-who of media elite looked on. The explosive exchange culminated in Sutton storming out of the party, with Bradford close behind.

While the motive for the brawl remains unclear, witnesses claim that Bradford wasn't trying to hide his animosity.

"It almost seemed like he was *trying* to cause a scene," one partygoer observed.

When reached for comment, Siren CEO and founder Cynthia Barnes-Cooke said in a statement, "It's unfortunate that this incident has distracted from the evening's fundamental purpose: to honor our many esteemed and accomplished women of influence."

Other employees were less diplomatic. "It's outrageous that anyone from Brawler would dare show their face at our event," sniped one Siren staffer who declined to be identified. "The toxic patriarchal culture they promote has no place in modern media." Another Siren source downplayed the spat, chalking it up to a "lovers' quarrel."

It's the latest chapter in the long-running feud between the dueling media companies and founders, at professional odds since the launches of their respective sites a decade ago. While their journalistic sparring is par for the course, an in-person clash appears to be a significant escalation.

News of the skirmish comes at an awkward time for Bradford, as industry rumors swirl about his future at Brawler amid reports he's selling his stake in the digital media juggernaut. Insiders voiced surprise at the brouhaha, noting that Brawler cofounder and professional provocateur Tom Bartlett is typically the one generating negative headlines, with Bradford widely regarded as the company's stabilizing influence. No word on how potential investors will feel about two erratic captains steering the ship.

Holy shit.

Well, this is bad. *Really* bad.

I set the phone down on the vanity with shaking hands, pulse pounding in my throat. There are so many thoughts ping-ponging around my brain that I can hardly make sense of any of them. *How did I get myself into this mess? Everyone I know is going to read this. Jack's trying to sell his stake in Brawler? My career is ruined. Why didn't I see this coming? Jack is going to be devastated.*

The last one leaves me frozen, and I think I'm going to be sick. *I have to go out there and show this to him.* I have to walk out of this bathroom and ruin his life, taking a chainsaw to all our beautiful memories of last night in the process. Even worse is the knowledge that I'm the catalyst for all of this. If I hadn't treated him like a pawn in my stupid game, none of this would ever have gotten this far.

I steel myself, take a deep breath, and open the door—then see the world has already beaten me to it.

Jack's sitting on the edge of the bed, his back to me, hunched over his phone. From his body language, I can tell immediately that he knows. "Jack?"

He doesn't move.

I cross the room and sit down on the bed next to him. "Jack." I put my hand on his back and he stiffens.

He turns his head to look at me, but his gaze is vacant. "What is this?"

"I don't know. I just saw it myself."

"Did you plan this?"

I recoil. "Excuse me?"

"You heard me." His voice is cold and hard. *Accusing.* "Did you have a hand in this?"

I gape at him in disbelief. *"Me?* You're the one who walked into a roomful of reporters and acted like a raving lunatic! Which you haven't exactly apologized for, by the way. What did you think was gonna happen?"

"So it's just a coincidence that for months you planned to write a story exactly like this, and today it just magically appeared? Wow, that sure is some *interesting* timing."

I stare at him as an old, familiar voice wakes from a long hibernation, shakes off the dust bunnies, and whispers in my ear like the ghost of boyfriends past: *Strike one.*

I push the thought away. *He's in shock; give him the benefit of the doubt.* "Look, I know you're upset. I'm upset too. But this affects both of us, and lashing out at me isn't going to fix it."

He snorts in derision. "Both of us. *Right.* This?" He holds up his phone. "Is a hit piece."

He stands abruptly and hurls his phone across the bed, and I flinch when it bounces off the headboard with a loud *crack.* He goes to the desk and grabs his pants, yanking them on aggressively while I stare down at my lap, nausea roiling my stomach.

Silence hangs over the room like a storm cloud, heavy and ominous, until one of the article's bombshells comes into sharper focus. "Wait a minute, what does this mean, you're trying to sell your stake in Brawler? Is that true?"

He doesn't respond, keeping his back to me as he jerks on his shirt.

"You are," I say in astonishment, awareness dawning. "Why wouldn't you tell me that?"

"Because the deal isn't done! If there even *is* a deal anymore," he says curtly, still turned away from me. "And it was supposed to be confidential. I couldn't discuss it with anyone, least of all you."

His spiteful words batter me like a spray of bullets. "What does that mean?"

He exhales loudly, finally spinning around to face me. "What do you think it means? You're a journalist! I obviously couldn't share sensitive details of a major financial deal with a rival."

It's jarring, how quickly he's swung from tender and flirtatious to cold and callous. Not five minutes ago we were cuddling in bed while he cooed sweet nothings in my ear, and now all I want to do is slink off like an injured animal and lick my wounds. "So now I'm a journalist? I thought I was your girlfriend."

He huffs as he buttons his shirt cuffs. "Yeah, I thought so too. And then I found out you were an undercover reporter trying to destroy my life."

You deserve that. Stand here and take it, Cassidy.

I'm not oblivious to what's happening here. Jack's looking for someone to blame and I'm an easy target, but he's taking it too far. I had nothing to do with this story, and I refuse to be his scapegoat.

I draw myself up to my full height, crossing my arms and doing my best to look intimidating—though I'm not sure how intimidating one can look in a fluffy white bathrobe and hotel slippers. "So that's what this is really about, then? I lied to you, and now you want to punish me for it. Any argument we ever have, months from now—hell, *years* from now—you're going to throw this back in my face."

"It hasn't been years!" he explodes, and I shrink back, my bravado evaporating in an instant. "It's been *one day* since I found out you lied to me! What do you expect me to say? That I believe you? That I trust you unconditionally? Trust is *earned*." He tugs a hand through his hair and pivots, pacing away a few steps before turning back and throwing out an arm. "I haven't even told my employees I'm selling, and now it's splashed across the front page! This isn't just some stupid article meant to smear me. It's my entire livelihood that's at stake. It's the past ten years of my life!"

I feel his fury like a stab to the gut. "Look, I understand why you—"

"No Cassie, you *don't* understand," he cuts me off, voice raised, and I take a step back. I've never seen him like this.

When threatened, most people choose fight or flight; Jack apparently chooses both. "You have no idea what I've sacrificed for this job—friends, family members. A *life*. I've put everything I have into building this company. I've been working on this deal for a *year*. You can't possibly understand how high the stakes are right now."

"Does that seem healthy to you? Seriously Jack, do you hear yourself? Is the success really worth it if it comes at the expense of everything else in your life?"

He smiles sardonically. "While I appreciate the concern for my work-life balance, you'll have to forgive me if I don't take career advice from someone living their life on the sidelines."

His words hit me like a sucker punch. "What is that supposed to mean?"

"It means how's that book coming, Cass?" His dark eyes hold a sharp glint and it's all I can do to maintain eye contact, so stunned am I by his vindictiveness. I'm a creature in distress and instead of handling me with care, he's going in for the kill. "For something you claim to be so passionate about, you sure aren't in any hurry to get started."

"Now you're just being cruel," I whisper, humiliation burning through me. *Strike two.*

"Am I? Or am I just being honest? I may have taken things too far last night, but I didn't say anything that wasn't true. You're the one who told me your job is unfulfilling. So why are you still there?"

I stare back at him, mute with shock, and now it's hurt pulsing through me, overriding the shame. He has no way of knowing that he's prodding an open wound, that in echoing Cynthia's harsh criticism he's confirming my worst fears about myself. *He thinks you're a coward, too.* My already shredded dignity goes from small to microscopic.

"Not so simple to walk away, is it?" he hammers me, failing to recognize that I'm teetering on the brink of a massive breakdown; one more jab and I'll topple right over the edge. "I've worked my ass off to get here and I'm finally at the finish line, and I'll be damned if *this* is going to ruin it."

His words pierce the air like a clap of thunder. "And by 'this,' you mean me."

Something in my voice must snap him out of his fit of temper because he blinks, the worst of the hostility draining from his eyes, and for the first time since he launched into this diatribe I see a glimpse of the Jack I know. "That's not what I said."

"But it's what you meant." *Strike three. Strike three through infinity, actually.* "I get it, Jack. Your job is your priority. It's more important to you than anything—or anyone—else. Message received, loud and clear."

And that's the truth of it, as much as I wish it wasn't. Jack's work is his North Star, his most valuable asset, his constant companion throughout a tumultuous and lonely personal life. It's driven his decision-making for more than a *decade*. Did I really expect to usurp that role overnight? Where can I expect to rank on his list of priorities—a distant second, if I'm lucky? Just because he's become the most important person in my life doesn't mean I am in his.

I feel like such an idiot; a lovesick puppy that's just been kicked. I've been serving my heart up on a silver platter to a man who's already spoken for, who will never fully offer his in return. My past concerns about being a weekend sports widow seem almost quaint now in retrospect. And the worst part is, anyone could have seen this coming a mile away. Cynthia sure did. The question she asked me in her office now feels painfully prophetic: *If this same opportunity was in front of Jack, would he be sacrificing himself the same way you are?*

I'm heartbroken to have gotten my answer.

His hand flexes at his side. "You're putting words in my mouth."

I force a laugh, mostly so I won't start crying. My throat feels like it's closing up. "I'm really not. But anyway, you should go." I hate that my voice trembles—if ever there was a time I wanted to project indifference, it's now. "You have things to take care of . . . messes to clean up. That's where you should be. Not here." *Please, please leave before I lose it completely.*

I'm giving him an out, granting him permission to do what I know he wants to—leave me behind so he can deal with the fallout on his own, assess the damage to his business without my emotional deadweight dragging him down. And as much as I wish he wanted to stay with me and weather this storm as a team, I don't want him doing so out of guilt. Even if all else is lost—my career, my reputation, this relationship—I still have my pride.

But he's not exactly rushing out the door. In fact, he looks so conflicted that I almost feel sorry for him. His haste to get dressed has left him looking a disheveled mess, like an alcoholic after an all-night bender: hair rumpled, shoes untied, shirt buttoned but untucked, tie spilling out from the pants pocket where he's haphazardly shoved it. He looks as wrecked as I feel. And yet, despite how angry I am at him and how badly he's let me down, he's still the most beautiful man I've ever seen. I'm still in love with him, and that knowledge is a crushing blow.

He's watching me closely, as though gauging my sincer-ity (or perhaps just guarding against a rogue right hook). Whatever he sees on my face prompts him to take a step to-ward me, but I hold up a hand to stop him.

"Please don't." *If you touch me, I'll lose my nerve.*

I can't identify the emotion behind his eyes—uncertainty? regret?—but I force myself to hold his gaze so he knows that I'm serious, that I'm not changing my mind. *I want you to leave*—and it's this lie, out of all the others I've told, that fi-nally breaks me.

I spin around, turning my back to him and pressing my knuckles into the corners of my eyes in a desperate attempt to stave off the tears. *Do not let him see you cry. Wait until he's gone to fall apart.* And I do exactly that, waiting until I hear the door open and swing shut behind me before I let out a sob and crumple onto the bed.

I lay there for a while, just letting myself cry and wal-low in my hurt feelings. I can hardly wrap my head around how quickly this situation soured, how swiftly things went from the highest high to the lowest low. I can hear my phone going berserk in the bathroom, which only intensi-fies my distress. The thought of dealing with the prying questions and inevitable gossip on top of this heartbreak is almost too much to bear. I want to crawl under these covers, pull the sheets over my head and never come out. I want to hide from the world, disappear from my own life, and trans-plant into someone else's like I'm in witness protection. I feel trapped; hunted. And because I'm part of this industry, I know exactly how this will play out: The press will circle me like vultures until they go in for the kill, picking my life apart piece by piece until there's nothing left worth saving. *Until I'm as dead inside as I am out.*

I breathe a sigh of relief when the buzzing finally stops, but it's short-lived; it immediately starts up again. And as much as I want to shut the world out and pretend this isn't happening, I need to face the music sometime (or at least call an Uber so I can escape this godforsaken hotel room). I heave myself off the bed and stumble over to the bathroom, and when I see who's calling—Christine—I'm suddenly desperate to hear her voice.

"Hey," I shudder out, trying to get my emotions under control.

"WHERE HAVE YOU *BEEN*?" she yells, and I have to hold the phone away from my head so as to not shatter my eardrum. "I've spent half the night trying to find you!"

"I was with Jack." Just saying his name aloud triggers a fresh round of tears and I have to take a couple of deep breaths before continuing. "I had my phone off. I know you're probably wondering what's going on, but I don't think I can talk about it without bawling."

There's a beat of silence. "So you talked to Mom and Dad, then? They said they couldn't reach you."

"Mom and Dad? No," I say, confused, sinking down onto the edge of the bed. "I haven't talked to anyone. Why?"

There's another pause. "Is Jack there with you now?"

"*No*. Christine, tell me what's going on."

She exhales. "Sorry, I'm just confused. You sound upset, so I assumed you heard about Gran."

My heart stops. "What *about* Gran?" *Please God, no.*

"She wasn't answering her phone, so Dad went over there and she was acting funny. Confused and slurring her words, couldn't get out of bed. They think she had a stroke."

I barely make it to the toilet before I retch.

Chapter 18

*T*HE NEXT FEW WEEKS ARE A TOP-TO-BOTTOM life upheaval—for both Gran and me.

Upon checking her into the hospital, doctors determined that Gran had, in fact, suffered a mild stroke, and while the left side of her body was not quite paralyzed, she was experiencing substantial weakness that would permanently affect her mobility unless she underwent aggressive physical therapy. Surprising absolutely no one, Gran flat-out refused to convalesce anywhere but her own home, which meant she needed round-the-clock, live-in care (which—you guessed it—she also rejected, insisting that she "didn't want strangers in her house"). As an alternative, doctors suggested a family member temporarily move in to oversee Gran's rehab needs— a job I quickly volunteered for.

It was an obvious solution. With both of my siblings busy raising families of their own and the physical demands of her care a lot for my sixty-something parents to take on, this was one circumstance where my youth and perpetual singledom could actually come in handy. I may not be adding any branches to the family tree, but this was a way in which I could positively contribute. Besides, I found myself with an abundance of free time ever since giving my notice at Siren. What better way to spend it than with Gran?

While my grateful parents lauded my selfless sacrifice, the truth is that the situation suited me perfectly. I wanted to go into hiding, and holing up at my grandmother's 1970s ranch in Connecticut is about as off-the-grid as it gets. Breaking my lease proved surprisingly simple; in fact, think I did Nat a favor—it gave her an excuse to move in with Gabriel without shouldering the guilt of abandoning me. It's about as much lemonade as I can make out of a situation with a serious dearth of lemons.

All I knew was, I needed to get out of New York. Everything I previously found romantic about the city now triggered heartache: the leaf-strewn paths of Central Park, the cozy couples huddled together at crowded sidewalk restaurants, the rows of stately brownstones, even the frenetic energy of Times Square. Every landmark was tainted, haunted by the ghost of him. Around every corner was a memory that stopped me in my tracks, stealing my breath and my peace, relentlessly reminding me of everything I'd lost.

It was like a nuclear bomb went off in the hotel room that morning, blowing up every area of my life at once. As I'd feared, the *Page Six* piece proved to be just the tip of the tabloid iceberg. In the weeks following the gala, a slew of additional news outlets picked up the story, the tale of another Brawler mogul behaving badly apparently too juicy to pass up. While I didn't escape unscathed—I probably deleted a hundred "request for comment" voice mails and emails in the days following the dustup—my no-name status in the media world clearly worked in my favor. I faded from the headlines fairly quickly, all things considered, while Jack bore the brunt of the bad press—though true to form, he never addressed the controversy in any sort of official statement.

Much worse than the sleazy gossip columnists digging for dirt on my personal life, though, is the fact that I haven't heard from Jack since he walked out the door of that hotel room.

It's strange. I think a part of me expected a cooling-off period, maybe even a couple of days of radio silence, or at least until he had a chance to take control of our (admittedly chaotic) situation. But I also assumed that once the shock wore off and he had a chance to calm down, he'd show up with his tail between his legs and apologize for reacting the way he did, for berating and accusing me, for leaving me to fend for myself when I needed his protection the most.

Boy, was I wrong.

It's been weeks and I haven't seen hide nor hair of him. Despite the way we left things, I'm stunned by his indifference, that he could cast me aside like yesterday's mail, then carry on like I never existed. *Like none of it ever happened.* How could he spend the night making love to me, confessing his feelings in a way I know was heartfelt and true, then walk away without looking back?

I've never been an overly emotional person, even-keeled and unflappable to a fault, but nowadays I find myself cycling through the five stages of grief multiple times a day. My mood swings from sad to hopeful to bitter so frequently I get whiplash. One minute I'm so angry I could kill him with my bare hands, the next I miss him so much I can hardly breathe. Some days I tell myself I'm better off, punctuating the point by taking a Peloton revenge ride and belting out girl-power anthems at the top of my lungs (*I can love me better than he can, damnit!*). But on others, the fog of depression is so thick I feel like I'll never claw my way out of it. Couple that with the anxiety surrounding Gran's fragile health, and my tears are on a constant hair trigger.

I think it's the unanswered questions that hurt the most; the lack of closure. I realize I could reach out to Jack myself (and you better believe I've fantasized about showing up at his apartment and demanding atonement for his sins like a disgruntled *Bachelor* contestant), but I can't ignore that in cutting me out of his life he's sent me a very clear message, and how I choose to receive it is the one thing that's still up to me. I don't know why he's ghosted me—the job, the breach of trust, the scandal, some combination of the three—but none of it really matters because he's made his choice, and there isn't a thing I can do to change it. I can fall to pieces or make a fool of myself chasing after a man who's rejected me, or I can accept responsibility for the role I played in our relationship's demise, learn from my mistakes, and move on with my life.

It was with that resolve in mind that I made another big decision: to quit my job at Siren and finally start writing my book.

Once the dust surrounding my newfound notoriety settled, I sat down with Cynthia to see if I even still *had* a job. I figured she'd welcome my resignation—it would save her the trouble of having to fire me—but was surprised to find it was just the opposite. After apologizing profusely for Jack's and my antics overshadowing the event, she informed me that the drama and subsequent press avalanche had resulted in a traffic spike that broke Siren records, making it the most widely publicized Women of the Year party ever. (And, ironically, netting me the week's $100 bonus. Cold comfort, but I'll take wins where I can get 'em right now.)

But after I explained the circumstances of Gran's health and my now not-so-secret dream of writing a book, she encouraged me to take the leap, even offering to get my manuscript in front of the right people when the time comes. Her vote of confidence helped solidify my decision to leave—as did her promise that no matter what, there'd always be a job for me at Siren.

Moving on felt both inevitable and sudden, but ultimately, it was time. I'd grown stagnant in that job, a fact I'd avoided acknowledging for quite some time. Siren had become a crutch, an excuse not to take risks, and there's nothing like being confronted by a loved one's mortality to make you reconsider your life choices in a hurry. Besides, would there ever be a better time to go after this big, daunting dream than while on sabbatical in Connecticut? (At least, that's how I'm framing this phase of my life to anyone who asks—it sounds better than "committing career suicide.") And while I don't want to jinx it, so far the writing's actually been going pretty well. Who knew intense heartbreak and personal anguish would be just the thing to break through my writer's block? (I mean, besides Taylor Swift.)

Another unexpected benefit of being in Connecticut? Proximity to my parents, as well as my sister, Greg, and my sweet nieces. I haven't spent this much time with my extended family since I left for college, and I'm determined to cherish every minute of this unexpected sojourn—starting today, with Adeline's fourth birthday party.

"Hellooo," I call out as I let myself in Christine and Greg's front door, juggling an armload of gifts and smacking directly into a wall of rainbow streamers hanging from the ceiling. I'm spitting crepe paper out of my mouth when I hear feet thundering on the upstairs landing.

"Aunt Cassidy!" the girls shriek as they race down the stairs, and I barely manage to drop the bags before Addie jumps into my arms.

"There she is! My big birthday girl," I exclaim, squeezing her as tight as I can while she squeals with delight. "Wow, you are really looking older. I forget, how old are you turning? Three?"

She looks deeply insulted, jaw dropping to reveal a bright blue tongue. "No!"

"Two?" I guess, playing dumb. "I don't know, you look too tall for two."

I can smell her sweet, sugary candy breath as she inspects my dangly earrings with interest. "I'm *five!*"

I tilt my head. "Hmm, I think you might be fibbing. And you know what happens to fibbers . . ." I warn in a mock-threatening tone, whipping my hand out from behind my back.

She shrieks. "Not the tickle monster!" She starts thrashing and wriggling, twisting out of my grasp, and I just barely manage to set her down before she takes off at a sprint. *Sheesh, these toddlers are stronger than they look.* I just got a better arm workout in two minutes than after an hour at Orangetheory.

I turn to Ella, patiently waiting her turn, and ruffle her hair. "How's my favorite big sister? Ready for the party?"

"Yeah. I wish it was my birthday, though," she says, gazing wistfully at my gift bags.

"Hmm. Does it have to be your birthday to receive a gift?"

Her eyes light up. "Did you bring me something?"

Pssh, did I bring her something. This ain't my first aunt rodeo, darlin'. I learned long ago that if you bring gifts for one kid and not the other, you may as well be firing the opening shots of World War III.

"This one's for you," I tell her, handing her a glittery pink gift bag, and she beams. *Thank God it's so easy to buy children's affection.* "And these are hers. Maybe you can go put them on the gift table? But don't let your sister tear into them yet, I want to watch her open them." And watch Christine's head explode when she sees what I got her: a set of "artist-quality" (read: permanent) markers, a toy bullhorn (with built-in siren function!), plus a few hideously tacky stuffed animals sure to make my clutter-phobic sister start twitching.

"We're in here," Christine calls out from the kitchen, and I *Mission Impossible* my way through the crepe paper maze crisscrossing the hallway until I make it to the kitchen, and *hoo boy*, does it look like a party store threw up in here. I greet Christine, who's standing at the island ripping open boxes of Capri Sun while Greg empties bags of ice into a galvanized metal drink stand.

I stash my purse away, then spin in a circle, surveying the room. *Talk about sensory overload.* Streamers dangle from every available surface, while bunches of balloons float up from chair backs and doorknobs and litter the floor. A color-coded array of chips, candy, and desserts cram a crowded snack table set up in the corner. The only thing I can't really make sense of is the . . . well, *eclectic* assortment of posters taped up all over the walls.

"So far I'm seeing unicorns, mermaids, flamingos, nar-whals, and . . ." I squint. "Are those pirates?"

Christine dumps the Capri Suns out on the countertop, knocking over a stack of Dixie cups in the process. "Addie took some artistic license with the under-the-sea theme."

Greg chortles. "What she means is that she took Addie to Party City at the end of a very long day and had lost her will to fight."

"Under the sea, huh? I'm not sure that would have been my first guess . . . or second or third," I say, picking up a skull and crossbones centerpiece and setting it down.

Christine blows some hair out of her eyes. "Just wait until you have kids and then talk to me about the weird shit you end up doing for them."

"Yeah, well, no danger of that happening anytime soon," I say wryly, then catch the two of them exchange a look out of the corner of my eye.

"How's Gran?" Christine asks as I make myself comfortable on one of their counter stools.

"She's fine. You know how she is, doesn't want us fussing over her." I grab a handful of gummy sharks from one of the candy dishes set out on the island and pretend not to notice her dirty look. "She sent a gift, which I just gave to Ella."

"I put the girls in charge of filling the goody bags. I realize that means they're probably eating more candy than is actually making it into the bags, but I just needed them out of my hair for a bit so I could get things set up."

"I don't think they were eating any," I lie, crossing my fingers behind my back. "Anyway, here I am, reporting for duty early as requested. How can I help?"

"Greg?" Christine prompts, but he just grunts, too focused on his ice task to respond, apparently. "*Greg*," she tries again, this time in a warning tone, and when he looks up they proceed to have an entirely nonverbal discussion consisting of laser stares, stern eyebrows, and aggressive head tilts.

I eye them warily. "Do you two need a minute? I can go check on the girls." *And definitely not sample any of the candy they're hoarding.*

"No, we do not need a minute." She gives him a withering look, and I'll say this for him, he holds up under pressure far better than I did growing up. Just one of her penetrating glares and I would have folded like a cheap suit.

Their standoff continues for another few seconds before she throws up her hands and turns to me. "So, slight confession: We asked you to come over early under false pretenses."

"What does that mean?" I slide my eyes between the two of them, trying to decode their bizarre body language. "You don't need help?"

"Actually, I do need help," she says, pushing a stack of paper in front of me and passing me a pair of scissors. "Will you start cutting those out? It's for their craft."

"Don't give her *scissors*," Greg hisses.

I exhale loudly and toss the scissors down. "Alright, enough. You guys are being weird, even for you. What's going on?"

Christine narrows a pointed look at her husband. "*Greg* has something he wants to tell you."

I swivel my head his direction and raise my eyebrows. "Well? Spit it out."

He presses his lips together and looks heavenward before meeting my eyes again. "It was me."

I look from him to Christine and back again. "*What* was you?"

He blows out a breath. "I was the one who blew your cover with Jack. I told him about your story."

A heavy silence descends on the kitchen, and I blink at him while he rushes to explain. "I swear I didn't mean to! We were at the baseball game and it just sort of slipped out. And then I tried to backtrack but it just made it worse, and he was asking me all these questions and I couldn't come up with a lie quick enough and it all just . . . came out." He closes his eyes and shakes his head, looking tortured. "I feel terrible about it, Cass. I can't believe how badly I screwed things up for you. Everything that happened is my fault, and I want you to know I will *never* forgive myself."

I listen silently, keeping my face carefully neutral. "I didn't realize you even knew about the story," I tell him, sliding my gaze to Christine.

Now it's her turn to look guilty. "I'm sorry. I ended up telling him later, after our double date. He kept making comments about how weird you were at that dinner and he wouldn't let it go, so I finally just filled him in. Which was obviously my mistake." She aims a sharp glare Greg's way and he hangs his head in shame.

"I see."

"I realize there probably isn't anything I can do to make it up to you, but if there is, please tell me," Greg says miserably. "You can hit me if you want. I deserve it." He braces his hands against the countertop, like I'm actually going to hurtle across the island and slug him.

I sigh. "I don't want to hit you."

"I really think you should hit me. It might make you feel better. It would *definitely* make me feel better. Seriously

Cass, I feel so guilty about this. I feel like I've ruined your entire life."

"Gee, thanks a lot," I say with a stilted laugh, trying not to feel offended. "Am I really that pathetic?"

He looks at me beseechingly. "You know what I mean. Jack dumped you, you got fired, you had to move in with your grandmother to wait out the scandal—"

Now I'm *definitely* offended. "Excuse me, I did *not* get fired. I quit my job."

He eyes Christine sideways. "Oh-kay."

I growl and grab one of the Capri Suns to launch at his head, but he ducks at the last second and it bounces off the tile backsplash behind him. "I did not get fired! But you know what, now I *do* feel like punching you."

"Okay, okay," Christine says, stepping between us just as I'm rounding the island. "Please don't beat my husband up before the party, visible injuries will be hard for me to explain to the other parents. And Greg, for the love of God, *stop* talking."

I fake-lunge at him like a schoolyard bully and smirk when he flinches. *Wuss.*

"The point is, Greg's been feeling awful about this. He didn't want to make things worse by bringing it up while we were dealing with all the Gran stuff, but we both agreed it was time to be up-front with you." She grabs my hand and squeezes it, offering me a sad smile. "We hate that we played any role in this, especially since all we want is to see you happy. We really are so sorry, Cass."

The sympathy in her eyes brings my simmering emotions right back to the surface, and now I'm fighting back tears for what feels like the millionth time this month. "I know you are." I exhale a slow breath, deciding to end

Greg's suffering. "And I appreciate you guys coming clean, but here's the thing: I already knew."

Greg's head snaps up. "What do you mean, you knew?"

"I guess I shouldn't say I *knew*, since Jack didn't tell me one way or another, but I strongly suspected. Think about it: One day everything was normal and fine between us and the next it wasn't—and the only thing that happened in between was you guys went to a baseball game." I shrug ruefully. "It doesn't take a rocket scientist to put two and two together."

Greg groans. "I'm the worst. Do you hate me? I would hate me."

"Stop, of course I don't hate you. Anyway, it's not your fault. Jack was going to find out the truth one way or another, and it should have been from me. I never should have asked Christine to lie for me to begin with. The only person I have to blame for all of this is myself." *And I'm certainly paying the price.*

"I think you can blame Greg a little," Christine quips, then leans in to whisper in my ear, "Milk this for all it's worth."

"Fine, and Greg." I wink to let him know I'm kidding.

Greg clears his throat. "Not to bring up a sore subject, but we couldn't help seeing some of the headlines this week." He glances at Christine, and *oof*, they're both wearing their "concerned parent" faces. I brace myself, knowing exactly where this is headed. "You hanging in there? It's got to be hard, seeing him in the news like that."

I shrug half-heartedly, because what can I say, really? Of course I saw the news—it was impossible to miss.

It appears that the momentous, decade-in-the-making business deal Jack was so determined to protect finally went through, so it's official: He's sold his stake in Brawler—and for a truly eye-popping sum. It's the kind of money that blows your hair back, that ensures you'll never have to work another day in your life. And while that big, impressive number might be the thing that preoccupies most people, the only thing I wondered when I saw the headlines was whether he had anyone to celebrate with; if anyone told him they were proud of him.

"Well, enough about him. I'm making it my mission to find you a new guy," Greg says decisively. "The *right* guy this time."

"Oh yeah? You'll be my own personal Chris Harrison?" I tease, sidestepping his offer with a joke. There is no part of me that would even consider dating right now, but I'll humor him because I know he's just trying to help and I don't want him to feel worse. And that's what someone who's heartbroken does, right? Pretends, goes through the motions, "acts as if" until suddenly, one day, you wake up to realize the ache is gone and your heart has healed.

Even if the thought of that breaks my heart in a completely different way.

"Absolutely," Greg avows. "But instead, what I will promise you is the *least* dramatic relationship ever."

"Phew," I tell him, mock-wiping my brow. "I've had enough drama to last me a lifetime. Though I think we may need to hold off on the matchmaking for the time being. I'm afraid I don't have much to offer a man at the moment." I feel like one of the girls' worn-out baby dolls: battered and broken, sporting a bald patch and missing a limb.

"How's the writing going?" Christine asks, coming to my rescue with a subject change.

"Shh," I whisper, giving her the *zip-it* hand signal.

"Why are we whispering?" she whispers back.

"It's going well, but we must speak of it in hushed tones, then knock on wood three times so as not to anger the gods or the Muse or whichever divine entity has blessed me with this small winning streak." I reach for another gummy shark and she smacks my hand.

"And you won't give me one single hint about what it is you're writing?"

I shake my head firmly. "You will find out when I'm finished and not a minute sooner. Sorry not sorry."

She snorts, then puts Greg to work cutting ("part of his penance") and pours us some wine ("if it's in a Dixie cup, it doesn't count") and bowls of Goldfish ("practically a charcuterie board").

She leans her elbows on the island, considering me thoughtfully as she munches, party prep all but forgotten. "I know these last few weeks have been hard on you, but I can't help thinking at least some of it was meant to be."

"You mean my entire life had to fall apart for me to finally decide to follow my dreams?" I joke. "Because I could do without that particular brand of karma."

"Oh stop, you know that's not what I meant. I just think maybe certain things worked out the way they were supposed to. You stepping in to help Gran, us being nearby to support you through a rough patch, you getting a chance to pause and catch your breath and focus on your future. I know you may not see it that way because the circumstances weren't ideal, but you made a lot of really big, brave decisions most people wouldn't have the guts to make. Honestly, I'm in awe of you."

Well, that does it—my eyes blow right past misty into full-blown fire hoses. "You know I'm not emotionally stable enough to receive compliments right now," I blubber, dabbing at my eyes with the anchor-print napkin she passes me.

"Too bad, you're getting 'em," she says, leaning over to hug my neck. "As Kris Jenner would say: You're doing amazing, sweetie."

Now I'm laughing through my tears. "Welp, I don't know about the *'brave'* part, but I am working on it," I say through sniffles. "You know what I was thinking about the other day? Mrs. Williams' class. Do you remember it?"

"Of course I remember! She was our kindergarten teacher," Christine explains to a bemused Greg. "She kept this giant iguana as the class pet."

"And on our birthday, she'd give each of us a birthday balloon."

"She had a helium tank in her classroom and everything!" Christine adds gleefully.

"That's right. So she'd give us our birthday balloon, and then we'd have to decide if we wanted to keep it to take it home, or"—I pause for dramatic effect—"pop it."

Christine hoots and smacks the counter while Greg just shakes his head at us wearily. *Tough luck, bud, you're getting dragged down memory lane whether you like it or not.*

"You have to understand how terrifying this was for a six-year-old," I insist. "She literally made you go after it with a thumbtack! The loud popping noise was bad enough, but I think the anticipation of it was even worse." I shudder. "So naturally, all the boys popped theirs because they needed to prove how brave they were."

"Let me guess," Greg says to Christine with a smirk. "You popped yours."

"Of course I popped mine," she says, indignant. "I had to impress Joey Watson, duh."

"And I, of course, did not. Because I've been a wimp since birth." I toss back my Dixie cup of wine like a shot and slam it down on the counter. "Fill 'er up."

"You're being way too hard on yourself," Christine argues while Greg pours me another thimbleful. "In fact, you were the smarter one in this scenario, because you got to enjoy and savor the balloon for longer than ten seconds. The rest of us bozos succumbed to peer pressure and cheap thrills."

I arrow her a look. "While I appreciate your generous attempt to rewrite history, I was, in fact, being a massive wimp. And you know what? I have spent far too much of my life running from risk. I am done playing it safe. From now on, I'm popping *every* balloon." *No one will ever call me a coward again.*

"I feel like this deserves a toast," Greg says.

"Hear hear!" Christine chimes in, linking her arm through mine as he tops us all off, and the three of us raise our Dixie cups aloft.

"To popping balloons," Christine says, her eyes shining at me.

I squeeze her arm and tap my cup to theirs. "To popping balloons."

Chapter 19

WHAT'S THE DIFFERENCE BETWEEN A twenty-eight-year-old single woman and a ninety-year-old widow?

About three weeks.

It's the joke I crack to anyone who asks how I'm faring at Gran's, and while my tongue may be firmly planted in cheek, there's more truth to it than I'd prefer to admit. I've only been living with her for a few weeks and I've basically turned into an old biddy.

Don't get me wrong—Gran is an excellent roommate. Top-notch, really. She's quiet, goes to bed early, doesn't smoke or steal my clothes. She's an excellent TV binge buddy. She's also the least demanding landlord I've ever had, since, you know, I'm not paying rent. What's not to love?

But in the span of just a few short weeks, I've noticed some alarming personality changes. I make comments like "It's getting late" around six p.m. I've started craving the disgusting Lipton iced tea packets she stirs into everything. Complaining about the cold dominates an increasing number of my adult conversations. I catch myself wearing house slippers to shuffle out to the mailbox. Oh, and let's not forget I'm now a cat lady.

Our nonstop togetherness does result in some amusing diversions, though. Once I filled her in on all the retro-inspired pranks I pulled on Jack—and as punishment for not including her in the con to begin with—she devises a fifties-style boot camp and puts me through my paces. She teaches me how to make a proper old-fashioned, down to expressing the orange peel. She back-combs my hair to new heights and makes me sport a bouffant to Sunday Mass. She barks at me like a drill sergeant until I can flawlessly re-create winged eyeliner. We watch more of those Old Hollywood movies and she schools me on celebrity scandals of the golden age until I could write a dissertation on Elizabeth Taylor's tumultuous love life. We laugh ourselves silly trying to mimic the Transatlantic accent and rapid-fire speaking style used by rom-com power couple Katharine Hepburn and Spencer Tracy. We raid her closet, which is so chock-full of vintage gems that I can't believe Nat and I wasted our time treasure-hunting through the city instead of coming straight to the source. Some pieces are so breathtaking I can hardly bring myself to touch them, but Gran insists I model each one while she regales me with glamorous tales of where, when, and with whom she wore them.

It's a gift, I realize, to be her caretaker, to be living inside this pocket of time with her. Behind every article of clothing, piece of jewelry, faded photograph, and antique knick-knack is a story, a memory, a priceless piece of family lore I'd never know otherwise. And as positive as her prognosis is, her stroke's served as a grim reminder that once Gran is gone, she's gone—and she'll take all her memories with her.

Which is why I'm shamelessly mining those memories for my book.

"Okay, so." I reposition myself on Gran's bed, crisscrossing my legs beneath me and settling my computer on my lap. She's propped up against the pillows, Pyewacket dozing in a puffy ball between us, tail occasionally flicking my way as if to remind me who's really in charge here. "I'm trying to show how my heroine is transforming. She's grudgingly adapting to her new world and starting to see both the culture and our hero in a new light, but I don't want her to lose herself in the process. I need to show her personal growth—while keeping her likable, of course."

Gran quirks a brow.

"Romance readers are much more judgmental about the heroine than the hero," I explain. "Basically, they'll excuse any bad behavior from him, but not from her. So she's allowed to have flaws, but they can't be too egregious. She can be strong and independent, but not *too* opinionated, or readers will say she's obnoxious and unlikable. It's a whole thing, don't even get me started."

"So you're saying she should be smart and capable, but in a nonthreatening way? Huh. Never heard that one before." We share a knowing eye roll.

"I guess I just don't want it to come across like she's sacrificing her true self for him, you know?" I say, twisting my hair up into a messy bun and sticking a pen through it. "I want the reader to root for her."

She nods, pondering that as she pets a softly purring Pyewacket. "I think you're still looking at this the wrong way, like anything you do for a man means you're losing part of yourself. A big part of relationships is sacrifice, of course, but it doesn't have to diminish you. For example . . ."

I nod eagerly, fingers poised and ready atop my keyboard, and she smirks.

"For example, I used to touch up my makeup before your grandpa got home from work. I didn't do it because I was afraid for him to see me without it, or because I thought he wanted me to look a certain way. I did it because I wanted him to know he was the worth the effort." Her eyes soften, the hint of a smile playing on her lips. "And I didn't view making him dinner as an imposition or an expectation; I did it because I wanted him to be excited to come home to me at night. I wanted him to feel as taken care of as he always made me feel."

As she recounts the memories, she gets a dreamy, far-off look in her eyes, some color returning to her cheeks. "He did things for me, too, of course. He made me coffee every morning. He always let me pick the movie. He even read the books I liked so we could talk about them. If I wanted to leave a party, he'd make himself out to be the antisocial one, or invent some embarrassing story, like he had the runs." She chuckles to herself, absentmindedly fingering the wedding ring she's never taken off. "Every Saturday morning, he would run some errand with the boys—getting the car washed, going to the hardware store, whatever—just to give me some quiet time by myself. And they'd always come home with flowers."

Just watching her reminisce, seeing the joy the memories still bring her, is enough to make my eyes well up. *Aw hell, not again.* I set my computer aside, leaning over to grab a tissue from the box on her nightstand.

"Oh sweetie, I'm sorry! I didn't mean to upset you," she says, worry bracketing her eyes. I think my parents must have called some secret family meeting about me, because

I've started to recognize everyone's identical looks of concern, their unflagging commitment to cheerfulness in my presence. And I get it, I suppose—I've been so weepy these past few weeks, I feel permanently waterlogged. I'm a blubbering Diane Keaton in *Something's Gotta Give*, only instead of looking out on a stunning Hamptons shoreline, I'm squatting in Gran's guest bedroom.

"You just lived such an incredible love story," I say, swiping at my tears. "I feel so far from that."

She clucks her tongue in dissent. "I don't think it's as far away as you think it is."

I groan through my sniffling. "Oh, come on."

"What? You told me all the things you did for Jack. You went out of your way to make him feel special, to let him know you were thinking of him. You gave him the emotional support he wasn't getting from other people in his life. You let your guard down with him in a way you haven't with anyone else. You even cooked for him and didn't spontaneously combust!" She pauses. "Well, kinda."

Even I have to laugh a little at that one.

She finds my hand and squeezes it. "Most of the lies you told were meant to protect him. You made some mistakes, sure, but you had his best interests at heart. I think that's a relationship to be proud of."

"Is this supposed to be making me feel better?" I say miserably. "That I had a great love story and lost it?"

I flop back on the pillow next to her and heave a watery sigh, staring up at her popcorn ceiling like it'll have the answers for me. I'm so tired of crying over him—especially since I know he's not doing the same.

She reaches over to stroke my hair, and Pyewacket gives me the hairy eyeball, as if to say: *Watch yourself, inter-*

loper. "You'll have to forgive yourself eventually," Gran says softly.

I pinch my eyes closed, as if doing so will somehow stop the tears from leaking out. This lump in my throat feels like a boulder. "I'm not the one who needs to forgive me," I say thickly. "And anyway, who says I've forgiven *him*?"

She hums. "A man's ego is a tricky thing. I was married for fifty years and I still managed to get on the wrong side of it a time or two. You both just have to be willing to work through the rough patches."

"Is this where you're gonna tell me not to go to bed angry?"

"No, I went to bed angry plenty of times. But anger is like fire—if you don't feed it, it eventually burns out. You just need to give it a little time."

I let out a hollow laugh. "Please, he's had *plenty* of time. It's been weeks and he hasn't reached out once. I'd say that's sending a pretty clear message." If there's one thing I refuse to do, it's hang on to false hope. "I'm not going to sit around crying and staring out the window, pining for someone who can't be bothered."

She arches a brow, side-eyeing the soggy, crumpled tissue balled in my fist.

"Fine, I will *occasionally* still cry, but I draw the line at the pining. Pining is a bridge too far! I need to move on with my life," I say firmly, hoisting myself up to a sitting position and sliding the computer back onto my lap. "And you need to hold me accountable."

"In that case, my friend Dolores has a single grandson . . ." she singsongs, and I raise my hand to stop that train of thought in its tracks.

"Not *that* kind of moving on. The kind where I write a

bestselling novel that takes the literary world by storm." I squint at my screen, reading over the notes I just made.

"Ah. Well, I suppose that's for the best right now anyway," she sniffs, giving me a once-over. "Since no man would take a chance on someone who insists on wearing a *blanket* as clothing."

I gasp in mock-offense. "It's called a Snuggie! And it's insanely comfortable."

"It's hideous, is what it is. Luckily I don't judge." She eyes me askance as she feels around on the bedspread for the remote. "Now if I *did* judge, I'd tell you it's an abomination that would scare off any man within a ten-mile radius."

I wave a hand dismissively. "*Pfft.* Who's here to see it? No one."

"I lost my mobility, not my eyesight," she huffs. "Besides, why would you ever hide that adorable figure? It is an absolute crime. If I were you, I'd be prancing around in a bikini."

"Oh really, in November?"

"*Especially* in November. Think of the attention you'd get! You wouldn't need an old list of husband-catching tips, I can promise you that much."

I bark a loud laugh, and Pyewacket signals her disapproval at the disturbance by arching her back. I scratch her head in apology.

"Laugh all you want, but you only have so many years before gravity turns on you, missy," Gran says reproachfully. "Blink and you'll be an old lady confined to her bed, with only the memories to keep you warm."

"Don't talk like that," I admonish, though I take the hint and tug the quilt (handmade, of course) up her legs. It's yet another thing her generation has on us—basic sewing skills. Lord knows a few home ec classes would have served me better than multivariable calculus. "Actually, scratch that, keep talking. I'll take as many of your stories and pearls of wisdom as I can get. Just don't come after me for royalties since, you know, I'm broke."

She points the remote at me. "If I'm going to look the other way on all this blatant plagiarism, then this book better be dedicated to me."

I wink at her as I slide on my noise-canceling headphones. "Obviously. Who else would I dedicate it to?"

IT'S SEVERAL DAYS later and I'm tapping away on my laptop in my newly commandeered writing space (aka Gran's study) when my phone rings, an unknown number popping up on the display. Normally I'd rather eat glass than answer an unknown number, but something about the location—Louisiana—tickles my memory just enough to hit *Accept*. "Hello?"

"Hi. I'm looking for Cassidy Sutton?" It's a female voice, soft and slightly hesitant.

"This is she," I respond, just as tentatively. I've had to block so many reporters over the past few weeks that my finger's already hovering over the *End* button.

She clears her throat. "My name is Olivia Sherwood. I got your card from my . . . well, from Eric Jessup."

My jaw falls open, and I'm momentarily struck dumb. I think I'd be less surprised if a cartoon coyote dropped an anvil on my head.

"Olivia! Oh my goodness. Wow." *Sheesh, are you a journalist or a fangirl?* I cast about for something normal to say.

"Um, how have you been?" I press the heel of my hand to my forehead, mortified. *What are you, her long-lost friend?!*

"Oh. Um, I'm well, thanks," she responds, politely ignoring the fact that I'm short-circuiting before her very . . . well, ears, I guess. "I'm calling because I'm looking to talk to someone about a potential story."

"I'm someone!" I blurt before I can stop myself, then close my eyes, pinching the bridge of my nose. "I'm sorry, you've caught me off guard. I swear, I'm usually quite normal and professional." I let out a self-conscious laugh.

"Don't worry about it, I know this is a little out of the blue." *Now there's an understatement.* "If it makes you feel any better, I'm definitely more nervous about this phone call than you are."

My interest is piqued. "What kind of story did you have in mind? I'd love to help you with it." *There we go. Better.*

She takes a deep breath. "Well, you may have heard some things in the press recently about me and Eric. That he . . . well, that we broke up."

"I did hear something about that," I say lightly.

"Most people have," she says dryly. "Only what's being reported isn't true."

"So you haven't broken up?" I ask in surprise. So much for that smug "*I told you so*" I lorded over Jack.

"It's . . . complicated. The important thing is, none of it is his fault, but he's taking the blame to protect me. He's always trying to protect me," she says under her breath, and she sounds . . . wistful. "But the things they're saying about him, they're just so far from the truth. I can't sit back and let him be vilified this way. I *won't*," she says firmly, all traces of her earlier hesitation gone. "I love him too much for that."

I straighten in my seat. *Well, this story just got juicier.* I put the phone on speaker and start rummaging through my workbag in search of my interview notebook.

"I couldn't help but notice that you said 'love,' present tense," I point out mildly, then shut up. One of the most valuable things I've learned as an interviewer is when to back off and let your subjects spill their guts.

"Yeah, the love part's never been our problem." She sighs. "You know that quote *If you love someone, set them free*? We're basically the poster children for it. We were so young when we met, so head over heels. I always knew he was going to have this big life, that he was going to be great, and I didn't want to hold him back . . . but I just couldn't sign up for that life. Being stuck at home while your husband's out on the road, raising kids alone, worrying about what he's up to or the women who'd throw themselves at him. I saw what it did to some of the players' wives, how many relationships collapsed under the strain, and I didn't want that for us. I didn't want that for *myself*. He tried to change my mind, but I thought I was doing the right thing by ending things, that we'd both move on and find other people." She exhales. "Only problem is, we never did."

I'm on the edge of my seat. I'm afraid to even breathe for fear she'll stop talking.

"He would check in with me periodically, and every time we talked it was like no time had passed. I used to think I couldn't forget him because he was my first love, and that's just how it is with first loves, right? You romanticize them so much that no one else can ever measure up." She pauses. "Of course, seeing him shirtless on the cover of every magazine for a decade didn't exactly help." She huffs a laugh.

"Anyway, fast-forward to last year. My mom had been

battling cancer for years, and when she passed away, guess who showed up to hold my hand through all of it."

I make a strangled noise in my throat.

"He's always been there when I needed him, no questions asked. I suddenly saw things so clearly: how wrong I'd been not to fight for what we'd had; how much time I'd wasted trying to find with someone else what was always there with him. I promised myself that I'd spend the rest of my life showing up for him the way he's always shown up for me." She goes quiet. "And yet somehow, I've managed to screw things up a second time."

Gah! That was a golden quote. *Where is my tape recorder when I need it?!* I scrabble around for a pen, and when I flip my notebook open to a fresh page, something falls out onto my lap—and when I see what it is, a tidal wave of memories washes over me, threatening to pull me under.

The US Open ticket stub.

It's a game we'd been playing for a few weeks. Spurred on by the notes I'd been leaving around his apartment, Jack had taken to hiding the ticket stub from our first date in random locations for me to find, like tucked into the pocket of my coat or zipped inside my gym bag. To retaliate, I'd slide it under his pillow, and the next day I'd find it slipped inside my sunglasses case. I'd stick it in his fridge, and he'd sandwich it inside my closed laptop. It was ridiculously silly and sickeningly sweet, like a sappy, love-drunk version of hot potato.

I pick up the ticket now, a kaleidoscope of emotions swirling in my chest: tenderness and longing, heartache and regret. In this, I feel a kinship with Olivia, a burning need to right past wrongs—and while I may not be able to repair my own relationship, I can at least try to help fix hers.

"So what happened?" I ask gently, staring at the ticket stub so hard my eyes blur. *Don't even think about it—there's no crying in baseball!* "And more importantly, what can I do to help you fix it?"

She tells me how she's been struggling with life in the limelight, how her need for privacy conflicts with her vow to show up for Eric the way his (very public) life requires. How Eric's desire to protect her from scrutiny has left him feeling guilty for the times when he inevitably can't. How her aversion to his celebrity has dredged up old wounds, straining their relationship and driving a wedge into their future.

"He wants a full-time partner, and he deserves that from me after all we've been through," she finishes. "And I refuse to make the same mistake twice. So this is me, breaking out of my comfort zone and making an effort to be part of his world."

I smile to myself, doodling a heart in the margin. "You want to 'grand gesture' him."

There's a brief pause, then an embarrassed half laugh. "I hadn't thought of it that way, but yeah. I suppose that's exactly what I want to do."

"Well, you've come to the right place." I hesitate, deliberating. "In the interest of full disclosure, I think you should know about some recent events in my life before you decide to work with me."

"If you're talking about what happened at the Women of the Year event, I already know about that," she preempts me. "In fact—and I hope you don't take this the wrong way—it's one of the reasons I decided to call you."

That throws me for a loop. "It is?"

"To be frank—and again, no offense—I don't trust re-porters," she says crisply. "But I read the original story you wrote about us and it was actually quite charming. And then when I saw your name in the news, I figured if I was ever going to do this, I'd be better off taking my chances with someone who's been through the ringer themself."

"Ah." *Every cloud has a silver lining, I suppose.* "Now I understand. Well, I can promise that I'll only include what you're interested in sharing, and I'll make sure you're happy with the final piece." I pause, knowing I need to say the rest. *I hope this isn't a deal-breaker.* "I do want to be up-front with you that I'm no longer with Siren."

"Oh." She's quiet for a beat. "Well, is there somewhere else you can place the story?"

I have to smother a laugh; every outlet in the world would die for this exclusive. "That part of it won't be a prob-lem. And I actually have an idea for where to run it, if you're open to something a little . . . unexpected."

"I don't care where it runs," she says, resolute. "I just care that Eric sees it."

I eye the ticket stub, making a game-changing decision of my own. "I can definitely make that happen."

IT'S LATE AFTERNOON a couple of days later when I hit *Save*, then lean back in the office chair and exhale a deep breath. *Finished.* Well, sort of. There's still one thing I need to do.

I make sure Gran's settled, then tug on my peacoat and pop in my AirPods before heading out the door for a walk. I need the fortification of fresh air, for my feet to be moving while I make this next call. *One I never thought I'd make.* I steel myself while I wait for his receptionist to patch me through.

"Cassidy Sutton? Now there's a name I didn't expect to hear," Tom booms in that signature Boston accent I'd recognize anywhere—and his voice actually sounds kind. "How the hell are ya?"

I'm a little thrown. I'm not sure what I was expecting from Jack's best friend—contempt, tension, animosity maybe?— but it wasn't *concern.*

"Hey, Tom." *I'm rather tragic and emotionally unstable, thanks for asking.* "You know, I'm uh . . . I'm okay, I guess," I stammer. "Yeah."

"Well, that was convincing," he deadpans.

Stellar start, Cass. I decide to skip right past the pleasantries. "I'm calling because I've got a business proposition for you."

"Oh?" Now he's the one who sounds off balance. "I'm listening."

"I have an exclusive interview with Olivia Sherwood about her relationship with Eric Jessup that I thought Brawler might be interested in." I wait for his reaction, but when he stays quiet, I press on. "I know it might be a little fluffy for your audience, but I figured—"

"No no," he interrupts. "We definitely want it. And just so you know, the relationship stories are actually my favorite."

"Oh please," I groan, not buying it for a second. "Tom Bartlett, a closet softy?"

"There's a lot you don't know about me," he says flippantly, then pauses. "But more importantly, stories about the sex lives of celebrities always drive our traffic through the roof."

Of course.

"I can pay you our standard contractor rate, plus a bo-nus based on click-through," he says briskly, all-business now. "Or is there a specific number you're looking for? Whatever it is, we'll make it work."

"Tom, you know this isn't about the money."

There's a beat of silence. "No, I didn't imagine it was."

"Jack's the only reason I have any connection to Olivia to begin with, so offering it to Brawler first just felt like the right thing to do."

He grunts a disbelieving noise, like *hmph*.

"I realize that may sound ironic coming from me, but I do still know what the right thing is," I say dryly.

"No, I just meant . . . you sure there's no other reason?"

The wind kicks up and I burrow deeper into my coat, bracing against the cold as the implication in his question becomes clear. "If you're worried this is just another trick, I can assure you—"

"You misunderstand me," he interrupts. "I'm not accus-ing you of anything. Just the opposite. I'm asking if you'd object to me running your byline in thirty-point font so that moron can't miss it."

My heart and stride stutter simultaneously, nearly sending me tumbling off the curb. I hardly know how to re-spond, the sentiment behind his words leaving me tongue-tied.

He exhales. "Look Cassidy, you and I don't know each other that well and my loyalty is to my friend, but the guy's acting like a total jackass."

I finally recover my voice. "You don't have to—"

"You were good for him," Tom cuts me off. "He was happy with you. Happier than he's been in a long time, and he deserves that more than anyone I know. You may have fucked up first, but Jack's the one fucking up now."

I don't know whether to laugh or cry at his blunt assessment. "I was happy too," I say thickly, and swallowing's never been so difficult. Just when I think I've banished that lump for good, it rises from the ashes like a damn phoenix. "He was . . ." . . . *the love of my life.* I clear my throat and try again. "He was good for me, too. Minus his temper," I amend. "I could do without that."

He snorts. "You and me both."

"I want you to know, I regret the role I played in all this. I know it affected you, too." I take a deep breath. "And even if I am mad at him, I still wish I could fix things . . . but I think Jack's made up his mind about me."

"The man's stubborn as hell, always has been. It's both his best and worst quality."

I hate that he doesn't even try to contradict my statement—and the worst part is, as his best friend, Tom would know *exactly* how Jack feels. Any residual hope I may have felt bubbling up vanishes as if pricked by a pin.

"Well, it certainly seems to have paid off. What with the deal, I mean," I say, trying to steer us back into neutral territory. "I'm glad everything worked out. I know how important it was to him."

He hums his agreement. "He's been ready to move on for years, though I sure did everything I could to get him to stay. I can't be too upset with him, though. We had a good run."

I pass a house with several giant leaf piles dotting the front lawn; some kids would have a field day jumping in those. "What about you? Going to cash out and live the high life?"

"Me? Hell no. I'm going down with the ship."

I chuckle at that. "Hope it's not too lonely up there at the top."

"One thing I rarely am is *lonely*," he says wickedly. *A cad 'til the end.*

I make a gagging noise. "Set myself up for that one, didn't I? Forgot who I was talking to."

He laughs, and there's a brief lull in the conversation as I fight a losing battle against the question I swore I wouldn't ask. "How is he, Tom?"

There's a pause. "He's doing okay. He won't really say much about what happened, but that's sort of par for the course with him. When he's upset about something, he throws himself into work. Although now . . ." He trails off. "Anyway, you don't need to worry. I'm keeping him busy."

Something about the way he says it—or maybe it's his reference to never being lonely—just makes me feel worse. What does *"keeping him busy"* even mean? Knowing Tom, he's probably taking him on an exhaustive tour of New York's finest strip clubs.

I feel sick. All this time, I've been imagining Jack alone in his ivory tower, shut away in his apartment full of extravagant, untouchable objects, mourning the loss of our relationship like a younger, hotter Miss Havisham. But who am I kidding? Jack's not sitting home alone, licking his wounds. I'm sure there's a long line of women who've been waiting in the wings for their chance to win over one of New York's most eligible bachelors . . . who are only too willing to help him forget the duplicitous ex who once tried to screw him over.

"You know what, Tom, I've gotta run." Literally run, away from the disturbing visuals now invading my brain.

322 + Devon Daniels

My hands start shaking in my pockets and I ball them into fists. "I'll email over the story as soon as we hang up."

"Sounds good. And hey, Cassidy—take care of yourself, alright? Don't make me have to look after you, too."

I force a half-hearted laugh, promise him I will, and hang up.

I exhale slowly, staring up into the rapidly darkening sky and taking a couple of cleansing breaths—then pivot and march back to the house with those leaf piles. *Because why the hell not? Kids shouldn't have all the fun.*

I pick the biggest one, throw my arms out, and fall backward into it like a snow angel, trusting that the world's going to catch me.

I'M BACK," I CALL OUT A COUPLE OF WEEKS
later as I let myself in the front door, trying not to drop any
grocery bags as I shrug off my coat. So Gran won't be left
home alone, I time my errand-running to coincide with her
thrice weekly in-home physical therapy appointments or, in
this case, a visit from Lois, her longtime friend and neighbor.

"We're in here," Gran calls out from the kitchen.

"Guess who I saw at the store," I singsong as I head their
way. "Your favorite, Bernie the butcher. And the first thing
he did was ask about you, so you can lord this over Dottie's
head at your next bridge—"

I reach the kitchen and stop so abruptly, my feet probably leave skid marks on the floor.

Jack is sitting across from my grandmother at her kitchen
table. Twin cups of tea are set in front of them, along with a
plate of table crackers and Gran's favorite garlic and herb
Rondelé cheese spread. *Wow, she broke out the good stuff.*

"Jack?" I say in disbelief.

I'm so stunned by his presence that I have to stop myself

from reaching a hand out to touch him to prove he's not a mirage, or maybe one of those creepy holograms of dead musicians concert promoters are so into these days. *Am I dreaming? Did I conjure him? Did I accidentally mix up my coffee with Gran's meds-spiked Ensure?*

Jack stands immediately, holding eye contact as he wipes his hands on his jeans. "Hi."

The mirage speaks! I'm so thrown by the sound of his voice that I jolt like I've been shocked by a doctor's paddles. My eyes drink him in, but instead of taking dainty birdie sips I'm gorging myself after a long spell of dehydration. I'm instantly inebriated, totally drunk on the sight of him. I don't know where to focus my eyes first, so I start at the top and work my way down: from the familiar tousled brown hair and piercing blue eyes to the rounded caps of his broad shoulders, over the soft fabric of the navy sweater that's hugging his biceps just so, to the solid chest and tapered waist I once fit so seamlessly against.

He looks . . . perfect. Brilliant and striking and so hand-some, I can hardly draw in a full breath. He looks like the exact thing I've been missing.

Every cell in my body wants to bolt across this kitchen, jump into in his arms and cling to him like a koala, but that would be crazy, right? I'm supposed to hate him. I'm *supposed* to be holding a grudge. Annoyingly, my first instinct is to fluff my hair, but I resist the urge to groom myself—he doesn't just get to waltz in here and fluster me, *no sirree*.

I suddenly realize I'm making this weird, standing here mute and motionless at the entrance to the kitchen. In an attempt to reanimate, I reach over to set my keys on the counter but miss entirely, sending them clattering to the floor, and when I bend to retrieve them I come face-to-face with a puppy, curled up contentedly underneath the table. *Okay, now I know I'm hallucinating.*

A thousand competing thoughts swirl around in my brain, jockeying for attention: *How did he find me? What took him so long? I'm so angry at him. I've missed him so much. How has he gotten even better-looking? The audacity! If he had even a shred of decency, he'd have shown up looking haggard and pale instead of healthy and fit (or warned me he was coming so I could've applied some self-tanner at least). How dare he just show up here like nothing's happened? How could he have abandoned me the way he did? Why is he here now?* But what comes out is:

"There's a dog in the kitchen." *Nailed it.*

"It's my dog," he says, taking a small step toward me. My eyebrows shoot up and damn, I just made eye contact again despite *specifically* ordering myself not to. "I know, it was a surprise to me too."

His explanation manages to leave me more confused than less, but since I'm already on the floor I reach out to pet this mystery pooch. It bounds over and licks my hand while I ruffle its dusty gray fur, its tail frantically wagging, before scampering back over to Jack and darting between his legs. When he bends to pick it up, I have to avert my eyes like he's doing something obscene. Separately, both Jack and puppies are irresistible—but Jack *with* a puppy might make my ovaries explode.

I belatedly remember something and shoot to my feet. "Where's Pyewacket?"

"She's fine, we put her in the laundry room," Gran says around a mouthful of crackers, totally unbothered.

Jack winces. "Sorry, I should've remembered your grandma had a cat."

I'm slowly regaining my bearings. "How long have you

been here?" I ask, turning to set the grocery bags down on the countertop (securely, this time), though I can still feel the weight of his gaze on me, burning a hole in my back.

"Not long," Jack says at the same time as Gran says, "A couple hours."

"A couple *hours*?" I spin around to frown at her, but she just smirks, unrepentant. "You don't think you should've texted me?" I scold, then slice my gaze to Jack. "Or did you lose my number, too?"

It's a direct hit. He visibly flinches, opening his mouth to respond before Gran beats him to it. "Jack and I have just been having a little chat, getting to know each other. Isn't that right, Jack?"

She raises her eyebrows at him pointedly and I have to stifle a laugh. *She is diabolical.* I take back my scolding—in fact, I'd pay serious money to have witnessed the brutal tongue-lashing he's surely received.

"That's right," Jack says, wisely agreeing, then takes another step toward me, still cradling his revoltingly adorable dog. The two of them even have matching blue eyes! *Seriously, God, can you cut me a break here? This isn't exactly fighting fair.* "And while I wouldn't blame you for wanting to kick me out, I'd very much like to talk to you." When I don't immediately respond, he adds a quiet, "Please."

We stare at each other in charged silence, the hum of Gran's ancient refrigerator practically deafening, until the scrape of a chair across the floor makes us both jump.

"What do you know, it's time for my soap. Cass, hun, could you walk me to my room?"

Jack springs into action, helping her up from the chair. "Where to?" he asks, but I wave him off.

"It's alright, I've got it. You okay to wait here?" Like he really is a mirage and if I blink, he'll disappear.

He nods. "Take your time. I'm not going anywhere."

He looks me straight in the eye as he says it, apparently failing to see the irony of his statement, and I'm not gonna lie: part of me *really* wants to punch him in the face right now. If this were an Old Hollywood movie, now is when I'd wind up and slap the leading man so hard, my hand would sting for a week. But before I can act on my impulse Gran squeezes my arm, and I don't even have to look at her to know she knows *exactly* what I'm thinking.

So instead of violence I choose guidance (heh) and lead Gran out of the kitchen, bracing myself for the earful of over-the-top commentary I'm sure she's about to unleash.

She doesn't waste a second. "Boy, is he a dish," she hoots as soon as Jack's out of earshot. "When I opened the door and saw that face, I nearly had a second stroke."

I groan as I push open her bedroom door. "You know I hate your gallows humor."

"Oh lighten up, it was just a joke." She pauses. "Don't have a stroke!" She throws her head back and cackles.

"Still not laughing," I remind her, helping her onto the bed. "What did you guys talk about for two hours, anyway?"

"What do you think we talked about, the weather? He's obviously here to win you back! And you better hear him out," she warns as I get her settled against the pillows.

"I thought you said he was a loser who doesn't deserve me." I switch on *Days of our Lives* and hand her the remote.

"I didn't know him then," she says defensively.

"Whatever happened to '*Don't give him the milk for free*'?"

Her smile is deviant. "Forget the milk—if it were me, he'd be dining at an all-you-can-eat buffet!"

"Alright, that's about enough excitement for you today." I lean over to tuck the blanket around her, and before I can clock what she's doing, she's reached out and pinched the apples of my cheeks—*hard*.

"Ow!" I swat her hands away. "What was that for?"

"You need a little color in your cheeks. Men like a little flush." She sits back again, pleased with herself.

"You are a *menace*." I rub my cheek tenderly; I swear there'll be a bruise. "And since when are you such a soft touch, anyway? Some smooth talker with a pretty face is all it takes to win you over?"

She holds up a finger. "Don't forget the money."

I groan. "Oh, *Gran*."

"What? It's like my mama always used to say: '*It's just as easy to marry a rich man as a poor man.*' I didn't listen, but you still can."

I exhale loudly and move to leave. "I was looking for some real advice, but I guess I'm on my own here."

"Fine, wait." She grabs my sleeve and sighs dramatically, mock–put out. "You want to know what I think you should do?"

"Please."

She looks me straight in the eye. "Swallow your pride, forgive him, and let yourself be happy."

I'm shaking my head before she's even finished talking. "And what, just pretend the past six weeks didn't happen? Pretend he didn't desert me at the first sign of trouble? How do I know he won't hurt me again?"

"You don't," she says, matter-of-fact. "He'll either prove

himself or he won't. But love is a leap of faith either way. It takes a strong person to apologize, and an even stronger person to forgive. And this won't be the last time you need to do it. But don't punish yourself by holding a grudge." She squeezes my hand. "I'm giving you permission to forgive him."

My eyes start to sting and I pinch my sinuses, willing away the looming waterworks. "How do you always know just what to say?" I whisper.

"Well, I *am* ninety. I've had some practice."

I let out a hoarse laugh, blinking away the tears.

"Actually, you should probably write down whatever I just said. I've already forgotten it."

I'm laughing harder now.

"Now get out there already, he's waiting for you," she says with a flick of her wrist, shooing me away.

"Meh, let him wait." I lean over and wrap her in a hug. "I love you."

"I love you too," she murmurs, rubbing light circles on my back—and this time, it's her voice that sounds thick.

"Hey, one more thing," she calls as I'm walking out, and I turn back with raised eyebrows.

Her lips twitch. "Leave the door open so I can hear you guys."

I impale her with my stare before shutting the door extra firmly behind me. When I turn I have a straight-line view into the kitchen, and I'm able to observe Jack for a moment without him noticing. His arms are braced against the stove's edge, his head bent as though deep in thought, or perhaps just weary. A superhero with the weight of the world on his shoulders. There's something so out-of-body about seeing him here in my grandmother's kitchen, standing amongst her dated appliances. It's incongruent, like a glitch in the matrix.

When he hears my footfalls, he straightens and turns my way, his expression determined. "Hey. Listen, I know I don't—"

His words cut off abruptly when I walk right up to him and let myself do what I've been wanting to since the moment I saw him: I throw my arms around his neck and squeeze, my pride be damned.

Jack releases a guttural sound and crushes me against his chest, holding me so tightly he's practically cutting off my air supply. But who needs air, anyway? For the first time in weeks the ache in my chest is gone, so if this is my last memory, at least I'll die happy.

"God, I've missed you," he grits out. His hand grips the back of my neck, locking me in place in the crook of his collarbone.

"This hug is not for you," I make sure to clarify, my voice muffled by his neck . . . but while I'm here, I decide to take a deep inhale of his skin. *Mmm, that's the stuff.* "It's purely for selfish reasons."

"I'll take it however I can get it." He clutches me tighter, his fingers threaded in my hair like a tether. I couldn't escape if I tried. "I thought you were going to slam the door in my face. Either that or hit me."

"Been thinking about it since the second I saw you. And you're not out of the woods," I warn, then snuggle tighter into his neck, directly contradicting my previous statement.

"I deserve it. I'll give you as many free shots as you want."

"Argh, you're too pretty. I can't have that on my conscience."

He lets out a soft chuckle and finally pulls back slightly, freeing me a fraction so he can look into my eyes, and his tender expression turns to alarm. "You're crying."

It's true, and I've given up trying to battle back the tears. I may as well grab a surfboard and ride the wave at this point.

"Please don't cry," he says, thumbing a tear from my cheek. "I have a lot of things to say to you and it'll make it *really* hard for me to get through."

"Can't make any promises," I snuffle. "I've never been much of a crier, but lately I'm like a leaky faucet."

The dog jumps up on our legs just then, looking for attention, and we reluctantly separate so Jack can pick it up.

"So is this your wingman?" I inquire, scratching behind the pup's soft ears.

His smile is sheepish. "Figured it'd be hard to turn away a guy with a puppy."

"I had a feeling. Soften me up, huh? Very underhanded."

"Hedging my bets." He laughs as I roll my eyes. "The truth is, I don't have the heart to crate him—but if I don't, he destroys everything he touches. But you'll be pleased to know my apartment isn't looking nearly so fancy these days."

I have to laugh at that. "So it's a *he*."

"Yes, and I'm actually terrified he's going to pee on your grandmother's carpet. I saw a patio out there, you think we could give him a few minutes to run around the backyard?"

"Sure. Although we prefer to call it the *lanai*," I joke, motioning for him to follow me. "You know, from *Golden Girls*?" I add at his blank expression. He shrugs, and *sigh, men.* "Never mind."

The dog takes off at a tear as soon as I open the sliding

glass door, sprinting in circles around the backyard while Jack and I settle into a couple of side-by-side lounge chairs. Thankfully, our mild fall seems to be hanging on, so the two of us can actually sit outside without freezing to death.

"So let's start with the big stuff first." I level him with a stern gaze, and he nods, seeming to brace himself. "Explain the dog."

He drops his chin to his chest and exhales a laugh, shaking his head. "It was Tom's doing. After everything . . . happened, I sort of shut down. I worked nonstop but never really left my apartment otherwise. And then once the deal went through, I *really* never left. Tom got frustrated with me, and one night he showed up and said he was taking me somewhere. I assumed he meant out to some bar, but instead he walked me to an animal shelter. Said he was sick of my shit and I needed a lifestyle change." He grins at the puppy running in frenzied figure eights around the lawn. "And he was right. I should've done it years ago."

"Unconditional love." I smile at him. "A pet actually seems like the perfect thing for you. Just what you needed." I guess this must be what Tom was referring to when he mentioned he was *"keeping him busy."* I beam him a silent thank-you for choosing puppies over strippers. "What kind of dog is he?"

"They think mostly Chesapeake Bay retriever, but with a bunch of other stuff mixed in." As if he can hear us talking about him, the pup races over to jump up on Jack, and he scoops him up. "I did a dog DNA test, but the results haven't come back yet."

"Of course you did." He is an *adorable* dog dad. "Does said puppy have a name?" I reach out with grabby hands and Jack passes him into my outstretched arms.

He clears his throat. "It's Asher, but I've been calling him Ash."

"Like the color? That's fitting." I scratch my fingernails through his smoky gray fur and hug him to my cheek, because the presence of a puppy means compulsory snuggling. I don't make the rules.

Jack watches the two of us with a lopsided smile. "Also like the tennis stadium."

It takes me a moment to connect the dots. "You mean Arthur Ashe?" He smirks at my shock. "You named your dog after the location of our first date?"

He nods, eyeing me, as though monitoring my reaction to that piece of information.

My cheeks are baking as I lift up one of Ash's floppy ears. "Your human sounds a little lovesick," I stage-whisper into it.

"A lot lovesick, actually."

Our eyes meet over Ash's head, and I can feel my resolve weakening the longer I look at him, the intensity of my anger fading in the face of the overwhelming pull I feel toward him. *The one I've always felt.*

But no. *No.*

"If that's really true, then how could you have left me the way you did?" I demand, finally blurting out what I've wanted to ask since I saw him in the kitchen with Gran—or actually, what I've been wondering for the past six weeks. "You *abandoned* me in that hotel room, Jack. The world was crashing down around us and at the first sign of trouble, you bailed on me. You vanished without a trace! After we'd . . ." My voice falters, and I shake my head and look away. "You never even checked to see if I was okay. You don't do that to someone you love."

He audibly swallows. "You're right. I screwed up. It was a mistake."

"A *mistake*?" I exclaim, incredulous. Sixth-sensing my change in demeanor, Ash escapes the line of fire by wriggling out of my arms and bolting. *Smart dog.* "A mistake is forgetting to text me when you're running late, not going AWOL for six weeks!"

"Six weeks and two days, actually. I counted every one."

I throw up my hands, exasperated by this man's contradictions. "I don't understand you!"

He raises a placating hand. "I'm going to explain myself, but I want you to know that *I* know there's no excuse for what I did. I got confused and I panicked, but that doesn't justify my behavior. I handled things the worst possible way I could have. And I'm so sorry for that, Cassie." He rakes a hand through his hair, his features twisted with regret. "I can only imagine what you must have thought of me. And then when I found out what you've been dealing with here . . . it makes me sick to think about it."

He does, indeed, look sick. And you know what? I'm not mad about it. I've been agitating in an emotional spin cycle for the past month and a half, so it's nice to see he's not as impervious as I'd imagined. And as apologies go, he's off to a strong start, at least. Admission of guilt: *check*. Taking responsibility: *double check.*

I'm as magnanimous as a saint when I raise my chin and say, "Go on."

He coughs nervously. "So for this to make any sense, I have to tell you about an ex-girlfriend."

Hold up, what? I make a face like he's just presented me with two-week-old rotting fish. I'm no longer a sensitive, peaceful empath. I'm a hardened street fighter ready to take up arms on the battlefield of love. I will crush my competition with nothing but a nail file and force of will.

"She was my first serious girlfriend, actually. Met her in college, and I was *all* in. I built her up to be everything. I thought she was 'The One,'" he says with a healthy dose of disdain, and I relax a skosh, mentally sheathing my sword. *Threat neutralized.* "In retrospect, I was clearly searching for the relationship stability I never had growing up. Not that I could see that at the time." He huffs a short breath. "Anyway, she wasn't as serious as I was, apparently, because two years in I found out she'd been cheating on me."

My jaw drops open. *How dare this jezebel?!* Outrage burns through me on his behalf and I'm seriously reconsidering my cease-fire.

"She knew about my parents, so the betrayal felt that much worse. I was angry and hurt, and I felt so fucking stupid. I was so certain I'd never cheat that it never occurred to me *she* would. It messed me up for a long time." He shakes his head, as if to cast off the bad memories. "This was around the time we'd started Brawler, so I threw myself into it and never looked back. And I promised myself I'd never let a woman make a fool of me like that again."

My stomach twists into a sailor's knot as I start to grasp exactly where all this is headed.

"So fast-forward to a few months ago," he continues. "Things were going well for me; better than they'd ever been, in fact. Brawler was doing well, and the deal was coming together. I'd met you. I thought I'd finally found the girl." We lock eyes, and his expression is so wistful—*longing*—that I lose my breath. "It felt like the next chapter, like everything I ever wanted was within my reach." He pauses. "And then I found out you'd been lying to me.

"I didn't want to believe it at first. There was no way I could've been duped that badly again, could I? Sure, you may have acted oddly at times, but I knew our relationship wasn't fake. And then when you admitted it and explained what happened, I decided to believe you. I *wanted* to believe you." He swallows and breaks my gaze, looking back at Ash as he barks at a squirrel. "And then we woke up to that story."

I feel sick. "Jack, I swear on my life—on my *grandmother's* life—I had nothing to do with that story."

"But how could I have known that? All I knew was you'd admitted to lying—about a *lot* of things—just hours before. It all felt like too much of a coincidence. In that moment, the only scenario that made any sense to me was that you were behind it, or involved somehow at the very least. I worried that my feelings for you were clouding my judgment, making it impossible for me to see you clearly. And I couldn't ignore my gut a second time." He lets out a tortured breath. "So I left."

"I wish you would've told me all this. I would've . . . well, actually, I don't know what I would've done," I admit after a pause. Even I can concede the evidence looked damning; I'm not sure how I could've proven my innocence.

"Afterward, I couldn't stop picking apart our conversations, obsessing over every detail, looking for any clues I'd missed. I drove myself crazy wondering what was the truth and what was a lie. The big things, of course, but also stupid little things, like do you really hate yellow Skittles as much as I do, or were you just telling me what you thought I wanted to hear?"

"Lemon candy should *not* exist," I say forcefully.

"My thoughts got pretty dark there for a while," he continues, and I want to clap my hand over his mouth so I don't have to hear any more. I hate knowing how unhappy he's been, even if I've been right there with him. "I worried there was more coming, that you might use the things I'd told you about my family against me. I wondered if you were working with other people, or if my dad had put you up to it. I even wondered if you slept with me that night to distract me."

"*Jack.*" My heart splinters at the haunted look in his eyes. "Tell me you didn't really believe that of me."

"I didn't say my thoughts were rational. I'm just telling you what was going through my mind."

Listening to him detail how royally I've messed with his head is messing with *my* head. I feel like I'm seeing him through new eyes, understanding him in a way I previously couldn't. It's incredible, really, the deep wounds and insecurities that can be hidden behind a confident exterior.

"If this is what you thought of me, then why are you here now?" I finally ask, unsure what else to say.

"The short answer? I came to my senses."

I snort a laugh and he flashes me a wry smile.

"But seriously, once the shock of everything wore off and I'd had a chance to settle down, I realized how insane I sounded. No matter what the circumstances were, I knew you weren't capable of the things I was trying to blame you for. I knew you weren't the person I was making you out to be. Of *course* you weren't. It seems so obvious to me now, that I was letting my past ruin my future." He shakes his head. "I knew I needed to fix things, but I wanted to close the book on Brawler first. Let's face it, this job has been an issue between us since day one. I figured if I could just see the deal through, then maybe we could move forward with a clean slate."

"I guess that explains the radio silence." Not that it excuses his disappearing act, but I suppose his rationale does make a certain kind of sense.

"The day I signed the deal?" he says, and I nod, urging him on. "It should've been the best day of my life. I'd finally reached the finish line I'd been running toward for so many years. Everything I'd worked for was coming true." He lets out a heavy sigh. "And I was fucking *miserable*. People kept congratulating me, and it made me want to scream. It all just felt so pointless. At one point Tom asked what I wanted to do to celebrate, and my only thought was that I just wanted to hear your voice." He meets my gaze. "I hated that you weren't there. And I hated myself even more because I only had myself to blame for it."

The corner of his mouth hitches up. "So I came up with a foolproof plan to get you back: I'd apologize for disappearing, then follow you around until you agreed to give me another chance. Imagine my surprise when I went over to your apartment and found out you'd ghosted me first!" He's indignant.

I cough a laugh, grateful for the break in tension. "Now *that* is a lie."

"Is it? Let's consider the evidence." There's a gleam in his eye as he holds up one finger. "You moved and didn't tell me."

"Had you been *speaking* to me, you would have known I moved," I say dryly.

He holds up a second finger, undeterred. "I went to the Siren offices to find you, which, incidentally, posed quite a risk to my personal safety. That place is full of women who despise me."

I suck in a breath. "You didn't."

"I did. I was told you no longer worked there and was escorted off the premises by Cynthia herself."

I cover my mouth. "You're lying."

His lips twitch. "Fine, that part was a lie. But they were *not* happy to see me," he says when I reach across the chair to shove him in the shoulder. "Things got a little dicey. I wouldn't be surprised if there's a restraining order out against me." He's kidding.

"I quit Siren."

His eyebrow spikes.

"Honestly, it was time. This whole thing just gave me the push I needed." I watch Asher lift his leg and take a nice long pee on Gran's rosebushes. "The good news is, I've been writing like crazy. I took your advice and finally got off the sidelines," I say pointedly. I can't resist the dig.

He looks properly remorseful, hanging his head. "I never should have said what I did."

"It was less what you said and more *how* you said it that was the problem." The word *coward* flickers in my brain but I banish it, this time for good. *You're not a coward. You're a fearless balloon-popper.*

"I was an asshole lashing out any way I could think of. I'm so ashamed of the way I behaved. An apology isn't nearly enough."

No argument there. "Well, sometimes the truth hurts. And despite your god-awful delivery, I suppose some tough love wasn't the worst thing for me," I acknowledge grudgingly. "I can't argue with the results, at any rate."

"You're being far too understanding." He shakes his head, refusing my compassion. "There's no excuse for the way I spoke to you. I want you to depend on me, not wonder if I'll disappear whenever the going gets rough. The way I behaved . . . it's not who I am. I hope you'll give me another chance to prove that."

My heart squeezes at the vulnerability in his voice, and any lingering vindictiveness I may have been hanging on to evaporates in a puff of smoke. "How about next time, we commit to actually talking things through instead of letting six weeks go by? Just an idea."

The corner of his mouth lifts, the phrase *next time* glowing in the air between us like a lightning bug. He reaches a hand out between our chairs—an apology, an olive branch, and a promise all wrapped in one—and lets it hang there, patiently waiting, until I clasp it and hold on for dear life. I may never let go.

I stare at him, letting my eyes travel a leisurely field trip across his face, taking a slow and steady inventory of all the little details I've missed so much: the dimple bracketing the corner of his mouth; his hair, ruffled and windswept, my favorite wayward front tendril misbehaving even more than usual; the stubbled jaw I'm desperate to graze my knuckles over; the gleaming blue of his eyes, clear as sea glass.

I love him. And no matter what potholes and speed bumps we've encountered on our path to get here, I know I always will. What was it Gran said? *All love is a leap of faith.*

Well, I've looked, and I'm leaping.

He gives my hand a little tug and I take the hint, sliding off my lounger and hopscotching over to his. His arms automatically open for me and I climb on, curling up against his side and resting my head against the solid cushion of his chest. This chair definitely isn't built for two—the wrought iron arm is digging into my spinal cord—but right now, it may as well be a bed of roses.

"I know who you are, Jack." I give in to the temptation

and trace a fingertip along his jaw, the familiar prickle of his stubble lighting a fire in my belly. "And I've already forgiven you. That is, if you can forgive me."

The words have barely escaped my lips when he presses his mouth to mine, kissing me so passionately that any mature, articulate thoughts I may have had about absolution instantly fly out of my head, leaving only raw desire in their place. This kiss is not patient or gentle; it's crushing, bruising, intense. It's weeks of pent-up emotion and angst, yearning and hunger. It's a pot boiling over, a raging wildfire consuming everything in its path.

I can't believe I've gone so long without this. It's been six weeks since he touched me, six weeks since he learned my body so thoroughly, and he makes it clear he hasn't forgotten an inch. His hands roam and rediscover and I let him take his fill, then steal mine in return. We kiss and taste and worship to our heart's content and I don't know how much time has passed before I come to, but when I do I'm straddling him like a horny cowgirl.

"Jack," I say breathlessly. I'm panting like a hiker at high elevation. "I hate to do this—and I mean I *really* hate to do this—but we have to stop."

"But do we really?" he murmurs, his lips placing swirling kisses beneath my ear, his hand slipped beneath my sweater and splayed against the bare skin of my rib cage.

"We do, because I can pretty much guarantee my grandmother has found a way to spy on us."

That stops him cold.

I drop my head into his neck and laugh as I roll off him. "If I'd known all I needed to say was 'I forgive you,' I would've done it sooner," I tease, fanning myself.

"You know who hasn't forgiven me? Cliff. He's barely

said two words to me since you stopped coming around. He won't even look me in the eye. Do you have any idea what it's like to be hated by your doorman?"

"I admire his loyalty," I say solemnly, then remember something. "Wait, so how *did* you find me?"

"Ah." He resettles us in the chaise, his arm nestling me against his side. "So I'd hit a dead end in my search, but worse, I'd started to think you really didn't *want* to be found. I worried I was being selfish, that if I did find you I might just end up screwing your life up all over again. So I paused to figure out my next move . . . and then the Olivia Sherwood interview came out." He clasps my hand to his chest and squeezes. "I couldn't help but think you were sending me a message? I nearly murdered Tom for not telling me about it."

"Tom understood the assignment."

He makes a frustrated noise. "I can't decide if I'm annoyed that you two colluded behind my back or happy that you're finally getting along." He lets out a long-suffering sigh. "Anyway, at that point I was out of options, so I had to play my ace." He pauses for dramatic effect. "I called Greg."

"Of *course* Greg spilled the beans. I swear, that guy needs a muzzle." I make a mental note to rename the villain in my book after Greg. "Though in this case, I suppose I owe him one."

"Well, actually, it was your sister who answered the phone, and boy, did she rip me a new one," Jack says, chuckling at the memory. "She chewed me out for a solid ten minutes about what a horrible human being I am and how I don't deserve you."

I wince. "Oof. Christine might be tougher than all the Siren women combined."

"You're not kidding. She told me—and I quote—that she'd

'cut my balls off' if I even considered coming back around before I'd gotten my shit together. And that I needed to be prepared to grovel."

I smile and kiss the tip of his nose. "I don't need groveling."

"Oh no, she was very clear about the groveling, and I do not intend to piss her off further." He is resolute. "She's rather scary, your sister."

"Yeah." I smile fondly. "I love that about her."

He brings our clasped palms to his lips and kisses the back of my hand. "So what do we do now?"

I hum. "I think maybe we just date like normal people who aren't professional rivals or secretly plotting to take each other down."

"Start over, then? What's so funny?" he asks when I immediately start cracking up.

"Can you just imagine us on a first date? Talk about a disaster," I say, wiping my eyes.

His brows knit. "Um, I'm feeling a little offended by how hard you're laughing."

I roll off him again and maneuver into a sitting position before sticking out my hand. "Hi, I'm Cassidy Sutton."

He eyes me quizzically but plays along. "Jack Bradford."

"So what do you do, Jack?"

He starts to speak, then stops, sheepish. "I'm actually between jobs at the moment."

I feign surprise. "Wow, what a coincidence. Me too! You think maybe one of us should be gainfully employed?"

"I do have a small nest egg," he says modestly. "And some ideas about my next move."

"Phew." I mock-wipe my brow. "So you can float me for a while as I write my book, then?"

He grins, getting into it now. "Sounds perfect, I've always secretly dreamed of being a househusband anyway. Speaking of kids, I hope you want them. I'm not getting any younger and my biological clock is ticking."

I've created a monster. "I think this first date is going *really* well."

He's on a roll now. "Whatever you do, just don't google me. I was recently involved in a bit of a tabloid scandal, and I wouldn't want that to scare you off."

"That's so weird. Me too! This app that paired us up really knows what it's doing."

"I do have to warn you about one thing. I'm afraid you won't think I'm much of a catch once you meet my family."

I pretend to think about it. "Well, you're super hot, so I think I can accept that trade-off."

He laughs, his smile cranking up to an eleven. It's blinding, stretching ear to ear, sunbeams shooting from his eyeballs. This smile is the eighth Wonder of the World.

"Here's the thing," I tell him once we've stopped snickering like schoolchildren. "I don't want to start over. I'd rather pick up where we left off. Our story may be messy and unconventional, but it's ours. And I wouldn't trade it."

His eyes crinkle at the corners. "I suppose if we can make it through all this, we can weather anything."

Truer words have never been spoken. "If there's one thing I've learned from all this, it's that there's merit to the old way of doing things. I've liked taking things slow, and I don't want to skip past the good stuff. I want you to hold my hand and walk me home and kiss me good night. I want to keep learning new things about you. I want to look forward to things with you. I feel like that was working for us, don't you?"

"Totally." He clears his throat. "Speaking of taking things slow, I think you should move in with me."

"*Jaaack*," I groan at the sky.

He raises a palm. "Hear me out. This is absolutely not for my benefit, it's a completely unselfish request." I raise a skeptical brow. "Asher needs a mother."

I exhale a laugh.

"I'm serious! The studies are clear: Children do better in two-parent households. What kind of father would I be if I let him start off life at a disadvantage?" Jack's giving me some major puppy dog eyes of his own. "Also, okay fine, his dad would sure love to have you around."

I take his chin between my fingers and kiss him, slow and tender. "You're very sweet, and I appreciate your entirely self-less offer. Especially as I'm technically homeless." I pull a face. "But this is where I'm supposed to be right now. Gran needs me, and besides, I have a book to finish."

His eyes narrow like I'm very shifty indeed. "I think you just don't want to live in my fancy apartment that you hate."

"I do not *hate* your apartment!" I insist, then rethink that. "I do hate your oven, though."

"Pretty sure the oven hates *you*."

"Hardy-har."

"What if I promise to do all the cooking?" He's really weaponizing those puppy dog eyes now. I'm in big trouble.

"Still no."

"In the nude."

I laugh out loud. "Very tempting, but I'm still going to have to decline. For now," I amend.

"Damn, I really thought that one would work." He laces our fingers together, eyeing me speculatively. "I feel like I'd be getting a different answer if I lived in a brownstone."

That one makes me hesitate, and he reads it all over my face.

He grins in triumph. "Brownstone. Got it."

"Jack, do not go out and buy a brownstone." As I say it, the ghost of Betty rolls over in her grave and I can practically hear her screech: *Let him buy the brownstone!*

"I won't," he says, nodding ever so slowly.

"*Jack* . . ." I say in a warning tone.

He grins, lowering his mouth to mine . . . and then I'm no longer saying much at all.

BESTSELLING AUTHOR CASSIDY SUTTON ON
LIFE, LOVE, AND ROMANCE ACROSS GENERATIONS

BY NATALIA KIMURA FOR SIREN

It's a Friday morning, the kind of crisp autumn day that makes Nora Ephron fans dream of bouquets of newly sharpened pencils and long, banter-filled walks through Central Park beneath a canopy of fall foliage—or at least, the fan sitting across from me sure does. We've been chatting all of five minutes before she blurts, "Don't you just *love* New York in the fall?"

If romance is a state of mind, then today's interview subject has a PhD in HEA (that's "happily ever after," for the uninitiated). I'm spending the morning at the cozy West Village brownstone of bestselling author-slash-screenwriter (and former Siren editor) Cassidy Sutton, discussing the extraordinary success of her debut novel *The Throwback*, life imitating art, and the unexpected joys of married life. (Full disclosure: Sutton is a friend, former colleague, roommate, *and* bridesmaid; I make no apologies for the blatant favoritism shown during this interview.)

The past few years have been a whirlwind for Sutton. She quit her job, wrote a bestselling book, sold the film rights in a fierce

Hollywood bidding war, and is now penning the script—and she somehow did it all while caring for her convalescing grandmother (better known to her three million TikTok followers as @GranKnows Best) *and* planning a wedding to Brawler-founder-turned-venture-capitalist Jack Bradford. If it made you tired to read all that, you're not alone.

"I crammed a couple of decades of life highlights into four years," Sutton jokes, reclining on her couch with a mug of tea and her Chesapeake Bay retriever Asher by her side. "Sometimes I feel like I just flipped a page and all my dreams came true."

Though it's hard to imagine there's anyone left who hasn't read the mega-bestseller, here's a brief synopsis: *The Throwback* follows Beth, an independent, career-driven, but unlucky-in-love Manhattanite working as an editor at a digital magazine (sound familiar?) who, on the eve of her thirtieth birthday, drunkenly laments her single status to her old-school traditional grandmother—only to wake up the next morning transported back to 1950s New York, where she's considered an "old maid," feminism isn't even a speck in the distance, and the only journalism job she can get hired for is secretary to the newsroom's chauvinistic star male reporter. Oh, and everyone's calling her Betty.

You can guess what happens next: Hijinks and hilarity ensue as she alternately tries to fit into her strange new world and drag her colleagues into the future. And that brash hotshot she loves to hate? He just might be the man—and sparring partner—of her dreams. But when the cosmic glitch threatens to correct itself, she has to choose between love in the past and life in the present.

"It's *Back to the Future* meets *Pleasantville* meets *His Girl Friday*," Sutton says with a laugh. "I never was much good at picking a genre."

The manuscript sparked a frenzy among publishers, eventually landing Sutton a six-figure book deal. Upon release, *The*

Throwback quickly rocketed up bestseller lists, where it's stayed for fifty-eight weeks and counting. "No one is more surprised than I am," Sutton says, adding coyly, "but I'll take it."

Why does she think the book's struck such a chord with readers?

"There's something really magical about that particular time period for so many people," she explains, pointing to the enduring popularity of such beloved stars as Audrey Hepburn and Cary Grant. "While there's certainly a tendency to romanticize and glamorize the past, I've heard from so many readers who long for a time that felt simpler and slower, when dating with intention was the rule rather than the exception, and courtship was a stage to be savored rather than rushed through or skipped over. But beyond the nostalgia, I think my heroine's journey resonates so deeply with readers because it reflects a struggle that's as relevant today as it was in the 1950s: the desire to strike a successful balance between a fulfilling relationship and family life and a purposeful career. As a writer, there's a really delicious tension between 'feminine' and 'feminist' that I had so much fun exploring."

It didn't take long for Hollywood to come calling. A film adaptation of the book is currently in development, an outcome Sutton says is beyond her wildest dreams. The role of Beth/Betty practically incited an industry-wide stampede, with just about every A-list starlet rumored to have been vying for the part of the modern girl next door. The role has been cast, though Sutton's been sworn to secrecy, saying only "it's a recognizable name" and "I think people will be very happy." Does she believe all the buzz around the film will usher in a new rom-com golden age, as some have suggested? "From your lips to God's ears," she says, knocking on her reclaimed wood coffee table. "It's the least the romance community deserves for carrying the entire publishing industry on their backs."

Something else she never saw coming? Her grandmother's newfound celebrity as a viral TikTok star. "It was a complete accident," Sutton shares, explaining that the idea was originally conceived as a gimmick to market her book. "As everyone now knows, my grandmother is a character, and we thought it'd be funny to film some videos where she'd dole out old-fashioned dating advice to the romantically disenchanted," adding that neither of them ever dreamed the videos would end up striking such a chord. "We get heartfelt messages from people around the globe who've lost their own loved ones and view her as a surrogate grandmother." One of their favorite comments? "Someone said Gran's filled the Betty White–shaped hole in their heart."

Indeed, die-hard fans of the snarky-hip nonagenarian say her pithy, politically incorrect commentary is not only reviving the lost art of courtship, but also inspiring a new generation to try out a more traditional, retro approach to dating that they've only ever seen in the movies. Her most viral video (up to twenty-four million views and counting) famously encourages men to hold their significant other's hair back when they're getting sick—"a tip I've become all too familiar with," Sutton confesses ruefully, rubbing her six-months-pregnant belly.

Which brings us to her husband—and rumored inspiration behind the book—Jack Bradford. While perhaps best known as co-founder of the controversial men's website Brawler, Bradford recently caused a stir of a different kind when he announced his venture capital firm would begin exclusively funding female-led start-ups, a shift Wall Street analysts were quick to attribute to his wife's influence (despite Sutton's claims to the contrary). "Jack would be the first to tell you he made a business decision. The female-run businesses in his portfolio were outperforming the men's two-to-one, and he believes the greatest growth potential lies in the women's sector, which is both untapped and underfunded." But seriously, she wasn't even a *little* bit responsible? "I think my husband discovered something Siren readers have known for a while: Women are used to doing everything men do—only backwards and in heels."

So how much of *The Throwback* was ripped from the headlines of her own love story? While Sutton insists comparisons are exaggerated, it's impossible not to notice the parallels to her personal life: the feisty, headstrong heroine disillusioned with the modern dating scene; the cocky, antagonistic professional rival turned chivalrous love interest; the battle-of-the-sexes power struggle that transforms the pair from bitter enemies into passionate lovers. Alas, it looks like the gossipmongers desperate for details on New York's newest power couple will have to keep guessing. Though she remains tight-lipped on the specifics, Sutton reveals the truth behind the duo's real-life love story is "way more romantic than my book."

Guess we'll have to hope for a sequel.

There's an old magazine article that pops up every so often on social media and never fails to cause a stir. It's called "129 Ways to Get a Husband" and was originally printed in the January 1958 issue of *McCall's* magazine (alongside a recipe for mincemeat-fig pie and an essay profiling "Three Women of Courage" by then senator John F. Kennedy). As you've probably guessed by now, this list of vintage dating advice provided much of the inspiration for *The Rom Con*, though I drew from plenty of other outlandish how-to pieces I found during research. The actual list of old-fashioned tips is a wildly entertaining read, a creative but comically absurd time capsule that paints a very clear picture of the social rules, roles, and expectations for women in 1950s America. As such, the reactions to it are about what you'd expect: amusement, disbelief, ridicule, and above all, a collective acknowledgment of how far we've come.

But what I found intriguing—and what ultimately sparked the idea for this book—were the surprising number of passionate, even wistful, reactions I saw making the case for embracing the retro advice and reviving the classic courtship rituals of the 1950s. Some commenters praised the article's hilarious, over-the-top meet-cute suggestions, while others debated the merits of each tip, brainstorming how best to tweak them for use in a modern world. Still others lamented the decline of such romantic gestures into contemporary "swipe culture," musing that their grandmothers may have had the right idea after all.

The divergent perspectives certainly got my attention. As a romance author, I'm forever on the hunt for relationship conflicts that feel both modern and timeless, that challenge me as much as the reader, that aren't so black and white. Is a "man-catching" list an antiquated relic or a gold mine of ideas? Which of the dating tips, if any, still hold up today? What have younger generations forgotten—or never learned—that older generations still have to teach us? My goal was to write an emotional and nostalgic love story that would celebrate how far we've come, while also exploring what may have been lost along the way. I hope you've enjoyed reading it as much as I enjoyed writing it.

One of the greatest gifts of writing *The Rom Con* (besides having an excuse to watch dozens of Old Hollywood movies) was how it brought my own grandmothers back to life for me in ways I never anticipated. Both women were incredible forces of nature: accomplished and resilient and effortlessly glamorous; exceptional matriarchs who were bold and independent in ways that were far ahead of their time. I felt them over my shoulders like guardian angels as I wrote (and kept fifties-era photos of them propped next to my laptop lest I forget). So many of the details I incorporated into the book were lifted directly from my core childhood memories, from Cassidy's vintage fashion moments to the hand-sewn Barbie clothes to Pyewacket the cat. While I may have been creating a fictional world, I gained very real appreciation for how fearlessly they lived, and how admirably they navigated a world that lacked so many of the freedoms and opportunities we now take for granted. In many ways, this book is a tribute to them and to all our grandmothers, who deserve more respect and gratitude than I could ever express.

Acknowledgments

First and foremost, thank you for reading *The Rom Con*. There are so many books out there, and I truly appreciate that you chose to spend your time with one of mine. I hope it gave you that butterflies-in-the-stomach feeling, an excuse to laugh, and most of all, a few hours of escape.

It's always difficult to distill several years of work, energy, and existential angst into a few paragraphs of thank-yous, but here goes.

To my editor, Kate Seaver: Thank you for your steady encouragement, your thoughtful and incisive edits, and most especially, your patience and flexibility in allowing me the time and space to make this book the best it could be. I am always calmer and more focused after talking to you, and I feel so fortunate to have you in my corner. Thanks also to the entire Berkley Romance team, including Amanda Maurer, Lauren Burnstein, Chelsea Pascoe, and Jessica Plummer, as well as artist Ana Hard and art director Vikki Chu for designing such a stunning cover.

To all my author friends: Your support, advice, and pep talks keep me sane! Thank you for brainstorming with me, for providing the best feedback, for hyping me up when I need it, and for talking me off more ledges than I can count.

There was quite a bit of research and real-life inspiration that went into this book, and I must give credit where it's due. As I mentioned in my author's note, Cassidy's "125 Tips to Hook a Husband" list is inspired by the article "129 Ways to Get a Husband," originally printed in the January 1958 issue of *McCall's* magazine. The legend of Engagement Chicken was first credited to a *Glamour* magazine editor back in the 1980s, though the story and accompanying recipe didn't make it to print until the January 2004 issue. I based Gran's book *I Do: Rules & Etiquette for the Military Wife* on a book called *The Air Force Wife* by Nancy Shea (revised by Anna Perle Smith, Harper & Row, 1951). Every woman has seen her fair share of silly lists printed in magazines, but the one I couldn't resist writing into the book was "Things to Do with Your Hands That Men Like" (Jani Gardner for *Cosmopolitan*, January 1970). It's by far the most bonkers list I found during research, and trust me, it's worth the google.

If you thought some of the Brawler antics sounded familiar, look no further than Barstool Sports, which provided me with a colorful foundation from which to draw inspiration. To help get into a fifties-inspired mindset, I went down many YouTube and TikTok rabbit holes. One of my favorite finds was a woman named Laci Fay (@LaciFayTheVintage GirlNextDoor), whose YouTube videos were so charming that I promptly wrote a similar character into my story. (When asked why she lives her life like it's the 1950s, Laci shared this delightful response: "Everybody is nerdy about something, and it might as well be about something that you love.") While I drew plenty of inspiration from my own grandmaternal relationships in crafting the special bond between Cassidy and Gran, I found a slew of sassy grandmas on TikTok that also helped. One account in particular, @gbandme, always had me in stitches—and inspired me to turn Gran into a TikTok star.

To my family: Thank you for being my biggest fans and earliest readers, for enduring my endless publishing-related texts, for always chiming in with your opinions, and for talking up my books when I'm too embarrassed to do it myself. Mom, with the example you've set for me, it's no surprise that I write strong maternal relationships into every book. There's no doubt this book was born from the thousands of conversations we had growing up. Dad, your energy in forcing my book on non-romance readers (mostly male) is unmatched. Please never stop harassing airport bookstore employees. Kristen, I hope you enjoyed your tribute character, even if Christine barely scratches the surface of your formidability. Thank you for being my protector and defender for the past forty years. Erin, thanks for always being my number one hype woman. John, thanks for being my expert on all things Barstool. Danielle and Dolores, I can always count on your early reader enthusiasm! And of course, the most significant thank-you must go to my grandparents. Without their steady, strong presences in my life, their hard-earned, passed-down wisdom, and their unwavering commitment to marriage and family, this book would surely not exist. I can only hope to one day inspire my future grandchildren the way they've inspired me.

To Kate, Kirsten, and Kim (collectively, Tusks): Thank you for tirelessly cheerleading me through all the ups and downs of our publishing journey—and I truly think of it as *our* journey, since you've been there with me every step of the way. I don't know why I spend hours obsessing over plot holes when you're always able to solve them in seconds.

In fact, if Berkley knew just how much influence you had on this book, your names would all appear on the cover.

It's a special treat that my kids are now old enough to help with things like brainstorming titles and taglines, judging the strength of my jokes, and keeping my pop culture references fresh (even if the majority are deemed deeply uncool). A, D, M, and G: Thank you for being patient with me when writing makes me cranky and distracted, and for being such good sports about my incorporating your unintentionally hilarious comments into my books (especially that Break & Bake joke, A; it's the gift that keeps on giving).

To Patrick: There's a special place in heaven for the spouses of writers, especially of those who are struggling through a challenging manuscript. The amount of whining I did while writing this book is something no husband should have to endure, and you deserve a medal for handling it and me with such limitless patience. I'm only able to accomplish half of what I do because of the selfless ways you take care of me each day, from making my coffee every morning to whipping up gourmet dinners for us at night. These daily acts of love are more romantic than any grand gesture I could write in a book. You're the best partner in life and love I could ask for.

And finally, to the Bookstagram community: Thank you for being such fierce champions of my work, for your excitement and energy, and for shouting about my books from the rooftops (I'm looking at you, M'Kenzee). Bookstagram is truly the kindest corner of the internet, and I feel so lucky to have been welcomed with such open arms. To hear that *Meet You in the Middle* is your comfort read, that it's the book you reach for when you're feeling down, that you've read it five, ten, even twenty times—I do not take any of it for granted. Being tagged in your posts and videos—which you create just for the sheer joy of it, because you *want* to, because you love books—will never stop being surreal to me. You are just the audience I hoped to find, and I'm so grateful for each and every one of you.

The ROM CON

Devon Daniels

READERS GUIDE

Discussion Questions

1. When we first meet Cassidy, she refuses to see Jack as anything more than her professional nemesis, but by the end of the book, she realizes that many of the assumptions she made about his character were wrong and that she's found her match in the one she least expected. What factors or events do you think were most influential in changing her mind?

2. At first, Cassidy scoffs at the antiquated social customs of her grandmother's generation, but she gradually comes to believe that much of the courtship advice has merit, even incorporating several of the suggestions into her relationship with Jack. Did any of Gran's tips resonate with you, and if so, which ones?

3. Throughout the book, Cassidy struggles to accept Jack's work and association with Brawler. Do you think it's possible to compartmentalize negative feelings about a partner's job, or is that type of conflict a relationship deal-breaker? Do you think Cassidy was right to judge Jack's work harshly? Why or why not?

4. Cassidy and Christine have a strong sisterly bond,
    with Cassidy deeply valuing her older sibling's ad-
    vice. How do you think Christine's opinion influ-
    enced Cassidy's decision to take her relationship
    with Jack more seriously? How do you think Chris-
    tine's example helped encourage Cassidy to take
    more risks?

5. The book follows Cassidy on her journey from risk-
    averse to risk-taker in both her professional and per-
    sonal life. What are some ways Cassidy grew and
    changed from the beginning of the story until the
    end? Would you describe yourself as a risk-taker or
    someone who plays it safe?

6. Cassidy opens up to Jack about feeling lonely and
    "left behind" as many of her friends get married and
    start families. Have you ever dealt with feelings of
    insecurity about your peers' personal or profession-
    al milestones, and if so, how did you navigate them?

7. Many women grew up reading magazines that pub-
    lished lists and quizzes similar to those mentioned
    in the book, like "125 Tips to Hook a Husband" or
    "Things to Do with Your Hands That Men Like." Do
    you think these lists of tips are sexist and outdated, or
    do you think they provide valuable advice? Has your
    opinion on this type of advice column changed over
    time?

8. One of the ways Cassidy attempts to behave like a
    stereotypical 1950s housewife is to cook Engage-

ment Chicken. Have you ever done something similar to impress a potential partner? How do you think gender roles and responsibilities inside the home have shifted since the 1950s?

9. Many actresses from Hollywood's "golden age" remain beloved icons and are as relevant in modern pop culture as they were eighty years ago, from Audrey Hepburn to Marilyn Monroe to Doris Day. Similarly, depictions of the archetypal 1950s housewife regularly pop up in contemporary books, films, and music. Why do you think people remain so captivated by this period in history and the concept of the perfect housewife? How have media depictions of wives and mothers evolved over time?

10. Cassidy enjoys a special relationship with her grandmother and treasures the extra time she's able to spend with her. What do you think younger generations can gain from spending time with their elder relatives? What stories or family heirlooms have been passed down that hold special significance for you?

11. Fashion plays an important role in *The Rom Con*, with Cassidy's wardrobe gradually morphing from the quintessential New York uniform of dark, sophisticated basics into the more colorful, whimsical, and feminine silhouettes of the fifties. How does Cassidy's shift in style echo her personal and professional transformations?

12. In the epilogue, we see that Cassidy has been able to build a fulfilling home life with Jack while still achieving her professional dreams. What factors and decisions do you think contributed to her success in finding that balance? What obstacles do women typically encounter in their quest to "have it all"?

13. The contrast between the more formal and intentional courtship customs of the past and the more casual, convenience-based contemporary dating approach is a recurring theme in the book. What do you think are some pros and cons of modern dating culture versus old-fashioned, retro courtship?

14. The story's setting plays a special role in *The Rom Con*, with scenes taking place at various famous New York City landmarks, from Arthur Ashe Stadium to Times Square to Central Park in the fall. What was your favorite scene or New York location to read about?

Devon Daniels is a born-and-bred California girl whose own love story found her transplanted to the Maryland shores of the Chesapeake Bay. She is a graduate of the University of Southern California and in her past life worked in marketing, product design, and music. Her debut novel, *Meet You in the Middle*, was chosen as one of the Best Books of 2021 by *USA Today*. When she's not writing, you'll find her clinging to her sanity as mom, chef, chauffeur, and referee to four children, or sneaking off with her husband for date nights.

Visit Devon Daniels online

DevonDanielsAuthor.com
DevonDanielsAuthor
DevonDanielsAuthor
DevonDanielsAuthor